BEAUTY *and the* BALLER

OTHER TITLES BY ILSA MADDEN-MILLS

All books are stand-alone stories with brand-new couples and are currently FREE in Kindle Unlimited.

Not My Romeo
Not My Match

Very Bad Things
Very Wicked Beginnings
Very Wicked Things
Very Twisted Things

Dirty English
Filthy English
Spider

Fake Fiancée

I Dare You
I Bet You
I Hate You
I Promise You

Boyfriend Bargain

Dear Ava

The Revenge Pact

The Last Guy (w/Tia Louise)
The Right Stud (w/Tia Louise)

BEAUTY *and the* BALLER

ILSA MADDEN-MILLS

This is a work of fiction. Names, characters, organizations, places, events, and incidents are either products of the author's imagination or are used fictitiously.

Published by Montlake, Seattle

www.apub.com

ISBN-13: 9781542034784
ISBN-10: 1542034787

Cover design by Hang Le

Printed in the United States of America

BEAUTY *and the* BALLER

Chapter 1

RONAN

"Hey, didn't you once buy some poster of *Star Wars* for like . . . twenty grand?" Tuck asks as he plops down next to me where I'm alone at a table for eight. It's after dinner, and most of the players have wandered off to dance with their partners.

"I have two, *The Phantom Menace* and *The Last Jedi*. Why do you ask?" I say, then drain my fourth or fifth whiskey, embracing the burn of the bourbon. The room isn't spinning yet, which means I'll need more. It takes a lot to forget that my NFL career is over, my fiancée gone.

"Dude . . . are you listening?"

I focus back on Tuck, faking normal. "Yeah, sure."

He grins. "Good. Your perfect woman just walked into our party. Like a gift from heaven. We must make a plan."

"Really." I arch a brow.

"I hear your sarcasm, but come on, would I lie to my best friend?"

"Is water wet?"

He says something else, probably some wisecrack, but I miss it when a woman laughs in the ballroom, light and airy. I close my eyes, inhaling a sharp breath. For a second, she sounded like Whitney. See, the body can be numb, but little things trickle in and haunt me. And football? Not playing cuts like a razor blade, sharp and vicious. I can barely breathe when my team takes the field without me.

I signal the server for another drink.

The waiter gives me a nod, pours it, and then rushes over and hands it to me. I take a hearty sip under Tuck's gaze.

"You never used to drink, Ronan. Don't you think you've had enough?"

Ha. This is nothing compared to those mornings when I wake up and can't recall details from the night before. "The girl? What's it about her that makes her perfect for me?"

"Look for yourself," he says, nudging his head toward where she must be. "You won't believe what she's wearing. Behind you and to your left. Check it."

With a heavy exhale, I loosen my tie and swivel in my seat and peer around various players. I focus in on the girl about twenty feet away and inhale as I get the full effect.

Whoa.

There's no way anyone could miss her. Not with that getup.

What the hell was she thinking?

"She's lost, yes?" he murmurs.

"Hmm," I say as my eyes brush over her.

Tall with pale-blonde hair, she's wearing a costume, legit, like Princess Leia—slave-girl version, the one where she was captured by Jabba the Hutt. It's a gold bikini with a red filmy loincloth over her hips. She's even got the sleek plaited high ponytail and golden knotted necklace. From the metal snake cuff around her upper arm to the green lace-up boots, the costume isn't one of those cheap knockoffs from a Halloween store. It's damn perfect, and she wears it better than Carrie Fisher did in *Return of the Jedi*.

A low whistle comes from Tuck. "She waltzed in the fanciest hotel in the city and crashed a Pythons party. Right in the middle of all these suits and dresses. Everyone's staring at her. Wait a minute . . . looks like someone isn't happy . . ."

His voice trails off as a black-clad security guy approaches her, clipboard in hand, headset on his head. A scowl settles on his face as he snaps out words to her. Security is tight at our events. Fans, crazy ones, will do anything to get a glimpse of their favorite team.

She doesn't look like a weirdo fan. Those are usually wearing black-and-gold Python gear and shouting players' names.

She *is* lost.

Tuck lowers his voice. "She's about to get thrown out—or arrested. They've done it before. She needs a Han Solo to save her."

I turn back to him. "Subtle."

He shrugs. "She's your type—into *Star Wars*, blonde, *and* a damsel in distress."

"Not interested."

"Liar," he says. "Bet you can't get her digits."

I lean back in the chair and shake my head at him. Before I got serious with Whitney, we used to compete at bars to see who could get the most numbers. Jesus. That feels like a million years ago.

"You wanna play that, huh?" I ask. "Is this you trying to motivate me to move on?"

"It's been almost a year since . . ."

"The wreck," I finish, my voice thickening. "The anniversary of her passing is in four days."

"I'm sorry." He sighs and glances away, then comes back to me, leaning his arms in on the table, an earnest expression on his face. "Look. I miss you, okay? Dammit. I sound like a silly schoolgirl. It's just . . . you're avoiding *me*, your best friend. You're drinking. A lot." He rakes a hand through his messy sandy-brown hair and sighs. "I'm sorry, man. This isn't about me, and I've got no clue what you're going through, and Whitney, the way it went down—it sucks . . ."

I stare at the table as his words ping-pong around in my head. He's not wrong. I'm in a dark place, a pit of hell, and I crave to crawl out. Some days it feels as if there's nothing left inside of me. No spark. No hope. No joy.

I sat out the season on the injury list, and that was mostly out of respect for my history with the team. Everyone knew I'd never play. I didn't even want to come to the end-of-the-year celebration, but I dragged myself here anyway. I just need something, *anything*, to numb this ache in my chest.

"Our team won't be the same without you," he says. "Maybe if you rehab another season, try different physical therapy—"

"I've done it all, Tuck." I endured two surgeries and rehab from some of the best doctors in the world—and that was just for my knee. I had a whole other round for my face.

He exhales noisily. "But you know I can't shut up, right?"

I tip my glass up at him. "Nine years together, and you never once stopped running your mouth."

An eager expression crosses his face, his words coming in a rush: "Let's play. 'Kay? Like old times? You rescue her from security, chat her up, and get her number, and I'll wash your Porsche and let you take pics of me and brag about it, post it on Insta, whatever. Anything else that happens"—he flashes a grin—"I'm talking maybe kiss her, will be icing on the cake; feel me? You don't need a lesson on how to woo a woman, do you?"

My lids lower. "No." I've been a phenom quarterback since I was fourteen. Women have always gravitated to me.

Or they used to.

I catch my reflection in the mirror behind him and see the scars on the left side of my face. Jagged and pink, the longest one starts at my temple, traces past my ear to my jawline, and ends midneck. Sixteen inches long, that cut was a quarter inch from an artery. Other scars, like jagged spiderwebs, slice into my cheek on the same side, then disappear into my dark hair. Last year, my hair was shaved around my ears and longer on top in a classic pompadour, but it has grown out, the longer length brushing my chin. Still, they're visible. Last week, one of the trainers dropped off some personal equipment I'd kept at the field. When I opened the door, he saw my face . . . and flinched. Might as well get used to it. They aren't going away. I rub the long one, my thumb brushing over it.

"They give you a dangerous vibe," Tuck says.

"Frankenstein—yeah, that's a good look." I drain my glass and set it on the table.

"All right, buddy, let's get you moving," he says as he tugs me up.

I weave on my feet—whoa—then straighten and frown. "What's the rush?"

He waves that off. "Listen to me. Go talk to that girl. For your best friend in the whole wide world. *Please.*" He bats his lashes at me.

"You're an idiot," I say as I glance back over at her.

While we were talking, the security guy called another one over. They moved her to a corner near the entrance, and she's got her chin tilted, a defiant look on her face as they question her. In a flurry of her loincloth, she nudges past them and gazes around the room, her eyes landing on me and sticking. Her face transforms, a radiant smile curving her lips.

Tuck lets out a surprised sound. "Huh, will you look at that? She knows you! This is perfect! You've got this!" He slaps me on the back. "Go get her, tiger. Go, go!"

"No," I mutter.

Then the security guard puts his meaty hand on her arm and half drags her to the door.

"Dammit," I breathe as a twinge of protectiveness rises. I heave out an exhale, shake off Tuck, and jostle my way through the crowd, leaning slightly on my right side to compensate for the prickle of pain on my left.

"That's what I'm talking about!" Tuck calls out. "Save the princess!"

Whatever. I flip him off over my shoulder.

I'll see what she's about, and that's it.

Maybe get her out of here without causing her any embarrassment. I grew up with two younger sisters, and there's a long list of escapades I've saved them from. Hell, I half raised them. What's the harm in helping the princess? It'll be a good story *and* get Tuck off my back.

As I approach, she's having words with the guy holding her arm. She fights free of his grasp—again—then rushes toward me, the slits of her skirt showcasing her long, toned legs. Security is hot on her heels, but she never looks back, her posture straight, her steps sure, as she keeps that "I know you" smile directed straight at me.

We meet in the middle of the ballroom underneath one of the chandeliers among the dancers, and I send a head nudge to the duo behind her.

"Ease up, guys. She's with me."

They shrug and leave. I'm sure crazier shit has happened at an NFL party.

My breath hitches as I take her in. I didn't appreciate her before at the table, but this close, it's as if someone created everything I love in a woman: tall, blonde, heart-shaped face, sapphire eyes, luscious tits. Toss in the costume . . .

My teenage fantasy in the flesh.

She takes both of my hands in hers, and the touch sends a buzz of awareness racing over my skin. I didn't expect that.

"Ronan," she murmurs.

Okay, she knows my name—not surprising.

"Hey, um . . . ?" What are you doing here?

"Help me," she implores dramatically. "You're my only, um, salvation . . . and stuff like that . . . to save the universe."

I huff out a rusty laugh. "Well, that's almost Leia's first line in *Star Wars*."

She leans in, and her fingers dance up my jacket and land on the lapels, stroking the black fabric. "I love this suit. You like my outfit?"

My gaze tangles in the soft curves of her body, lingering on her bikini-clad breasts. Gradually, I move up to the smooth line of her throat, to the dark winged eyebrows that contrast with her hair and frame her face. Even without the kick-ass costume, she's the kind of girl you see on the street and do a double take. Hourglass shape, classic features, and a perfect pouty bottom lip.

"Yes," I murmur.

"I could get used to this skirt." She moves her hips, swishing the fabric.

"Loincloth."

"You don't say? I'll make a note of that." With a sly yet sweet smile, she does a little twirl, then stops in front of me and places a hand over her heart.

"What?" I ask.

"It's sinking in. You really came to help me."

My lips twitch. "To save the universe. And stuff like that." I glance around the room. "Can I escort you somewhere?"

Disappointment flickers over her face before she quickly hides it. "No. I'm fine. Really. It was nice of you to come over. I'll go. I just wanted to pop in and see . . ." She stops, seeming to think about her words, then smiles ruefully. "Never mind. Thank you. Goodbye, Ronan."

When she turns, I grab her hand. "Wait."

I don't know why I stop her, but . . .

My eyes lock with hers, several breathless moments passing as our hands cling. Acting on instinct, my thumb caresses her palm.

Her lips part, heat flashing in her irises.

A long breath comes from me. I miss *this*. Desire, not pity, in a woman's eyes.

I swallow thickly. There's been no one since Whitney. I've had opportunities, mostly Tuck dragging me out to dinners and get-togethers, and girls have offered, but my body—and my heart—wasn't ready.

It's been forever since I flirted with a girl, but . . .

Lowering my lids, I tug her closer to me until our chests brush. "Who are you, gorgeous?"

Silence, thick and sweet, stretches between us. "Yours."

A shot of lust, fueled by her whispered words, hits me. The lizard part of my brain, the primitive side that reacts on instinct to fighting and fucking, rears up. *This one,* it demands. *Take it.*

She's not the right girl, the other side of my head shouts, even as my index finger strokes her cheek. She turns her head into the touch, sighing softly, and my chest seizes at her automatic response.

You wanted something to push that grief back.

"Dance with me," she murmurs and doesn't wait for my reply but leans her forehead on my shoulder, her body starting to sway to the slow song the DJ plays.

I dip my head and sway with her, slow and easy. My hands slide around her waist, almost tentatively. Moments tick by, heavy with expectation, as if waiting to see what happens next. My thumb finds the small of her back and circles the soft skin there. It's my favorite part of a woman, and I can't resist. My breath snags as her fingers trace designs on my shoulders, then press harder, her nails dragging down my back, then up. I bite back a groan. Touch. It's one of the things I've missed, the smooth glide of hands over skin, the feeling of connection.

We go from one song to another, the music bleeding together as the DJ spins slow tracks. I keep my eyes shut, my body relaxing against hers. Even my knee feels better. A long exhale comes from my chest as the tension from the last few hours vanishes. It was hard to walk in here. To sit at a table with couples, recognize their sorrow-filled glances, and realize that once again, I'm alone.

The truth is it's the nights that eat at me the most. I'm sick of spending them by myself.

Vaguely, as if from a distance, I'm aware that "Say You Won't Let Go," by James Arthur, is on the speakers, a song about two people connecting . . . maybe it's a message.

Her lips brush against my neck, almost hesitantly; then, braver, she moves back and kisses my throat. Electricity flares, and I toy with the top of her loincloth, rubbing the fabric. I ease my hand underneath it, my fingers grazing the curve of her ass. My heart hammers as she responds by swishing her leg in between mine, brushing against the bulge in my pants.

Powerful and greedy, desire slams into me.

I stop our dancing and slide my hands up her arms to her neck, tilting her face up. Need soaks her features, eyes dilated, cheeks flushed.

She isn't one of Tuck's party girls who flirts with me to be nice.

And I'm not misreading her signals.

I didn't see this (her) coming, but . . .

"You wanna get out of here?" I ask in a gravelly voice. "Maybe do some role-playing, hmm?"

She knows what I mean. Her. Me. One night.

Her pink tongue dips out and dabs at her plump lower lip. "All right."

"Good," I purr as my thumb brushes her mouth.

I crook her arm through mine and lace our hands together. We move through the dancers as we leave the ballroom. Outside, the foyer is crowded with people, and we dodge past them with heads bent. I'm doing it to not be recognized; she seems to understand.

With each step, the air thins, my chest tightening. I'm not sure if it's because this is an impulsive decision I'll probably regret tomorrow or if it's her. We get inside the elevator, and I slap the button for the top floor, then ease her against the wall. Words don't feel necessary as I run my nose up her throat. She smells fresh and tart, like apples, and I'm rushing, totally—I don't know this girl, even her name, but I don't care. Nothing has stemmed the darkness, even alcohol, but I'll sink myself into a beautiful woman to bring on oblivion.

She looks up at me. "I—I don't normally, um—"

I stop her with a finger to her lips. "I'm going to kiss you. Is that okay?"

She nods.

I slant my mouth across hers, our breaths mingling as I part her lips. She melts against me. A shudder ripples over me as lust, long banked and hungry, strains to be unleashed, to crush her beneath me. I hold it back, for now, and learn her mouth, the shape of it, the dips and valleys. Her breath hitches as I tug on her bottom lip with my teeth, then kiss it softly. I move from her cheek to her ear, my teeth biting on the lobe.

"I don't normally either," I breathe.

Later, she takes the card from me and opens my door. We walk inside the suite and pause in the foyer as she takes in the penthouse I booked. The decor is mostly white with a low-profile, black gas fireplace burning in the den. The views of Manhattan are glorious from the windows, which is where she drifts, but my gaze goes to the kitchen . . . and the whiskey bottle.

I offer her a drink, and she says no. I pour a glass for me; then we wander into the master bedroom, where an empty bottle already sits on the nightstand. Tuck was right about me not being a drinker. For years, I set high goals, studying how to be a great leader and quarterback for my team, pushing my body to its limits with training, eating right, rarely consuming alcohol. For me, it was the game I lived for.

I won three Super Bowls in a row.

Look at me now.

There's a moment of clarity, my mind debating if bringing the girl here was a good idea. I'm supposed to see Whitney's parents tomorrow—

I kick that thought away.

She gives me a heart-stopping smile and does a pirouette in front of the window, her loincloth billowing around her. She repeats her quote, correctly this time, then laughingly admits she doesn't know any more. I tell her I'll teach her all my favorites. I finish my drink, then another. Time passes fast, yet slow, as she flits around the room. She talks, telling me things, maybe her name, and I soak her in, the graceful way she walks, the way her overgenerous lips curl when she smiles.

Propping myself against the wall to keep steady, I find music on my phone, some slow pop song.

"You're incredible," I murmur in her ear when she glides over to me.

How did I get here with you? How did you find me?

With our arms draped around each other, we sway as she sings along with Savage Garden's "I Knew I Loved You." Her voice is rich, each note perfect and clear. She's good. Or maybe I'm just trashed and anything sounds good.

When the song ends, there's a silence as we face each other.

The air thickens.

I brought her here, but she can walk out that door.

With that thought, I twine our fingers together and dip my face into her neck and inhale deeply, deciding this spot is my second-favorite part of a woman. I rest my hands on her clavicle with ownership, my thumb brushing against the goose bumps on her skin.

"It's game time. Are you staying, Princess?"

"Yes." Her gaze is steady and sure.

It's all I need as I try to remove her costume, but my fingers don't know where all the snaps and buttons are, and she does it for me, quickly, tossing her top to the floor, then her bikini bottoms, revealing a white lace thong. Sitting on the bed, she loosens her green boots, tugging at the laces. She undoes her hair, the curls from the braid spilling around her shoulders. My mouth dries as she stands unabashedly in front of me. There's no shyness. No pretention. She's lush and decadent, her tits heavy, her nipples a rosy red. The curve of her waist gives way to full hips and long legs. Her toes are painted a shimmery gold—

My thoughts halt as she jerks the duvet and blankets to the floor, leaving the sheet and pillows on the bed.

My adrenaline spikes. We're doing this. *I'm* doing this.

"Come to me," I demand softly.

She walks over and strips me of my jacket, then tosses it on a chair. She unknots my tie while I tear at the buttons on my shirt. They fly across the room. My pants are next, both of us fighting for the zipper as our breaths mingle. I shove down my underwear, and she takes my length in her hands. A long guttural sound comes from my chest as our bodies fall to the bed.

I shove down the pain in my knee and cage her in underneath me. She looks fragile and vulnerable, and my blood heats, the alpha in me rearing up to protect her. I capture her sapphire eyes, and something there is eerily familiar. Shadows of pain.

I nudge my nose against hers softly, then give her tender kisses as our scents mingle, my whiskey with her sweetness. I tell her she's perfect, that she's safe with me, that she's mine. "And I'm going to eat you up," I purr.

"Ronan . . ." She runs her hands through my hair, pulling on the ends and dragging me down for a wet, openmouthed kiss that turns frantic. My hand cups one breast as I suck the other nipple into my mouth. I move between the two, my five-o'clock shadow brushing over her soft skin. She tastes like . . . I don't know . . . joy.

I kiss down her body, my hands following. I touch the curve of her waist, her inner thigh—then I'm at her center. I lick the nirvana there, my hands clenching on top of her thighs as I feast.

Moaning, she tugs on my hair, and I rise up.

An unexpected flicker of disconnect hits, almost choking the desire, as the chain around my neck, the one with Whitney's engagement ring on it, swings between us, glittering. I shove the ring to my back as guilt washes over me.

A dark road flashes in my head, the scratching swipe of windshield wipers, hail pinging, wind battering the car. I should have paid more attention to the storm and slowed down, taken a different road, insisted she put her seat belt on—fuck, how did I miss that? She hated wearing it, the one rule she refused to follow, and I wasn't paying attention; then a bolt of lightning hit the bridge—my breath shudders. No.

I don't want to think about that.

Not here. Not now.

I kick back the ache of those memories; I try, even as the condom gets rolled on. I slide inside her, all the way home, a primal roar coming deep from my chest. I stare down at the beauty in my bed, and finally, she's the only thing I see in my head.

We become a whirlwind of carnal need, straining to crawl into each other. We're wild, grasping, finding new positions, new places to touch. I'm voracious; she's ravenous. I grunt with every thrust, my eyes eating her up as the headboard clatters against the wall.

"Ronan . . ." Her head thrashes back and forth on the pillow.

"I'm there, Princess . . ."

My fingers circle her nub, and she explodes brilliantly, magnificently, her body undulating in sinuous waves.

My cock thickens, eager to follow, ecstasy a heartbeat away.

"Whitney," I call out as I come.

My body trembles as I rest on top of her before rolling off and falling to my back. I shove my damp hair off my face and suck in gulps of air. That was incredible. My hand reaches over the space between us and toys with her long blonde hair, carding it through my fingers. She's already flipped over, facing the other direction, the sheet around her shoulders.

Some of the blood returns to my brain.

Wait . . .

A sinking feeling trickles in.

Did I . . . did I call her . . . *Whitney*?

No way. Impossible.

My heart drops to my stomach as realization kicks in.

Jesus, I totally did, but . . . it wasn't like that.

It just wasn't.

I don't know what to say. She heard me, of course. Grimacing, I stare at the back of her head and wrestle with how to explain about Whitney's death, how she died in my arms, how it was my fault . . . but those memories are full of thorns.

I search for words, but my tongue feels thick, my brain sluggish, fighting through the haze of bourbon. I should say I'm sorry, I should ask what her name is, I should tell her that she's the best thing that's happened to me in a year . . .

Exhaustion wins and drags me under.

◆ ◆ ◆

When I wake up, my head is stuffed with cotton balls. Sunlight glints in through the blinds, and I rub at the grit in my eyes. Tensing, I turn to look at the pillow next to me. There's no one there, not even an indentation. The room is dead quiet except for the blaring horns from the traffic outside. A heavy feeling settles in my chest, and I can't decide if I'm relieved or disappointed she left. I rake my hands through my hair, frowning, as I try to piece the night together. It might take a while.

I hiss when I see that it's two in the afternoon, and I've missed lunch with Whitney's parents in Connecticut. Cursing under my breath, I yank my pants off the floor, fish out my phone, and then fire off a text apologizing.

I collapse back on the bed. One thing is clear. *I had sex.*

Guilt chews me with sharp teeth, then spits me out in disgust. Couldn't I have waited until after Whitney's one-year anniversary?

Doesn't she deserve that? I loved her with my whole heart, with everything inside me, yet it feels as if I betrayed her.

Swallowing thickly, I get up and grab my clothes, when a golden arm cuff rolls out of my shirt. I rub my fingers over the thick metal, my head flashing to last night. I recall us dancing, the sex, yet . . . I frown, squinting. She was blonde, yes. She had blue eyes, yes, but the rest is vague and blurry.

Sure, I've been blackout drunk, but how can I remember the awe in her eyes when we met, her bubbliness, the smell of her neck . . . yet *not* her features?

Maybe I don't want to? Guilt over Whitney? I exhale. I don't know.

Another memory trickles in, ugly and harsh, and a curse escapes my lips. I called her Whitney. A fresh wave of remorse settles over me. Jesus. No wonder she left without a word.

My insides twist as I glare at the whiskey bottle on the nightstand as if it's to blame.

Deep breaths come from my chest as I pace around the room, my head churning. I pick up the bottle and toss it in the trash. Something has to give. I can't keep doing this to myself, to my body. The truth is I'm numbing myself, wallowing, spiraling closer and closer to destruction. This isn't me. I'm not a drunk. I'm a former superstar. I'm Ronan Smith and . . . I pause as clarity runs through my head. I want my life back, no matter what that may be.

Closing my eyes, I touch the ring around my neck.

Today is when everything changes.

Chapter 2

Nova

Two and a half years later

A white Jeep roars into my yard, barely missing my mailbox; stalls for a second; and then mows through my flower bed. Azaleas, monkey grass, pampas grass, all driven over, but when it takes out my yellow rosebush—the one Mama planted for my first birthday—I'm ready to murder someone.

I stamp my foot and pull out my earbuds in the middle of "Unchained Melody," by the Righteous Brothers.

Sparky hisses, his back arching.

There. I'm justified in my anger. He only hisses at bad shit.

Standing on the sidewalk under the glow of a streetlight, I lift Sparky up and rub his head, his blue cat eyes still glaring at the car as it backs out of my yard (without acknowledging us), then jumps the curb and lands on the road. The vehicle zooms through the stop sign at the end of our street, then takes a harrowing right turn onto the highway.

"Thank God we weren't in her way," I mutter, and by *her*, I mean the girl who burst from the house next door shouting "It's over! I mean it this time!" and then threw herself into the Jeep that nearly killed us.

Someone new is living in the old Locke house.

And if this Jeep is indicative of their company, we're going to have problems.

Usually, I'd go meet them, "do the pretty," as Mama used to say, but life's been hectic since her funeral. In the few weeks I've been here, I've dealt with the bank and lawyers, gotten my sister enrolled in high school, and arranged for my things to be shipped to Texas. My clothes still haven't arrived. All I have is what I stuffed in my duffel in my apartment in New York when I heard Mama had passed from an aneurysm.

A swell of roaring grief threatens as I twirl Sparky's purple diamanté leash through my fingers. She's gone at fifty-five. Too young. *My mama.* Fighting back the tears, I glare at the majestic two-story white house next door. Stately with Doric-style columns and a fresh coat of white paint on the bricks, the focal point is a big front porch, bookended by fancy wicker swings. The Party People have put a lot of work into the house since I've been gone.

My childhood home, by contrast, is a small two-story bungalow in need of multiple repairs. The worst part is I don't have the money to keep up with the payments. I made September's, and I have enough until the end of the year, but I don't know about the future. Mama had savings, but most of it is earmarked for my sister's college. She did have a small life insurance policy, but it hardly counts, and it may take a few months to trickle in. For the hundredth time . . . *what am I going to do?* A desperate feeling curls in my stomach. Money doesn't buy happiness, but a little right now would go a long way to easing my stress.

Anger burning bright at the Jeep, I turn my attention back to the party house. Cars are parked two by two in the long drive. Adding more insult to injury, one of them, a white Mustang, has partially pulled up behind my driveway, blocking Mama's (my) older-model pink Cadillac.

The front door opens next door, and several women spill out, holding drinks as they line dance in the yard to "Cotton-Eyed Joe." The girls appear youngish . . . hang on . . . is this a college party? Blue Belle is a small town, but we do have a community college on the west side of town.

My ire rises. I need to establish some rules with my new neighbor. One, invite all the neighbors when you throw a party in the cove (it's called southern hospitality); two, control your parking situation; three, play decent music; four, don't let your party go past ten on a Saturday night.

I march toward the house—

"Nova! Wait a minute," calls a voice from across the street, and I stop and turn. Illuminated by her porch light, Mrs. Meadows stands on her steps, somehow appearing regal in her floor-length blue robe, fuzzy house shoes, and Stetson. In her sixties, she's tiny, about five feet, with shoulder-length gray-blonde hair. Don't let the short stature fool you. She's a powerhouse.

She moves off her stoop and hurries over to me, squinting at Sparky in my arms. "That thing looks like a rat. Oh goodness, why is the skin wrinkly? It looks evil, dear. I like a calico cat, the ones with fluffy tails, but I prefer dogs. I've got a little Pomeranian. His name is Bill, after my late husband. He adores hot dogs. I shouldn't give them to him, but when he begs, I can't resist."

I'd forgotten how much she loves to talk.

"Ah. Great. Sparky here is just hairless—but not harmless," I say, then point to the flower bed. "One of my neighbor's partiers took out my special rosebush and my sister's. I can't let that pass. Aren't you on the HOA for our neighborhood? These cars are everywhere on the street. That has to be against the rules."

"Yes, I'm on the HOA, the school board, the beautification committee, and the booster club," she says proudly, then sighs as she checks out my flower bed. "I'm sure it was just an accident. I'm sorry about Darla, dear. It was so sudden. I came to the visitation and the funeral. She was a good woman." She winces. "And of course, her jelly was amazing."

I bite back a smile. Mrs. Meadows and Mama were friends but rivals when it came to food. Mama had taken the blue ribbon at the county fair for her jelly for the past five years: her strawberry versus Mrs. Meadows's apple.

"Thank you for the casseroles you brought over," I say. Which reminds me to add thank-you notes to my list of things to do, right next to *get a job*. With few employment opportunities here, I picture myself driving around town with a Pizza Hut thingy on my car. Worse, I imagine myself delivering to the houses of people I went to high school with. Nova Morgan, homecoming queen, delivering a deep dish right to your front door.

"You plan on staying in town?" she asks.

"This is Sabine's home, and I'm her guardian now." Me. In charge of a fifteen-year-old.

She tips her Stetson up. "Well, at least you didn't have to relocate a family down here. Bless, you never did get married, did you? Of course, everyone thought you'd marry Andrew, but . . ."

I wince at my ex's name and hear the southern subtext. I haven't snared a man; therefore I'm a failure.

"Nope. On the shelf at twenty-nine. Now . . . if you'll excuse me, I need to talk to my neighbor."

She takes my arm gently, being careful around Sparky. "Dear. Just let Coach have his party. We beat Wilson High last night—and it's his birthday. The boosters are throwing him a small thing. You know how important football is to Blue Belle."

I physically recoil. A Texas high school football coach is living next door!

She's oblivious to my horror. "We made it to the state finals last year with him. He used to play pro ball—"

I glare at my decimated bushes. "I don't care who he is."

"I understand you're upset, but let the flower beds go for a moment." She gives me a reassuring smile, one I'm sure she's given many Blue Belle citizens who need managing. She herds me away from the party house. "How are you? Really? I heard that quarterback from the New England Cougars broke your heart for a supermodel. Just terrible. What was his name?"

I'd bet a hundred bucks she knows his name, stats, and salary.

My chest tightens. "Zane, and she was a flight attendant."

We dated for six months; then things started to fizzle. He was in the middle of football season, and I was working two jobs. It felt like a lull, but I assumed once we weren't so busy, it would fire back up.

I didn't know he was looking for greener pastures.

We should explore options but still see each other, Nova.

In other words, *I'll keep you on the line while I bang this hot, younger girl I met on a Delta flight.*

A long sigh comes from me.

Since high school, athletes were my kryptonite, but Zane was the last straw.

I'm done now. No more jocks. No more sexy muscles and cocksure attitudes. I swear to God and Jesus and the Holy Ghost.

"Ah," she murmurs. "I see. So you'll be looking for a man. Maybe you *should* meet Coach, but don't go over there angry. Let me see if I can get him to the Waffle House for breakfast tomorrow, and you can drop by, yes?"

I come to a stop. "I don't need a man, Mrs. Meadows. I have a life. A career." This is a lie. I have nothing. The Manhattan preschool where I worked has already hired someone. The Baller has tons of servers who wanted my position.

"Call me Lois. Remember that time I caught you stealing apples from my prize tree in the backyard? The green ones I use to make my jelly?"

"Yes." I'd taken them several times before, successfully, but that day I fell out of the tree and skinned my knees. She scolded me for half an hour, pacing around her backyard and waving her hands as she warned me about the perils of a life of crime. I was ten.

"Lordy, you were a handful growing up. I never told your mama about any of it."

"Thank you?"

She nods sagely. "All I'm saying is I know when to preserve the peace. Instead of telling your mama about you stealing my apples, I gave you a good talking-to, and that was the end of it."

"I see. You want me to preserve the peace. With the coach?"

"Yes. I'll chat with him for you." She leans in. "Look, things are precarious right now. I'm worried he might not stay in town, so we got a special committee together to find him a nice local gal to settle down with—" She lets out a squeak as I flip around and march toward his house. "Wait!"

I walk toward my neighbor's. "I get it, Mrs. Meadows; you don't want me to rock the boat, but I'm not going to . . ." I inhale a breath as I search the sky for words. "Ruin anything for the team or you. I just want to talk to him." And get a look at him because she's made me wonder just who the heck this man is. A person needs to know their enemies, and yes, right now, he's the bad guy who's having a party, and I must assess. "Plus, there's a vehicle parked behind mine, and I want ice cream." Just now, I decided it.

"Take my car."

I halt and gape at her. "You're serious, aren't you? He doesn't get a pass just because he's on a pedestal."

She reaches for her inhaler in her pocket and takes a shot. "I knew you were going to be trouble."

"*Trouble* is tattooed on my ass," I reply.

She follows me down the sidewalk to his house, her fluffy house shoes keeping step with my Converses. "My grandson, Milo, plays wide receiver. He's really good, Nova, and we're hoping he can get a football scholarship to UT next year. I need Coach to stay in town if it's going to happen."

"That's wonderful that Milo's talented," I say gently as I recall a rambunctious blond-haired little boy who used to play with my sister. "I can understand that you want the best for him. You're a good grandma."

"Right. Let's me and you go back to my house. I have this essential oil, lavender, that I put in a diffuser. It gives you calm, and I'll fire it up; then we can have some tea and cookies. I can get out my apple jelly and give you a jar to—"

"That sounds fabulous. Some other time." I march up the newly redone steps of the house to the porch, taking in the mounted ceiling speakers where the music is blasting. Nice.

I dodge around the dancing women. She follows, panting slightly.

Points to Mrs. Meadows for determination, but my roses demand recompense. Seeing them mowed down is a metaphor for my entire life, and now that I know he's an ex–football player, I find it even more despicable.

Through the glass door I have a view of the kitchen that leads to an open area, a huge den where several women are watching a football game on the big screen. Some lounge on the kitchen stools, chatting as they sip drinks and munch on the appetizers on the countertop.

Not a man in sight.

Frowning, I pause, realization dawning. "You mentioned a special committee. Did they invite these women?"

"Yes, I planned it. I'm head of the Blue Belle Booster Club. In hindsight, I should have invited you. My mistake. I'll be sure you're at the next football event."

"Don't bother. You're trying to get him married?"

She lets out a gusty breath. "How many times do I have to say it? We want him to stay, Nova. We've introduced him to some of the prettiest girls in town. Melinda Tyler is here. She was Miss Texas. Very good family. She might be the one."

Ohh, a beauty queen. Only the best for a coach.

I huff out a rueful laugh. I'm not surprised at all by the machinations. When I was in high school, the Blue Belle Booster Club bought a new Escalade for our coach after he won state. Once they rented a $2,000-a-month billboard in Huddersfield—our biggest rival—with just *34–10* on it and kept it up all year. Everyone knew what it was. The score from the game where we'd decimated them. The boosters—and their special committees—will do whatever it takes to keep the team happy. Need a million-dollar jumbotron? Done. Want a college-size stadium? You got it. Want a wife in a small town? We'll find her.

"Unbelievable," I mutter.

She shrugs. "He had a woman, but she lives in New York, and you know how those city girls are."

"I'm a city girl."

She harrumphs. "Not in your heart, dear. Anyway, she's some model and never would have settled down here. She came to some of the games last year and was highfalutin, just plain old pretentious. That's who took out your bush, dear. I saw her peel out of here, and if you let me, I can call a landscaping company to fix them, and I'll even pay for it—"

"Aunt Lois! Great party!" calls one of the girls from the other side of the porch as she swings in the wicker seat. She waves. Round face, brown hair. Pretty. Chewing gum.

"How old is your niece?"

She bristles. "Twenty."

"How old is he?"

"Thirty-two today. He likes them young."

My teeth grit. "Well. I can't wait to meet this fine, fine man."

I murmur sweet words in Sparky's ear and set him down on the porch. I adore my cat, the only male who's never let me down, but he's not a people person per se, which is why I keep a firm grasp on his leash.

Straightening my shoulders, I open the door, step into the kitchen, and scan the room.

Eventually the women take notice a few at a time and turn to look. They are all younger than me and look fabulous: cute shorts and skirts, low-cut slinky tops, hair long and styled. I don't recognize a soul. Most of my high school friends have moved on to bigger cities, or I've lost touch with them. Part of me wilts as I take in the fashionable crew—then I shove it aside. Not here to impress anyone.

One of them, a leggy redhead in a shimmery green pantsuit with a belted tie, arches a carefully manicured brow at me as she sips on a martini. There's a small diamond headband on her head. Hello, Miss Texas.

She rises from her seat in the den, as graceful as a swan, and glides toward us in that way that beautiful women have when they've had classes in posture. I had those same classes.

She gives a perfect smile to Mrs. Meadows, then takes me in. "Hi there. Who are you?" She says it like I'm a five-year-old and lost.

I'm wearing gray joggers with a hole in one leg and a wrinkled Johnny Cash shirt, and my hair is scraped up in a messy bun. I'm desperately in need of highlights. Not a stitch of makeup.

You wouldn't believe it now, but a long time ago, I was a beauty queen. The memories of those days prick at my heart, and I shove them down and give her my sweet, sweet smile. I add a little extra Texas to my voice as I run a sweeping gaze over the ladies. "Hey, y'all."

"Hey . . . ," comes from a few as they size me up.

Yes, an interloper is here. Someone not in fashion and considered elderly.

"Come on, Sparky." He prances ahead of me as I walk to the island and grab one of the cold sodas that are resting in a cute little tin tub—a woman did that. I twist off the top, then take a long drink as I glance at the myriad of food, streamers, and balloons, all in maroon, gold, and navy, Bobcat colors. **HAPPY BIRTHDAY, COACH** is written on a large banner that's been draped from the ceiling over the fireplace in the den. Whoever this guy is, they're laying it on thick, and if he's winning games, well then, he's their new favorite person.

I note the stainless steel appliances and the large white marble island. The new cabinetry. The ash-colored hardwood floors, the rustic wood-and-metal pendant lights. It's all very urban farmhouse. The renovations make me yearn to fix Mama's—my—house. That knot of responsibility tightens again in my chest. One day at a time, Nova.

"And you are . . . ?" comes from the redhead, her voice inquisitive. She's followed me.

"I'm Nova Morgan." I grab a chip, swoop it through what looks like homemade guac, and chew. "Great party. 'Cotton-Eyed Joe' on repeat is just fantastic, but I'd love it if you turned it down. I have a sister next door who's trying to sleep." Lie. She's not even close to going to bed.

Someone moves in the room, and the music is turned down considerably. My bets are on Mrs. Meadows. I shake my head. She really is something, trailing me to the party in her nightclothes.

"Oh. I've heard of you," Miss Texas says, a light dawning in her green eyes. "You went to school with my sister."

I squint at the glossy red hair. The Tyler family had four girls, all gingers with M names. It dawns on me. "You're Marla's little sister?"

Miss Texas sniffs. "Yes. She lives in Dallas now. She married Brad."

I wince. I might have kissed Brad, Marla's long-term boyfriend, in tenth grade, and I might have made sure Marla knew about it . . .

"Good for them. Where's Coach?" I ask the room.

"That would be me," a deep voice says from behind me. There's arrogance mixed with exasperation in his voice, and my lips tighten. Metaphorically, I pull up my big-girl panties and mutter, *Bring it on, jock-ass.*

Steeling myself, I turn to face him, seeing the french doors from the den have been opened, which is probably where he came from. The back entrance leads out to a glittering blue kidney-shaped pool, lit by underwater lights. There's even a waterfall. Modern, sleek-looking chaise lounges dot the area. Girls in bikinis walk around. A few men. Finally.

I focus on him, gasp, and then shut my eyes, hoping he'll disappear. But when I open them, he's still there.

No, this can't be right . . .

But the logical side of my mind says, *Fate just bitch-slapped you.*

I bite back a groan.

Holy shit.

Ronan Smith.

The worst, most horrible, can't-even-think-about-it-without-cringing one-night stand ever.

Chapter 3

Nova

I feel dizzy, as if I've been suddenly transported to another dimension. My hand finds the edge of the island and clings to it.

It's been over two years, and he looks the same yet different. Wearing plain navy swim trunks, his body is exquisite, with broad rippling shoulders that taper down to a muscled chest, a six-pack, and then a sharply defined V. He's shockingly tan and healthy looking, a stark contrast to the pale, gaunt-faced man from before.

His height is around six-four, and his legs are slightly parted in a warrior stance. A towel is around his neck, and he reaches up with a muscled forearm to rub it over his face.

I look at his lips. That night, at certain moments, they were thin and tight, but now they're plump, the bottom one lush and extravagant. That kissable mouth *almost* softens the scars on the left side of his face.

I don't dwell on the scars or the jagged line down his face, although part of me appreciates them, wonders how they've changed him, if they've created depth. I itch to paint him, scars and all, but mostly, it was always his eyes that fascinated me. Tonight, they're a blue-gray color, an icy winter storm. The night I met him, they were a hot gunmetal color, smoldering with heat.

Dark, straight brows frame his chiseled face, and his wet hair is slicked back. When it's dry, it's a mink-brown color, chin length, and wavy.

Someone—a pretty girl, twentyish—comes up between us, thank God, says something cutesy, and puts a glass of iced tea in his hands, and he murmurs a low "Thank you." I use the time to gather myself as the girl chats him up. He never takes his gaze off me, though, the lines around his eyes tightening in a way that tells me he's clocked me—he remembers.

An arc of electricity hums over my skin, and my breath quickens.

How is it possible that he's here?

He doesn't *fit*. I always pictured him still in New York, maybe in that penthouse room at the Mercer Hotel, lying on his stomach, his lips parted as he breathed the sleep of someone who'd had too much to drink. The top sheet was tangled around one of his legs, his bare ass taut and firm. One arm hung off the bed, the other curled under a pillow. He never stirred when I gathered my clothes and slipped out the door in the early hours of the morning. I ran through the hotel, and it wasn't until I got in the cab that I let the tears fall. What I'd thought was special . . . wasn't.

I used to gaze at his billboard in Times Square on my way to work. You'd see professional players hawking cologne or underwear or sneakers, but nope, his thing was literacy. **Transport Yourself with Reading.** He sat on the steps of the New York Library with a book in his hands and a wide smile on his Henry Cavill face. It made my heart flutter.

He drapes his gaze over me, one that hints at keen intelligence. He lingers on my faded shirt, scans my joggers and black Converse, and then moves slowly back up to my face. He takes a sip of his drink, slow and easy. "You all right?"

Hell no.

I expected some mediocre ex-baller, and it's *him*.

I open my mouth to say—

Miss Texas slyly eases the other girl vying for Ronan's attention out of the way, then juts between me and him, a plate of chips and dip in her hands as she offers it to him. At my feet, Sparky, a great predictor of nice people, hisses, breaks my hold on his leash, and lunges for Miss Texas.

She shrieks as she drops the plate, and it shatters. Sparky screeches, darts between her legs, pauses for a moment to swipe at the flowy leg of her pantsuit, gets his claw stuck in the fabric, fights to release it, and then roars triumphantly when he gets free.

Back arched, he runs and hisses the entire way out the back door.

I have the insane urge to laugh but stifle it as I dash out the french doors to the open pool area, my head tumbling with thorny thoughts. Oh my God, I never would have come if I'd known it was *him*. Should have listened to Mrs. Meadows! I rub my forehead in disgust. Mrs. Meadows never said his first name, and since I haven't kept up with the local gossip, I came in clueless. *Brought a knife to a gunfight*, as Mama used to say. Of course, she never told me about the new coach. She knew I was wary about our hometown team and the memories it brought.

I heave out a deep, weighted sigh. Holy . . . he's been here for a year! Sure, I came home periodically to see Mama and Sabine, but things were usually hectic . . . and he was just next door. At Christmas I noticed that someone had renovated the house, and when I asked Mama about it, her reply was *A Mr. Smith from out of town*. Such a common name.

You'd think someone might have mentioned the coach while I've been here, and maybe they did, but my mind has been a hazy cloud. Yesterday, I stared at a can of green beans for ten minutes at the Piggly Wiggly.

I make for a group of chaise lounges under a pergola where I see the end of Sparky's leash. I bend down and scoop him up and tap him on the nose, a reprimand for hissing. His eyes say, *Miss Texas is a bitch,* and I tell him that we don't call women those names and that we'll discuss it later.

"Hey, Nova!" calls a male voice, and I glance over my shoulder. I'd know that handsome square face and wavy auburn hair anywhere. Wearing jeans and a maroon Bobcats polo is Bruce Hamilton, a.k.a. Skeeter because he moved like a mosquito on the field. Relief rolls over me.

"Heard you were in town," he says in a slow drawl.

"Yep." I glance behind me. Ronan hasn't come out. Maybe he's organizing a cleanup of chips and guac in the kitchen. Maybe Mrs. Meadows is running interference. I ease back into a slice of a shadow created by the purple wisteria vines that drape from the top of the pergola.

Skeeter follows. "How are you?"

"Great!" I say brightly. *Terrible! I really want to get out of here!*

"I heard you came back. I can't believe you're staying."

I nod. This is the same conversation I've been having since I arrived. Everyone expects me to pack up Sabine and move her to New York.

"How are you?" I ask him.

"Still single and living with my mom. Happy as a pig. For real." He smirks, shrugging broad shoulders. "She cooks me breakfast every morning, packs my lunch for work, and doesn't complain when I leave my underwear on the floor."

"Basically, it's Club Med," I say with a smile. It is good to see *him*. And he hasn't changed a bit since we went to school together.

"I knew you'd be a coach someday," I say as he fills me in on his position as a coach for the Bobcats. He's in the middle of giving me a play-by-play from last night's game when I sense someone walking up.

"Nova, right?" comes Ronan's voice from behind me, unmistakable, rich, and husky.

"I met your mom," he says. "I'm sorry for your loss."

I turn slowly. "Hmm. Yes. I'm your new neighbor. Thank you. Mom never mentioned you were a coach." I mentally shake my fist at her in heaven.

He's grabbed a white T-shirt, and it sticks to his damp chest. The towel is still in his grip and hangs next to his leg. He clutches it with strong hands and long talented fingers. I can still see him on TV, catching the hike, jogging back to throw the football, and then letting a perfect pass fly. He took Michigan State to a national championship, won the Heisman, was drafted as the number-one pick in the draft, and then brought home three Super Bowl trophies to the Pythons. He was Peyton Manning and Tom Brady on crack.

After working at the preschool, I bartended at night at the Baller. The bar was a private club, with a clientele of mostly professional athletes, yet he was never one of our customers. I never gave up hope that he'd walk in one day. My fascination wasn't with how hot he looked in football pants—which he did—no, it was about the masterful way he played the game. You'd think that after my heart was broken in college by my first love, Andrew, I'd be jaded about the game, but when you grow up in a Texas small town, football is ingrained in your soul.

"Ah, I see," he says in a distant tone as he glances around at the party. "Nice to meet you."

Wait . . .

Really?

We've "met."

I frown, and he notices, a quizzical look appearing on his face as our eyes cling . . . and oh my God . . . not a hint of recognition is there. Nada.

Did I misinterpret in the kitchen?

I step out of the shadows, and his face doesn't change. Not a flicker of *I know you.*

I should say, *Nice to meet you too*—it's the proper southern thing to do before I bring up the roses—but . . .

He doesn't recognize me. *For real.* Okay, okay, maybe I have put on a few (ten) pounds, have a few lines around my eyes, and am not dressed like some stupid princess from a galaxy far, far away, but obviously he's the kind of guy who's slept with so many women he can't recall one—even the girl he called by the wrong name.

Bitterness rises. I've replayed the Awful One-Night Stand a million times in my head, berating myself for going to his hotel room, for believing we shared a connection.

He'd been drinking—okay, I'll give him that—but the alcohol didn't hinder his sexual performance, and he didn't slur his words either.

You're perfect. You're safe with me. You're mine . . .

We were effortless and natural, almost instinctive, two people sensing familiar souls, ones with cracks but not completely broken. And when he kissed me in the elevator . . . a long sigh comes from my lips. I wanted to be *his*.

My hands clench as I wrestle with my emotions. He really doesn't remember me.

Skeeter slaps him on the back. "Ronan, this lady was the prettiest girl to ever attend Blue Belle High. We did some crazy shit together. Remember that time we put popcorn in the Huddersfield quarterback's truck, Nova?" He glances at Ronan. "It was the night before our big game, and we popped about a hundred bags and dumped them in his car."

I smile. "And our own cafeteria ladies let us in their kitchen to pop them. Five microwaves. We hit the jackpot."

"I bet that jerk quarterback is still finding kernels in his car." He chuckles as he glances at Ronan. "Me and Nova and Andrew. We got up to some trouble."

I nod and smile. "Good times for sure." But not all of them, especially with Andrew. I toss a quick glance around the pool area, a sigh of relief coming. He's not here.

Ronan gives me his unmarred profile, his tone annoyed, seemingly uninterested in our reminiscences. "Ah, great. Look, Lois told me about the flower bed. Sorry. It was Jenny. She came in and made a scene—"

"Your girlfriend," I state, my chin tilted up. "Young. Blonde. She said it was over, by the way, and she really meant it this time. She might have been chewing gum."

He frowns and gives me his full attention. "Not my girlfriend. She showed up unannounced."

"Tricky," I reply. "What was she, then?"

His scowl deepens. "That's none of your concern."

I shrug. "Whatever. Sounds like a communication problem between you and her. I'd be upset, too, if I walked into this hen party."

A long pause follows. "You're angry with me."

"Gold star for you."

Hello. I don't care that you're a fancy-pants coach, nor do I care about your relationship status.

And . . .

Come on . . .

You don't remember me?

Skeeter guffaws, his eyes darting between us. "Gotta give it to the boosters. If the party had been left up to me, we'd be out at the gravel pit shooting rattlesnakes. Maybe driving some four-wheelers through the mud."

"That sounds like a real good time, Skeeter," Ronan replies in a soft tone, but his gaze never leaves mine.

Whispering sweet words in his ear, I set Sparky down and cross my arms.

Ronan arches a brow as the cat sits at my feet and looks up at him.

"Look. Your Jenny in a Jeep took out my roses, just ran right over them, ones my mama planted for my first birthday and my sister's. The yellow ones. She picked them out at the store in Austin, dug the holes herself, painted our names on a rock, wrote a sweet note to us, put it all in a little metal box, and then placed it inside with the bushes. Every birthday, we took a picture of us next to the roses. We have an album for them that sits on the coffee table." I want him to know the significance. Every time I came home, I'd look at those lush, creamy blooms and know that no matter where I roamed or lived in the world, *this* was home. It's where my life began. My roots are in those roses. "What are you going to do about it?"

He throws the towel on a lounger, and his hands go to his hips, his fingers clasping that V. "Lois said she'd take care of the flowers. Also, this party was a surprise to me. I don't normally entertain. I'm sorry it inconvenienced you, all right? We good now?"

I smile tightly. "Absolutely. I see how it is. Send one of your boosters. Let everyone in Blue Belle bow and scrape to take care of your problems so you can keep on entertaining your guests and winning football games. I get why Mama never mentioned you. You're a pompous jerk."

Even though I kept my voice low, there's a lull in the conversations around us, and I can feel heads turning, eyes lingering on us. Mrs. Meadows makes one of her squeaks. Clearly, she hasn't let me out of her sight.

Skeeter clears his throat. "Wow. Nice night. And the stars are so bright. This pool is amazing. That waterfall, man, love it . . ." His words trail off.

Ronan's chest rises. "I'm a pompous jerk?"

"Oh, you're so much more than that, but children are present, so I'll temper my language," I say.

Skeeter's forehead furrows as he looks around. "I thought this was an adults-only party."

"She means the women," Ronan says, his jaw popping.

"Oh, yeah, um, lots of them here . . . ," Skeeter replies and sticks his hands in his pockets. "Think I'll go get some chicken fingers. Be right back. Good to see you, Nova."

He isn't coming back.

Ronan shifts on his feet, then takes a step closer to me. He smells like summer, sun, and man. My heart does a flip-flop in my chest, but it's because I'm pissed. Several moments tick by as we stare at each other.

"Perhaps we should talk in private, Ms. Morgan," he says curtly.

I'm not sure I can handle being alone with him. Not without some armor, and by *armor*, I mean a kick-ass dress and stilettos. Maybe that would get his attention.

He takes my elbow before I move, surprising me. I let him guide me and Sparky past staring girls in bikinis, through the french doors, into the den, and down a hallway to a door. He opens it and ushers me inside. I step in as he stalks around me to a big oak desk, crosses his arms, and leans on it, a flat expression on his face. "Now we can chat without either of us causing any more chaos tonight." He looks at Sparky.

I ignore him and gaze around.

It's a trophy room—an office but huge, maybe twenty by twenty feet. There's a lot to take in. Shiny golden football statues sit on a shelf on the wall behind him, and holy football legends . . . there's the Heisman.

Framed photos of him are on the right side of the walls, him and his team accepting the Super Bowl trophy. I see Tuck and wince. Ouch. There's a memory . . .

The left side of the room is full of memorabilia. Signed movie scripts under glass with lights on them, autographed posters of the *Star Wars* actors, Funko Pop figurines, a model starship. It's like the galaxy threw up.

In the back is an elaborately carved pool table, a movie screen, and several theater-style recliners. My eyes flare when I see a life-size Chewbacca and Darth Vader in the corner side by side, looming at each other. I huff out a laugh.

"Is something funny, Ms. Morgan?"

Ignoring him, I leave Sparky to waltz around the room, heading to the trophies, grazing my fingers over the Heisman. About fourteen inches tall, it's smaller than I thought it would be.

"Go ahead. Pick it up," he says.

Biting my bottom lip, I pick up the trophy and gasp at the heaviness, then carefully set it back on the shelf.

"It weighs forty-five pounds. Cast bronze," he says gruffly. "I nearly dropped it when they gave it to me." There's a hint of emotion in his voice, and I recall the way he accepted it at twenty-one, his jawline sculpted perfectly, a devilish light in his eyes, a man born in the inner city who climbed to the top, ready to take on the world and win.

What must it feel like to lose it all?

I throw a look at him. "It's only given to one player out of hundreds and represents talent, integrity, diligence, and perseverance. Do you still have those qualities?"

His tone is dry. "My talent is gone, sadly. I wasn't aware my integrity was in question. It's this party and your annoyance with it. Please say your piece, and we'll be done." He moves his hands in a "Give it to me" motion.

"I said it already. You're a jerk." I wave my hand at the hairy monster in the corner. "How tall is that thing?"

"That thing is Chewie. He's seven feet, five inches. He's a Wookiee, a mechanic, a smuggler, and Han Solo's copilot. Darth Vader, the man in black, is the bad guy. He's six-eight. Would you like to see my Princess Leia?"

I start, then spin around. "Where?"

"In the closet."

Now that just hurts my feelings.

He heads to a door near the back, and I trail behind him.

The door opens, and I blink, my heart flipping over. My costume didn't look that good. "You don't make out with it, do you? Like those blow-up dolls? A synthetic partner?"

"No," he says on an exhale. "I like real women."

I cock my head, studying the wax Carrie Fisher look-alike.

"The bra is copper, and the bottoms have a metal plate at the front and back." He fingers the links around her neck. "The chain and collar bound her to Jabba the Hutt."

"Who?"

He glares at me. "A big ugly alien crime lord who captured Leia. She used it to kill him. Any more questions?"

"I know who they are," I say rather defensively. "I've never watched the movies, though. I'm a unicorn." I smile at him. Just because.

"Fascinating."

"You're a geek." A grumpy geek god. I always knew it. I kind of liked it. Not anymore.

"Unapologetically. Now . . ." His words trail off as I leave him. I hear him huff as I pass a glass case mounted on the wall—what the . . . ? I back up. There's a golden snake cuff inside the case, looking small next to a poster of the white-clad Princess Leia.

That cuff is *mine*. I reach out to touch—

"Ms. Morgan, please don't touch anything."

I place my finger on it, smear it, and then turn around. "Oops."

"You're trying to antagonize me."

"Your brain is, like, super amazing."

"Why make the effort to be rude, Ms. Morgan? Is there something about me you don't care for?" His eyes glitter at me.

Oh, I like poking at him. A lot. He's kind of infuriating, but underneath . . . my skin shivers. He's a wild man. Vicious. A beast. *I* remember.

I smile knowingly at him.

He blinks, then frowns. "Have we met before?"

Someone knocks on the door, and it swings open, Miss Texas poking her head in. She poses in the doorway and gazes at Ronan. "We're about to light the candles and sing 'Happy Birthday.' Are you ready?"

She gives me a cool glance, then checks the dainty Rolex on her wrist. "It's getting late, and some of the guests are wanting to get started."

I pick up Sparky and move toward the door and slip out. Honestly? I need away from him to recover myself. I put on a good front, but underneath there's a mix of anger and sharp disappointment simmering . . .

Anger is just sad lashing out, Mama would say.

God. I miss her.

"Ms. Morgan. Wait—" he calls after me, but I'm gone.

By the time I find my way back to the kitchen—the house is a maze—Miss Texas has beaten me and holds a sheet cake, the fancy kind you get at a bakery. There's a carefully detailed football field with little players and people in the stadium on top of it. **We love you, Coach Smith,** it reads. Another girl lights the candles.

"Leaving so soon?" Miss Texas asks me sweetly.

A quick scan tells me Ronan is back outside, surrounded by women, waiting for the cake to come out, I guess. He captures my eyes, a scowl deepening on his chiseled face. Nope, not going to get caught in a staring contest.

I flip around and brush past Miss Texas, giving her a smirk. "Tell Marla—and Brad—I said hi."

Mrs. Meadows follows me into the foyer, a look of sympathy on her face, one that's surprising, and I deflate slowly, my shoulders slumping. "Did I cause a scene?"

"It wasn't *too* bad. You got his attention, that's for sure, which is more than I can say for most women." She searches my face. "There seemed to be some . . . long pauses and tension between y'all. You both lived in New York at the same time. I'm wondering if you ever came across him?"

She is the last person I want to know about my night with Ronan. "Never."

"Ah, I see, hmm. Anyway, breakfast tomorrow—you and him? I can set it up. Just to mend fences. Maybe freshen up a bit when you come. Wear some makeup."

"I have no interest in being one of the women you throw at Ronan." Been there, fucked him. It wasn't great.

"Ronan, is it?"

Exhaustion flares, and I inch toward the front door to exit. "See you later."

She frowns. "Are you okay, dear?"

I'm really *not* okay.

And it's not just Ronan. It's Mama's death, Sabine, the house, being in my hometown with painful memories I can't seem to shake, the total upheaval of my life. I left behind two good jobs and a nice apartment, and now I'm starting all over from scratch. Sure, I've done it before, but I was younger and more optimistic. Blue Belle needs to stick.

I push up a smile. "I'm fine."

Leaving her there, still watching me, I walk through the foyer and out to the front porch as a chorus of female voices sings "Happy Birthday."

"Hope it's a good one," I mutter as I take the sidewalk and let Sparky down. He prisses in front of me, his tail twitching.

"Have fun, hmm?" I ask him.

He throws me a look. If he had eyebrows, one would be arched.

I recall him stuck in the pantsuit, and a grin curls my lips. "You're my ride or die, Sparky. Forever and always."

Sabine stands on our steps as I come up to our house. She's wearing cutoff shorts and a baggy Bobcats shirt. Her face is a replica of Mama's, high cheekbones and pointy chin, mercurial hazel eyes. With deep-chestnut hair that's long and thick with a slight wave to it, she's startlingly beautiful with an IQ that makes me feel like an idiot. Born a month after our dad died, she didn't speak until she was three, and then it was in complete sentences. She taught herself to read by four.

Her head cocks. "You went for a long walk. Why?"

"Met some neighbors." They suck.

"There's one hundred and seventy-nine days of darkness in Antarctica. Most of it is covered in ice over a mile thick."

My heart swells at her dedication to geography. She has stacks of books in her room, all about different countries and locales. "Want to move there?"

She sets down the paint cans she was holding but doesn't let them get too far. Like me, she's an artist, and painting her bedroom different colors has been her therapy after Mama's death. We go to Ace Hardware and pick out new colors every other day.

"No. This is where I was born, and this is where I want to live."

"I was kidding."

"I knew that." She shrugs.

"I hate the cold anyway." I inhale the September air, catching the scent of the magnolia trees nearby. The familiar sounds of crickets and frogs surround us, and it loosens some of the tension in my chest. "Did you come to find me? You wanna talk?" I sit down next to her on the steps.

We've talked a lot. *Mama is gone. I'm here. I won't leave you. Ever.*

She rubs the jewelry on her finger, a white quartz ring with a gold band that Mama gave her. Diagnosed with high-functioning autism when she was five, she uses the ring to release stress. "What happened to the flower bed?"

"Ah, someone accidentally drove over them." I briefly explain about the Jeep and the coach's party, skating around the part about me confronting Ronan. She tells me she's been upstairs in her room painting with headphones on.

"Mama would be pissed."

She learned *pissed* from me. Must do better.

"Coach Smith is not your usual coach," she adds.

"Oh? You've talked to him?"

"He's my World History teacher."

Mr. Smith *was* on her course list. I give myself a facepalm. School's been in session for only two weeks, and we haven't had an open house yet, but . . . "How did I miss that? You didn't think to tell me he was the football coach?"

"Why would I? Everyone knows."

Right. She assumes that if she knows it, then I should.

"We almost won state last year. We would have, but Huddersfield took the title. Football is the most exciting thing in Blue Belle."

"Yet I missed him being the coach."

"You stare off into space a lot," she says.

"I'm working on that."

"In eighth grade, when I took US History, Coach Mitchell sat at his desk and told us to read the chapter and answer the questions at the end. It was tedious and pointless. I don't think my classmates learned anything about our country. Coach Smith talks to us; he explains." She pauses. "Did you find a job today?"

The preschool in town is fully staffed, Piggly Wiggly doesn't need cashiers, Randy's Roadhouse has enough waitstaff, and the Mini Mart said I was overqualified. That fear skates down my spine again, and I swallow as I tighten my messy bun and feign confidence. Sabine has sensory issues, elastic in her clothing is a big no-no, and social interactions can baffle her, but she's more intuitive than all the books I've read would suggest. Maybe it's because she's my sister. Maybe her diagnosis gives her a special psychic superpower. Whatever it is, she senses when I'm worried no matter the brave face I wear. "It could have been better, but it will work out," I say.

I pull the keys to the Cadillac out of my joggers. "I'm in the mood for ice cream. How about me and you head to Dairy Queen?" We limit her sugar, but their menu has options. "There's a car behind us, but we're Mighty Morgan Girls, and nothing keeps us from a Blizzard."

"Can we do the drive from the Dairy Queen to the Pig?"

Ah, the old cruising loop in Blue Belle. "You want to see who's out and about?"

She ticks off her fingers. "I am a teenager. I do have social interests. It is Saturday night. Toby has a car. I might see him."

"Toby?"

"He's a football player. Quarterback." She smirks. "I asked him if he liked me, and he said yes. Then he touched my hair and twirled it around his finger."

No. Jesus. I'm going to kill him.

"Of course he's an athlete," I mutter under my breath.

"We sit together in study hall. He's very hot. Great ass."

A long sigh comes from me. "Oh, Sabine. You remind me of . . . me."

"Am I old enough to date?"

"I . . . don't . . . know." I was allowed to date at fifteen, but what's the norm now? I want to protect her, but I'm not sure how . . .

"Mama gave me an anatomy book when I turned fourteen, but it didn't go into detail about sexual intercourse. I read the entire thing. It was four hundred and sixty pages long with pictures. Not the dirty kind, just diagrams. It was skimpy about orgasms. It's harder for women to have them, and I have questions."

"And I want to answer them, but can we discuss this later?"

"When is later?"

"Let me think on it, okay?"

"When will you be finished thinking on it?" She's very exact.

"Give me a week."

She nods. "One week, starting now."

We stand up and pile into Mama's car. She straps herself in, then reminds me to do mine.

Using the mirrors and her help, I back up as far as I can get without dinging the car blocking us, then pull forward and turn the wheel into the yard. Being easy on the accelerator, we ease forward to the porch and skirt around a big holly bush.

"Thelma and Louise!" I call out as I drive through the yard and over the sidewalk, hit the curb, and then plop down on the street.

"Who are they?"

"Female road trip movie. Excellent. Sadly, we don't have Brad Pitt with us—oh, and don't worry, we won't drive off a cliff."

"Joke. Funny." She rolls down her window and looks up at the stars. "I woke up this morning and forgot Mama was gone. I thought everything was the same; then I remembered it wasn't. Can we sing Dolly in the morning like she used to do when I had breakfast? Her singing—" Her voice stops, and I reach out and take her hand.

I swallow thickly. "You bet."

She takes a deep breath. "I'm glad you're here."

"You're just happy Grandpa isn't your guardian."

"He smells like peppermint and farts a lot."

"And he lives in Phoenix," I add.

She nods. "Everything will be fine. We're different flowers from the same garden, but we're perfect together. Mama always said so."

Mama did say that, not necessarily because of Sabine's diagnosis but because we're opposites in personality and have a fourteen-year age difference between us. She had me at twenty-six and tried for years to have another baby, gave up, and then got pregnant at forty. Then my dad had a massive heart attack while mowing the lawn.

It's just been me and Mama and Sabine for fifteen years, the Mighty Morgan Girls, and I try to cling to that thought, to be strong . . . like Mama.

She's going to be a lot to live up to.

We're different flowers from the same garden, but we're perfect together.

My throat tightens with grief, with fear that I'm not enough, at the trust I heard in Sabine's words . . .

We're going to be okay.

Maybe if I keep saying it, it will be true.

Chapter 4

Ronan

My dreams wake me up, twisted and dark, and my hands clench the sheets as images flit through my head: a stormy night, lightning hitting the road, my Tahoe slamming into a bridge and then rolling down the embankment, Whitney's scream piercing my ears—then her in my arms. She begged me to help her, to let her live, and I could do nothing as the light went out of her eyes. The memory crawls over me, and I sit up and scrub my face with hands that shake.

There haven't been any thunderstorms here lately, yet something brought that dream on . . .

My dog, possibly an Irish wolfhound, puts his head on my shoulder, disrupting my thoughts. He showed up at the back door the day I moved in, mangy, skinny, and ugly, with no collar. I figure someone dumped him in the nice neighborhood. Or maybe he just found me. I give him a pet. "Morning, Dog." He licks my hand, then rolls back over and puts his head on the pillow next to mine.

After I shower, my phone rings—Lois asking if I want to have breakfast at Waffle House and suggesting I focus on a rushing game against Wayne Prep next week. I hum a noncommittal reply, decline breakfast, and get off the phone.

Later, after I've gotten my workout clothes on and had a cup of coffee, another booster calls and invites me to First Baptist. "It's the biggest church in town," he tells me, "and oh, by the way, my daughter is just lovely and would love to meet you."

My jaw grinds. I bet she would. The women are coming out of the woodwork to lock me down.

The people love me, but they're meaner than a big-ass linebacker making a tackle when it comes to getting me a girlfriend.

Dog bumps into me, nearly knocking me down as he dashes to the french doors and barks. I hush him and follow his gaze out to the pool and see a naked cat standing on a chaise lounge. The thing is screeching like a banshee. Dog growls, and I push him back and go outside. The cat sashays over to me, rubbing in between my legs. Then it darts for the french doors to glare at Dog through the glass. Brave little bastard. I snatch him up by the scruff of his wrinkled pink skin—weird as hell—and read his fancy collar.

"Hello, Sparky," I say in a dark tone.

I hold him in the crook of my arm, and he squirms to get away as I head to the pool house for a plastic container. I could call Nova—her cell was on the collar—but by the time she gets here, he might run.

I place the cat in the bin, gently, leaving the top vented. He doesn't go in easy and scratches my arm, making blood bloom in a long line. "You're a little shit," I tell him as I frown at the memory of her, the *only* person to give me lip since I arrived in Blue Belle. *Pompous jerk.* Indeed. Even when I was young and brash, no one dared call me arrogant.

I heft the container up and start for the gate that leads to the sidewalk of the neighborhood. Her house is the smallest in our cove, a bit run down but charming, with faded-cream bricks, soft-blue shutters, and a wide stone front porch. In the driveway is a pale-pink Cadillac. I used to see Mrs. Morgan in it, a tall lady with dark hair. She brought me strawberry jam the week I moved in, and that was about the extent of our interactions.

I get to her front porch, then pause at the flower beds, my jaw grinding. Jenny. Dammit. An acquaintance of Tuck's, I met her a few months before I moved to Texas last year.

A long sigh comes from my chest as I bend down and check out the two taller bushes, her birthday plants. They took the brunt of the Jeep, their stalks bent, bright petals littering the mulch.

After everyone left last night, I replayed Nova's words several times, unable to sleep. Insomnia is a regular occurrence, but this felt different. Around two in the morning, I took Dog for a walk, but it was too dark to see her flower beds from the sidewalk. I stood there for half an hour trying to figure out why meeting my neighbor made me antsy. It was guilt, I decided, over the roses. I came home, googled *yellow rosebushes*, and went down a rabbit hole for an hour.

Leaving that behind, I rap hard on the door. "Jolene," by Dolly Parton, comes from the house as the door opens slowly. I lower my lids as I take her in. Messy long blonde hair, one side flattened. Sleepy sky-blue eyes. Drool on her cheek.

Tall, maybe five-eight, she's wearing what look like men's boxers and a white tank top. A slice of her stomach is revealed, tanned and toned, and a pink feather boa is around her neck. My lips quirk at that; then I freeze when I see her nipples pressing through the fabric, erect and hard. I force myself to move back to her face. She takes a slow sip of the coffee in her hand, a bored expression on her face, but I don't miss her nose flaring or the slow, steadying breath she lets out.

She leans against the doorjamb, cool as a cucumber, and her voice has thickened since last night, a slow Texas drawl. "Goodness. Ronan Smith at my house. Long time no see—like for real, you have no idea. Is residential cat catching part of your job description as head football coach?"

She's got a mouth on her.

"I was worried this ugly thing would get eaten by my Irish wolfhound."

"Huh." Moving with grace and a good deal of *I don't care*, she steps out to the porch with long legs, sets her coffee on an outdoor end table, and then takes the bin from my hands. She puts her face up to the clear plastic and talks in a baby voice: "Poor wittle Sparky, got caught by the big bad football coach."

He puts his paw up and makes a "Help me" meow.

"He isn't ugly; he's an adorable Donskoy of Russian heritage," she says, the accent gone, her tone flat. "They're affectionate, clever, and protective. They're the dogs of the cat world."

"He scratched me." I show her the dried blood on my forearm.

"Should we call the boosters for medical help?"

So. It's going to be like that, huh? All right. Fine. I *was* dickish last night. I had good reason. I thought I'd be spending my birthday with Skeeter and some of the coaches watching football at Randy's Roadhouse. We did that for about an hour; then they cut it short, and we drove back to a houseful of people. Then Jenny showed up—surprise—saw girls in the pool with me, and had a meltdown. A twenty-two-year-old model, she pushed back the loneliness in New York like a few women have. When I moved here, I told her long distance wasn't feasible for me, but then she claimed she was in love and started showing up in Blue Belle.

After I got out of the pool, I took Jenny to my office, where she announced she was dumping me to date a Wall Street guy. I told her good luck; then she marched upstairs, found a dress she'd left, and stormed out.

I'd just recovered from that episode when Nova appeared in my kitchen. I assumed she was another candidate for the future Mrs. Smith.

"Thanks for the concern. I'll live." I stick my hands in the pockets of my Nike shorts, then change my mind and pull at the collar of my shirt. Still twitchy, I tug my hat down lower on my head and glance away from her, giving her my scarless profile. It's become a habit—not that I'm vain, but I know they're ugly.

"Your dog-cat was in my backyard," I say curtly. "You should watch Sparky better."

"There's an old dog door at the back of the house. He must have slipped out before I got up." She places the bin down, and Sparky jumps out, walks through the open door, and then jumps up on the back of a chair in one of the front windows. He stares at us with a smug look.

"Without hair, he's very expressive," she murmurs. "I love that little jerk. I wonder if he went back to your house to take a poo. It would serve you right."

I frown. "I think we got off on the wrong foot last night."

"Hmm, it was before that."

I huff. "You're not a Pythons fan, huh?"

A hesitant expression flashes on her face.

Right. Lois mentioned she'd dated Zane Williams, the current quarterback for the Pythons' rival team. I've played him and beat him. He's not up to my caliber. Or what my caliber used to be.

"You're famous," she muses. "I can't figure out how you got here. I know the booster club has a private plane and tons of money, and we've had some great coaches, but . . . you?"

"A friend went to college with the current principal. He offered, and I like Texas football." The fans are devoted, I dig the kids, and I didn't have any other offers.

And . . . I needed a fresh slate. A new focus. Away from everything I'd messed up.

I shift on my feet, my eyes flitting over her again, sticking on those pink lips, the bottom one fuller, the top with a deep V. It's the kind of mouth a man wants to crush—

My frown deepens. Something—

My peripheral vision catches sight of Melinda's Mustang pulling onto the main street that leads to our cove. Cursing under my breath, I duck down behind the stone that surrounds Nova's porch.

She shakes her head. "You're supposed to face your problems, not run from them. Is this another one of your communication issues with women?"

"I don't have issues," I growl. I just don't want to see Melinda. Last night, she hung on me like glue, even insisting on staying and cleaning up the party mess, not leaving until midnight. There was an uncomfortable moment at my door when she wrapped her arms around me, then tilted her face up for a kiss. *I'm so sorry about Jenny, Ronan. I'm here if you need me.*

Nova takes a slow sip of her coffee. "I predict an engagement by Christmas, then a spring wedding. Your china will be classic white, your pots and pans stainless steel."

"No one's getting married. Where's she now?" I say as my leg sends a pang from my crouched position.

"She's taking the turn onto our street. She's got the top down, a scarf tied around her hair, and big sunglasses on. Did you see her pantsuit last night? Divine."

An exasperated noise comes from me. "I didn't notice." Yet . . . I noticed Nova in her Johnny Cash shirt. I saw the curves under her joggers, the finely drawn features of her face, the languid way she moved. The moment she turned around in the kitchen . . . I tensed.

"I hear Britney Spears coming from her car. Yep." She flips her boa, then sings a few bars of "Oops! . . . I Did It Again." She stops and gives me a curious look. "Are you sleeping with her?"

"What? No!" A long aggrieved sigh leaves my chest. I can't get involved with anyone from Blue Belle. I don't want to lead anyone on. "Lois is trying to hook me up. I'm not oblivious to their plans."

"Hmm." She moves to sit on the top step as she gazes out at the street, giving me her profile, and it allows my eyes time to roam her face uninterrupted. Her pale-blonde hair hangs straight around her shoulders as the sun catches the honey highlights. Long dark lashes, winged brows, straight nose . . .

"She's pulling into your driveway. Should I let her know you're here?"

I narrow my eyes at her. "Just . . . tell me what she's doing."

"Really? I used to do radio work. I'm a jack-of-all-trades, really; I can do just about anything if I set my mind to it. My voice is quite good."

My brow pulls down. "Okay?"

She looks at my house, then clears her throat. "A striking redhead walks up to the front door of the house and knocks, waits, then knocks again. Holding a box of what looks like Dunkin' Donuts, she looks at her watch and taps her heels, clearly not expecting to be denied entry to the coach's lavish home."

"I wouldn't say *lavish*—"

"This Texas beauty queen is not deterred and moves to the doorbell."

"A play-by-play? Really." I glare at her.

"Mama always said if at first you don't succeed, try to make more noise . . . and wait . . . she presses the doorbell again. And again." She tsks. "That's right; she's broken Texas polite norms and rung three times. Whatever she had planned to talk about with the fancy-pants coach is important and couldn't wait. She wants him to eat her donuts, folks."

"You are insane. What kind of radio—"

She slants an eye at me. "It was a talk show about women who love football, if you must know. I did recaps of games. It didn't pay much, but it was fun." Her gaze goes back to the house. "Wait, what's this? She's pulling out a yellow sticky note made by the 3M Company."

"You're making shit up—"

Nova throws up a "Be quiet" hand and continues. "She takes a pen out of her Louis Vuitton—which is spectacular, one of the limited editions you can't find anywhere—and writes a message, something that could probably be said by text, but this beautiful man magnet seems to feel the personal touch is best. She has written her note and is now placing it . . . wait . . . nope, she's pulling it back. Her pride has reared up. Good girl. Don't chase him, honey, even if it's clear that Coach is the town's adopted favorite son. Pretty soon, they'll buy him an Escalade—"

I find a better position and lean back against the walled porch.

"And . . . that's it, folks. She's walking away from the house. Stops, turns! Will she go back? No. The beauty has failed and is leaving the property. She arrives at her car with a pout. Dang. Her lover has missed out on some yummy goodness—"

"Not her lover," I mutter.

"She places the scarf back on her head. She turns to get in the car—wait—she's turning and . . . holy shit . . . waving . . . at . . . me?" Nova rises from her seat and sends her a wave, a smile plastered on her face. "Damnation. She's in her car. Destination: my house."

I groan. "Don't tell her I'm here. Please."

She fluffs her hair, then rubs at the drool on her face. "How do I look?"

I skate my eyes over her, lingering on the curve of her breasts in her tank top. "I think you know." Hot.

"Delightfully disheveled?" She shrugs. "This reminds me of that time I had Jimmy Lockhart hiding in my closet. He'd crawled in my window, and we tried to be quiet, but he accidentally knocked a lamp off my nightstand. I covered him up with clothes and stuffed animals. Nearly peed my pants when Mama walked in my bedroom to check on me. Of course, I *liked* Jimmy. He had a great personality. You do not." She stands and straightens her tank top. "She's here. Sit tight, Fancy Pants."

And she's gone from my view, walking down the porch in her bare feet.

When I can't catch their words, I crawl closer to the edge to get a glimpse of what's going on. My foot hits something—dammit—and I turn to see a planter rocking back and forth, an orange pot on top of a wire plant stand. I reach over to grab it, but the pot topples over the porch and lands with a thud on the grass below.

"What was that?" Melinda asks, her voice rising. "Your plant just fell."

"Sparky. He adores pushing plants around."

"Isn't that him in the window?" Melinda asks.

Shit. I glance at the front window and see the cat on the back of the chair. His eyes lock with mine and convey, *Busted*.

Nova clears her throat. "Yeah, um, well, you see, I have lots of cats."

"Are they all as vicious as that one?" Melinda asks.

Nova goes into her spiel about Sparky being the dog of the cat world, and I stifle a laugh.

"Is someone on your porch?" Melinda asks.

Nova coughs. Once. Twice. "Nope. That was me. I, um, think I have the flu. You shouldn't get too close."

"It's not flu season."

Nova coughs. "You never know. Sorry. You'd better go."

I hear more murmurings between them until finally the engine of the Mustang comes to life. The radio picks up with Britney, then fades as she drives away.

"She thinks I'm a sickly, crazy cat lady," Nova grouses as she climbs back up on her porch and plops down next to me. She crosses her legs and puts her elbows on her thighs, her hands resting under her chin as she gazes at me. She doesn't look at the scars—no, those irises lock with mine and don't let go.

"You owe me a petunia," she says. "On the flip side, Melinda apologized for parking behind my car last night and promised she wouldn't do it again. According to her, she'll be over here a lot, and she'll be using the driveway. Also, her father adores you. He's a booster, yes? I recall he was a football player back in the day."

I nod.

"You have to buy me a cat as well. I hate lying to people."

I mimic her position and face her. I hear the chirp of a bird, the knocking of a woodpecker, a car, but it all fades . . .

There's a strange tension around us, a thickening of the air.

She breaks it by looking away from me. "Sparky needs a buddy. I warn you; they're expensive. I'll pick one out, yes?"

"Sure. Thank you for the help."

"I like seeing you squirm," she murmurs.

"Why?"

"Payback." A slow blush works up from her neck to her face as she mutters something under her breath.

"What was that?"

She clears her throat. "Just . . . life has a funny sense of humor."

Before I can ask her to elaborate, my phone erupts with the chorus from the Steve Miller Band's "Take the Money and Run."

"Excuse me a moment." After standing up, I walk to the other end of the porch, keeping my voice low, my back to Nova. "Reggie. Hey, man. Been a while. Whatcha got for me?"

He lets out a gruff laugh, and I picture him in his high-rise in Manhattan, his huge U-shaped desk, the pictures with his arm slung around athletes on the wall behind him. One of the biggest agents in sports, the man never stops working. "How's it going down there in Podunk, Texas? You bought yourself any cowboy boots? I'd like to see that, actually."

"It's Blue Belle, and no, I don't have any."

"Pity. How's the high school gig? Heard you won your first game. Your quarterback looks good. How old is he?"

Leave it to Reggie to be on top of the news, scouting.

"That would be Toby. He's seventeen. What's going on with you?" I ask.

"I got a lead on a possible college job. How do you feel about Stanford?"

"California. I love the sun. What job?"

"Quarterback coach. Half a mill is what Dunbar is pulling in there, but rumor is he got caught by someone on staff doing coke. He was arrested last year on a drug charge, and the team looked beyond it, but this is the second time, and I feel like he'll go into rehab, then maybe resign. William Hite is head coach—you know him—and he's incredible. I threw your name up in a call, and there was some tentative interest, but we have to play it close to the vest."

"Hmm."

"It's a prestigious school with a long tradition in football. You'd look great in white and red."

I grimace. It's not about the money. I pulled in twenty-five million a year with the Pythons. My financial situation is set for life. And Hite is a great coach—the kind I want to be. I want to be in charge, have control of a team, mold it, and make it mine. I want *his* job. A long exhale comes from me. I don't expect the offers to come pouring in—not when I haven't proved myself on the college level—but my name does carry clout, and I can always hope.

He continues in a rush. "I know it's not what you're looking for. You want to be in charge, and someone is going to snatch you up, but we need to do this one step at a time. How do you feel about Stanford if Hite calls me?"

"I need to think on it. I can't leave my team midseason." I scuff my feet on the porch. "Keep your feelers out. Get back to me if you hear any more chatter."

I hang up and turn back around. Nova stands a foot away.

"So Mrs. Meadows was right," she says. "The rumors are true. You're looking to leave. That woman truly does know everything."

"You like to eavesdrop?"

"It's a lesson all southern women learn early." She shrugs an elegant shoulder. "We don't care if we get caught."

My jaw pops, frustration rising. I do want to move up the ladder. Once I set a goal, I give it my entire focus. I almost won state last year, and this year's goal is to get that trophy, then elevate to a higher level, either college or professional. I never planned on coaching high school the rest of my career.

But I'm not discussing that with her.

I huff and raise my arms. "Fine. I'm going to check out your flowers, maybe replace them. It's why I came over here—besides delivering your cat! Then I'll leave you in peace."

She takes a step closer until we're nearly toe to toe. The smell of green apples wafts around her as she pushes a finger into my chest. "No, you're not, Fancy Pants. I am. You wouldn't know what to do with them." She deflates, her shoulders dipping. "Plus, they can't be replaced. Not the roses anyway. They mean something to me." Her eyes shine with emotion as she takes a step back.

Shit. My frustration ebbs as I whip my hat off and run my hands through my hair, then clutch my cap. I know grief, that feeling of grappling with death, when you want to cling to any reminder. I wore Whitney's ring around my neck for a year.

I search for the right words. "I've hurt your feelings. I said the wrong thing. Of course they can't be replaced and you'd want to keep them. I'm sorry."

She gives me a surprised glance, then chews on her bottom lip. "Right. You understand."

"Yes. I've lost someone." My wreck made the news for weeks; plus if she dated Zane, I'm assuming she knows.

Something catches her attention across the street, and her eyes flare as a groan comes from her. "Uh-oh. Mrs. Meadows has us in her sights."

Lois stands on her front porch, purse in hand as she walks down to her car wearing a blue flowered dress, heels, and her Stetson.

"Hey, y'all! Glad you two are getting along!" she calls. "Don't mind me. Y'all keep talking! Get to know each other! I'm headed to church if you want to come!"

"Maybe next time, Mrs. Meadows!" Nova says brightly.

Lois gets in her silver Mercedes and backs out, then pulls away slowly with a satisfied smile on her face.

"Great. She'll be pushing you on me now," I mutter.

"Good thing I'm not interested," she snaps.

"Same," I say, slamming my hat back on.

A female voice calls Nova's name from inside the house; then Sabine comes to the door, dressed in shorts and a baggy T-shirt. There's a spatula in her hand, and a purple boa is around her neck. She gives me an unsurprised look. "Oh, hey, Coach Smith. Are you here for pancakes? I can make a few more. They're gluten-free."

"Hey, Sabine," I say with a smile.

"He isn't staying," Nova says with her chin tilted up, her eyes on me. "He just brought Sparky home."

I exhale. "Right. I'll see you around." My hand brushes against Nova's when I move, and sensation ripples over my skin, my body tightening.

Weird. The same thing happened last night when I escorted her into my office. I made sure to keep my distance after that, but . . .

I make it to her sidewalk before my curiosity eats at me, and I stop and watch her flip around, her heart-shaped ass swaying back into the house.

She. Is. Beautiful.

And dammit . . .

Since the moment she turned around in the kitchen, her face pricked at me, tantalizing, like a memory out of reach.

I've enjoyed women over the years, and most of those sexual interactions tend to fade into the background of my mind. Then there are certain women who take up real space in your head, the ones you react to in a way you never forget.

Even if you can't recall their faces . . .

Those tingles . . .

Then . . .

Long time no see—like for real, you have no idea.

Then there was her mention of payback and how life has a funny sense of humor . . .

And those lush lips . . .

Her fascination with Leia's cuff . . .

I stop in my tracks, my hands clenching.

No way. No fucking way.

What are the odds? The mere idea is impossible!

Walking down the sidewalk, I pull out my phone and call the person who knows about the party. Tuck answers on the third ring, his voice groggy. "Ronan?" I hear the sound of fabric rustling. "Dude. I just woke up." He pauses. "Fuck, happy birthday. I missed it. I suck!" he calls out, then curses again, several times. "I'm sending you a big-ass fruit basket today! Jesus! My brain is mush on these meds!"

I chuckle. "How's the ankle?" He fractured it last week at practice.

"Hurts," he moans. "I'm out for a while. Slowly dying of boredom. Send tequila and strippers, stat! Better yet, take a break, and come see me. I miss your ugly face."

I laugh. "You're a baby. Buck up. Can you talk for a few?"

"All right." He lets out a grunt. "Let me get up and hit the start on coffee. I have to hobble, so hang tight." He puts me on hold, and I picture him limping through his spacious apartment in Manhattan, the one we shared for years. We bonded from day one—me the serious one, him the party boy. He was there for me when I woke up and made a plan for my life.

He makes his coffee, complaining about his injury. He bitches about a new wide receiver who's young and fresh, River Tate, then tells me about his love life, his voice escalating. His latest girlfriend left him for a violinist. He mopes about it, then lets out several long sighs.

"So what's up with you?" he asks.

I reach my house and face the neighborhood, my gaze on the house next door. I sit down on the wicker swing and trace my hand over the smooth wood. "Remember that night of the Pythons party? The last one I went to?"

"You were throwing back bourbon like it was water—yeah, I recall."

"Remember Princess Leia?"

There's a beat of silence, then: "We've never talked about this. You insisted. You said it was none of my business what happened."

I'm not one to discuss my sex life, but that incident was particularly hard. I let out an exhale. "Right. Things change. She came into that party because she knew I'd be there. She was looking for me. You remember that?"

"Hmm, right. Maybe. Who knows? I just thought she stumbled in the wrong ballroom. You know they have those cosplay parties where people dress up all the time. You ever do that? Dress up as Luke Skywalker and wave a sword?"

"It's a lightsaber, and no, that isn't my thing. I'm just a collector." I push up out of the swing and pace around the porch. "You pointed her out to me."

"Everyone saw her, but maybe I showed her to you—I don't remember."

"You insisted on the bet with me."

"Which I never collected because you clammed up and didn't give me any deets." There's wariness in his voice, which means . . .

I sit down on the porch steps, making connections. "You told her I'd be there. Admit it." Part of me has always suspected, but I let it go, not wanting to deal with it.

He lets out an exhale, and I hear a chair scraping back as he sits. I picture him running a hand through his sandy hair, maybe pulling on the ends. "Took you long enough to ask. Of course I fucking sent her. You needed to move on."

"Shit. I knew it—"

He continues. "And don't give me grief, because I'm your best goddamn friend in the whole world, and I was looking out for you, trying to knock some sense into you—"

"Stop your tirade; I'm not angry."

"You were different after that," Tuck says on a sigh after a few moments of silence. "You stopped drinking. You got healthy."

"Did you date her?" Tuck goes through women like a frat boy guzzling beer. He falls in love; they leave, usually giving up on him committing; and then he moves to the next one.

"No."

"So . . . elaborate. How the fuck did it happen?"

"You are pissed!" He groans. "You know I can't stand it when someone's got beef with me. I screwed up. I meddled like a mom, and now you're—"

"Just tell me who she is."

He clicks his tongue. "Let's see. Her name, shit . . . she worked at the Baller, that bar we used to hang out at. Remember? You had to have a membership to get in?"

"No." I wasn't hanging out in bars the last couple of years . . .

"You were seeing Whitney then."

"Right. You met this girl there?"

"Yeah, she bartended. Gorgeous, like I took one look and thought, *If Ronan was single, he'd be all over that.*"

"Hmm. You totally hit on her."

"She turned me down. Weird, right? I mean, I am amazing, but I digress . . . anyway, one night at the bar, one of our games came on the TV, the last Super Bowl win, and she was really into it. We started talking, and maybe I was drunk, but I had the best idea ever."

"Dress her up as Leia and crash our party." I shake my head. "You had her memorize a line."

He grunts. "When you say it, it sounds ridiculous, but I am brilliant. That outfit cost me two grand. It was a replica made by someone in LA."

"Wow. You went all out. Did you pay her?"

"Ronan, it wasn't like that. She wanted to—"

"You did."

"No, I didn't, asshole! Okay, okay, I initially told her I'd pay her, I did, but she insisted she was cool, and I gave her my digits in case she changed her mind, but she never got back with me after the party . . . come on—don't be angry. You *liked* her."

I did . . . but . . . God, the guilt I felt. I wore it like a mantle, part of it anchored with Whitney, the other side full of self-reproach that I'd hurt an anonymous person. For months, every time I walked into a party or a restaurant—hell, even on the street—my gaze searched for every blue-eyed blonde.

My gaze goes back to the house next door as Nova comes out to take Sparky for a walk. She turns in the opposite direction of my house, and I watch her disappear.

"Give me a name," I say as dread builds up.

I hear him slurp his coffee. "It was something different. Star? Nope, hmm. Wait, wait! Nova! It was Nova!" He heaves out a sigh. "You mad?"

My chest rises, my jaw flexing. He manipulated, intervened, and set me up. She did too. She knew exactly what she was doing when she walked into that party. Yeah, I'm simmering. Disappointment hits me, unexpected. Part of me liked to believe that my night with the beauty was serendipitous, a message from the fates to move on—when in truth it was planned.

I click off, my head tumbling. He tries to call me back, but I ignore it.

Yeah. A long breath comes from my chest.

I get it now. I get it now—that tightening in my chest when I saw her in my kitchen.

It's her.

The question is, What am I going to do about it?

Chapter 5

Ronan

Two landlines ring simultaneously on my desk in my office in the field house. My cell pings next to them. I ignore them and stalk to the walk-in closet, unbuttoning my dress shirt from class, then grabbing a polo for practice. Just as I've slipped it on and tucked it in my khakis, I hear the squeak of my office door opening.

I step out, and Lois stands there in a denim skirt and a Bobcats jersey with Milo's number on it. "Hey!" She tips her hat up. "I just want a minute—want me to get those phones?"

I slip a cap on my head, then put my hands on my hips. "I want you to find me a personal assistant."

She plops down in one of my chairs. "I'm working on it. You seem tense, Coach. I've got this book about breathing exercises that help you relax. You should read it."

I nod absently as the team spills into the locker room, and I watch them with discerning, eager eyes. We've got a good crew of athletes. Even though I don't play in the NFL anymore, my competitiveness hasn't dwindled. In Texas, it's a necessity.

Toby, Milo, and Bruno stop at my door, three of my best. All juniors. I've been working with them for a year, shaping them into winners.

Toby, my quarterback, sends a head nod. "Coach. What you got for us?"

I point to the folders. "Get the playbooks. Study. Then we hit the field. I want to see some quick play action. Got it? How's the arm? Loose?"

Tall and dark haired, he grins and rolls his shoulder. "I'm ready. More than ready. Sir."

"Did you get enough hours in at the bookstore this weekend?" He works to supplement his family's income.

He nods. "Saturday and Sunday. I ran five miles before I went in."

"That's good. I like the dedication."

Bruno, my running back, reaches over and scrubs Toby's head. "He's been jawing all day about how we're gonna decimate Wayne Prep, bragging to all the girls, especially Sabiiiiine."

Toby shoves him, and they scuffle around.

"Cool the ribbing, boys," I say. "Wayne Prep went seven and three last year. Their defense wins games. Never underestimate an opponent."

Bruno touches his chest with his fist and calls out, "Win the heart! Win everything!"

Several whoops come from the guys out in the hall, echoing our motto.

"All right, all right," I say. "I like the spirit, Bruno. Now get those binders."

He snatches them up off the table, and he and Milo leave, while Toby lingers, a hesitant expression on his face.

"Coach? Um, my mom's fortieth birthday is coming up. She doesn't know a lot of people, and I—I know how y'all are friends . . ." He licks his lips. "She hasn't had many good days lately, and I thought . . ."

I've spent a lot of one-on-one time with Toby. Visits to his house. Talks with his mom.

"We'd love to do something for her," Lois chimes in as she gets up and pats Toby on the back. "I'm the party planner. What day, dear?"

"The Friday of our bye week. I don't think she wants to do anything big. Just . . . she's been talking about getting out of the house, maybe going out to eat." Red blooms on his face. "My dad . . . he hasn't called in a while . . ."

His mom has a debilitating heart condition. She gets breathless easily and tires fast. His father works in the oil fields. When he's home, he hangs out in bars. Toby hasn't seen him in months.

I nod, my gaze steady on his. "Lois will plan something. I'll be there."

Toby gives me a broad smile, a relieved look on his face as he walks to the locker room.

"He's a good kid," Lois murmurs.

"Yes." His situation—and his talent—reminds me of my own childhood.

Skeeter pops his head in. "Cheerleaders have lice. I'm shook. It's gonna be everywhere by the end of the week." He whips his hat off and scratches his head.

"And?"

He gives me a glare. "You ever have lice, Coach?"

"Not that I recall."

"It's awful! My mama used to put mayonnaise on my head to kill 'em. Then she'd comb out my hair with this tiny little pick. She gave up one time and shaved my head in fifth grade. Worst school picture I ever took." He takes a breath. "We need to disinfect the helmets, uniforms—hell, maybe Lysol the whole field house. I've got a pressure washer at home. We can mix up some chemicals and let it rip." He motions spraying the walls.

"No pressure washer or man-made chemicals, please," I say as I pinch my nose. "Get someone on it—"

"Who? We've got practice. Our flunky left us."

Frustration flares. Hayden, our all-around helper and my PA, was a local college kid who ran errands and did whatever we didn't have time for. He got married last year, and his wife delivered a new baby a couple of weeks ago. He quit for another job, and no one has thought to hire anyone else.

I lift my arms at him. "We've got five assistant coaches on staff. Figure it out. If you're that worried, do it yourself."

He ambles away, muttering.

The lights on both landlines start up again, and I groan and snatch one up. It's a news station asking for an interview before the Huddersfield game two months from now. "Fine," I growl and pencil in a date on my calendar. I grab the other phone. It's Randy's Roadhouse offering to host a celebratory party after we beat Huddersfield. "We may not win," I mutter, then get off.

"You're going to get a reputation as rude," Lois murmurs as she files her nails. "You should try some peppermint oil for your stress. Just rub a little on your temples, and voilà. It smells nice." She points her file at me. "I'll bring you some."

"Not rude. I don't have time for this . . ." I wave my hands around at the office. "Extra stuff." When I played professionally, I never had to worry about answering phones, arranging fundraisers, getting interviews. My agent did it. I just kept my body in top physical form, listened to my coaches, and performed.

Bruno juts his head back in. "Coach, the cheerleaders want to know if we're doing a big pep rally before the Huddersfield game. Their sponsor wants to do this dance routine to 'Another One Bites the Dust,' and I was thinking, you know, we need to be lit too—like jazz it up a bit. Usually, we just walk around the gym in our uniforms and wave. Miss Tyler is nice, but she has certain ideas . . ."

Melinda planned pep rallies last year, but I asked Principal Lancaster at the beginning of the year to find someone else. It just created more time when she was around me.

I point at him. "Bruno. Where are those plays? Sit your butt down, and study. Worry about Wayne Prep, son. Cheerleaders and pep rallies can wait."

"My girlfriend—"

"Has lice. I don't care. Locker room. Now."

He leaves, and I plop down with an exhale, then give Lois a long look. "My birthday party was over the top."

"It was a small thing." She tucks her file away in her big purse. "But I understand. I can't always plan the perfect gig. Apologies. It won't happen again. Also, I've been making sure we send meals over to Bonnie and Toby a couple of times a week. I heard you bought her house, then gave it to her."

I narrow my eyes. Bonnie's disability checks weren't enough to cover her bills. I stepped in this summer to help. Toby needs to know his food and shelter are taken care of. A kid can't perform if he's worried about basic needs. "Who told you that?"

"Someone at the bank."

"That's confidential information."

She gives me a half smile. "Nothing is secret in Blue Belle."

Fine. I'm not surprised. I wave it off . . . "Lois. The women you invited to my house—"

"Were so sweet! Don't you love how Texas girls can cook? Those coconut-battered shrimp . . . delicious! I saw you chowing down. It was unfortunate that Jenny showed up. I mean, y'all broke it off in New York—that's what you told me—but she never got the message. It's good she saw you with Melinda. Jenny really isn't your type. You need—"

"No more matchmaking."

"Don't you get lonely in that big house? With that ugly dog?"

"Football is why I came to Blue Belle. It's why you hired me. I don't want every woman in town throwing their hat in for me."

"Noted, but here's the problem: Melinda *is* smitten. She's a teacher here, and dealing with her is a slippery slope. Her dad is our biggest booster. Plus, you want to maintain a decent working relationship with her."

"No relationship."

She sighs. "We don't want you to leave."

"I'm still here, Lois," I say in an exasperated tone.

"But I want you to stay forever. For Milo." She pulls out her inhaler and toys with it.

"He's going to be fine next year if I don't come back. Hell, we don't even know if I'm leaving or not, but you're trying to set me up. And it's not just you. Everyone is. The checkout lady at the Piggly Wiggly put three different phone numbers in my bag. A woman at Ace Hardware followed me out to my car last week. I can't go anywhere without someone suggesting I meet their daughter or niece or cousin." I exhale. "I was clear with the board from the beginning. I signed a yearly contract for a reason."

"How do you feel about Escalades? In black? Or we could give you a bonus?"

"No."

She bites her lip. "Fine, but I can't stop a moving train, Ronan."

"What do you mean?"

"Melinda claims to be in love."

Jesus! No! That's just not true. She's just caught up in the competitive nature of being the one to snag the coach . . .

The landline rings, and I curse, pick it up, and then hang it up.

Lois gives me a smile. "What did you think of Nova? You know, as a neighbor?"

I pause, remembering that first kiss in the elevator, the fact that I hadn't touched a woman in a year—

For the past few days, I've been circling around that night, waffling from being pissed off that she was part of a plot to wanting to, shit, atone for how it ended? Fuck if I know. The best thing to do is pretend we don't know each other.

"She's beautiful . . ." Lois keeps talking, but I've zoned out as I think back over the past few years with women. I've shunned commitments, isolating part of myself for simple self-preservation. No serious entanglements means no anguish, no responsibility for someone else's safety. Jenny once said my heart was made of stone, and I guess she's right. I'm just a lurker, watching the world go by as I coach football. I can easily go on like this for the rest of my life.

"Not interested in her." I stand, grab my clipboard, and put the whistle around my neck.

She follows me out the door. "Funny. I didn't ask you if you were interested."

Ignoring her, I walk down the hallway, past the locker room, and outside to the field. My eyes rake over it, scanning the perfectly trimmed grass, the bright-white lines, the Bobcat in the center. Calm washes over me.

I grew up in a poor neighborhood outside Chicago with a mom who waited tables and worked at a paper mill. My dad deserted us by the time I was six. I can't even recall what he looks like. Tall, I guess.

He spun out of our driveway on a rainy March evening, my mom with one baby on each hip, me at her feet, crying. *Too much too soon,* she told me years later, which was a fuck of a lot nicer than how I'd put it. He was weak. A loser. My jaw clenches. A kid never forgets being abandoned, and if anything, it's made me more determined, smarter, and very, very careful about my commitments.

When my middle school gym teacher saw I'd sprouted six inches over the summer, he took me to the coaches. I tried shooting hoops but couldn't make anything from the three-point range, but when the football coach placed that pigskin in my hand, my body hummed. I threw a perfect spiral down the field—and my life goals were born.

I never looked back.

Whitney came along at a time when I longed for something permanent, tired of the revolving door of girlfriends. I loved her deeply and planned a life with her.

"Have you ever met her before?" Lois asks, making every step I do. "In New York?"

"Who?"

"Don't pretend—"

I stop. "Lois. Get your ass off my field."

She sucks on her inhaler. "Got it."

The waitress at Randy's Roadhouse stares at the long scar on my face, and I pull down my hat and look at the menu. I meant to sit in the seat across from me, the one that puts my scars to the window, but Skeeter took it first. "I'll have the brisket with steamed broccoli, a plain salad, and water to drink."

She turns to Skeeter, who orders a double cheeseburger, large fries, and a draft beer. We eat together most weeknights after practice. He was already doing offense when I came, and I kept him. Mild mannered and jovial off the field, he becomes a force of nature when he coaches.

After our food comes, Sonia Blackwell, the science teacher, walks in the door, pauses when she sees us, and then comes over. Petite with shoulder-length dark hair and glasses, she's wearing a bright-green shirt with an avocado on it and slacks. We murmur our hellos.

She adjusts her glasses. "Skeeter. So I heard about the lice—"

"What? Has another team got it?" He slams down his beer. "I knew it. It's gonna be an epidemic."

She shrugs. "No, um, I was just wondering if you come across one, maybe save it for me? You could bring it to the science lab in a cup or something." She smiles, a dimple in each cheek. "We're studying reproduction, and the female louse doesn't need the egg to be fertilized to have a nit. Those things are bloody fascinating."

I put down my bite of brisket. Ready to watch the show.

Skeeter shakes his head, a large bite of burger in his mouth. He chews furiously, then wipes his face. "Hell no, Sonia. I ain't touching those things with a ten-foot pole, and neither are my boys. They're a menace. Remember fifth grade?" He glares at her. "I do. And today I cleaned fifty-two helmets with Lysol. If I see a louse, I'm gonna stomp on it, then flush that fucker."

Red steals up her face. "Oh, yeah, well, I, um, just thought it would be cool through a microscope." She looks away from us.

This is what I know. They've known each other since school. Sonia has a crush. Skeeter is clueless. She's a fearless teacher, but when it comes to him, she flops around like a fish. My take is he was popular and she was the shy nerd.

"If I see a louse, I'll text you, Sonia. You want to join us?" I ask, noticing she came in by herself.

She glances at Skeeter, and I kick him under the table. He grunts, then darts a look at me. I nudge my head at her, and he gets a confused look on his face; then realization dawns. "Um, yeah, you wanna eat with us?"

"You guys have already gotten your food." She shrugs. "I guess not."

"We don't mind," I offer as Skeeter focuses back on his burger.

The hostess, who's been lingering, asks Sonia if she wants to go to her table, and she gives her a jerky nod. She stops about halfway to her table, her voice rising. "Nova!"

My head snaps around to the girl who just breezed in the double doors and heads to the bar area. She's wearing denim shorts and a blue T-shirt with red cowboy boots, and her hair shines under the light, straight as an arrow down her tanned shoulders. She sees Sonia, then rushes over to give her a hug.

Skeeter follows my eyes. "Nova really let you have it at the party." He chuckles. "She's usually sweet, but you had to go and ruin her roses."

I scowl. "It was Jenny."

He smirks as he chews on a fry. "In college, she talked me into a tattoo. She couldn't get anyone to go with her, and I was game." He pushes up his shirt and shows me the number fifty-seven. "That's my high school number when we won state. She got *Trouble* at the top of her ass. With yellow roses around it. Those are her thing, so you really messed up when you ruined them."

"I didn't," I growl.

"She was crazy fun. Spunky." A frown flits over his face. "Then everything went to hell . . ."

"And?" I give him a look after the pause goes on too long.

The waitress interrupts us, asking if we want refills, and when she's walking away, Skeeter gets up to go to the bathroom. I bristle. What went to hell for Nova?

I glance over as Nova wraps up her chat with Sonia, then heads back to the bar, where she plops down on a stool.

Before I think too hard about it, I grab my water glass, which I didn't want refilled, and head to the bar. Tuck's words keep tumbling around in my head. Who is she? Really? Why did she agree to come to the party if it wasn't for money? Is she just like the other crazy fans who would do anything to see a player? Was the emotion I felt in her arms fake?

My chest twinges. Did I hurt her? Or did it mean nothing at all?

She's leaning in over the bar, her face supported by her elbows, chatting to the male bartender, when I slide in next to her. I motion to him. "Water, please."

She stills, then turns to look at me, those blue eyes cool. "Hello."

"We meet again. Nice boots."

"Bound to happen. It's a small town." She kicks out a long leg. "The shoes are a throwback to high school. I begged for Mama to buy these, and she wouldn't, so I saved my money from my tips at the diner."

"I used to work at a diner. I washed dishes."

She shrugs. "We have something in common. Did you buy boots?"

"No."

The bartender slides my water over, and a tense silence settles between us when I don't leave.

A server walks behind the bar, and Nova raises her hand. "Hey. I'm here for a pickup order. Under Morgan. I called it in about half an hour ago."

I take a sip of water. "So. How are you?"

She frowns, probably wondering why I'm trying to talk to her. "Fine. How are you?"

"We have lice at school." Ugh. Stupid.

"I'll check Sabine tonight."

"You want a Coke or something else while you wait, Nova?" the bartender asks. He's in his early twenties with a baby face and a trendy fade hairstyle. His eyes roam over her breasts. "On the house, darlin'. Anytime you come in, ask for me, and I'll fix you up." He taps his name tag. "Riley."

"Aw, thanks, Riley; that's so sweet. I'd love a Coke," she says, batting her lashes as he slides one over. She tips it up at me, a little smirk on her face. "Free drink. Yahoo." She glances back at the bartender, who's moved away to help someone else. "Hmm. He's cute. You think I'm too old for him?"

"Yes."

"But you can date a twenty-year-old?"

"What? No." Whitney was my age. Jenny was young, but I also thought since she was, she wouldn't expect much. Wrong.

My waitress shows up next to me, a disappointed look on her face. "Coach, I would have gotten your drink for you."

"I got it," I say. "No worries."

She shrugs, then pulls a piece of paper out of the green apron that's tied around her waist. "I was told to give you this. It's that lady's"—she points at a young, attractive brunette across the bar, who smiles brightly at me—"phone number. I know you said to stop giving them to you, but she used to babysit me, and she's super nice. She just came out of a nasty divorce and got a big ranch in the settlement. I think y'all would make a cute couple." She leans in. "She also gave me twenty bucks."

I grimace/smile at the lady, then tuck the number in my pants.

Nova smothers a laugh. "Wow. Women are paying for the hope of you calling them. Will you?"

"She owns a ranch, and I do like horses."

She chuckles.

I take her in over the rim of my glass. Her beauty is like a blow to a man's chest. With her height and that face, she could have been a model. Somehow, I don't think it's something she ever aspired to be. Not with that serious glint in her eyes. She might be trouble, but there's a deeper side to her than what's on the surface.

"Order up for Morgan," the server calls and sets a white bag on the counter.

Nova swipes the bag, then jumps off the stool. "See you later, Fancy Pants."

And before I can think of anything else to keep her here, she's waltzing out the front door, those boots accentuating her perfect ass.

Chapter 6

Nova

With the windows rolled down, Sabine and I belt out "The Climb," by Miley Cyrus, as we pull up to a bookstore. I'm tapping my fingers on the steering wheel while she moves her shoulders with the beat. Like me, she sings with heart. It's a song about an uphill battle, about struggles and mountains in your life, but you don't stop; you keep climbing.

I throw the Caddy in park and inhale a lungful of late Texas summer as I gaze at the new bookstore. On Main Street, and just a few blocks from our house, it's inside an old barn.

We step inside to the cool air. Completely renovated, the inside is bright and spotless with white walls and big industrial lights that hover over the space. On the right side are red-and-black tables and booths, most of them packed. The left side features an order counter with a long bakery case. The back of the barn is lined with tall rustic-looking shelves.

Sabine's face glows. "We're studying the French Revolution in Coach Smith's class. I want some books about France," she tells me, her gaze already scanning the shelves.

"France? I always wanted to try the Alps. Do I need to buy skis?" I smile.

She squints at me. "You'd have a hard time finding ski equipment in Texas."

"True, but I could get behind a trip to France. Eiffel Tower, museums, wine, cheese . . ."

She cranes her neck to look around me. "Right, we could do that, but beginners can't ski Mont Blanc in France. You need mountaineering experience, and you'd have to be in top physical shape. You are not ready for that journey. You'll need an intense cardiovascular exercise program, maybe some Pilates to stretch out your muscles. I suggest you start on the bunny slopes somewhere in the US, perhaps Colorado. There's Aspen, Vail, Breckenridge—really I could go on and on . . ."

I do a thumbs-up. "Got it. I need to work out, or I will die skiing. Also, we're on a budget. Look in the used section when you pick out your books," I call out as she rushes off.

A tall young man in a bookstore uniform—white pants and a polo—pauses mopping, leaning on the stick as he watches the sway of her hips.

"You missed a spot," I say tartly when he still hasn't taken his gaze off her.

"Oh yeah." Red colors his face as he gets back to work. See, I can guardian.

I mosey to the front counter, where there's a blackboard menu behind a young girl in a red apron with **Dog's Book Barn** scripted on the front. I order a regular coffee and a chocolate croissant. I need sugar. It's been another two weeks of no job, and anxiousness hangs over me like a wet cloud.

As she hands my drink and wrapped pastry over, I lean in. "Are you guys hiring?"

She smiles at me, braces shining, sweet as the pie. "The owner mostly hires high school and college kids." She gives a coffee to a customer who's been waiting, then bounces back to me. "He says it's to give us purpose. He's, like, the best! The pay is better than Dairy Queen.

Plus, the books are cool. Our prices are competitive with any online place."

I take in the girl's name tag. "That's super great of him, Allie. I used to bartend. I think he'd be happy to have me. And I know my coffee." It comes in beans, and you grind them. I can totally be a coffee barista. "Is the manager here?"

She pushes up white glasses. "I'm the weekend manager."

Her attention goes to the entrance when the bell rings, indicating that someone new has entered. She flashes a bright smile at them, then focuses back on me. "Hang on one moment. Let me get you an application." She darts into an office, then comes back.

"Great," I say as she hands it over.

"I'd be happy to talk to you after you've filled it out. Please use a black pen, ma'am."

Ma'am. Please. Interviewing with a perky teenager. What has my life come to?

I turn, trying to juggle the application with my drink and food, but collide with a hard body. Coffee drenches us as my croissant sails out of my hand and plops on the concrete floor, a gob of chocolate oozing out.

I look up at the sculpted, broad chest now wearing a liberal amount of hot liquid.

An internal groan comes from me. I'd know that six-four muscled body anywhere.

Dammit. Ronan.

And I'm *still* not wearing a dress and stilettos.

I've seen him several times since the front-porch incident. Last Monday evening, he dropped by to pick up the box he left at my house when he brought Sparky. Why does a man worry about his containers? It's just a box. Mama has hundreds. I had my sleep shorts and a tank top on, my hair tangled and damp from a shower. He stood at my door for several moments after greeting me, then abruptly left. Then there was the awkward encounter at Randy's Roadhouse. I meant to inquire about work again, but he showed up, and I chickened out, took my food, and left.

Then this week, on Wednesday night, when I couldn't sleep, I went for a midnight walk, saw him ahead of me, and ducked behind a tree while he passed.

"I'm so sorry! Did it burn you?" I say as I scurry around and pick up the mess on the floor.

We both grab napkins from the counter and wipe at our clothing.

"No, it's fine. Are you okay?" His face is impassive, nearly inscrutable, hidden by the shadow of his ball cap. Part of me—the stupid, silly part—longs to see his whole face.

"Yes. You got most of it."

He dabs at his shirt. "Nice to see you again too, Nova."

I wince. "*Nova* actually means a star that releases a sudden burst of energy. Mama said she named me aptly. It's derived from the Latin *novus* or *new*. I always took it to mean 'a new star.'" I stare at a point on his chest. Why does it have to be so spectacular? Why am I rambling?

The less time I spend with him, the better.

"*Ronan* is Irish and means 'little seal.' We're neither Irish nor do we know a thing about seals. My mom just liked the sound of it," he says as he takes his hat off, pushes a hand through his wavy hair, and then settles it back on his head. The brief moment gives me a glimpse of his face, the brutalness of the scars juxtaposed with his chiseled jawline and straight, Greek nose.

I say his name, dragging out the syllables. "It sounds kinda strong. Invincible."

He gives me a glance, then takes the damp application and napkins I have clutched in my hand, tosses them in the trash, and puts his hands on his hips and levels me with that steely gaze. "So. Why are you avoiding me?"

"You saw me duck behind the tree? Dang. I thought I was being stealthy. Guess I'm not quite the ninja I thought."

"Hmm."

I chew on my lip. "Looking back, *perhaps* it was impulsive." I point to the scratch on my arm. "The branch of the tree got me. Satisfied?"

"No." He flicks at a piece of croissant on my shoulder, then focuses back on me. "You don't like me. Maybe we should discuss—"

Allie comes around the bakery case, vibrating as she gives him a wide smile. She hands him a coffee and a chocolate croissant. "Coach, here's your usual," she says.

I gaze at it longingly. *Where's mine?*

"Congrats on the wins against Wayne Prep and Payton High. We really kicked their asses—um, butts." She bats her lashes. "I didn't think you'd be coming in today."

"There's someone I wanted to see." He looks at me.

"Me?" I squeak.

"Hmm. I drove through town and saw your car."

Allie cuts in. "I've got the cookies laid out for tomorrow, and the new mango tea has come in. I can't wait to put it on the menu. Oops, another customer. Catch you later, Coach." She stops as she turns. "Oh, this older lady is looking for work."

She leaves, and I grimace as realization dawns. Dammit, why are the stars aligned against me? "You're the person who owns this place? Wow. Football coach and a business entrepreneur." I shake my head. Of course Sabine wouldn't think to tell me. She'd assume I knew. "Why open a store if you're leaving?"

He gives me his profile, ignoring my question. "Lois mentioned you were looking for a job."

"There's always the strip club at the end of town."

His lips twitch. "I see you got your roses fixed."

I nod. "Mama had tools in the shed. I did some pruning and said a little prayer. I was tempted to steal some holy water but chickened out. Mrs. Meadows sent a crew over this week, and they replaced the rest with new plants and mulch. It looks better than it did before."

"I called them. I sent them. I paid for it. I didn't let the booster club bow and scrape to take care of my problems while I'm winning football games." He finally looks at me, a smile curling his lips as he repeats my words from the party.

My heart does that flip-flop thing, and I blink rapidly at the effect of Ronan Smith being nice. "Over and done, then. We have no need to talk about it anymore."

"We still have unfinished business, Nova," he says, his voice lowering. "I've been thinking . . ."

Behind him, the entrance to the barn opens, and two women sweep inside. Melinda Tyler and Paisley Lennox Carlisle. My hands curl. Paisley is one of two people in Blue Belle I don't want to ever see. Still as willowy as ever, she looks like a million bucks in dark skinny jeans and a red silky blouse with strappy heels. A designer purse is slung over her shoulders. Her makeup is perfection, her brown hair up in a chignon, golden highlights framing her oval face. I want to spit.

Following my eyes, Ronan stiffens and groans. "Jesus! I can't get away from Melinda. She's at work. She's at the games. She's here." He mutters under his breath, then says, "She showed up at my house last night."

He motions for me to follow him as he walks to the end of the bakery case. They haven't seen us, but we're still partially visible, and they'll be coming up to order. Sweat pops out on my forehead. I do *not* want to see Paisley. Not when I'm in frayed shorts and an old Aerosmith shirt from high school with coffee stains! It's too much!

He gives me a pained look. "You won't believe what she did . . ."

"Who?" I say distractedly, eyeing the women.

"Melinda . . . aren't you listening? I wish someone would. No one understands that she's driving me crazy. This town is driving me crazy."

I ease closer to him. He's big. I can hide behind him. "Of course I'm listening. You're rambling about your stalker while I'm trying to avoid being seen . . ."

Ronan is still muttering, and I've missed part of it. "She came to my door and was wearing this shiny black trench coat—"

"In this heat? Why?"

"With lacy lingerie underneath. She dropped her coat right in my foyer and threw herself at me."

My eyes flare, and I give him my full attention. "Ballsy. Was it pretty? The lingerie?"

He lifts his shoulders. "Who cares?"

I frown. "Wait, let me get this straight. She came to your house to have sex, and you said no. Just clarifying." Melinda *is* beautiful, and he is a man . . .

There are several beats of silence as his gaze lowers, skating over me. "I don't want to have sex with Melinda. She's not my type."

"Which is . . . ?"

"Blonde."

"Just blonde? Pathetic."

"No, smart-ass. I need a connection to someone. A spark. I don't have sex with just anyone."

"Curious. Again. How old was Jenny?"

He huffs. "Old enough!"

"Uh-huh. Forget that. I'm worried about me. I know that woman with Melinda, and I look like something the cat dragged in. Dang it. I forgot the Tylers are related to the Lennox family. That explains why they're together. Ugh."

He glances over at them, tugging his hat lower. "Let's hide, then. Seems to be your go-to to avoid people."

"Me? Didn't you hide from Melinda on my porch?"

"That was different. She's insane."

I smile. "You know, you just might be back in my good graces with the hiding idea. And I take those nighttime walks to think, so don't be all huffy that I hid from you. I can't think with you around—now get us out of here."

He pauses, his lips quirking. "You can't? Really?"

I wave at him. "Ronan. Where can we hide? This is your store. And who the heck is Dog?"

"My dog. His name is Dog."

"Dumb. You have a giant Irish wolfhound, and you didn't name him something cool like, I don't know, Goliath or Hercules or Maximus—"

"You talk too much. Come on. Follow me." He takes off to the back of the barn, where we slide into the slice of shadow created by two looming shelves. Thankfully, there isn't anyone around us. He positions us so that he's behind me and tells me to be the lookout since I'm smaller.

"They're ordering," I tell him over my shoulder.

"Did they see us?"

I pause to savor Ronan Smith depending on me, sounding all kinds of sweet. It's a direct contrast to the in-control, überserious quarterback he portrayed for the media. "I don't think so." I peek around the corner and run envious eyes over Paisley's ensemble. Damn her sense of style. Those red stilettos are gorgeous.

"Who are you running from?" he asks. "She looked familiar."

I suck my cheeks in, then blow them out. "Paisley Lennox Carlisle. Also known as my best friend in high school until she stole my boyfriend, Andrew. And I'm not running, just preventing a social disaster."

There's a long pause. "Andrew Carlisle's your ex? Our basketball coach?"

"Yes." I turn to face him, starting when I realize how close we are. He's wearing a blue workout shirt and shiny silver gym shorts with sneakers. The heat from him feels like a furnace, and he smells like man and sweat—with a little coffee. His well-defined forearm muscles ripple as he shifts around.

My eyes race over him as he sets his drink on a shelf. There are three things that make me instantly horny: a man in a lushly tailored suit, muscled forearms, and a male fresh from a workout. He's hitting two right now, and I've seen him in a suit. It was divine.

Deep breath. I'm done with athletes. Especially this one.

"What happened?" he asks.

I lean against the shelf with him. I shouldn't divulge my past to Ronan—he works with Andrew—but then I've never been one to do what I'm supposed to do.

Plus, I left all my friends in New York, and I'm bursting to vent.

"In a nutshell: everyone thought Andrew and I would get married. *I* assumed."

"Ah. Tell me more."

I stop and rub the back of my neck. "We were a big deal in high school, junior to senior year. He was the quarterback, and I was the cheerleader. It was true love, whatever. There were four of us who did everything together: me, Andrew, Skeeter, and Paisley. We graduated and went to UT together. Paisley and I joined a sorority, and they had football scholarships. I went there because of him—like, I followed him. I'd always wanted to go to school in New York . . ." My words trail off as I swallow thickly.

"They hurt you." His gaze searches my face. "Fuckers."

I huff out a laugh. "Yeah. Fuckers."

He takes a bite out of his croissant. "That's the spirit."

"Give me half of that, and I'll tell you anything you want to know. I might even make stuff up."

He breaks off a piece and hands it to me.

I pop it in my mouth and chew. "First, I need to back up and give you the backstory—which is true, by the way."

"Okay," he muses. "We're stuck here anyway."

"My mom was a homemaker who sold Mary Kay makeup, but don't let that fool you. She grew up with money; her family owned several banks in Dallas. Very strict, old-school, conservative people. She went to private school, had etiquette classes, even a debutante ball.

They cut her off when she married my dad. They wanted her to marry someone from their circle, but she was in love. My dad was ten years older than her and a big rodeo star," I say wistfully. "He was your typical cowboy on the circuit but didn't see a future there long term after he met Mama. He quit the rodeo and managed a construction company. They were so happy . . ." I stop, a tug in my chest.

"You miss them."

"So much." I smile wryly. "Skipping that . . . Andrew came from money. Oil and cattle. Big sprawling mansion. Fancy cars. Paisley too. Her dad was in business with Andrew's. They were all good friends and a lot like my mom's family; they had certain expectations for their kids."

He nods.

"My mom used to clean their houses on the side, and that's how I met Andrew and Paisley as a kid, and I was drawn into their little circle. Mama insisted on putting me in pageants, right there with Paisley. Maybe it was because she wanted things for me that she had growing up—I don't know, but she'd scrimp and save to buy my dresses or sew them herself. Sometimes I wore Paisley's hand-me-downs."

"Two friends slash rivals in a Texas pageant."

I smirk. "Yep. Our senior year, it was me and her against everyone else in the pageant; then when it came down to just me and her, and I won the crown . . . she changed." My nose scrunches. "But I wouldn't see it for what it was until later."

"She wanted your tiara." He tears the last bit of his pastry and gives me half.

"Thanks. She wanted everything I had, no matter what. She took Andrew—"

"Then he was a fool," he says. "Sorry to interrupt this episode of *As Blue Belle Turns*. Please continue."

Our chests brushing, I take his Bobcats ball cap off and put it on my head. "My payment for the rest of the story. It's a bad hair day."

He huffs. "You marched into my party, your cat attacked a guest, then you told me off in front of everyone. You've eaten my pastry and taken my favorite hat, yet you're chicken to face your high school nemesis?"

"You wanna see Melinda?"

"Well played."

"Right. So back to the saga. We made it to our sophomore year at UT, and I kept expecting an engagement from Andrew, but he grew distant. I'd text him, and he'd reply hours later." I frown at the swell of emotion that digs into my chest, the hurt that never goes away.

Ronan tenses. "Hey. You don't have to explain if it's painful. I was just trying to . . ."

"No, I started this. Maybe it's good to talk. I loved him. Madly. He'd been my sole focus for four years." I take a breath. "A lot of weekends, I came home to help Mama with Sabine, and I missed a lot of his games, but that Sunday I came back early. I had a key to his place and went over to surprise him. I walked in the kitchen, and on the table were candles and leftovers from a dinner. It was chicken breasts stuffed with mozzarella and spinach, and there's only one girl who loved to cook that . . . Paisley. I stood in the kitchen for a long time, taking in the food, my head processing. Then I heard them. I eased open his door, and they were having sex . . ." This is definitely TMI, but I can't stop. Maybe it's the images in my head. Their feet tangling on the bed, their soft whispers. "I—I didn't stop them. I just sat down outside his bedroom and listened. I needed to hear it all, to really let it sink in . . ." I pause. "Have you ever been betrayed like that?"

He shakes his head.

"You're lucky. I still can't eat chicken—which is stupid. Do you know how much chicken food there is in the world? Chicken parm, lemon-pepper chicken, *fried* chicken." I count them off on my fingers. "Paisley ran out crying. Andrew said it was only that one time, that it was a stupid mistake, that he'd only ever slept with me and he had a weak moment, wondering what it would be like with someone else, and she'd been chasing him. He begged me for a month to take him back. Got down on his knees outside my window at the sorority house. Followed me to class. Called me repeatedly. Called Mama for help." My lips twist. "Then Paisley came to me and said she was pregnant." A long breath comes from my chest. "Andrew's parents got involved and insisted he marry her if he wanted their money. I left and went to NYU."

There's a beat of silence as he stares at me. "Now you're living in the same town with them."

I lift up my hands. "You see my problem. I swore I'd never live here, yet . . ."

"Right," he says rather distractedly, a calculating gleam growing in his eyes as he shifts around. "Melinda is here with Paisley, and both of us need to make a statement. No more hiding. I have an idea. It's a little risky and might require some faith in me, but I have a good feeling . . ."

He takes my elbow and tugs me out of the stacks.

"What are you doing?" I exclaim.

"You want payback, right? For what Paisley did?"

"Mama always said 'Never wrestle with a pig. You'll get dirty, and the pig likes it.' I don't know where she heard it—"

"Bernard Shaw. Famous playwright."

"Look at you and your brain."

"I enjoy reading."

I gaze around at the store. "Noted."

He pushes a hand through his messy-pretty hair. I sigh at it and reach up and touch it.

"What are you doing?"

"Nothing. Fixing your hair."

"Why?"

"I considered a job as a beautician when I couldn't get a job after college."

He stares at me.

I shrug. "I like hair. I can do a french braid, a fishtail, a triple fishtail, a lace braid." I pause. "Huh. I see where Sabine gets it."

His lips twitch. "Let's focus. I want to put this Melinda thing to rest. I don't have time to mess with her machinations. It's war."

"War sounds rather ominous," I say warily. "What about the pig thing? Do we want to lower ourselves to their level?"

"I do whatever it takes to win." He pulls us to the center of the store and throws a wave up at Allie, who sparkles at the attention.

"The entire town is in love with you," I mumble.

"Not you," he replies. "Which makes this even easier. You don't even like me."

Oh. I've had time to process seeing him and that Awful One-Night Stand. Yes, my self-respect—and heart—took a beating that night, but perhaps I've softened . . . he was still grieving. I suspect he still is. That kind of pain can ease, but it never quite goes away.

He leads me to a table near Melinda and Paisley's, then presses a book into my hands, one he grabbed off a display on our way to the front. "Speaking of books, here's one of my favorites, *The Art of War* by Sun Tzu, a Chinese military strategist. Take it. It was written in the fifth century and has thirteen chapters, each one devoted to a skill set related to war tactics. Now people use it for business, lifestyle discipline, legal strategy, whatever. I use it for football. For life, really. You'd be surprised at the wisdom."

"Who? What? And you think I talk too much? I probably won't read it, but thanks?"

His face transforms with that genuine smile, and I inhale a breath.

"What?" I ask after a few moments pass.

"You're surprising," he murmurs.

"In a good way?"

"You're not like anyone I've ever met."

"Very vague," I grouse. "I'm not obtuse. I've heard of the book, of course. I have a BA in art history from NYU." A degree I'm still paying for.

"'The whole secret lies in confusing the enemy so they can't fathom our real intent.' We're using that one today. You ready?"

"Got it. Confusing the *enemy*. This sounds violent," I say as he pulls us closer to their table, then stops under one of the big lights hanging from the ceiling.

Then . . .

With an adoring look—*whoa*—he takes both my hands in his.

His plan clicks in my head. "Ronan, no, this is not a good idea—"

He ignores me, his fingers lacing with mine. "Babe, thank you for the coffee date." Warm and deep, his voice carries over the store.

There's a long silence; then I hear a gasp. Melinda. I glance over, and Paisley meets my eyes and drops her fork, her face paling. She breathes my name. *Yeah, that's right, sweetheart; Nova is back in town,* my eyes say. *Ignore the T-shirt. My clothes are coming . . .*

I look up at Ronan, my voice low. "Technically, I never got my coffee. Your big body bumped into me."

"You bumped into me, babe." He smiles as his hands move up my arms to my throat. It's a tantalizing, possessive action. He lets one rest there, holding me as our eyes cling. I feel the pulse in my neck throbbing. I picture how it must look: me in his hat, us in the middle of the store, our chests nearly touching, his fingers toying with the neckline of my ancient T-shirt.

Intimate.

"I think that's enough," I murmur as I bat my lashes. "She's probably going to sneak in my house and murder me after this."

"I won't let her. Plus, don't you want Paisley to think you're banging the hot football coach?"

"Who said you were hot?"

His eyes glitter at me. "You, Nova Morgan, may not like me, but you think I'm sexy. I know this."

"You're an egotistical ass."

"Hmm. I think you like that too. Let's test a theory."

"What theory?"

"A primal one," he purrs as he drags his thumb over my bottom lip.

I'm too shocked to move. It feels like I'm back at the Mercer Hotel, his undivided attention laser focused on me.

My breath quickens. In for a penny . . . "All right. Quit stalling, and get it over with."

"I'm making sure they see us. Be patient." His fingers trace up my jawline to my hair, rubbing the strands through his fingers.

"Oh, I can feel people looking." My body is hyperaware of everything, especially him. I don't drop his gaze, but I know Allie is looking. Maybe the mop boy.

He bends down into my neck and bites my earlobe. "You smell like apples."

I gasp. "Perfume . . . reminds me of home . . . long story about Mrs. Meadows's trees . . ."

"Hmm." He tilts my chin up, and his eyes are that hot, stormy color. Oh . . .

He takes my mouth hesitantly, with small brushing kisses. One, two, three times, testing and tender. He wraps his arms around my waist and slants his mouth differently, deepening the kiss. I pause, tempted to push him away, but instead part my lips, my tongue touching his. Sparks ignite inside my body. His fingers slide around and cup my scalp as he kisses me, tasting, exploring every corner of my mouth. Heat rushes over my skin, and my hands, which hadn't known what to do, move up his broad chest and tangle in his hair.

He steps back, his chest rising rapidly.

We breathe for a good five seconds.

"Not bad for a fake kiss," I manage.

"I'll see you tonight," he announces with me still in his arms. "My place."

My gaze darts over to Melinda and Paisley. Both are staring, mouths slightly ajar. Melinda has a flush on her face, her eyes brittle, and Paisley blinks at me in disbelief.

"Sure," I reply, then whisper, "Not," before I twirl away.

I'm still recovering my pulse rate when he stops at the entrance and sends me a smile and a heated look. Give him an Academy Award. Then he sends me a thumbs-up and is out the door, all business. A long sigh leaves my chest.

Leaving the dining area, I head to the stacks to find Sabine. By the time I make it back to the front with her, Melinda and Paisley have gone.

I touch my lips . . .

How am I supposed to forget that kiss?

He probably already has.

I laugh.

"I found a book on orgasms," Sabine says, and I start and take it out of her hands and set it down on a shelf. We finally had the "orgasm talk." I focused on being factual, which is how she relates best. I found a photo in Mama's sex book and used a pen to point out the part of a woman's anatomy that's likely to lead to climax. I was detailed and scientific. Being honest and practical with her does not encourage her to engage in sex. Knowledge gives her power and prevents her from feeling shameful about her body.

"What? It's about surprising new science that can transform your life. See, it says so right on the front. You're single. Maybe you can read it."

"I don't have a sex life. And I've told you everything I know. That book is a gimmick."

"I don't have a sex life either, but I will someday."

"Not tomorrow or anytime in the next ten years," I say.

"Were you a virgin at fifteen?"

"Yes." Andrew was my first. At sixteen. It was too soon.

She sets her books on the counter. The guy at the checkout is the mop boy; then I see his name tag.

"Hello, Toby," I mutter. So. This is why she wanted to come today.

He's attractive: tall with short dark hair, soft brown eyes, and broad shoulders. She has good taste.

He gives me a hesitant glance. "Hi, Ms. Morgan. Nice to meet ya. Hey, Sabine, did you find everything you wanted?"

My eyes tighten. Was he with her in the stacks?

"You're looking pretty freaking amazing," she tells him, and I sigh gustily at her frankness. "Nice uniform," she adds.

"It's just white pants and a polo," I murmur under my breath.

"Ah, well, I'm just working." He blushes as he scans her books, never taking his eyes off her. "Can I text you later?"

"Yeah," she replies

Oh my God, they're texting?

"You scanned this one"—I pick up a book—"twice. Look alive, Toby." I give him a sweet but deadly smile. *And keep your paws off my sister.*

Finally, we finish and exit the store, a sigh of relief hitting.

"Back to this sex book," I say. "Your brain is still cooking, which means your body isn't ready to make those kinds of decisions. Twenty-five is when an adult's brain is fully formed. You told me that." I give her a triumphant look, which she ignores as she gets in the car and sets the France books on her lap.

"Sometimes you just have to trust me, Nova. I won't rush into anything. Maybe you need sex." She counts off her fingers. "It boosts your immune system, prevents heart disease, improves bladder function, relieves stress—and I can keep going. Just because I want to talk about it doesn't mean I want to hook up with some rando."

"Well. I'm grateful for that."

"I'm not Celia Keller."

"Who's that?" I throw the Caddy in reverse.

"Lacey's older sister."

"Ah." Lacey has been her bestie since their elementary days.

"She picked up a cowboy at the Roadhouse, fucked him in the bathroom, then ended up pregnant with twins. They cry all the time when I'm at Lacey's. Two boys. They poop, and it's disgusting."

"Fucked?" I give her side-eye.

She shrugs. "Cursing is actually a sign of intelligence. NPR did a study—"

"Not in the South and not from a lady's mouth."

Sabine cocks her head. "It's true, then."

"What?"

"That when you get older, you turn into your mother. You sound just like her."

Great.

"Dammit."

She rolls down her window. "Exactly. Different flowers, same garden . . ."

Chapter 7

Nova

Life is strange indeed.

It's Friday, and I'm sitting in a job interview at the high school—the very last place I considered working.

Nervous, I stare down at my hands, carefully manicured and painted a navy blue by Sabine last night while we watched *Downton Abbey*. My clothes finally arrived from Piper, my roommate in New York, and I'm dressed like a professional: maroon silk blouse, a snazzy little navy blazer, a gold pencil skirt—Bobcats colors. Best of all, I have killer gold Gucci stilettos with crystals over the tips of the toes, just a tiny bit of bling because too much might scare the people of Blue Belle. My hair is tamed, scraped back in a sleek, high ponytail. My understated makeup says, *Hire me. I'm a serious professional.*

I hold my breath as Principal Lancaster checks out my résumé—which I typed up last night on my laptop, then printed out on regular paper. Mrs. Meadows told me about the opening when she popped by for a chat on Monday. *My dear, they're hiring at the high school. I'm not sure what for, but you should go . . .*

I should start calling her Lois. She's been helpful—even though I did catch her flipping through Mama's personal recipe book. I had to wrestle it out of her hands. Okay, not really, but nobody gets Mama's jelly recipe.

I squirm in the straight-backed chair as I take in the man across from me at the big oak desk. New to me, he's in his late fifties, stately looking with a full head of short gray hair and black glasses.

The administrative offices have been updated since I walked the halls of Blue Belle. A soft beige color is on the walls, along with photos of Principal Lancaster with various townsfolk. Lois is in two—one of her cutting a yellow ribbon for the new football stadium a few years back and another of her with the team last year at the state finals. Ronan is front and center, his arms around players, a happy grin on his face. A sigh leaves me. I remember that grin. It reminds me of the one he wore when he accepted the Heisman. *The world will be mine.*

"You taught at a preschool?" he asks, glancing up and breaking me out of my reverie.

My hands twist in my lap. Being an art teacher was an unexpected career choice. I wanted to work at a gallery or in graphic design, but those jobs were competitive and hard to come by after graduation. I did odd jobs—radio work, office clerking, bartending—until I scored a small gallery job that I adored. It lasted for two years; then the store unexpectedly closed. My roommate worked at the preschool and got me a position there.

I clear my throat. "Yes, the Blair Preschool in Manhattan. I was in charge of the art department for five years." I taught three- and four-year-old toddlers how to finger paint—with a little Van Gogh thrown in. Parents paid fifty grand a year to send their kids there, and I enjoyed it, but the salary was barely enough to pay my bills.

"You have some experience in education. Nice."

"Yes."

He steeples his hands together and gives me a friendly look. "Well, Ms. Morgan, we'd like to offer you a position here at Blue Belle High."

Surprise ripples over me.

No questions about my strengths and weaknesses? No calling my references?

I scoot a little closer to the edge of the seat. "I don't have a teaching degree."

He nods. "Our enrollment exceeded our expectations this year. Basically, we're overcrowded and scrambling to get our class size down and hire new teachers. This position has been open for two weeks, and no one with a teaching degree has applied. Thankfully, the state allows special accommodations for this, and, well, Mrs. Meadows vouched for you. She's one of our board members." He smiles. "She came to my barbecue this weekend and told me this story about you climbing her apple tree."

I let out an unsure chuckle.

"Anyway . . . we'd love to have you on board as a Bobcat. And . . . if you find that you want to continue here as a teacher next school year, we'd ask that you find classes to get teacher accreditation. Many places are online these days. You can even count your teaching experience this year as your practicum credit. I feel confident our enrollment is going to soar, especially with our football program. Everyone wants to be at a winning school, right?"

"Yes."

"Of course, we'd have you back next year if things work out." Then he tells me the salary, one that's considerably more than I made in New York.

"What would I be teaching? Art?" I ask hopefully. Whatever it is, bring it, but please don't let it be algebra . . . or English . . . or history . . . or, Jesus, any kind of science.

He removes his glasses and sets them on the desk. "You'll have a part-time English position. Juniors. How do you feel about *Julius Caesar*? I do believe that's on the curriculum."

I know nothing about Julius except that he got stabbed in the back by his best friend. I can relate.

He must see the disappointment on my face.

"Miss Burns has taught art for years," he says, studying me. "Perhaps one day that position will be open, Ms. Morgan, but not today."

"I see."

"We already filled the algebra job, and the English one is the only—"

"I love English," I gush. "Adore it. My favorite subject. You said part time?"

He nods. "Officially, you'd be a Blue Belle teacher, and you'd report to me for those duties, but we also need a personal assistant for Coach Smith, which makes it a full-time job. The booster club is covering that portion of your salary. Does that sound doable?" He smiles. "Lois mentioned you're quite the football fan."

A sharp breath comes from me. This feels a little like a bait and switch. Get the girl excited about teaching America's youth, then throw in the wrench. "Right . . ."

He pulls a sheet of paper from his desk and slides it over for me to take. "Here's the syllabus for the classes if you want to be sure you're up for this."

I glance over it, the words running together. Yep, there's *Julius Caesar*, poetry, a term paper—oh my God. I may have to study for this.

"As far as helping Coach, here's a list of some duties, but you two can work that out. It's up to him." He gives me another paper. "Our goal is to free up time for Coach. He's hardworking and talented as hell—pardon me—and we want him to stay. He put in a request for a part-time PA, and we've been waiting for the right person . . ."

He says more things, and I'm nodding, my mind racing as I think about Ronan. Yes, we had a chat in the bookstore where I said way too much to him, and we fake kissed, but I haven't heard a peep from him or noticed him walking at night. Which is fine. I don't want to see him.

Plus, that kiss is going to complicate things if we work together.

Honestly?

I'd rather teach a bunch of horny teenagers throwing spitballs at my face than be his PA.

He awakens something in my body; therefore, he is dangerous.

I glance down at the duties.

Answer phones in Coach's office. (Doable.)

Manage calendar/Book travel. (Fine. Anyone, even Sparky, could do this.)

Social media. (Take pics and post them.)

Management of fan mail. (People do that? Yes, this is Texas.)

Manage personal appearances. (Ronan needs help for the Waffle House?)

Manage pep rallies. (Seriously?)

I'm in high school all over again—only I'll have to hang out with the super hot, full-of-himself football coach.

Sweat rolls down my back. Plus I'll be around my ex . . .

"Well. What do you think, Ms. Morgan? Can you handle this?"

This is money and stability, and it might mean a job next year. Hope rises, a little thing that flutters in my chest, painting a vision of me teaching art someday . . .

My fingers tighten around the paper as I look up at him with a smile. "I accept."

The door opens, and Ronan stalks in, filling up the office with his height. Wearing khaki pants that hug his ass, an expensive blue dress shirt, and a navy baseball hat with his hair curling around the edges, he should look like any coach, but dammit, he just doesn't!

He stops when he sees me.

"Sorry, Denny. I didn't realize you had someone in here," he says to the principal, but those ice-blue eyes track all over me, from the top of my ponytail to the tips of my stilettos. I ease one out so he can get a better view. That's right. Check it. I've got great legs. And sexy shoes. I don't always wear joggers and boxers.

His gaze skates up my face and ends on my ponytail. His lips twitch as he puts those hands on his hips. "Nova."

"Me," I say with what I hope is optimism.

"Thanks for coming in from your class, Coach." The principal stands and sends a head nudge in my direction. "The hunt is over. We hired Ms. Morgan, a hometown girl, to be your part-time PA. Her credentials are amazing."

I bite my lip. That is just not true.

"She's just what we're looking for. Just perfect," the principal adds.

I hear a *lot* of satisfaction in his voice. My gaze lands on the photo of him with Lois. One, Lois told me about the job; two, she vouched for me; three, she went to his house; and four, she's head of the committee to get Coach hitched. Even an idiot can see right through this. I'm the new girl up to bat. Only they don't know that we have a history . . .

Lois is a meddling minx, but this is exponentially better than Pizza Hut.

"Is she?" Ronan says, crossing his arms. "I thought you usually hired a college intern."

Principal Lancaster nods and murmurs about how there weren't any interns available this semester, and with the extra enrollment and the need for teachers, he decided to kill two birds with one stone, thus giving me a full-time position.

Ronan nods during his spiel, his gaze entirely on me.

Before he can argue that he doesn't want me for the job, I stand up—gracefully, using all those classes Mama put me through—and glide over to him and put my hand out. I use my sweet smile on him and infuse my voice with excitement. "I can't wait for us to work together, Coach."

I literally have no idea what I've gotten myself into. On the outside, I'm cool, but on the inside, I'm quivering with uncertainty. Not only do I have to figure out high school English, but I'll be assisting Ronan, and I'm not sure he's on board.

The three of us walk out of the principal's office to the front desk, where a secretary sits, her head cocked with a phone to her ear. She hurriedly gets off the phone and rushes over to us.

Principal Lancaster explains that I'll be starting next week; then the secretary leaves to get paperwork and a laptop for me. Principal Lancaster shakes my hand and goes back to his office while Ronan heads for the exit. I trail after him. He's not getting away from me now. We've got to talk about this.

Melinda breezes in, red hair twirled up, a tight green dress on. I inhale. Dang. She is pretty. But a little evil.

"Coach Smith? Do you have a moment?" she calls sweetly, ignoring me as she walks up to us.

"Hmm," comes from him.

"I baked a pie for you. Pecan. I put your name on it in the staff lounge. I remember you said that was your favorite . . ." She gives him a glossy smile and touches his arm. He eases it away.

"Ah. Thank you," he says tersely, then shoots me a pointed look, as if to say, *See?*

I lift my shoulders. What does he want me to do about it? If our kiss didn't work, then I'm out of solutions. I can't be kissing him every time we see her.

"Why are you here?" she finally asks me, her lashes shielding her gaze as it darts from me to Ronan.

"I'll be teaching English."

Her nose flares. "Oh. You're the fill-in when they couldn't find anyone else." She gives me a tight-lipped smile. "I teach English. If you need any help, let me know. I have a master's in English literature."

"Of course," I say. "Thank you for the offer. It's very kind of you."

"You're very welcome," she says in a syrupy tone, then walks past us.

"Not on my life will I ask her," I mutter.

Ronan's lips curl. "But she was so nice. And so were you."

"Southern girls are born being nice, but they don't always mean it. Now, if she'd said 'bless your heart,' we might have had a tussle. Everyone knows what that means. It's pity with a dash of condescension."

"I learn more and more every day," he murmurs.

"How did the ranch lady from the Roadhouse work out for you?" I ask, reaching for normal before I bring up the job.

"Awesome. We roped some cows. Rode some stallions."

"Never called her, huh?"

"Nope."

A bell pings for the class change, and there's a rush of other faculty in the office and down a breezeway adjacent to us that connects other offices.

My breath hitches when Andrew enters, then walks toward us, his head down, papers in his hands. My eyes eat him up: the short dirty-blond hair, the square chin, the dimple that softens his angular jawline. He's wearing slacks and a striped dress shirt, his shoulders broad, his build lean and muscled.

His lips quirk up in a familiar way—one he used to do when he was amused—and my chest feels a rush of emotion, most of which I can't define. My hand reaches out and clutches Ronan's arm. He covers it with his hand and gives me a squeeze.

"Don't let him see you sweat," he whispers.

"Is that another Chinese military strategy?" I swallow thickly, not moving. Not yet. I haven't laid eyes on him in almost nine years. I skipped our five- and ten-year reunions, and when I registered Sabine for her classes this year, we came early and left immediately. I mean, I knew I'd probably run into him at some point at a school function, but I pushed it to the back of my mind. I had other things to focus on.

Someone calls his name, and Andrew glances up, sees me, and stops in his tracks. His mouth opens. "Nova?" Shock colors his voice. He flicks his eyes at Ronan, his brow furrowing, then back at me. "What are you doing here?"

Sure, I'm a confident girl; I've supported myself in the city, I made friends, I worked my ass off, and I lived happily. I fell in and out of infatuation several times—a surface feeling, mostly with athletes, those easy-come-easy-go relationships.

But . . .

He's the reason I hid a small piece of myself from every man. There's no trust in my heart, and a part of me picked risky relationships on purpose, knowing they'd end the way I expected, and as long as I knew it was coming, then I wouldn't be devastated. I'm not surprised Zane's eyes wandered and found a flight attendant. I always knew he wasn't permanent because *I* wasn't permanent. I've never loved anyone but Andrew.

He comes closer, rising amazement on his face, and I inch closer to Ronan.

The last time I spoke to Andrew, he'd shown up at my dorm room at NYU, reeking of alcohol, his face haggard. It was a week before his wedding, and he'd gotten on a plane and flown to New York. He came inside and begged me to come back. *I'm lost without you. I miss you. I love you. I need you. I made one mistake. Can't you forgive me? You're the one I'm supposed to be with. You're my sunshine. We can't let them keep us apart . . .*

We sat on my bed while he made his case. We'd grown up together, he'd loved me from the moment of our first kiss, he'd carved our names in the oak tree at the front of the school, he'd give up his inheritance, we were meant to be forever and ever . . .

He looked deep into my eyes, crying as he got on his knees and asked me to take a chance on him, to come back to UT, and we'd find a way to figure out the baby and Paisley.

I said yes.

And when I woke up the next day, he was gone. Betrayed. Twice.

I still can't find my voice, and Ronan takes over, his voice curt. "She's the new English teacher and my PA."

Then he's sweeping me out of the office and into a busy hallway.

I wrestle with my feelings, leaning against his hard frame, and I straighten, but he tugs me back. "Not yet. He might have come out. Let him know you don't care—even though you obviously do."

A long exhale comes from my chest. How on earth am I going to do this job with Andrew here?

Keeping me next to him, Ronan maneuvers us through a crowd of teenagers. All eyes are on us, the students giving him appreciative, admiring glances and calling out, "Coach Smith! Hey! Good morning! Great game!"

We make it through the throng to an empty area, and I focus on what's front and center.

After clearing my throat, I ask, "How unhappy are you that I got this job? If you wanted someone else, you could have spoken up in his office."

He doesn't reply.

We've turned a corner in the hall, and he stops at a door, opens it quickly, and tugs me inside.

I look around at the . . . storage closet. It's shadowy and small, about ten feet by ten, with shelves stacked with paper towels, hand sanitizer, pencils, pens, paper . . . "Nice office. Where do I put my desk, Coach?"

"It's Ronan when we're alone," he says gruffly.

"Is this going to work between us or not?"

"Nova. Are you okay?"

His hands land on my shoulders as his gaze searches my face intently. His thumbs stroke my tense muscles, but I don't think he's aware of it. Sparks zing over my skin, goose bumps rising where he touches me, and I will them to disappear. This isn't sexual. He's truly worried about me.

Carefully banked emotion rears its head, and I swallow, blinking back the tears that have been hiding under the surface since I saw Andrew.

"I—I knew it was coming. I just . . ." Kinda flaked.

"I'm sorry for it."

"Thank you for getting me out of there. Next time will be better."

"Sure." He drops his hands, almost reluctantly, then gives me his profile, messing with his hat. Realization dawns. The hat and collar pulling is his tic when he's unsure. I saw him do it at his party, then on my porch and at the bookstore. Those scars.

"I wish you'd look at me."

He starts at my frank words, then turns to take me in. "Okay."

"I need this job," I say softly. "I've been foisted on you, and maybe it is unfair, but there's Sabine and the house and my school loans . . ." I bite my lip. "I'm sorry. We both know Lois got me this job."

He leans against the door, and I do the same, our eyes holding. The sound of students out in the hall fades as the silence builds between us, but it's not uncomfortable. We seem to have created our own little bubble.

"I see," he murmurs as he searches my face. "Money troubles."

I nod. "I gave my word to Mama that if anything happened to her, I'd do the best for my sister. And when I give my word, I mean it. Honor and loyalty are important to me. We don't have any other family close by, and I can't take her back to New York. This is her home."

After the moments stretch, I ask, "What are you thinking?"

A deep exhale comes from his chest. "I'm thinking about a lot of things. We're going to have to take them bit by bit. First is that kiss."

I feel color rising on my cheeks. "What about it?"

His voice grows husky. "It's kept me awake at night."

My skin hums with electricity. "Oh."

He dips his head, breaking our gaze. "With that aside . . . I have a plan—or a proposal, whatever."

"What is it?"

His head rises. He gives me a long look, pausing at my sparkly shoes. His face softens as a huff comes from his chest. "You are something in that outfit. I like the mascot colors."

"I like fashion. You've never seen me dressed up."

His lips twitch. Ah, that's his amused tic. "Haven't I?"

"What do you mean?" I ask, narrowing my eyes.

"Nothing." He takes a step closer to me, until I can smell his cologne, something with hints of wood and leather. "Here's a quote for you: 'In the midst of chaos, there is also opportunity.' Sun Tzu. Keep that in mind."

"Okay." My shoulders straighten. Here comes the strengths-and-weaknesses interview . . .

"First, here are the facts. You just saw Andrew, and based on your reaction, it's going to be hard for you, yes? You'll have to see him at faculty meetings, in the hallway, at lunch . . ."

I wince.

He nods. "My proposal is . . . since we'll be spending time together, we help each other out. I want Melinda to ease off, and you want to show Andrew you aren't pining—"

"Not pining," I mutter.

"Regardless, he is here," he says gently. "He and I don't have the best relationship. We're polite on the surface, but he was slated to get the head football job; then I came along and took it. He was offered an assistant's job but declined and went back to basketball."

"Oh."

"My proposal is . . ." He bites his bottom lip with his top teeth, pulling at it slowly, and the gesture is somehow vulnerable yet sexy. "We pretend to date."

My chest takes a deep breath. "Oh."

"You can say no. I don't want you to feel as if you have to say yes. The job is yours regardless. I mean that."

"Okay."

He lets out an exhale. "The booster club keeps throwing women at me; you saw my birthday party. The whole town is involved. Melinda works with me. Hell, she came to my house in lingerie. I need to date someone as a buffer. Plus, she's already seen us kiss, so it wouldn't be a big surprise."

"I see." My mind races. Who on earth pretend dates? It's silly and ridiculous.

"They picked you for a reason, and once they think we're together, everyone will back off, especially Melinda. Plus, you aren't interested in me like that . . ." He arches a brow, as if waiting for me to reply.

"Hmm, right," I say.

"HR allows teachers to date, and if you say yes, I can let them know, make it official, and get the ball rolling. Once they know, word will get around fast, and there's not much we'd have to do."

My eyes thin. "You know the HR rules for romantic relationships?"

"I've looked into it."

"Interesting. Have you considered dating anyone here, ever?"

He frowns. "Of course not. I don't plan on being here long. I don't do relationships."

So why was he looking into dating someone he worked with?

"You'll break their hearts when you leave." I saw those faces in the hall, those looks of admiration and hope. "They want you to stay."

A frown furrows his forehead. "I'm not a bad person, Nova. The administration knows my plan."

Right, but that high enrollment for next year would mean a job for me and probably more people. Sabine told me that the last coach here hadn't gotten us to state in five years—and now we have Ronan Smith, a winner. Those athletic scholarships mean everything to these kids. To the community.

A bell rings, signaling class has started.

He whips off his hat and rakes a hand through his hair. "Well? What do you think?"

"What does fake dating involve?"

"A date to a function. A kiss after a game. Whatever you want. I would never do anything you didn't want to . . ." He trails off, heat flashing in his eyes. "We have chemistry, Nova."

The air in the room thins. "We don't."

He stares at me for at least five seconds, and with each moment that ticks by, my body becomes more aware of his. My nipples pebble under my bra.

As if he knows, he laughs under his breath. "Right. Come by the house tomorrow, and let me know your decision. Later, Princess." He opens the door and leaves.

The halls are silent as I exit the school. *Fake dating* dances in my head. It would make things easier for him, and it would provide me with a *Hey, look who I'm with* whenever I see Andrew. Plus, it's not like I'm interested in dating anyone else. I have a career to think about now, and being his arm candy would help my street cred with the whole town.

The issue is . . .

What if I like spending time with him?

What if I miss him when he's gone?

And we can't forget . . . I'm inherently weak when it comes to jocks.

Nope. Not a good idea at all.

It's not until I've cranked the Caddy that it dawns on me.

He called me Princess.

I bang my head on the steering wheel.

Chapter 8

RONAN

The bell rings for the end of my freshman history class, and the students grab their books. I gather my things, my head still thinking about Nova—

"Coach!" Bruno, Milo, and Toby fill up the room with their shouts as they rush to my desk. All three are wearing jerseys for spirit day, their faces sweaty. It's Friday, our bye week.

I raise an eyebrow. "I'm headed to lunch—"

Toby's face is red, his usually kind eyes hard. "Someone's snuck on campus and left us a message in the stadium. The maintenance person just saw us in the hall and told us. We ran out there and checked it out, then came here."

I frown as I come around the desk. I was just at the stadium this morning before I came inside. I've heard of pranks from opposing teams in the past—toilet paper, cows let in, trucks that tear up the field . . .

"What is it?"

"You have to see it for yourself to get the full picture. Words don't do it justice. I mean, it's unacceptable," Bruno calls out as he slams his fist into his palm. "They're messing with our heads! Literally!"

"I see." I grab my clipboard and whistle. "All right, show me."

Skeeter joins us in the hall, and I fill him in as we muscle through the lunch crowd, leave the building, and head to the stadium. We enter and step out on the grass.

The sun is high in the sky, and I squint at the field. Holy shit . . . "Are those stuffed animals?" There are hundreds, from one end zone to the other, bits of tuft and mangled bodies covered in fur, red splatter dripping.

"Yep," comes from Skeeter. "Mutilated."

I put my hands on my hips and stalk out to center field, where our mascot is painted. There's a life-size stuffed bobcat lying on top of it, decapitated and covered in red paint. Its jaw is open with a note crammed in. I take it out and unfold it.

Bobcats are dead meat. We will tear you apart piece by piece on the field just like we did these animals. We beat you last year and we'll beat you again. You're not good enough to make it to state. And Coach Smith is a loser. He's only there until he can get a better job. Go fuck yourselves, dickheads.

"Well. That's uncalled for," I mutter.

The trio has followed and is trying to read it over my shoulder, but I tuck it into my pocket. No reason to fan the flames.

"This is a squirrel head!" Bruno grouses, jerking one up off the field and waving it around. "And here's a tiger. Stupid fuc—I mean jerks. They didn't even use the right animal!"

"I found a teddy bear!" Milo calls from the end zone.

Toby's mouth tightens. "They must have had to go to every Walmart in the state to get this many stuffed animals." He kicks one of them, and it sails through the air.

I grit my teeth. Last year, our team had a hill to climb, and we were the underdogs but ended up with a good season, but now that we're slated as one of the top teams in the state . . . "Who did this?"

Toby gives me a steely look. "My bets are on Huddersfield."

"That game isn't for weeks," I say.

He shakes his head. "Doesn't matter. They're vicious."

I whip my hat off and slap my leg. "We don't have a million-dollar stadium for nothing. Let's check the cameras."

We march to the control room upstairs, but before we get there, Toby stops us, his tone bitter. He's got his phone in his hands. "Huddersfield has already claimed it. They posted on Instagram." He shoves a phone at me, and I stare at a picture of our field littered with red-splattered animals. They must have been up in the stands to get this pic. Fuckers.

"Who is this person?" I ask.

Toby takes his phone back. "A fake account by the looks of it—which means they'll get away with it."

Bruno grabs it. "Dude! It's got over five hundred likes and all kinds of comments." His shoulders heave as he points out to the field. "This demands revenge."

Bruno can be a hothead, Toby is the peacemaker, and Milo just goes along, but Toby nods his agreement. Skeeter does, too, and I frown. No, Skeeter . . .

We check the cameras and see a white SUV pulling up and three masked figures getting out, all dressed in black and carrying garbage bags. They seem to be guys, but it's hard to tell with the view. The license plate is covered in paper. Well planned.

"They knew our schedule," Toby murmurs.

"They're watching us," Bruno says, looking over his shoulder. "They could be right now. Maybe hidden cameras."

I keep the eye roll in. "More than likely, they got lucky and moved fast. They scattered those toys in less than ten minutes." I heave out an exhale. "Probably athletes."

"The players," Toby says grimly.

"Yeah, they won state last year, and now they're worried about us," Bruno snaps. "Trying to fu—I mean mess with us."

"Back in my day, we'd get them back and make sure everyone knew," Skeeter mutters.

"That's what I'm saying! We can't let this go," Toby says.

"Where are we gonna get stuffed rams? They have the stupidest mascot. I mean, they keep a live goat in their stadium and pretend it's a ram. Idiots," Bruno grumbles.

"That poor goat, all tied up. No family or friends," Skeeter adds. "Animals deserve to live in the wild."

"Steal the goat! It's been done before!" Bruno shouts. "That's it, Skeeter!"

"Yeah!" call Toby and Milo as they fist-bump each other.

Skeeter starts, then gives me a wild look. "Nah, nah, Coach, I wasn't suggesting they—"

I cross my arms. "No one is stealing anything. We're going to let this go."

The boys gape. "Coach, if we don't, then we're pussies," Bruno argues. "Bobcat pride means something."

Toby and Milo nod in agreement.

I shake my head. "This team is about integrity. We dress up for games, we use polite language in front of others, we try our best in class, we work our bodies, we practice, and we prepare our hearts. Win the heart, win everything. You can't do that if you're consumed with getting back at Huddersfield. That's what they want. It's a ploy." I put my hands on my hips. "Besides, just like on the field, it's the second person who gets caught. They'd be waiting on you. Don't stoop to their level. Be better."

There's a long silence, the guys not meeting my eyes. Skeeter shuffles his feet, a mumbled "Yeah, what he said" coming from him.

I look at Skeeter. "Get maintenance on this, stat. We need it cleaned up before practice. Call the office, and have someone call the principal over at Huddersfield and see if they had any students absent today. I doubt it will help, but we can see. Also, see if we can get that Insta account down."

I take in the sullen faces before me. "You three walk with me back to the school. I want you to keep this between us and the team. There's no need to go half-cocked into the school and start spouting off. It will only make things worse and make fans angry. Got it?"

"But those poor stuffed animals—" Bruno starts.

"No *buts*," I say.

He lets out a gust of air. "Yes, sir. My lips are sealed. Can I tell my girlfriend? She and I share everything. She's a cheerleader, super hot—"

I inhale. "We all know your girlfriend, Bruno. This is just for the team. We can use this as an opportunity. If you see a Huddersfield person out somewhere, be nice, pretend like it never happened, that it didn't make a blip on your radar. That's the ultimate revenge."

They give me doubtful looks.

Bruno's shoulders dip. "Are you going to give us one of your *Art of War* quotes?"

"No, Toby is. He's your captain. Toby?"

I turn my gaze to him, waiting for the leadership I know he has inside him. I've heard him repeating our mantras at practice and on the field. He's my best player, the most dedicated, the one who has a lot to lose if he doesn't get a scholarship. That thought makes me pause, the idea of leaving him next season; then I push it away. Whether I'm here or not, I'll make sure Toby gets his education.

Toby straightens his shoulders and paraphrases one of the quotes. "Ponder before you make a move. Think about your enemy and where he'll be waiting. If you think they're laying a trap, they are."

I nod. "Tell them what we should do."

"Ignore it. They did this to piss us off, hoping we'd have a knee-jerk reaction, maybe get caught and have to sit out a few games and ruin our winning streak," he says.

Pride soars inside me, and I slap him on the back. "All right. Now, do you mean it?"

"Yes, sir."

"I want a promise from each of you that you'll let this go," I say.

"We promise," they say.

We exit, and by the time we get back to the building, we're talking game strategy and workout routines. Crisis averted. No goats stolen on my watch . . .

◆ ◆ ◆

"Thank you for my birthday at the Roadhouse. The cake was so good. Chocolate's my favorite," Bonnie, Toby's mom, says as we walk into their small house. It's on the south side of town, a more run-down area, the houses built in the fifties, the yards small. Toby holds the door open as we head to the den.

Toby settles her gifts and balloons on the counter. Lois picked her out a bedazzled jersey with the number fifteen on it, Toby's, and a gift card to a ladies' store in town.

Bonnie and I end up in the den, and I turn on the TV so she can watch a previous game where Toby threw three touchdown passes. She couldn't go because she was sick.

"What are you having trouble with?" I ask Toby as I come in the kitchen for water. He's at the table, scowling over his notebook.

He pushes his hair back and groans. "Algebra two. I've kinda hit a wall. It's solving quadratic equations . . ."

I settle down next to him. "Let me see it."

We huddle over the textbook and go through the problems, step by step. Bonnie comes in and puts the cake and gifts away, asking if we need anything, but we say no and keep at it.

When I was in high school, I focused on my studies, terrified my athletic talent wasn't enough or would be snatched away from me.

Between school and work and taking care of my sisters, I barely had time to do anything else.

"I think I have it," Toby says a few minutes later. "You can go."

"You sure? I'm not in a hurry. Trust me. No plans."

He chews on his lip.

"What's up?"

"Nothing. I think Mom's ready for bed, and I haven't talked to her much," he says hurriedly, standing up and taking my glass to the sink.

I frown. "Is this about the field today?"

"No, sir. It's nothing. I swear."

I study him for a few seconds. I hear him. He wants some alone time with her. Or perhaps something *is* eating at him, and he isn't ready to talk.

I clap him on the back. "You've got my cell if you need me, 'kay?" I point at the books. "If you get stuck, give me a ring, and we can work it through FaceTime, yeah?"

"Yeah. Okay."

"See you Monday." I leave for home.

After changing into joggers and an old practice shirt, I head to my office. Dog trots behind me as I grab my guitar and sit in one of the leather recliners. I learned to play from Tuck. I'm not as good as he is, but the more time I spend alone, the more I pick it up.

Dog settles at my feet as I strum a few lines to warm up, then play the opening to "Hurt," by Johnny Cash, a cover from a Nine Inch Nails song.

I'm humming the lyrics when the door opens, and Nova enters my office. Dog raises his head, yawns, and then plops back down. I give him a glare—*Thanks for noting the intruder.*

My french doors must have been cracked from when he went out.

She's wearing shorts, a green tank top, and those boots, her hair up in a high ponytail that reminds me of her in that Leia outfit. It makes my cock twitch. There's a lightsaber in her hand, and she waves it around, then sets it on my desk as if it's a king's scepter.

I keep playing, restarting the song as she approaches.

Her head bobs, fingers tapping the rhythm against her leg; then she starts to sing.

Her voice startles me with its purity, the lyrics clear and spine tingling. It's a different perspective from Cash's woeful ballad, her voice sweeter. A memory flies at me, one of her singing in my hotel room. I tug my eyes off her and focus on the guitar.

A quietness fills up the room as the song ends. The hair on my arm is raised, and I drape my eyes over her hungrily and admit, fuck, that the fake kiss in the bookstore was total bullshit. I wanted to kiss her. And yes, I asked her to pretend date, and yes, I cleared it with HR first. What was I thinking?

"Another one," she says. "It helps me relax."

Sweat beads on my forehead, and my fingers feel numb as I switch to "Jolene." She laughs under her breath and belts it out, adding a country twang to her vocals.

"You sing like an angel," I say after the song as I settle the guitar at my feet. "Did you ever pursue music?"

"Not really. I'm all right, I guess; it was my talent in pageants." She exhales a long breath, her lips twisting. "So. How long have you known who I was?"

Ah, so that's why she came over a day early . . .

And here it is.

The part where I need to explain about that night in New York . . .

"It was the day I brought Sparky over. Something about . . ." Our electricity . . . "Anyway, I called Tuck for your name."

Her eyes glitter. "Ah. My buddy. He can talk a girl into anything."

My lips flatten. "He said something about offering you a fee—"

She frowns. "Hold on. I never agreed to the money."

"So why did you do it?" I ask gruffly.

She mutters under her breath.

"What was that?"

She glares at me. "I wanted to meet you, you big doofus."

"You wanted to meet a washed-up, drunk former quarterback in an outlandish outfit—"

"Tuck presented the idea, and I . . . I . . ." She waves her hand.

"Yes?"

A gust of air comes from her. "I love football, and you played it better than anyone ever had. There. I've complimented you." She shrugs elegant shoulders. "It was a fan moment for me. I didn't show up to have sex with you. Please. I have sex because *I* want to."

Relief washes over me. I smirk. "So. You are a crazy fan."

She rolls her eyes. "Not anymore—as you know."

"Right. That night was . . ." I lift my brows, waiting for her to finish.

"You clearly don't remember what happened—"

"I recall most of it." I chew on my lip. "It . . . it was a hard time in my life."

"I see," she says, her blue eyes softening.

I glance away from her, not prepared for her gentle tone. I recall the state I was in that night, how grief ate at me, and it wasn't just Whitney I mourned; it was my career, my life. One moment I'd been about to start my tenth year in football and get married—then it had blown up in my face. Something inside me died. My dreams. My faith in my ability to take care of people. My desire to love.

The morning after was a turning point for me; the realization that I was on a path of self-destruction reached a crest and tipped over. I'd hit rock bottom, and Nova was the stepping-stone that pushed me out of that dark pit.

"I was celibate when we met," I say quietly. "I was rehabbing at first; then later, I just didn't have the heart to be with anyone else; then you showed up . . ."

A rueful smile rises on her face. "Your teenage fantasy in the flesh. I've already forgiven you, Ronan. It was a long time ago."

But I need her to *know*. "I knew it was you. I swear." I shift around. "I'm sorry. The car wreck wouldn't get out of my head . . ."

She pauses. "I knew her. Not well," she adds at my inhale. "She did the photography for the kids' yearbooks once a year. I shared half of my BLT with her once when she forgot her lunch. You kept your private life under wraps, and I didn't realize who she was, not until the papers wrote up the accident. She seemed really sweet."

"She was." I met Whitney at a photo shoot for the team. We dated for nine months, then got engaged. She was petite with blonde hair, and I fell in love with her laugh, her bashfulness, the way she curled her hand around her face at night.

There's a long silence as we gaze at each other.

"Done. Fresh slate," Nova murmurs, breaking our gaze. "I brought the lightsaber—found it in Sabine's old toys—as a gift. It's completely worthless, but I thought it was cute." Her chest rises. "And perhaps it will soften my answer: I can't be your fake girlfriend."

Chapter 9

Ronan

Disappointment slams into me. My gaze drinks in her plump lips, the elegant line of her throat. "Why?"

"It will make things complicated. We have a history."

"I'm going to change your mind," I hear myself saying, stepping closer to her. "First, we can keep the arrangement professional."

She winces. "And when you leave, I'll still be here dealing with the aftermath."

I brush a piece of lint off her shoulder, my hand lingering as if it has a mind of its own. "I'll make sure you aren't to blame, Nova."

Her tongue darts out and touches her lip.

"Let's play for it," I purr.

"Play?"

"Hmm. You worked in a bar. I'm sure you've played pool or thrown your share of darts?" I nudge my head at the back of the room.

She thinks about it. "I'm not great at games. Sabine decimates me in chess. Strategy was never my thing."

"I'm not good either."

"Please. I'm not sure this is fair."

"You don't seem like the kind of woman to turn down a bet, Nova. I bet you can't beat me."

She stiffens, her eyes narrowing. Gotcha.

"Come on." I take her elbow and guide her to the back.

She picks up the dart shaft and runs her fingers over the flight on the end. "Let's do darts, then. What are the stakes?"

"If I win, you'll agree to be my fake girlfriend. You decide what you want if you win."

Her gaze drapes over me slowly, taking in my loose nylon sports pants and an old Pythons shirt. She cracks her knuckles. "Let's make this interesting. We throw three darts. The one who hits the closest to the bull's-eye gets something each time. A boon."

"Hmm, sounds like you've done this before."

"You have lots of pretty things in this room." She nudges her head at the big-screen TV. "Very nice."

"All right. I'm in." I am so going to kick her ass.

She inclines her head. "We should practice."

"Please." I move and let her stand behind the throw line of the dartboard.

She throws one, and it hits the wall.

I huff out a laugh.

"I'm warming up," she snips.

Her next five darts hit the outside of the bull's-eye, and my lips twitch.

"Here, let me help." I move behind her and take her arm. "Don't put too much weight on the front of your feet, or you'll lose stability."

She leans back against me as I hold her throwing hand. My other hand goes to her hip, and her body aligns with mine, fitting. I take a deep breath, sparks flaring over my skin.

I clear my throat. "The way you hold the dart is called the grip. First, don't apply much pressure. Use your index finger . . . here . . ." I caress her finger, putting it where it goes. "Find where it's level . . . that's it . . .

support that with your thumb, and then use your other fingers . . ." She moves to get a better position, and her ass brushes against me. I force my cock to settle. We stand there for several moments, neither of us moving.

I step back. "Now, relax your posture, and release the tension. Keeping your eyes on the board, let your elbow be at a comfortable fixed position. Good. When you throw, move your arm, throw like it's a paper airplane, but don't change your elbow. Try to release all your fingers at once. If you don't, you'll screw up the stability of the dart. Extend your arm as if it's aiming for the target you want to hit."

She throws, and it hits the triple-score ring outside the bull's-eye.

A grunt comes from her. "Dammit."

She throws several more, missing, then scowls at me.

I take my practice round, being a little reckless with my throws to bolster her confidence.

The contest begins, and I go first, my shot hitting inside the bull's-eye and to the left.

She steps up to the line and gives me a sweet smile, one that I know is a little sly, then throws her dart and hits the middle of the bull's-eye. She gasps, then claps, a delighted expression on her face. "Will you look at that? I win the first one!"

"Lucky shot," I mutter.

"What should I ask for?" she says as she taps her chin.

"Please don't take my TV. I need my football this weekend."

She laughs as her gaze lands on my shirt, and I pop an eyebrow, amused. I tug up the end of it. "You want my shirt? You *used* to be a fan . . ."

"Nope." She sits and spins around on a barstool. "I want the Heisman. I know you won't give it up forever, but I want it for at least, let's say, a month."

I burst out with a laugh. "That's my baby. I kiss it every morning!"

"You agreed to *anything*. Plus, it won't be far from you. Just next door."

I exhale. "You can have it for one week. You must keep it away from Sparky. Keep your air between sixty-eight and seventy-two. Don't set it near anything—"

"Done!" She jumps off the stool and marches over to the Heisman and picks it up, hugging it. "It's so pretty. And hard."

"Don't use it for sexual pleasure," I reply with a grin.

"M'kay. Maybe." She sashays back to the dartboard, setting the trophy next to her phone on a table. She uses her phone to turn on music, and the sound of Otis Redding's "My Girl" fills up the room. "All right! Let's do the next round." She hums the song as she picks up her dart, throws, and hits dead center.

"You're a dart shark," I accuse as I take my spot. "Admit it. Your practice shots were total bullshit."

"I said I wasn't good at strategy games . . . but I love me some darts."

"You played me."

I shake my head, then throw, hitting close to hers. We both rush to the board to check the darts.

"Tie," I say. "We each get a boon."

She bites her lip. "You go first."

My gaze lingers on her tank top.

She uses her Texas drawl on me. "This isn't strip darts, honey. My shirt isn't coming off."

"Fine. I want your bra for a week."

"No."

"You got my trophy, and you can't spare a simple bra? Wow."

"Ugh. You're a whiner." She tugs her arms inside her shirt and moves around, obviously unhooking it, then pulls it out from her neckline. All very skilled. Her nipples poke through her shirt as her breasts sway. She tosses it at me, and I catch the red lace fabric.

I hold it up to my face, then run my tongue along the edge of one of the cups.

Breath whooshes out of her, her lashes fluttering. "Ronan . . . I . . . what are you doing?"

Something I shouldn't, but . . . "I never said I'd play a clean game."

"Don't use it for sexual pleasure," she grouses. "Okay, my boon is . . ." She pauses. "I want you . . . to put my bra on."

"You wicked woman."

"Rules are rules."

There are no rules to this game. We're toying with each other, and we both know it.

"I've never worn women's undergarments before," I say as I dangle it in front of her. "I need help."

She takes the bra from me. "Can't even dress yourself. Poor thing. Bless your heart."

"Ah! I know what that means. Just put it on me and swear to never tell anyone."

She slips the armholes on me, then sets the straps on my shoulders. She eases behind me and pulls, then grunts. "Of course it won't snap." She turns me around to face her, then puffs out the cups. They end up between my throat and the top of my chest.

"Oh yeah, you're so sexy," she murmurs, and I laugh; then I catch myself in the reflection of the mirror behind the minibar and groan.

"This is outrageous."

"Yep. Ronan Smith in lingerie. I have *TMZ* on speed dial—" She reaches for her phone, and I toss it out of her hands.

"No pics. Prepare to lose, sweetheart. Let's do this again." I'm ready to win this thing.

She gives me a pointed look. "I'm wondering why you didn't ask me to be your fake girlfriend."

"Because I'm confident." And this bra is the fucking sexiest thing I've ever seen. Totally going to jack off with it.

We throw again, and I win. "Yes!" I pump my fist while she scowls, her hands on her hips.

"What do you want?"

I think on it. "First, we should do more than three throws. You in?"

"Maybe." She looks over at Darth Vader. "I'd like a dark villain. I could hang clothes on him—or dance with him. So what do you want?"

I skate my eyes over her. "You don't have much on you."

"This is true. I'm rather poor." She sticks out one boot, showing a long, shapely, tanned leg. "How do you feel about boots?"

"They're not my size."

"But they are one of my prized possessions."

"Lie. They're from high school. I want a kiss," I murmur.

She waltzes over to me, hips swaying. Then, fast as lightning, she reaches up and brushes her mouth over my scarred cheek.

My breath hitches as she lingers, her fingers lightly caressing the line from my temple to my neck. My heart twinges, shifting in my chest, aching for . . . something I can't have.

She stares at me. "I like your face. It's you. Oh, you were pretty before the scars—in fact, I liked to call you Henry Cavill . . . that jawline is wicked hot—but now . . ." Her shoulders shift. "You have character. Meaning. You survived and came out on the other side flawed . . . yet beautiful."

I frown, grappling with how I feel about her words. "I'm not beautiful."

"Beauty isn't on the outside. I learned that in the pageants. I met some beautiful women who were ugly on the inside and some who were incredible. Beauty is how we go on, the life we create around us. Living a life that's meaningful. I'm not sure I'm there, to be honest. I'm trying hard. We all are. I know that coming home was good for me, even though the reason is sad. Truthfully . . ." She sighs, a contemplative expression on her face. "I needed an anchor in my life, a sense of belonging, and Sabine and home are it." A laugh comes from her. "Look at me. I'm making us talk about serious things when we should be throwing darts."

It dawns on me that I don't have an anchor—unless you count coaching.

She might be the first woman to ever kiss my scars. Sure, I've been with women since that night with Nova—carefree, lighthearted young women, the kind I could forget—and usually they just pretended my scars weren't there. Perhaps they didn't know what to say. Perhaps they just wanted to forget they existed.

"Let's move on," I say and ease away from her.

She throws first and hits just outside the bull's-eye; then I go, and my dart hits the wall.

"Dammit."

She's chanting "I beat Fancy Pants" while I glower in the corner. Stopping, she stands in front of me. "I want Darth Vader for a week. You have to deliver him to me."

I groan. "He's very expensive. And heavy."

"This game was *your* idea. Let's go again. I can do this all night," she sings.

I line up and throw, but my dart goes off center. I curse again.

Her stance is spot on, her elbow perfect as she throws straight to the bull's-eye.

I heave out an exhale as she waltzes around the room, stopping at the Princess Leia snake cuff. "I want the bracelet. Forever. It's mine anyway. I need it to complete my outfit." Her head turns, and she cocks an eyebrow. I stalk over to where she is, flip open the case, and slap it in her open hand.

"You don't even like *Star Wars*," I mutter.

"You hate losing, don't you?"

"Yes," I growl.

She fiddles with the cuff, not able to work the clasp, and I take it from her, push her sleeve up, and attach it. On its own accord, my hand grazes down her arm.

"This game feels like foreplay," she murmurs, then sways away from me.

"I never envisioned foreplay with me in a bra," I complain.

She laughs. "Round six is up." She throws, and her dart is off center.

I step up and send the dart straight into the middle of the board. Score. I face her, smiling.

She toys with the end of her ponytail. "I'm not taking off my clothes."

I take a seat on one of the stools. "I need to think on this."

She sits across from me, cupping her chin in her hands as our gazes cling. I fucking love looking at her, and it isn't just her beauty. There's an infectious quality about her smile, a sense of irrepressible joy that surrounds her.

Playing darts with her might be the best time I've had in this big house.

"Tell me something about you," I say. "Something I don't know. A secret."

"A secret . . . hmm . . ." There's a long pause; then, abruptly, she yells and hops around the room.

"What?"

She plops on the floor, yanks her boot off, tosses it away, and then rubs her arch. "Cramp. All that positioning in front of the dartboard . . . maybe the stilettos I wore. It's been a while since I wore them. I don't know. Ugh. My calves hurt too." Her face scrunches in pain.

I bend down and take her foot. "Here, let me." I press my thumbs into her arch, rotating them with deep pushes. "It hurts at first, but try to relax your leg muscles, okay?"

"Okay." She winces, little puffs of air coming from her. "Sorry. I ruined the game. I was going to make you dance around in my bra on the next round. Or take the big-screen TV. Mama's is ten years old . . . ouch! It hurts. Why?" she wails.

"Could be dehydration or the shoes or just about anything."

"I can't stop the shoes. I'll be seeing Andrew!"

"You'd dress for a man who hurt you?"

"I'll be dressing to make him see what he missed."

My lips tighten at those words. "Flex your leg again," I say and massage into her foot, pressing on the top toe, then drawing my hand out to her heel.

Relief crosses her features, a sigh coming from her. "It's gone. God. Your hands are like magic. Thank you."

"No problem. I've had a million cramps." I sit down next to her on the floor. Her tank top has ridden up, and I see her stomach. I pull it down just as she does, and our hands meet. Our fingers pause, then lightly lace together. My thumb brushes over the top of her hand. Small circles on soft skin . . . heat ripples over me.

"Tell me your secret," I murmur, leaning closer to her face.

A slow blush works up her throat. "I can't."

"Why?"

A shuddering breath comes from her as she gazes up at me, pupils dilated.

My breath quickens. "Nova . . ."

Her mouth parts. "Ronan . . ."

At the sound of my name on her lips, the desire I've been pushing away rushes in like a tsunami. Forget fucking Andrew. Yes, she's still in love with him, but . . .

Her hand tangles in my hair, cupping my scalp. "What is this . . . ," she murmurs.

This is crazy. It's undeniable spark. Desire.

Part of me tells me to stop, to not go down this road, that I'm crossing a dangerous line . . .

I lean down, and she meets me halfway, our breaths mingling as our mouths cling in a desperate kiss. Her lips are pillowy, like satin, and I groan at the lush feel of her. Our lips pull away and go back again, searching for more. I tug on her lower lip with my teeth, and she does the same to me. Our tongues tangle, tasting each other, until we pull away gasping. It's as if our mouths recognize each other, syncing in an age-old rhythm.

I hover over her, aligning my body with hers as my forearms support me.

"Pull up your shirt," I breathe out.

She eases it up, exposing her full, creamy tits, and I take a nipple in my mouth and suck. Her areola is a dark pink, and I tease my tongue around it, then nip with my teeth. I move to the next one as my mouth learns the shape of her, the curves, the freckles on her chest, her collarbone. I taste it all. My dick rotates against her shorts, slow and easy, then harder. Her hands slide around my waist and under my pants to my ass, pulling me closer.

Sparks explode when she reaches around to cup my cock through my joggers. I push into her hands, groaning.

"Nova . . . ," I whisper as I stare down at her. Her sapphire eyes glow with heat, and something inside me pauses, terrified, a war inside my mind.

This is the moment . . .

When I should stop.

But—

And that's when the office door flies open.

Chapter 10

Ronan

"Ronan!" Lois calls as she and Skeeter barge in my office. "We've got to help—oh dear, sorry, um, I didn't mean to interrupt your . . ." Her eyes widen at the bra around my chest; then she blinks rapidly and looks away. "Goodness. I didn't know you had company. We rang the doorbell, and when you didn't answer, we tried the door. I told you you can leave your door unlocked in Blue Belle, but if you do, people might just walk in, especially in an emergency. Bless."

"I hadn't gotten around to it," I snap as Nova stiffens under me and jerks down her shirt. I pull her up from the floor, then turn down the music, trying to even my breathing.

What the hell are they doing here?

I rake a hand through my hair and put my back to Lois and Skeeter, wincing as I push down on the tent in my pants. I pretend nonchalance and look down at Dog, who wags his tail. "No wonder they dropped you off at my house. You're pathetic." I give him a pet, then move to my desk, wadding up the bra, then tossing it in a drawer and slamming it shut.

Nova sits on a barstool, her face pink.

I face Skeeter and Lois, my arms crossed. "What emergency? Start at the beginning."

Skeeter grimaces, his auburn hair a mess. "The Wayne County sheriff pulled Bruno, Toby, and Milo over on Loch Ness Road out by the lake. He called Lois; then she tried to call you. Then she called me when you didn't pick up."

I pick up my phone, seeing twenty missed calls. "It was on silent."

Lois waves her hands. "We've got to get down there and fix things."

"If they're arrested, our season is over," Skeeter mutters, stuffing his hands in his jeans. "We beat Wayne Prep, and they're out for blood—"

"Jimmy Lockhart is the sheriff of Wayne County," Lois grouses. "He's a big Wayne Prep fanatic. We have no friends in that county."

"What the hell were they doing way out there?" I ask. "It's eleven at night."

Skeeter grimaces. "Stealing the Huddersfield goat. You have to drive through Loch Ness Road. It's a back road, and I'm guessing they were hoping to sneak into Blue Belle."

"Dammit!" I roar and pace around the room. "They stole the mascot."

"They say it's a ram, but the horns aren't right. It's a goat," Skeeter grouses.

Lois whips her hat off and glares at us. "We're wasting time. My poor Milo. He's only sixteen! We've got to save them."

"How?" I ask.

"We go down there and beg. And pray the sheriff will listen. Skeeter's car is at my place, so he's with me," Lois says, shoving her hat back on as she flips around. "You follow."

"Where the hell is this lake?" I ask, grabbing my keys.

"I'll show you," Nova says, coming around to stand next to me.

"You want to come?" I ask.

She nods. "If you want. I'll need to grab Sabine. We may be there awhile."

"All right." Relief hits that she's coming. I'm not ready to let her go yet.

Lois and Skeeter walk out my front door. I lock it; then Nova and I head out to the garage. I open the passenger door to the Suburban for her, make sure she's buckled, and then get in the driver's seat and crank it up.

Five minutes later, Sabine comes out of her house, dressed in shorts and a T-shirt, and crawls in the back seat, strapping herself in.

We pass through Main Street and go several miles; then Nova gives directions that lead to a deserted, wooded gravel road that's barely big enough for two cars.

We go around a curve, and blue lights flash in the night sky. Bruno's white truck is pulled off the side of the road with a police cruiser behind it. Lois and Skeeter are already out and talking to the sheriff. Leaving Sabine and Nova, I jump out of the car, my jaw clenching when I see a goat tied to a tree. Wearing an orange Huddersfield football jersey, he blinks at me, then dips his head to chew on the grass.

The boys sit in the back of the police car. Yeah, this is going to be tricky.

The sheriff is tall with a khaki uniform and a cowboy hat, a holster at his hip. He steps away from Lois, who had her hand on his arm, and meets me. He gives me a firm handshake. "Ronan Smith. Nice to meet you. Jimmy Lockhart."

I give him as much of a smile as I can muster. "Heard my boys got in a little trouble."

He jabs his finger at the white truck. "I was out here on a call and thought I'd check out the lake area. I saw Bruno Miller driving with a busted taillight, and I pulled him over for a warning citation, then saw the goat in the back seat. Thought it was a dog, but, well, it's the Huddersfield mascot. It lives at the stadium. That's breaking and entering and theft." He gives me a hard look. "I called Lois out of respect for you. I'm a fan of the Pythons."

"But not of the Bobcats?"

He scoffs. "I played quarterback for Wayne Prep. Born and raised in Wayne County. I was at the game when you beat us a couple of weeks back."

Great.

"What happens now?" I ask.

"I'm gonna take them in and book them in juvenile custody. Call their parents. They'll make bail, then go to juvenile court. Theft is serious business, Coach." He looks pointedly at the goat. He's brown with white spots and not very big, about the size of a German shepherd.

My eyes land on the guys in the back of the cop car. Their heads are turned as they look back at me with wide eyes. "They're my starting lineup," I say tightly. "The Huddersfield people trashed our field, and they're reacting. They're good kids, dedicated on the field, and *usually* uphold the law."

"They didn't tonight."

"Is there anything we can do to handle this . . . in private?"

There's a tense silence as frogs croak in the distance. His face flattens. "Are you offering a law enforcement officer a bribe?"

"Of course not, but I love to sign footballs." Yes, this is a bribe.

Skeeter slides in next to me. "Come on, Lockhart, we used to face off on the field. We know each other. What would it take to forget this ever happened?"

He hooks his thumbs in his belt. "Nothing."

I scrub my face, searching for words. "Don't you remember how it was to be a football player and another team pulled a prank? They're kids. Those hormones can get out of control."

He nods sagely. "I remember, but they can't be sneaking into a stadium and taking property—even if Huddersfield does keep it in a cage."

I pinch my nose, then hear one of the Suburban doors slam. Nova comes up from behind me, and her hand curls around my arm. "What's going on, darling? Are your guys going to be arrested?"

I look down at her upturned face. *Darling?* "I think so," I mutter.

"What the hell? Nova Morgan?" says the voice of the sheriff.

She fluffs her ponytail, her voice easing into her drawl. "Jimmy! I didn't know that was you!" Her face glows as she sweeps toward him with open arms. He lets out a hearty laugh, picks her up off her feet, swings her around, and then sets her down.

"I thought you were in New York. It's been forever since I saw you!"

She tells him about her mom passing, and he squeezes her arm, a familiarity there that makes me scowl. "Loved that woman. She made the best oatmeal chocolate chip cookies." He guffaws, a grin spreading on his face, his voice lowering. "I'll always remember her catching me in your closet under all those stuffed animals. She nearly whipped me out the door. Then she told my mama. I couldn't call you for a week."

"Longest week of my life," she teases.

He chuckles. "I was terrified you'd forget about me."

I think he's forgotten about us.

And why is she still standing in his arms?

"I heard you got promoted to sheriff. You look so handsome." She plucks at his badge and smiles. "You were always my favorite ex-boyfriend. And that's the truth."

"Fifteen and thought we were in love; then you had to go and dump me for Andrew." He bends down and gives her another hug, and I freeze, remembering she doesn't have a bra on. His hand lands on her lower back, easing close to her waistline—

"Anyway . . . back to the boys," I snap.

He throws me a side-eye, then looks down at her. "I take it you're seeing Coach?"

Nova turns and smiles brightly at me. "We're dating, yes. He's adorable."

I roll my eyes . . . of all the things . . .

"He's completely devoted to me. Aren't you, darling?"

"Completely," I say with a grim smile.

Lois appears next to me, wiping her eyes. She's been over at the police cruiser talking to Milo through the glass. "What's going on?"

"Nova and Jimmy are having a reunion," I mutter as Nova hooks her arm with the sheriff's and they walk to the goat. I can't hear what they're saying.

Lois exhales as she watches them. "I forgot they had a thing. It was so long ago." She throws me a look. "So . . . you and Nova? Did I hear her right? Adorable?"

I close my eyes. "Please never walk in my house again unannounced. And I don't know what Nova is doing."

Skeeter smirks. "You sure move fast, Coach. You just met her and y'all—"

"Whatever you saw in my house, wipe it from your memory," I growl.

"I think it's fine if you wear women's clothes," he says. "I ain't got a problem with it. The guys might be surprised if you wore it out to the field, but they admire you, and I'm sure they'd get used to it. I have a male cousin in Austin who wears heels and dresses. He changed his name from Mark to Mandy. No one turned a hair in my family."

"Skeeter! I don't wear lingerie. It was a dart game. She won a round, and I had to . . . ugh. Never mind . . ."

He pats me on the arm. "I'm like Fort Knox. Nothing's getting out of my mouth."

"People's sex lives should stay private. When my Bill was alive, we got up to some fun stuff," Lois adds.

I exhale. "This is not the place to discuss it."

Nova pets the goat and laughs up at Jimmy. He takes his hat off and sets it on her head.

"She's working her magic," Skeeter says, relish in his voice. "Nothing like stoking an old flame." He nudges me. "Be good to her, Coach. Just sayin'. She had it rough with Andrew. You feel me?"

"Of course," I say with a frown. I'd never want to hurt Nova.

She crooks her arm back in the sheriff's as they head back to where we wait. Her face is uptilted toward him, and he's patting her hand. It looks very cozy.

Jealousy whips over me, and my hands clench.

Totally irrational behavior.

They stop in front of us, and the sheriff gives me an up and down, sizing me up.

"Since Nova is vouching for you, I'm going to let them go with a warning for the taillight," the sheriff says. "I want them to check in with me on Saturday for some public service work. They'll be picking up trash on the side of the road. In Wayne County. Best not wear Bobcat attire."

Lois sucks down a shot of her inhaler, then murmurs a heartfelt thank-you.

I head to the cruiser with the sheriff. The boys file out as I put my hands on my hips and give them a glare.

They start with a rush of apologies—

"No. This is unacceptable. You promised me," I say, cutting them off. "Huddersfield almost got what they wanted: you in trouble."

They bow their heads and nod. "Yes, sir."

I heave out an exhale. "Every day next week. Five a.m. Be dressed and on the field for running. Do you think I want to get up that early? I don't. You won't be playing Friday night against Collinwood. You're out. You'll spend the rest of the week working with your backups. And if we lose against them, that might ruin our whole season. I expect commitment. I expect trust. I expect integrity. I expect heart. Are you showing it to me?"

Their faces fall as they shake their heads. "No, sir."

"Do you want to win it all or not?"

"We do," they shout.

"Then why did you come tonight?" I call. "It was reckless. You can't be reckless in football, boys! Every moment counts! Every decision you make can affect your team!"

"It was stupid, sir. We see that now," Toby murmurs, and I focus on him.

"I left you working on homework, and now this?" It stings. I expected more from him.

"I'm sorry," Toby says, his head down.

Bruno raises his hand. "It was my idea, Coach. I talked them into it."

"And you're all going to pay the price," I say.

After I'm done, the sheriff stands next to me and goes into a lecture about theft. Once the boys look suitably chastised, he turns to me and points at the goat. "I'm not putting that thing in my cruiser. It's up to you how you get it back to the stadium without getting caught."

"I can take him back," Bruno says.

I glare at him. "Get your butt in your truck."

Lois grabs Milo by the sleeve and drags him to her Mercedes. "I've got this one." She opens the passenger door and shoves him in the back seat. "Your mama is gonna whop you," she tells him.

"She doesn't do that," Milo calls as Skeeter sits in the front of her car.

"She should!" Lois snaps as she shuts the door. She walks around to her side, gets in, and throws gravel as she pulls away.

Toby and Bruno get back in his truck.

"Straight home," I tell them. "I'm calling your parents first thing tomorrow morning."

With grim faces, they drive away.

When I flip around, Sabine and Nova are loading the goat in the back seat of my Suburban.

I close my eyes and lift my hands up to the sky. "Only in Texas."

I get in the car and sit, stewing for several moments. My hands twist on the steering wheel, and I exhale, letting the anger ebb as I lay my head back on my seat and stare at Nova. "There's a live goat wearing a jersey in my car."

Her lips curl, merriment in her eyes. "Things you never thought you'd say."

"This whole thing might be funny in a few days, but I'd never let them know that. Thank you for saving us from the sheriff."

"You're welcome. I did agree to meet him for lunch."

I twist in my seat. "No way. He asked?"

She pops her lips. "Yep."

"Do you want to?"

"I like Jimmy. We'll catch up and have a great time."

I frown. "You don't have to go. I mean . . . because you feel like you have to."

"I want to. He's a friend."

I pause. "Am I?" I want us to be.

The goat makes a strange chuffing sound, and she doesn't reply but turns to look in the back seat.

I look out the windshield, my head racing back to us on the floor in my office. That was a whole lot more than friendship, that delicious tension and chemistry, the taste of her nipples . . .

No.

No.

I need to stop these thoughts.

Sabine giggles as the goat pokes his head up to the front. He licks my hand, and I grimace.

"Do we have to give him back?" she says.

"Yes," Nova and I say at the same time.

"I love his little horns. And he's silky. Can we get a goat? Pretty please."

"Goats are farming animals," Nova says to her. "I like house animals."

"This one lives in a cage," she counters. "We need to save it from a life behind bars." The goat sits on Sabine's lap. "Look, he's trained. I said *sit*, and he sat. I could train ours to get the mail or get beer out of the fridge."

"Ten years before you can drink, and you didn't say *sit*; he just sat," Nova grouses.

"Wow. I must be twenty-five for sex and alcohol. Nice joke," Sabine says.

"Not a joke," Nova replies tartly.

I laugh as I pull out on the road. "Okay, girls, any ideas on how to sneak this goat back in?"

Nova gives me a squinty look. "Um . . . yesssss."

It dawns on me. "Fu—I mean, don't tell me you've stolen this goat before?"

"Senior year, me . . . and a few others." She grimaces.

Andrew.

"I left a note describing where to find him, some field outside of town with some cows. We didn't hurt Lambert," she says.

"Lambert?" I ask.

"Maybe Lambert the first. I don't know how long goats live," Nova says.

"Between fifteen and eighteen years. I just looked it up," Sabine says. "We could train him to shake hands and roll over. I could sleep with it."

Nova shakes her head. "Still not feeling it, Sabine."

"But they have those pygmy ones!"

"No means no."

That chuffing sound comes again, and Sabine abruptly puts Lambert on the floorboard.

"Um, Coach?" Sabine asks.

"Yeah?" I look at her in the rearview.

"Lambert puked in your car."

Chapter 11

Nova

"Are you going to tell me what you did with that goat?" he asks me.

It's almost one in the morning, and Sabine has gone upstairs. I'm not sure why he didn't just drop us off, but he said he wanted to talk. I replied that talking is better after a cup of coffee in the morning, but I didn't resist much.

I plop down next to him on our blue couch.

The den is shadowy, just the lights from the kitchen illuminating us. His gaze skates over me; then he looks away and glances around at our den—a small room but cozy in grays and blues and lime greens. A portrait of Mama, me, and Sabine is over the fireplace, taken the year I graduated NYU. Sabine is a little girl, her face serene, looking somewhere off camera. Mama is dressed in a pink pantsuit, her dark hair coiffed up, makeup on point.

"If I don't tell you, then you're covered under deniability," I say.

"Hello. I was driving the getaway vehicle. I'm expecting state troopers to pull up at my house at any moment."

I smile. "You let us off at the corner, so you're fine. We walked to the stadium and stayed in the shadows on the sidewalk with Lambert.

If they had cameras, it was just two girls returning a goat who escaped. Totally believable."

"Fucking Lambert."

I laugh. We spent about ten minutes after we got here cleaning out the "gift" Lambert left us.

"How did you get him inside?" he asks.

"I climbed over one of the low fences outside the stadium—see, I banged my knee." I point to my bruise. "Then Sabine handed over Lambert. Thank God for small goats. We snuck inside an open door and found where they keep him. It's a small pen now, so not a cage, so at least there's that. Maybe people just say he's in a cage because we hate Huddersfield so much."

"I'm picturing you in boots climbing over a fence." He rubs his hand over my knee, his fingers lightly brushing the bruise. I bite back the tingles it sends over my skin. "You're okay, though? I can get you some ice for it."

"I'm fine."

"I never want you to get hurt over something that's *my* responsibility. You should have let me do it." There's a serious tone in his voice.

"Honestly? I had fun. I haven't been bad in a while." I smirk.

He leans back on the couch. "So this fake-dating thing. You pretty much announced it tonight, but we can always tell everyone it was a joke or that you said it to help us out."

"True." I nod. Lois heard me, though, and I saw that gleam in her eye. She believed it—especially after seeing us in his office—and she's probably already told the booster club via a mass text or email, which means everyone will be telling everyone by tomorrow morning. They'll be toasting each other with coffee at the Waffle House. Throw in the bookstore kiss, which several people saw, and the foundation has already been laid for a fake relationship, so it wouldn't be hard. Show up to a few games, smile and flirt at school with Ronan in front of Andrew and Melinda. It seems easy, but a tingle of unease rises. I haven't admitted it to myself since seeing him again, but I can't deny that my heart *is* vulnerable to him. I'll have to guard it. Carefully.

"Let's do it," I say.

He gives me a surprised look and smiles. "Really? All right, all right. Thank you. Again. Is this the album you mentioned?" He leans over and picks up the photo book on the coffee table and flips it open.

I nod.

"This is you?" He points to a picture someone snapped of our family in front of my rosebush.

Smiling, I lean over. "My fifth birthday. I remember that red gingham dress. Mom always wore pink, of course, and the small wiry man is my dad," I say, pointing to him. "Mama was taller than him. Bull riders are usually around five-five to five-ten, and it's all about strength. He used to tell me he was the strongest man in the world, and I'd brag to all my friends." I laugh. "He wasn't a man to dress up—jeans and flannel were all he ever wore—but I picked out this white button-up at the store and begged him to wear it for my birthday pic. He took it off as soon as the camera clicked."

"When is your birthday?" He chuckles. "We need to know these things, I guess."

"June eleventh. I'm a Gemini, the social butterfly of the zodiac. Take me to a party, and I will shine. They're also flighty."

"I'd never describe you as flighty. You're here for your sister unconditionally; you say unexpected things."

"Like what?"

His lashes lower. "Like about what beauty really is . . . and what you said about my face."

I feel a blush rising. Yes, I said that. And I meant it. "It's the artist in me. You should know that about me in case anyone asks. I draw and paint, mostly flowers, cows and horses, cowboy hats, barns, and churches. I lived in New York, but the things I love to draw are from where I grew up. Maybe I missed home more than I realized. I should have come home sooner and spent more time with Mama." I sigh. "When's your birthday?"

"September seventeenth. Virgo. They're logical, hardworking, and systematic. The bad trait is stubbornness." He pops an eyebrow at me, and I laugh and bump my shoulder into him.

"That is so you."

"I know. Lois said your dad passed years ago . . ."

"Heart attack." I chew on my lips, my head circling back to the afternoon I heard Mama scream, then run outside. She started CPR on my dad while I called the ambulance. I tell Ronan about it. "Every time I hear a lawn mower, I recall that day. He was gone before they got to the hospital."

A darkness shadows his eyes. "For me, it's storms. Lightning scares me, like something bad is going to happen to someone. Tell me something else about you."

"Hmm, I like to cook. My favorite color is yellow."

"That's boring as shit."

I gasp and put a hand over my heart. Dramatically. "Fine. You want juicy? I broke a toilet in Ryan Reynolds's penthouse, and he doesn't know it was me."

He bursts out laughing. "Oh, you have to explain."

"He was having his party, and Harry Beauchamp and I went—"

"You dated a New York hockey player too? Damn."

I raise my hands. "Athletes are my weakness."

"Is that right?" he says dryly. "Let's see. There's Andrew, Harry, Zane—who is a dick—then me—"

"Whoa. You and I, we never 'dated.'"

He dips his head, grimacing. "Yeah, I guess not. Who else?"

I tick them off on my hands. "A baseball guy, another footballer, a basketball star . . . hmm . . . I'm sure there's a few more in there . . . they kind of run together."

"You have a type."

My eyes drift over him, lingering on the sharp line of his jaw, on his blade of a nose, on his sculpted body, toned by years of exercise . . .

I clear my throat. "Back to this Ryan Reynolds party. Celebrities were everywhere. Blake Lively is the sweetest ever, America Ferrera, Jake Gyllenhaal. I tried not to gawk. Then Harry decided to dance with this actress." I roll my eyes. "One dance. Two. Three. I was pissed and slung back several glasses of champagne, which then led to what I like to call the Bathroom Crisis."

"Did you pee your pants?"

"No! The first floor had a line—that's where I met Anna Kendrick, but I was doing the pee dance and couldn't talk to her. We weren't supposed to go upstairs, but in my defense, there wasn't a person there to tell me I *couldn't* go past the velvet rope that blocked it off. If they were serious, they'd have had a guard, right? So I huddle crawled up the stairs, and voilà, there in the hallway was this beautiful megabathroom. I'm talking glossy black subway walls, gold faucets, and a glittery chandelier."

"Lavish."

I laugh, recalling me describing his home that way. "I finish my business, flush, then the toilet starts to overflow—like there's a waterfall gushing out on this fancy marble floor. I jiggle the handle, gold, and it falls off in my hands. I take the lid off the toilet to see if I could adjust the inside of the tank. Nope, the toilet is so high tech it's beyond my mechanical experience. I drop the lid—it made an awful noise. It cracked just a little. I dragged towels out and cleaned up the water, dumped them in the tub, then set the broken lid back on top of the toilet. Then I fixed my hair like everything was okay, slipped back downstairs, grabbed a glass of champagne, told my date to fuck off, and called a cab. I kept the toilet handle. By accident!"

He gets a funny expression on his face. "When was this party?"

"Five or six years ago? It was springtime—"

"Did Anna Kendrick trip over someone's leg and sprain her ankle?"

"She did! She had an ice pack wrapped around her . . ." I stop, my eyes widening. "No way . . ."

"I was at that party."

"But . . . how did I miss you?"

"How did I miss you?" he says softly.

Oh. I look down at my lap and chew on my lip. "Huh."

"I was with Tuck."

"You weren't with Whitney?"

He shakes his head. "I hadn't met her yet."

My heart dips, my mind racing. What if . . . what if I had seen him that night? Would he have noticed me? I stop that train of thought. He met Whitney later and loved her.

"Why do you keep Leia in a closet?" I ask.

He stills, frowning. "I bought her last year, and when I got her in the house . . . she didn't look right. Something . . ." He shrugs. "Anyway, I figured she might be too sexy looking if the players came over to swim on the weekends."

"Is it because she reminds you of a night you'd rather forget?"

He gazes at me searchingly. "I don't want to forget that night. It opened my eyes."

Oh.

His forehead puckers in a frown. "Nova . . ." Emotion flits over his face, and his hands tighten as they rest on his thighs. "Earlier . . . in my office. You're beautiful and incredible, and we have this past between us, but we should keep things light."

I stiffen, a curl of anger rising. Got it. Don't develop feelings for the baller. Which is totally fine! I'd already decided that myself.

He looks up at me. "After Whitney, I swore I'd just chill—you know, not catch any feelings for a while—and . . ."

"You don't have to worry about me getting the wrong idea." Rode that roller coaster in New York. It crashed and burned.

"Are you okay with what I said?"

He's afraid I'm going to just roll over and fall in love? Pfft. I frown. "I'm not Jenny, Ronan. I'm not the kind of girl who chases you down and demands we 'determine the relationship.' We don't have a relationship—and hello, I like the guy to chase me, so there."

"Wait . . . you're nothing like her, okay. It's just I want this—"

"To be light! Message received." Jeez.

"I'm sorry about earlier—"

"It's forgotten! Let it go, okay?"

That furrow on his forehead grows, as if he wants to say more.

"We can pretend in public and be done with it. Check." I stand up and stretch and yawn, needing some distance from him. "It's late, and I'm ready for bed."

He studies my face for several moments, then stands, thanks me again for helping with the sheriff and the goat, and walks out my door.

I drape myself back down on the couch, and Sparky curls up in my lap, a soft meow coming from him. I give his ears a scratch, my throat tightening, part hurt, part *I should've known better than to kiss him!*

Ronan doesn't want to get involved with anyone. He's emotionally unavailable. I get it. It's an understandable feeling after losing someone like he did.

We'll keep things easy and fun with no attachments.

I swear.

Chapter 12

Nova

My first day at Blue Belle High begins with me dressed in a cream leather pencil skirt, a sleeveless white silk blouse, and three-inch black stilettos, with my hair up. I'm going for the angelic look. *Me.* Nova Morgan back at BBHS. I push down my anxiety and smile at Sabine as I walk through the double doors. Adjusting the lanyard with my name on it, I head to the teachers' lounge while Sabine leaves to find Lacey before class. In my leather satchel are the school-issued laptop and a bundle of materials Principal Lancaster gave me. I crammed this weekend. Me and Julius Caesar are now best pals.

I'm staring down at the floor when I bump into someone, a tall, thin, gaunt-faced boy with caramel-colored hair. He's maybe fifteen or sixteen, and his pinched face gives me pause.

"I'm sorry," I say, smiling. "Are you okay? I wasn't looking where I was going."

He reels back, grimacing. "Whatever. Be careful, will ya?" He turns around to stalk off.

"Hey!" I call. "What's your name?"

He flips me off over his shoulder and keeps trucking.

I squint. Well. Good start.

I enter the staff lounge and introduce myself around. I say hi to Miss Burns, the current art teacher, someone I don't know. She's older, maybe sixty, and I wonder if she'll retire soon. Please.

Melinda flits around the room, dressed in a killer blue pantsuit—how many does she have?—her diamond headband in her hair. She studiously ignores me.

I head to a coffee bar, get a large cup, and pour in a liberal amount of creamer.

Someone comes up next to me, and by smell alone, Ralph Lauren's Polo, I know exactly who. My entire body prepares for war.

Fortifying myself, I plaster on a fake smile and turn.

"Nova, oh my God," he says as he takes me in, his golden, warm eyes eating me up. "I tried to find you Friday but missed you in the hall. I can't believe it's you!" He gives me a sheepish grin. "I drove past your house this weekend, but you weren't home."

I flinch. "Why?"

Color rises on his cheekbones. "Oh, I had a congratulatory gift for you on getting the job. Nothing big. Honestly, I felt like I was in high school again, cruising past your house—only now I drive a Range Rover instead of a Corvette. Those were the days, right?"

I nod, my spoon furiously stirring my coffee. He's tall, about six-one, his hair a blond color that complements his topaz eyes. Wearing gray dress slacks and a blue button-up shirt, he's still a fastidious dresser. Annoyingly, he hasn't gained weight. At least he has a few lines in the corners of his eyes.

"You look the same," he says. "Still beautiful, Nova."

Ah, but beauty was never enough, was it?

I reply back with the usual "Oh, you look great too" while my head tries to decipher how I feel about *him*. His smell makes me feel nostalgic, recalling us in his red Corvette, his arms around me, fingers playing with my hair. I remember how he'd moisten his lips with mango ChapStick before we kissed—

"I'm separated from Paisley," he says quietly, dropping that bomb as easily as saying the sun is shining. A frown flits over his face as he takes in my expression. "Sorry. I wasn't sure if you knew, but everyone else does . . ." He shifts around me, his arm brushing against mine as he picks out a mug and fills it with coffee. "It happened several months ago. It'd been rocky for a while." He takes a long sip, holding my eyes over the rim. "I'm sorry about your mom. I sent flowers."

I continue to stir my drink. I hadn't known about him and Paisley. I never checked his socials or asked anyone. "Maybe it will work out."

"Yeah, well, sometimes fate decides those things for you. What's meant to be will always be, right?"

"Hmm."

He eases closer, and I don't move away, part of me transfixed by him, by the reality that *Oh my God, we're having a normal conversation.*

His head dips, then rises up to capture my eyes. "It's funny. I feel like I want to tell you everything that's happened since you've been gone. I guess once you grow up with someone, once you share everything we did, it doesn't matter how much time passes—you feel as if you're still close . . . but then, I'm not sure if you feel the same."

There's a heavy silence.

He sighs, overlooking my silence. "Anyway, my daughter is eight now. Brandy. She's in third grade and a damn good soccer player." He chuckles, then sobers. "Paisley and I are splitting custody. It's been hard, the sharing and going back and forth, but for the best." He takes a sip of his coffee, his eyes going to my left hand. "You never got married?"

"No."

His gaze softens. "Is it nuts that I'm glad?"

Anger and hurt flare like a lit torch. How dare he? Does he expect me to be flattered? If he hadn't cheated, then abandoned me in New York, I would have been married to *him.* My hands clench around my mug, and I open my mouth to lash out—

Thankfully, Skeeter marches in the lounge, whips his ball cap off, and wipes at his hair. "Lice alert on the baseball and volleyball teams! I knew we'd have an epidemic, and it's happening!" He looks at Principal Lancaster. "We might need to shut school down for a day or so. Call it a snow day!"

"I'm sure it will pass," the principal murmurs.

Skeeter ambles over to us, reaches for his mug, and then fills it, not quite meeting my eyes as he turns red. "Good to see you, Nova. Thanks again for, um, Friday. Sorry about, you know, before, um, well, when me and Lois . . ."

Don't bring it up, Skeeter! You and Lois probably saw my boobs!

"Did you guys ever have lice?" he asks me and Andrew.

Forget lice.

Ronan walks in, filling up the room, towering over everyone, wearing black slacks and another crisp pale-blue button-up. His hair falls around his face, softening the scars that don't need softening at all.

I tear my eyes off him and check my reflection in the mirror on the opposite wall. My makeup is superb—lots of heavy eyeliner, smoky eye shadow, thick lashes, red lipstick—and best of all, I have two little buns on the sides of my head. They're less fluffy and sleeker than Leia's but stylish. Sabine watched a YouTube video on how to make them and did them this morning. Mighty Morgan Girls for the win!

Ronan's eyes roam over me, noticing the hair, then the snake cuff around my upper arm. His lips twitch.

That's right. I look amazing. I stand a little taller, take a hasty sip, and burn my lips.

A broad smile crosses his face as he holds my gaze. "Hey, babe. I would have given you and Sabine a ride this morning. I must have missed your text."

He doesn't even have my phone number! Oh, he's good at this . . .

He came by on Sunday morning, the Heisman wrapped in a blanket. He followed me inside and upstairs, where I set it on my dresser.

There was a tense moment when our arms brushed, but we both ignored it. Sabine invited him to eat pancakes, and he surprisingly said yes. We made normal conversation about football, about his mom, about mine.

That afternoon, he showed up with Toby, Bruno, and Milo with Darth Vader. It took the three of them to carefully maneuver him into the house while Ronan gave directions. We moved the chair in front of the window and put him there so he could watch the neighborhood. Sabine placed a boa around his neck, and I waited for Ronan to flip out, but he only smiled.

The room goes quiet, eyes darting between us. Andrew lets out a surprised sound at Ronan's *babe* while Principal Lancaster's face glows at me approvingly. Melinda slaps down her mug on the table a few feet away.

Let the games begin . . .

I smile brightly. "Oh shoot. Sabine and I wanted to get here a little early, darling. Sorry. I meant to text you."

"No problem." He stalks toward me and kisses me on top of my head. "Excuse me, Andrew," he says curtly. "I need coffee."

Andrew moves, giving me a curious look as he takes my hand for a brief squeeze. Mine feel clammy; his are warm, the grasp achingly familiar.

"I'll talk to you later, Nova. We have a lot of catching up to do. I want to hear all about New York." He gives me a lopsided smile, the one that used to tug at my heart, then walks over to Skeeter and Sonia.

"I see you've reconnected with your past," Ronan mutters, watching Andrew with a hard gaze. "You all right?"

Is it Andrew or Ronan or my new job that has my nerves in a twist? Likely answer is all three. "Yes."

"Are you aware that you're dressed similarly to Princess Leia?"

"Really? What a coincidence."

His lips curl. "I don't believe in coincidences. Regardless, you look stunning."

"Thank you."

"Did you dress for me, then?"

"Obviously. Tomorrow it's Chewie. Then . . . um, what's that guy's name, the one who saves everyone?"

"Luke Skywalker?"

"No, the green one. I think he was a wise man?"

"Yoda."

I snap my fingers. "That's it! Hmm, wait. I could dress as one of those robot thingies, the gold one . . . what was he called?"

"C-3PO. God, you know nothing."

I smile as I take a sip of coffee. I know some of their names, but it sure is fun messing with him. "I'm picturing a gold dress, lots of buttons."

"He didn't have buttons. He had wires in his midsection—dammit. You need to watch it. No one hangs with me and hasn't ever seen *Star Wars*."

"But I kind of like being one of the few people who haven't. It's the same with *Titanic*. Mama and Sabine watched it over and over, but I never could bring myself to see Leo drown. He's too pretty. I mean, there was room on the boat!"

"You mean the door."

"What?"

"Rose was saved on a door, not a boat."

"See, I didn't know that. I never saw it."

"The *Star Wars* franchise is not *Titanic*. It's about hope in the galaxy, with laser guns and starships. It's the belief that one person can conquer an empire."

"Wow."

He rolls his eyes as I chuckle. See, we've got this. Just friends. Keeping it light.

The bell rings, signifying we have fifteen minutes before class starts.

I let out a gusty breath. "Here I go."

Ronan gives my shoulder a squeeze for good luck, and since Melinda is still watching, he places his lips over mine in a gentle kiss. He smells like virile man, and his pale-blue eyes are warm (fake!) as he gazes down at me. "You can do anything you set your mind to, babe."

I glance over as Melinda flounces out of the lounge.

"It's working," he whispers in my ear, his lips skimming my skin.

I push down the tingles as Sonia approaches.

We ran in different circles in high school, but she and I had a horrendous PE class together senior year. I remember her as a little awkward but feisty when the time called for it. With straight dark hair to her shoulders, big white glasses, and a pert nose, she's pretty.

"I like your shirt," I say. It's white with a peace sign and says **PEACE LOVE AND VEGGIES.**

"Thanks. Want me to show you around?" she asks.

"Sure," I say. "I'm room 333."

Telling Ronan goodbye, we exit the lounge and head down the left side of the hall in the opposite direction of where Ronan led me last week. She points out the cafeteria, the way to the gym, and other important landmarks. We work our way back, and I peek into different classrooms, wincing when I see that mine is directly across from Andrew's.

She checks her phone. "Looks like we still have six minutes. Awesome! Follow me to the special place. You can't tell anyone, okay?"

"Um, okay?"

Walking briskly, she rounds a corner, ducks down a dark hallway near the student restrooms, and then opens a door and ushers me inside.

I blink at the dim light. "Oh my God, how many storage closets are in this school?"

She waggles her brows. "Three. I know them all. The lounge is always crowded, and these are the best places for alone time. There's a rumor that Melinda tried to corner Coach in one, like, she locked the door and wouldn't let him leave, but I don't know if that's true. It might have been his office? It's no secret she's after him."

"Tell me about it," I grouse.

She reaches in the pocket of her black pants. "Here, take a toke on this. It's my extra. Hope you like peppermint flavor. I might have a vanilla or strawberry. I have so many. I get them off the kids on the daily." She holds out two e-cigarettes and a handful of pods.

My mouth opens. "You vape on school grounds?"

"Don't be a snitch, Nova, but hell yeah. Everybody needs a break."

I giggle. "I always thought you were a goody two-shoes except for those times we skipped PE."

She sucks on an e-cigarette, the vapor billowing around the closet. She grins. "Are we gonna be friends?"

"Definitely."

"I can tell you're nervous about the deviants you're about to face—"

"Deviants?"

She smirks. "I'm kidding. Trust me—I love these kids, and teaching science is amazing, but the English teachers will have given you the kids they don't want. Mrs. Pettigrew is head of the department and a wanker. I have a thing for British words, by the way."

"Bloody hell, all kids should be wanted," I mutter.

She giggles and takes another toke. "I spent a summer abroad there, and it stuck with me. So yeah, here's the skinny: there's good and bad teachers just like in any profession. All I'm saying is, Petty Pettigrew cherry-picked who got your class, and guess who her bestie is?"

"Melinda?"

"Yep, and Melinda also teaches junior English. But don't worry about your first rodeo into the life of horny teens. I'm going to help you." She flashes a smile. "Also, Principal Lancaster asked me to be your mentor."

"And my mentor smokes." I grin as I take the e-cigarette and take a toke, then choke on the flavor. I hand it back. "I'll pass on this, but thank you, and yes, I'm nervous. Any tips?"

"My advice is to walk in there like a badass. Pretend they're prisoners, even though they aren't, of course. Come out of the gate tough. Slam your fist on the desk, march around like a sergeant, rant and rave about how mean you are, and don't let them give you any lip. If you start out soft, they'll eat you alive. You can always be nicer, but they won't buy it if you suddenly become hard. You've already lost them."

My eyes widen. "Got it. Be tough."

"Now, let's get to the good stuff. Spill the tea—you and Megacoach a thing?"

I pause, then nod and smile. "Oh yeah. He is . . ." *Off limits.* "Amazing!"

She narrows her eyes. "That sounded fake. You put your accent in. What's going on?"

Another bell chimes.

"Bullocks. No time." She stands up and waves at the air frantically. "I'll see you at lunch. Good luck, and let me know if I need to beat anyone up. Cheers!"

We slip out of the door and into a crush of students rushing to their lockers. I tell her bye, then walk toward my classroom.

I pause as my eyes catch Andrew as he stands at his podium. A few students are around him, and he's smiling, his stance easy and confident, and it hits me that he loved US History in school. I wonder if he's a good teacher, not one of those boring ones like Sabine talks about. He glances over at the door, sees me, and smiles tentatively.

My chest does a weird tightening thing.

After he left New York, I forced myself to become stronger, to wear armor around men, to never get too close. I packed him away in the dark closet of my mind like a forgotten sweater. I told myself I moved on.

Have I?

He comes to the door. "You okay? I can go in and introduce you?"

A memory hits me, one of him giving me a promise ring on our graduation day in front of the entire class. Dammit. Why am I remembering the good things about him? He hurt me. Horribly.

"I'm good. Thanks." I'm about to turn when he says my name. "Yes?"

He sticks his hands in his slacks. "Does it feel weird to be back here, you know, where we . . . dated?"

I stiffen. "We're different people now. It doesn't feel the same."

"You and Ronan, huh? That was fast."

"We met in New York years ago."

"Ah. I'll be honest. I'm disappointed . . ." He stalls and looks away from me, then rubs his neck. "Sorry. That's not really appropriate since . . ."

"No, it isn't," I snap.

He winces. "I'll see you at lunch."

And I'll have Ronan as my buffer.

I turn to go in my classroom.

◆ ◆ ◆

Bruno leans his elbows on his book. "Ms. Morgan, this crap is boring."

I zero in on him. A dark-haired boy with a big smile, he's part of my third period.

I cross my arms and blow at the hair that's falling around my face. Also, my lipstick is gone, I stapled my finger, *and* I got a paper cut.

I'm worn down to a frazzle.

When I walked in my first period, everyone was talking, two girls were out of their seats arguing over a boy, and the boy was in the middle egging it on. One girl was at my desk going through the teacher's textbook, and another was trying to be her lookout. Someone had written

Suck My Cock on the whiteboard, and my chair was turned upside down.

I raised my voice and pretended like they were the worst toddlers I'd ever encountered. I crossed my arms and glared as I announced my one and only preschool rule: *Sit down and listen with eager ears!*

By the time everything was put back together and I called roll, I realized they hadn't read their homework from their previous teachers, so we read Shakespeare aloud. Some of the students grumbled, one called me the b-word under his breath, and one student—a guy named Caleb Carson, the one who'd bumped into me when I'd walked in this morning—abruptly stood and left my class when I called on him. Something about his hunched shoulders pricked at me, but I couldn't leave my class. I wasn't taking my eyes off this bunch.

Second period was minimally better, and now I'm on my last class.

Bruno flashes me a charming smile, but I don't trust him an inch. "You agree it's boring," he announces.

"Absolutely not." I shake my head, my face in what I hope is a "This literature is fabulous" look, then sweep my gaze over the class, mostly football players, with a few girls. Most of this period read the assignment, and we had a decent discussion earlier.

"Do we have to answer the questions at the end of the scene? We have a game Friday, and I need to focus." Bruno again.

I pinch my nose. "Friday is four days away."

Milo, who's sitting across from him, gives him a fist bump. "Ms. Tyler let us talk and hang out in class. And she was going to let us watch the movie instead of reading the play. She was cool."

"I'm not cool," I reply.

Bruno lets out a jaw-splitting yawn and stands up. "I need to hit the restroom. Where's the hall pass?"

I ease up from my desk. "Sit down, Bruno. You're a big boy. Running back, right? You can hold it for five minutes, then *hit* the bathroom between classes."

He lingers near the door, debating, and I narrow my eyes at him.

"Don't test me. I will give you a time-out." I have no idea what a time-out means for a teenager, but I can come up with something on the fly . . . "You can stand in the corner for the rest of the period. Your choice. Your consequences."

He heaves out an egregious exhale and plops down at his desk.

I walk to the front of my desk and lean against it. "You're more than just football players; you're smart young men who need this class. You need to pass to play football."

Bruno rolls his eyes. "Just give us an easy A. Or a B. We won't tell."

I resist the urge to tap him on the nose like Sparky.

Toby shifts at his desk. "We can do the questions at the end, Ms. Morgan."

Bruno guffaws. "You're just being nice because you like Sabiiiiine."

I take a step to Bruno's desk, my voice sharp. "No talking about my sister."

"Yes, ma'am," he replies, eyes widening. "She's a nice girl. Real cool for a freshman. Like super awesome."

I open his book, flip the pages, and point. "Read this aloud. Act one, scene two, here."

Looking annoyed, he leans down. "'But, for mine own part, it was Greek to me.'"

"Good," I say. "It's a common saying we use every day, although most people get the actual quote wrong. Instead, we say, 'It's all Greek to me.' Do you know what it means?"

"That the speaker didn't understand what was said." He smirks. "A lot like this play. I keep reading it, and nothing makes sense."

Everyone laughs.

I nod. "Maybe reading it *is* like slogging through mud . . . or tackling a big defensive player. Do you let those players beat you?"

"No," he mutters.

"Right. So let's pretend *Julius Caesar* is an opponent, one you must beat to get to state. One step at a time."

He sighs and opens his notebook. "All right. You did save us from the goat thing. I'll cut you some slack and get to work."

One of the girls raises her hand.

"Yes?"

"Is it true you're dating Coach? Is that who left you the rose on your desk?"

I glance over at the long-stemmed yellow rose that was here when I came in. Andrew. He said he had a gift for me this weekend—

"Granny told me you were dating Coach," Milo says.

"Milo told me," Toby says.

"My hot cheerleader girlfriend told me," Bruno adds.

"Does everyone know?" I ask as I raise my arms.

They all nod.

"He's pretty hot," a girl murmurs under her breath.

"Don't tell him," I mutter, and then I'm saved from further comments when the bell rings and they grab their books and laptops.

Bruno stands and walks to the door, grinning back at me. "You sure we have to do the questions?"

"Yes!" I call out. "Ask me again, and I'll double it."

He scoots out of the room, and I wilt and lean over the desk with my head in my hands. God help me. I need a drink. Maybe a toke of that e-cigarette.

"Ms. Morgan?"

Shit, I thought they were gone. I rise up from my desk. A long sigh comes from my chest. "Toby, what do you need?"

He shuffles his feet. "Uh, I wanted to, you know, talk to you about Sabine. I—I really like her."

Yeah, buddy. I've noticed, and Sabine and I have discussed her going out with Toby, but . . .

"She's a freshman, and you're a junior. In the grand scheme of things, that may not seem like much of an age difference, but for her . . ." I squint. I really don't know what kind of young man he is, but I'm protective of my sister. And the truth is I'm winging this.

He nods, his throat bobbing. "The first day I saw her, I—I thought she was the prettiest girl in the whole school."

"But do you *know* her, Toby? Her personality? How she's different, and when I say *different*, I mean that in a brilliant way."

He straightens his shoulders. "She has autism. I got some books about it from Dog's."

"Okay."

"I want to, like, ask her out, officially, on a date. Maybe to the movies. Actually, I've already asked her, and she said I had to ask you, so . . ." He shrugs.

Movies? In a dark auditorium? Hell to the no.

But at least she told him to ask me . . .

"She isn't allowed to date yet, Toby," I say gently.

He looks at the ground, then back up at me. "I know you don't know me, but I think she's incredible. Smart. She helps me with my history. I know she doesn't like to touch her eraser and that the fire alarm makes her jittery. She rubs her ring when she gets anxious. She doesn't always get what people say, and I *like* that about her. She's not like other girls. She says what she thinks, too, and there's no pretending."

"How many girls have you dated, Toby?"

"A few. I had a girlfriend last year."

"How long did you date her?"

"Six months." He gives me a wary glance.

"And you kissed her and . . ." More . . .

He reddens. "I know she's never had a boyfriend. I'd treat her with respect. I haven't even kissed her."

That's good to know. There's a silence as I study him. The earnest face. The boy-next-door looks.

Sabine dashes in my door, sees Toby, stops for a moment, and then rushes forward. "You're dating Coach?" she calls. "I thought you told me everything I needed to know, and everyone knows but me!"

I close my eyes. She didn't hear me tell Jimmy during the goat incident. "Yes. I'm sorry. It happened fast. Is everything okay?" I've been putting off telling her because I can't tell her it's pretend. I'm not sure she wouldn't tell someone—not with the intent to make trouble but because she doesn't always understand the necessity for a white lie. If I asked her if my butt looked big in this skirt, she'd tell me the truth.

"If you're dating Coach, then I want to go out with Toby," she says.

"Sabine, it doesn't work that way. You can't use this as leverage—"

"We can double-date," she says. "You and Coach can be there. Everyone does that. Even Lacey's mom lets her boyfriend come over while she's home."

I pick up my satchel and stuff my materials in. "We'll talk later."

"When is later?"

"I don't know," I say.

"I need to know when later is. Tell me!"

What would Mama say? She'd stay calm. She wouldn't yell back at her. I inhale a deep breath. "Watch your tone, Sabine. This isn't the place. It's where I work and where you take classes."

"But . . . when?"

"Later is when we're at home. Get to where you need to be."

She exhales, and Toby murmurs to her gently, takes her hand, and laces it with his.

I watch them go, my head tumbling. What to do, what to do . . .

Eating my peanut-butter-and-strawberry-jelly (Mama's jelly) sandwich on the run, I head to the administrative offices to check in with the guidance counselor about my student who walked out. We chat for fifteen minutes as I cram food in, and she explains his situation.

When the bell chimes, I realize I've missed seeing everyone in the staff lounge. I fast walk to the field house, my makeup melting in the warm October air.

I reach the offices and read the names on the doors to find Ronan's. His is last, the biggest one next to the locker room. It's big, about fourteen by fourteen. Two TVs on the wall, several chairs, a table with folders on it, and a big desk against the wall. Two phones are ringing. His cell is on the desk next to them, vibrating with text messages.

I plop my satchel on a chair and answer one of the landlines. "Coach's office."

There's a short pause. "Who's this?" a woman's voice says.

"Nova Morgan, his PA." I roll my eyes in case this is one of his admirers. "And his girlfriend. Can I help you?"

"His girlfriend?" the woman asks. "Really? Oh, um . . . hi. I'm his mom, Bernice. I've been trying to reach his cell, but he must be on the field."

I flounder. "Hi! Great to meet you on the phone. I'm not sure where he is, but I can take a message."

"I didn't realize Ronan was seeing someone—well, there was Jenny, but we never met her." She pauses. "How old are you?"

"Twenty-nine."

She lets out a hum of satisfaction. "And you work together?"

"It's actually my first day."

"That's wonderful! He needs someone, and if you work together, well, that's progress. I mean, you're going to be spending lots of time together. How serious is your relationship?"

Holy shit. She's one of those moms . . .

"Um . . ." I stop when I see the closet door to the right is open and Ronan is unbuttoning his dress shirt. His head is bent, his finger working down his shirt, one slow button at a time. He tosses it on a small table in the closet. Pulling by the neck, he tugs off the white T-shirt underneath. His broad shoulders flex, his six-pack rippling, the V of his hips clear from his low-slung slacks. He reaches up to a rack and pulls down a polo, then eases his muscled arms inside. His pants are next. I swallow as he unzips them and bends over and pushes them off. His legs are massive, toned, and hard. He slips on a pair of blue shorts, then sticks his feet in sneakers. He slides his fingers through his messy-pretty hair—oh, wow—then settles a cap on.

He turns his head and sees me.

I start, then send up a wave and point to the phone and mouth, *It's your mother.*

He stalks out and takes the phone from me, our bodies close. He smells divine, and I don't move away. Plus, the electricity is addictive.

He looks up at the ceiling. "Mom . . . stop . . . no, it's not serious . . . no, she's a girl I met here in town . . ."

He keeps chatting as I move away to one of the chairs.

Not serious. A girl I met in town.

We're playing pretend. Just pretend.

Chapter 13

Nova

I settle myself in a chair, twirling the yellow rose between my fingers before tucking the stem back inside one of the outside pockets of my satchel.

I glance up, and Ronan's eyes glitter.

"From Andrew," I murmur.

"Really."

"He always gave them to me. When I won homecoming queen—he was king—he sent me four dozen, for the four years I'd been in high school."

He sticks his hands in his pockets. "You're keeping it, then?"

"It's a flower. I like it."

"Huh." He dips his head and shuffles around the papers on his desk. "I didn't see you at lunch. How was your first day?"

I chew on my lips. "No one threw spitballs at me. There was a paper airplane, though. Do you know a student, Caleb Carson?"

"No."

"His parents were killed in a car wreck back in April." I shake my head. "Before that, he was a solid B and C student, and he wasn't getting truant notices." I chew on my lips. "Something about the way he left my room got to me."

"Maybe life put him in front of you. You lost your mom; he lost his parents. I believe things can be interconnected."

"You mean like destiny?" I capture his gaze.

"Mm-hmm."

How absolutely fascinating.

"Do you mean like Tuck showing up at my bar, me being Leia, then us meeting again being in Blue Belle?"

He looks away from me, grabs one of the notebooks, and walks to the door. "There's a list of things for you on the desk. I wrote down the passwords to the social media accounts. My cell number is there. You good?"

I nod. "Sure."

Without looking at me, he walks out the door.

Well. Talk about avoidance . . .

After answering calls and jotting down messages, I dust the filing cabinets and the TVs and straighten up his closet. I clean the helmets and the benches with a disinfectant, then let the laundry guy in when he shows up to collect last week's uniforms and Ronan's dress shirts. Feet aching from my shoes, I walk out to the field and take pics of them practicing, careful to not post any of their plays or formations.

By the time the bell rings, I'm exhausted. Sabine is going to soccer with Lacey, so I point the Caddy to a house near the entrance of the stone gate that leads to our neighborhood. I stop at Caleb's house, a rambling two-story colonial, a bit newer than some, but weeds have taken over the yard and landscaping. I slip my shoes back on and walk up the sidewalk.

An older lady, maybe seventy, answers the door warily.

Caleb appears in the foyer, a scowl on his thin face. "I've got it, Granny," he tells her, then steps outside.

I wave. "Hi. Remember me?"

Dressed in dark jeans and a Rolling Stones shirt, he crosses his arms and glowers at me. "What do you want?"

"I was hoping we could talk."

"Nope." He flips around to head back in the house.

"Wait!" I catch the door before he can slam it in my face. "Caleb, I know what happened to your parents."

His jaw clenches, anger flashing. "So? Everyone does! A drunk driver ran a traffic light and killed them."

"Just give me five minutes, okay? Please."

His throat bobs as he steps back out. I sit down on the steps of his porch while he stands in front of me. "You walked out of my class today, and you've missed six days already, which leaves a lot of work to make up."

"So?"

Okay, he's belligerent. I kind of get it.

"Your state scores are good; you used to play baseball and be part of the drama department."

"And?"

"You're a smart kid—" I stop and yelp when a foot cramp hits. I kick my shoes off and lean over to massage my foot. I groan, the pain rippling up my calf.

Caleb's hazel eyes widen. "Um, are you okay?"

I throw my hands up, all professionalism gone. "No, I'm not. I really wanted to wear these . . . stupid freaking shoes . . . and I can't because they hurt, but they look great . . . ouch!" I press my fingers into my foot. "And you know what? It's been a doozy of a day. In case you're the only person at BBHS that doesn't know, I'm dating the football coach, and he's freezing me out, and I think he might have left me a rose, which is dumb, because he didn't—it was my ex. And then I had to deal with three classes of kids who don't even care about Julius Caesar, and maybe I agree with them, but I want to be a good teacher and a good sister, and to top it all off, I'm still angry about my mama . . ." I blink rapidly at the rush of sadness.

Caleb's brow furrows. "What did your mom do?"

"Nothing on purpose. She died." My cramp eases away, and I let my foot fall back down to the porch. "Wow. You didn't want to hear all that. I needed to vent, and you were available. Sorry."

He uncrosses his arms. "You're the first teacher to come to my house."

"Here I am."

"Eager much?"

"Sarcastic much?" I reply.

"You talked to us like we were babies."

I wince. "Yeah, I need to work on that." I pause. "I really am sorry about your parents."

Emotion flits over his face, his eyes shiny. He sits down next to me.

"Death sucks," I say, then lean back on the porch. "Tell me why you left today."

He looks away from me. "I got mad. Miss Tyler just lets us hang out." He shrugs. "They say I have anger issues."

"I understand. Let's do this again. Hi, Caleb. I'm Nova, and I'd really like it if you came back to my class tomorrow. I might not be a great teacher, but I think it might be entertaining to watch me try to teach Shakespeare. Don't you?" I smile. "Truth? I'm holding out for the poetry unit. I was thinking we could draw or paint or, I don't know, pick a song that hits the theme. What do you think? Is that a good idea?"

He shrugs.

"You're angry about your parents. I'm there with you. And . . . and . . ." I'm not a counselor, but I have thoughts about what he's going through. "There are some days when it's overwhelming, and I get pissed that she was taken too soon, that I hadn't talked to her in three days, that I don't know how to do the things she did for my sister."

He stares at the ground.

I sigh. It's tough to talk when the other person doesn't talk back. "How do you feel about Dairy Queen?"

"Um, it's okay, I guess."

"Wanna go?"

He grimaces. "I can't be seen with a teacher, Ms. Morgan. Street cred and all."

"Right, it's just . . . ice cream solves a lot of problems. Break up with someone, eat an M&M Blizzard; get angry about a loved one passing, eat another one."

He huffs. "Sounds like a you problem."

"You're right." I rub my hands down my skirt as I stand and pick up my shoes. "Caleb . . . I don't want to be a pest"—I kind of do—"but I live down the street from you. Every day that I don't see you, I'm coming back to this house."

He lets out an exasperated sound as he stands. "Why are you so weird?"

I lean in. "Mama always said, 'Keep your heart open, even when it feels like breaking.' Then she'd talk about opening our wings and sing 'Little Sparrow,' by Dolly Parton . . . I know that might be odd, too, but the point is . . . I'm where you are, Caleb. We have something in common. Loss. You have scars that people can't see, but I can because I have them too. I'm on your side, you know. If you want to talk—"

"I have a counselor."

"All right. I'll see you tomorrow, then."

"Don't come back," he calls.

"No promises! Bye!"

Then he's gone, shutting the door in my face.

Chapter 14

Ronan

"Hello, darling," Nova says sweetly as she breezes into the staff lounge. Wearing a tight black leather skirt and a low-cut red blouse that hugs her breasts, she sashays to us and takes the seat next to me. She kisses my cheek, and my face tingles as a small silence fills up the room like it usually does after our PDA in the lounge. We're at the end of week one of our pretense, and it seems to be working. We play it up in the lounge, *darling* and *babe*, then go our separate ways in the field house. I've made up my mind to keep her at arm's length, and so far, it's working.

She unpacks her lunch and pulls out wrapped cookies. "You forgot these when you left after dinner." Thick lashes flutter at me. "You ate two before they even cooled last night. You're so adorable."

I open the chocolate chip cookies and take a bite and nod appreciatively. "Thanks, babe. You're the sweetest. I loved that, um, casserole you made."

"What kind of casserole was it?" Skeeter asks.

"Beef," Nova says as I say, "Sausage," at the same time.

Melinda frowns. "Which was it?"

Andrew raises an eyebrow, his eyes darting from me to Nova.

Nova nudges me with her shoulder. "Darling, it was a beef thing with black beans and sour cream and, um . . ."

"Pasta," I say as she says, "Rice."

Jesus!

Andrew squints. "Pasta and rice?"

Nova nods. "Yep. That's right. Both. Very tasty. It was one of Mama's recipes."

"So good . . . ," I add, then squeeze her leg under the table. I chance a glance at her, and her lips are pressed tight, as if she's trying not to laugh.

Thank God I didn't have dinner with Skeeter last night . . .

Melinda frowns at me. "It sounds gross. How can you mistake beef for pork?"

"Sometimes a man just thinks about food, Melinda. Images run through your head, and you just want meat," Skeeter answers for me, around his double hamburger. A drip of mayo gets on his chin, and he wipes it away. He nods approvingly at me. "Builds up that protein so you can stay in shape."

Nova strokes my arm. There's a sly look on her face that's unmistakable. "This guy, hmm, he's already in great shape."

I lean into her. "Ah, you'll make me blush, babe."

Sonia hoots. "Keep it clean, you bloody deviants; you're making me horny."

Skeeter puts a fry in and chews. "Y'all are enough to make a man want a girlfriend. Dinner and cookies. I can get behind that."

Sonia drops her piece of tofu as her eyes drift over Skeeter. "Oh?"

He nods at his burger, oblivious to her wide-eyed stare. "As long as she likes football and knows how to cook, we'd get along." He glances up. "You like football, Sonia?"

"Um, yeah. Since high school," she says, her face reddening. "I cook."

Skeeter nods, then gets pulled into a conversation with one of the other assistant coaches.

She slowly deflates.

"Ronan, has Nova ever told you about some of the crazy things we did?" Andrew says.

Nova stiffens, and out of instinct, I take her hand in mine under the table. It's not the first time this week either.

"I've heard some stories," I say, my voice lowering, daring him to say anything that hurts her.

He chews on his sandwich, then swallows. "Let's see. There's the night the entire senior class ran around in our underwear on the football field. Nova's idea. Then one day we skipped school and went to UT. Nova wanted us to pretend to be students and crash frat parties. We drank too much to drive and had to get a hotel room." A knowing laugh comes from him. "She got in trouble with her mama. For a month, she had to crawl out her bedroom window to meet me—"

"That's enough, Andrew," I say sharply.

He shrugs. "It's no secret we dated for a very *long* time—"

"Yet it feels like a million years ago," Nova says with a sugary smile, then looks at me. "You ready for the field house, darling?"

I glare at Andrew, who's got a smirk on his face—what a dick. Then we stalk out of the lounge, our fingers laced together.

"You okay?" I ask as we reach the sidewalk. I should unclasp our hands since no one is looking, but I don't.

Her forehead furrows. "Yes, but let's not talk about him."

All right. I can understand that. Sometimes a person just needs to process, and I get the feeling she's still figuring out how she feels about Andrew . . .

"He isn't worth worrying about." I brush my lips against her forehead, a total impulse.

"Totally." She squeezes my hand as we walk, our steps in sync as she keeps pace with me in red high heels.

"Let's talk about this 'adorable' thing. It's a word for puppies and little girls," I say a few minutes later. "Can you find a new adjective?"

She turns her face to me and laughs, her lips curving up as her eyes dance. "Nope. You're stuck with it. I *adore* it. I'm going to post it on the team's Insta."

"I think *sexy* would work," I say. "You already think I am."

"So cocky, Ronan, but it will forever and always be *adorable*." She giggles and leans into me, her shoulder brushing mine. Her scent wafts around me, sweet and tart. We've been careful around each other, but today we're still stuck together like glue, naturally and effortlessly.

Loneliness rises and taunts me, at the idea of going home after practice, just me and Dog. Unbidden, I picture Nova in my house, sitting next to me on the couch. We'd have dinner and talk about her lack of *Star Wars* knowledge or football or New York or goats. She'd be pressed against me, her face upturned and animated as she told me a story about high jinks she might have gotten into in New York.

I inhale a sharp breath. I mustn't think about things I can't have.

I ease away from her when we walk into the office. "I need to change."

"Okay." She nods, all business, as she picks up the ringing phone.

I shut the door and yank off my shirt, my chest rising. I toss my slacks on the table and jerk on my shorts, reminding myself . . .

Keep it professional. No attachments means no pain. Don't forget it.

My cell rings as I park outside the stadium in Collinwood, a small town an hour away from Blue Belle. I snatch it up.

"Yo. Tuck. What's up? I'm about to head to the locker room. It's game night."

He lets out a noisy exhale—as usual—the sound of disco-tech music in the background. "What's up? What's fucking up? I don't care if you have a game! Your mom called me is what's up! You're dating Nova? When? How? I'm hurt, man, hurt! I'm your best goddamn friend in thc world! I did that! I did that! I found her for you, and you wouldn't give me a call and let me know?"

"Calm down. You are my best friend."

"I am calm! It's loud in here!" He groans. "You never told me she lived in Blue Belle when you called me."

"Go outside so I can hear you. And shouldn't you be recuperating?"

"I left the apartment so the maid could clean." I hear rustling, the sound of the music dampening. "I'm doing some kick-ass physical therapy. I'm dead every time I leave the therapist. I needed to get out. I miss playing, bro; I miss the team so fucking much." He pauses. "Ah, shit . . . I'm sorry. I wasn't thinking."

"I'm good. Don't worry about it." I want him to feel free to talk to me. My loss still cuts, but it always will.

"Tell me the deets about Nova. Every single one. How did this happen?"

I wince and run down her being my neighbor, then her job at the school. I remind him about the machinations of the town, then tell him about Andrew. "We're, um, fake dating." Jesus, it sounds stupid when I say it out loud.

"What are you, an idiot? Why isn't this a real thing?"

My hands twist around the steering wheel as an image of Nova flits through my head.

"I'm just . . ." I can't explain it to him. He breezes through girls, one after the other, and he's never been broken.

I was. The pieces inside of me aren't meant to fit back together. I don't want them to.

There's a silence. "Ronan. Dude. You don't seem like the type of guy to initiate a fake relationship for the sake of warding women off. That's bullshit. You can fend off women yourself—"

The bus pulls up alongside me. Posters with **Go Bobcats** decorate the sides. "Gotta go, Tuck. My team's here. I'll call you later. Miss you, bro."

He's still talking when I get out of the vehicle.

◆ ◆ ◆

In the pouring rain, one of the Collinwood players, a big defensive baller, tackles my backup quarterback, shoving him down in a pit of mud. A late hit.

"These refs are a joke!" Skeeter says as the Collinwood crowd does the wave to cheer on their team. "They're not calling shit!"

My guy stumbles to his feet and shakes his head.

I call a time-out, our last one. We're on our third down with ten seconds left on the clock until the end of the game. We're down by six, and my frustration rises. I hate the early rainfall that ruined the field. I hate that I can't play my star players.

Mud smears the players' uniforms as they jog over to the sideline.

"Put Toby in!" someone on our side yells.

"Yeah, Coach!" another person calls. "And Bruno!"

I ignore them, not even turning around.

Skeeter stops his pacing and stalks over to me. "Should we?"

I glower. "No."

He nods and joins the huddle, slapping the guys on the back.

"Okay, what's the play?" Skeeter says. "Hail Mary?"

My backup quarterback's eyes flare. He's a freshman, a good player, but he can't throw that far.

Rain pelts us, and I tug my hat down. "We're on the fifty, and that's what the defense will expect." I pause. "Let's do a hook and lateral."

The players gape. "Coach?" comes from one of them. "Are you sure?"

"We've done it in special teams practice." My tone radiates confidence, but there's a knot in my gut. It's a complicated play that depends on everyone being in the right place at the right time.

I lean in. "We haven't lost a game yet. And you know why?"

"Our heart!" one of them calls.

I nod.

"Win the heart, win everything!" they say in unison.

From the bench, Toby and Bruno and Milo come into the huddle and encourage their backups. They form a circle with their arms around each other. Bruno leads them as they yell our motto.

I slap the backup quarterback on the shoulder pads. "Shotgun formation—three wide receivers on the right, tight end on the left, and the running back is next to you. Fake that big pass. You got this!"

My hands are on my hips as the center snaps the ball. The wide receivers spring to the end zone on the right, and it looks like a perfect long-pass opportunity for the backup. The tight end fakes blocking, then runs fifteen yards down the middle of the field. The ball sails to him, and the Collinwood defensive players run toward him. Before he's tackled, the tight end throws a backward pass to the running back, who's alone on the left side. He dashes for the end zone, nearly thirty yards away. I stiffen as a Collinwood defensive player figures out the play and runs to tackle him. Skeeter jumps up and down, waving his arms as our guy runs down the field. From the other side, the opposing coaches yell out what's going on, but . . .

My running back hits the end zone.

Yes!

Our fans cheer as our kicking team runs out.

"We still need one point," I say under my breath.

The kick juts into the sky and splits the goalpost.

Elation rolls over me, and I shut my eyes.

The buzzer goes off, and Skeeter runs for me and attempts to pick me up, then gives up and laughs.

"Another win in the books!" he yells as the crowd and local reporters rush the field.

I shake the opposing coach's hand, then give a few statements to the media, then fight through them. I stop at the entrance to the locker room. Underneath an overhang, spinning a closed umbrella, is Nova.

Her hair is damp, her cheeks flushed. She's wearing tight jeans and a Bobcats jersey she picked up in town. She gives me a blinding smile, and my heart skips a beat. She walks toward me, and I pick her up and twirl her around.

"Wow. Is this part of the plan?" she says on a laugh.

"If Jimmy can do it, I can too," I murmur in her ear.

"No one expected the hook and lateral," she says as I ease her down, my arms wrapping loosely around her waist.

I dig that she knows the plays. "It's been a long time since a girl waited for me after a game."

"Oh."

"I like it," I murmur.

"Is everyone staring at us?" she says, her fingers toying with the ends of my hair that stick out from my hat.

"Hmm." Reporters are lingering, fans and parents waiting to see the players. "Pretty sure there's some photos being taken. Hope you don't mind being on the front page of the *Blue Belle Gazette*."

"Poor people. They have no clue how devious you are."

"At least they aren't throwing their daughters at me anymore." I keep my voice light. "I saw Andrew sitting with you."

"He sat next to Lois, actually." She shrugs. "Are you jealous?"

"We're together, and he's your ex. People will talk."

Her eyes search mine. "Give them something else to talk about, darling."

I press my lips against hers, taking her mouth like I own it. It's the first real kiss since that night in my office, and I admit part of me has wanted to do this for a while. She tastes like rain and sweetness. God, she feels good.

"That'll do it," she breathes, then steps out of my arms, her chest rising. "I'll see you later tonight," she adds loudly, probably for the female fan club waiting by the locker room door.

I grab her hand before she gets away. I look up at the sky, anxiousness flitting over me. "Hey. Drive safe in the rain. Go slow, and put your seat belt on, okay? Are you stopping anywhere on the way home?"

She searches my face, and I see the dawning in her eyes. "Slow. Got it. And no, we're going straight back."

"Text me when you get there, okay? For real."

She nods, and I let my hand trail away from hers as she walks away, finding Sabine and Lois.

I'm still watching her when Skeeter hits me on the arm. "Killer game. You ready to talk to the team?"

"Yeah." I turn and head to the locker room, reminding myself that my anchor in life *is* coaching football. Nothing else.

◆ ◆ ◆

The following week, I'm midbite of my turkey sandwich when Melinda breezes in the teachers' lounge carrying a cake. "Ronan! I'm so glad I caught you."

"Here we go," Skeeter mutters under his breath, a knowing smirk on his face.

"Bloody hell, she can't catch a clue," Sonia whispers, then glances at Skeeter. "Like some people."

Skeeter shoves a Philly cheesesteak sandwich in his mouth and chews. "What do you mean?"

Sonia turns red. "N-nothing."

Melinda places the cake on the table, then touches my shoulder, her hand lingering. "My dad sent this over. I thought you might want to share it with the team."

A triangular sheet cake, it has the score from the game last week and **Great Game, Bobcats!**

I murmur a thank-you as she sits across from me. She crosses her legs, her foot brushing against my knee for a little too long. I set my sandwich down and pull out my cell.

I need u asap. Stat. Not a drill. Where r u?

Maybe this isn't exactly an emergency, and the truth is I can handle Melinda on my own, but Nova's usually in here by now. Andrew is noticeably absent as well.

She sends me an eye roll emoji. On my way. Hold your horses.

A few minutes later, she comes in the door, and my eyes rake over her hip-hugging yellow dress. The neckline is cut deep, showing the silky skin of her cleavage. Her blonde hair is straight and glossy, framing her features. Her sapphire eyes are outlined in dark makeup, her lashes thick and black, her lips a lush red. She's absolutely dazzling—like a fucking star—and watching her walk in the lounge is my favorite part of my day. She gives the table a sweeping look, then her "Hey, y'all," making my lips twitch.

She moves away from Andrew—where his hand was on her lower back.

My blood pressure spikes.

"Hullo, mate!" Sonia calls. "How were the deviants today?"

Nova replies to Sonia. "Caesar is officially dead in the Senate! Stabbed twenty-three times by his best friend and the rest!" She pumps her fist, then grins. "And no one was put in time-out."

She leans down, brushing her lips over my cheek, then sits next to me, our shoulders touching. "Hello, darling."

"Hey, babe."

Andrew sits down next to Melinda and opens his lunch as Sonia reaches over the table to give Nova a fist bump.

"Did Caleb show today?" Sonia asks.

Nova's face radiates hope as she nods. "I wore him down when I showed up the next day with Blizzards for us and his grandmother. He said it was embarrassing to have my pink Caddy in his driveway when everyone could see it . . ." She takes out her sandwich. "He's still surly—"

Melinda laughs abruptly, interrupting her. "I'd be surprised if you get anything out of him. I never could."

"A kid's personal life can affect their performance at school," Nova says, frowning at Melinda. "Maybe he just needed someone to show they cared. I lost my dad when I was fourteen; it was the toughest year of my life. My grades were terrible. I'm glad Mrs. Pettigrew put him in my class."

"You've got the A students now. That must be sweet," Sonia says to Melinda.

Melinda narrows her eyes. "I don't know what you mean."

"Read the subtext, Melinda," Skeeter grouses. "You picked the good kids."

Nova pats his hand. "They're all good, and I love the students I have." She pauses. "I invited Caleb over for dinner, but he said no, then dashed out my door. Toby is coming, though. It's his and Sabine's first 'date,' which is me cooking pasta and watching a movie with them. I plan on sitting between them." She laughs, then sobers. "I'm serious. Is that nuts?"

Sonia smirks. "Maybe."

"What time are we eating?" I ask, my tone casual, like I was invited. Part of me wishes I had been.

"Six," she says.

I capture her gaze. "I'll be there. I need to pick up the Heisman ,
check in on Vader. What should I bring?"

She takes a bite of her sandwich, frowning, as if she knows I
serious. "Um, well—"

"Speaking of dinner, who's coming to the big fundraiser gala
Melinda says, cutting Nova off. "My dad mailed out over five hundre
invitations, and most of them replied they'd be there. At a thousan
dollars a person, it's pretty amazing." She glances at Sonia's T-shirt anc
sniffs. "The attire is dressy, by the way."

"I want some of those bacon-wrapped mushrooms they had last
year," Skeeter says, then throws a look at Sonia. "You're going?"

A carrot stick falls from her hands. "Uh . . . why are you asking?"

"Just making conversation," he mutters. "So? Are you?"

She blinks. "Um, yeah, I guess so."

Skeeter nods. "Is that accountant guy coming with you?"

"Um . . . he . . . uh . . ." Sonia stops and jumps up and dashes to the trash, where she coughs, then spits out a piece of carrot.

Nova gets up to go check on her, patting her on the back. Sonia nods that she's okay, and they come back to the table.

"Are you coming, Nova?" Melinda asks, her gaze hard. "Staff gets to come for free, of course."

Nova smiles at Melinda, her sweet/sly one. "Of course. I'll be with Ronan."

"How fun," Melinda replies as she stabs her broccoli with a fork.

With her elbow on the table, Nova puts her face in her palm as she gazes at me. "I'm trying to decide which jacket you need. The gray one. Oh! The tie . . . hmm . . . maybe the blue, the one with the little checks, or that pretty maroon one for the Bobcats?"

"Whichever one you want me to wear, babe. Should we match? Which dress are you going for? That black one looks great on you."

She gives me a "You're so amazing" smile. "Or we can contrast? You wear the maroon tie, and I'll do a navy or gold dress?"

"Perfect," I purr.

"It's a date," Nova says dreamily. "I can't wait to dance with you."

Melinda slams down her glass of tea. "Well! Aren't you two just . . . perfect!"

"Yes, we are," I say as I meet Andrew's stare. Satisfaction ripples through me. That's right, asshole. *She's mine.*

He drops his gaze, but he doesn't fool me. I recognize the emotion simmering behind his eyes. Want.

Nova reaches over to caress my shoulder, then touch my hair.

"You like my hair, don't you?" I say, lowering my voice.

"So much," she purrs. "Messy pretty. I need to try a braid on it, give you a Viking look."

"Not for the gala, though. Maybe tonight after dinner." I give her a kiss on her nose.

"I do love Vikings," Nova says on a soft sigh.

Sonia grins. "Bloody hell, you two are sickening!"

"Sorry, I guess we get carried away," I murmur. Not sorry.

Nova's lashes fall to her cheeks. "We're just"—she bites her lip—"so in love."

There's a silence, and my breath hitches as the air in the room seems to disappear. In love? My hands clench under the table, pushing back the fear those words bring.

"Totally," I manage to say.

Melinda jerks up from her seat and flounces out of the lounge. Andrew chews his food as if it's nails, a scowl on his face.

"Coach, do you think you could spare some of your players to dress out for the basketball scrimmage this week? Bruno is my best man, and we need him," he says, his tone sharp.

I shake my head. "I need them on the field. We're ranked two, and Huddersfield is one. It's down to the wire."

Skeeter nods. "True that, Andrew. We've got to tighten our game."

"The analysts are saying Huddersfield has the best defense," Andrew replies.

"And we have the top offense," I counter.

He lets it drop, then pulls a small wrapped box out of his satchel. "Hey, Nova. I've been meaning to give this to you for a while. My gift. Congrats on becoming a member of the staff."

Nova unwraps the box and pulls out a maroon coffee mug with **BBHS** on it. She stares at it with a frown, blinks, and then gives him a blinding smile. "Wow. Thank you! I love it."

I take my hat off and run a hand through my hair, feeling twitchy. I glance over, and Nova's eyes are on me, narrowed. She glances at Skeeter, then motions her head to the door. She's trying to tell me something . . . I lift my shoulders. *What?*

She rolls her eyes at my lack of understanding, then murmurs, "You ready to head to the field house, darling?"

There's still fifteen minutes left in lunch, but I nod and pack up my things. Andrew watches us as we toss our trash, then head out the door.

As soon as we're out in the hall, I glance at her. "What's up?"

"Let's get to the storage closet."

Chapter 15

Nova

He opens the door to the closet, the big one from the first day, and we slip inside. Our bodies brush against each other in the dark as I fumble on the wall for the light switch. It clicks on.

He leans on the door. "What's going on?"

I reach up and take his cap off.

"I'm running out of hats, babe."

I huff. "Do you seriously call your girlfriends *babe*?"

He laughs, a full, deep sound. "No."

"What do you call them?"

His eyes brush over me. "For you? Princess. What would you call me if it was real?"

"Beast—but only when we're alone."

"Why?"

I chew my bottom lip. Might as well say it . . . "Because you fuck like an animal."

There's nothing but silence; then a long shuddering breath comes from him. "Nova . . . the things you say . . ."

I glance away. I should be embarrassed to be so blunt, but it's true; he devoured me that night, and when it comes to him, I have zero inhibitions. My head tells me to keep the walls up around us, but the other side of me—my stupid, weak heart—*clamors* to tell him things. You know how it is when you've gone through a friend drought, and you get a new one, and all signs point to a wonderful comradery, and you *want* them to know your secrets? Yeah. It's like that with him. "I have the types of sex categorized."

"And they are . . . ," he says softly.

I shiver, aware of the tension between us. It's always present—in the staff lounge, in the field house. Here. We're two people who know how good the sex was between us, yet we're pretending it never happened . . .

"Nova?"

I hold his gaze. "There's the holy-shit-I-can't-believe-he-put-that-there sex. There's makeup sex, which can be slow or fast. Next is sweet I'm-so-in-love-with-you sex. There's lazy I'm-so-tired-from-work-I-can-barely-have-sex-but-let's-knock-one-out. There's act-like-a-crazy-person sex, where you break the bed, knock lamps over, maybe roll around on the ground. There's sad goodbye I'm-leaving-you sex—not a fan of that one. There's the anal-beads-and-whips, which can also be combined with holy-shit sex. Literally. There's you-just-lay-there-and-let-me-do-all-the-work sex. Then there's vicious I-can't-get-enough-of-you sex. Beast mode from start to finish. You."

His hand touches my shoulder, his fingers stroking my skin. "Nova—"

A bell rings, making us both start. He pulls back, and I push out a laugh.

"Anyway, moving on from that word vomit." I pause for dramatic effect. "Ronan . . . you have lice."

He flinches. "What the . . . no fucking way."

I nudge my head at his cap in my hands. "There's a little critter in your hat. He's about the size of a seed, tan, and very fast. Here, look."

"Those things are in my hair?" he calls as he scratches his scalp.

"I thought I saw something crawling in your hair in the lounge, and that's why I wanted to leave and get you away from Skeeter. He's going to freak. He's going to hose down your office, the entire field house."

"We can't tell him. What do we do?"

We.

I laugh. "*Darling*, this is all you."

"It's not funny," he mutters, shaking his hair out as he paces around the room.

"Don't throw them around!"

He stops and puts his hands on his hips and glares at me. It's what he does when he's on the sideline. I could catalog many things about him: the way he raises his eyebrow—just one—the way his full lips twitch, the texture of his scars under my mouth. Most of all, I like how protective he is of me around Andrew . . .

"Nova! Are you listening? What's the plan?"

I chuckle.

"I repeat, this is not funny," he grouses.

"It kinda is."

"Yeah, what if you have it? You like to wear my hats."

"That was weeks ago. All right . . . a plan. First, you're going to get my empty water bottle . . . the one I set on that shelf when we walked in. Then, we'll catch the one in your hat and give it to Sonia."

"No way in hell. Skeeter was right. Dump it on the floor, and I'll stomp on it."

"Normally, I'd be behind you one hundred percent, but Sonia is my only chick friend—besides Lois—and she desperately wants one under her microscope . . ." I smile tentatively. "Please."

"No."

I ignore him, my gaze on the louse. He's crawling up the side of the cap, and I shake him back down. "He's a feisty little bugger."

"Look, the water bottle has a narrow opening. It was a decent idea—"

"I was working with what I had, thank you."

He pulls out his phone.

"What are you doing?"

"If Sonia wants a damn louse, she can come get it herself. I'm not a procurer of menacing rodents."

"It's a bug."

"It's a pest, and I'm texting her now."

"I love that you said *procurer*," I say, mimicking his deep voice. "Your big brain is amazing—and has lice on top of it."

"Real funny, Princess." His fingers fly over the phone; then he looks up at me. "Question: Do they bite?"

"They're biting your head for blood. They lay eggs on your hair called nits? I can't remember it all. I had it once. Mama treated me for a few days."

"A few days!"

"I'm sure Mama went overboard." I stretch my arm way out and pat his.

"Sonia better get her ass down here as soon as—"

Sonia whips open the door and steps inside. "Show me the little wanker."

"Shut the door!" Ronan calls.

She clicks it closed, a jar in her hands. In her excitement, she jostles into me, and the hat falls to the ground. I yank it up but . . .

"He escaped!" I get on my knees and search.

Ronan groans.

Sonia wails, then points at Ronan. "I need to find another one."

He looks up at the ceiling. "Sonia, I swear to God, I am not letting you—"

"Pleeease," she begs, her hands up in a prayer, the jar between them. "Come on. Let me. It will only take a minute, and this is your contribution to science. Think of the bright young minds that will benefit from your donation."

His shoulders slump. "God, you're ridiculous. Fine."

We hunt around the room and find an old stool tucked away in the back corner. After pulling it to the center of the room, he sits on it. I pull out a little flashlight I have on my keys and waggle my eyebrows. "We'll find 'em."

Sonia gives me a side hug. "You're the best mate ever!"

"Can you two stop the girl party and get your louse?" Ronan mutters.

"Grump," I say with a grin; then, just to spite him, I turn music on from my phone: "You Got It," by Roy Orbison. I'm so happy with my selection that I do a little shimmy, and Sonia joins me to dance.

Ronan glares daggers at us.

"So, so funny," he bites out.

I click the song off, wiping the tears from my eyes. Who knew high school could be so fun? I love that he has lice!

"Let's get this over with, Sonia."

We get down to business. He bends his head over while I hold the flashlight, leaving Sonia's hands free to pick up Ronan's hair.

Skeeter opens the door, not looking up, his phone in his hands.

"Shut the door!" Ronan snaps, and Skeeter jumps, his eyes big as the door clicks behind him.

"Uh, Coach, is this one of your, you know, sex things?"

"I don't have sex things! It was a bra! Just a bra."

"There's a good story," Sonia hums. "What happened?"

"Ronan put on my bra. Red lace. It was very sexy," I reply. "He likes to wear lingerie."

Ronan heaves out a gusty breath. "Girls. Please. I have lice. Focus."

Skeeter's been silent, his eyes darting from Ronan to us. He pales and presses back against the door. "No, no, no." He gulps air. "Coach . . . you . . . have . . . lice?"

"Apparently," Ronan mutters. "One got away already. On the floor."

"That's it. I'm out of here—" he calls, his hand on the doorknob.

Sonia throws him a glance. "Best not. You might have it if you've sat in the same chair or worn the same hat. I'll do a check. Just stay over there."

He gapes at her. "You think I'm going to stay in this closet? I came in here to call my mom! She was going to tell me what's for dinner!"

She shrugs. "You're safe, Skeeter. They can't fly or jump. They're attracted to people with clean hair. Has your scalp been itching, particularly at night?"

Horror rises in his eyes. "I did wake up last night and scratched my . . ." He pinches his nose. "Oh my God!"

"Gotcha, you little bugger!" Sonia swoops a small thing into her jar, then twists the lid on tight. She glances around. "All right, that's done. We need to check each other. Who's up?" She snaps her fingers. "I have class in five minutes, and these things only live for forty-eight hours, and I don't know how long it's been alive, so let's get this thing going."

"Me! Check me!" Skeeter skates around Ronan and sits on the stool. Her fingers dance through his hair while I hold the light.

"So, um, is head lice—can it get on my, um, my privates?" Skeeter asks.

Sonia snickers. "That's called crabs, and it's a different parasite. They like your genitals and make you feverish or irritable. And itchy, of course."

He breathes out a long exhale. "Thank God. I'd hate to put mayonnaise on my balls."

"No mayo," she says. "But if your privates are itching, get that checked out by a doctor."

He flushes. "They aren't! I was just trying to learn, you know, for science stuff, and I figured since you're so smart, you'd know."

She blinks. "You think I'm smart?"

He shrugs. "Hello. You were our valedictorian. I remember your speech at graduation. The opening line was 'Live a full life . . .' I don't recall the rest."

Amazement flits over her face. "I didn't think anyone was listening."

He shrugs. "We done?"

She gazes down at his head for a few ticks, her hands dropping to pat his shoulder. "You're good, Skeeter. I don't see anything."

He moves to the corner of the closet, his eyes on me. "You're next, Nova. I need to know who I can and can't be around."

"Oh, for God's sake," comes from Ronan as he rubs his fingers through his hair, then looks at his fingers, as if one might appear there.

I laugh as I sit on the stool.

Ronan marches over to hold the light while Sonia's hands card through my long hair.

She pauses, and the room grows quiet.

"What?" I ask.

"Lice, babe," Ronan murmurs, satisfaction in his voice. From his phone, he turns on "Who's Sorry Now," by Connie Francis. Kudos to him for the oldie, but . . .

"You're lying. I'm not itching," I say and flip around.

Skeeter jumps back. "I saw it. Creepy-crawly was right freaking there in your part." He points his finger at me and Ronan. "Y'all are contaminated and must be quarantined!"

I gape as my head suddenly feels itchy. I try to keep my hands down. I don't want to touch them either.

"Skeeter, you need to check me," Sonia tells him.

His eyes flare. "Me? No!"

"Yes," she says. "You're the only safe one!"

He grimaces. "Okay."

Sonia sits on the stool as Skeeter swallows, then moves his hands through her hair. She lets out a *hmm* sound. Skeeter is oblivious.

"What's next?" Ronan asks me quietly as he clicks off the song.

I exhale, twitchy. "We leave school, go to the pharmacy, then take care of business."

"You're lice-free!" Skeeter announces a few minutes later, then gives Sonia's shoulders a squeeze. "We're the lucky ones. Those two are in for a hell of a day." He smirks, then helps Sonia up. She stumbles a little and falls into him and tilts her face up to his.

Skeeter gazes down at her . . . one second, two, three, four, five, six . . .

"Are they having a 'We don't have lice' moment or 'I'm into you' thing?" I murmur.

Ronan smiles. "Let's let them figure it out."

We slip out of the closet and shut the door. He texts the principal to let him know we're leaving, then sends a mass text to the coaches to handle his practices and do a head check of all the players. I get busy sending one to Sabine to catch a ride home with Lacey and stay until I can decontaminate our house. I don't mention the situation. I'll check her when she gets home.

"We have lice," I say in a wondering tone as we walk down the hall.

"Little fuckers," Ronan mutters.

Andrew turns the corner, looking only at me.

Ronan laces his fingers through my hand.

We step outside and head down the steps as he walks me to my car. I open it, and right before I slide in, I give him a long look, recalling Andrew's gift in the lounge. "You left that rose on my desk the first day."

He drapes his eyes over me, face completely straight. "Really."

"Yeah, baller, you did. Really. And I like it." I scratch my head, blow him a kiss, and then shut my door and crank my car.

◆ ◆ ◆

"You are way too peppy about this," Ronan mutters as we sit in his office at his house on the recliners.

I was humming "Jolene" but stop as I take in the pale-blue plastic shower cap thing on his head. Seeing a deliciously hot, virile man in a lice cap is up there as one of the best things ever.

We drove separately to the pharmacy, spent half an hour half-horrified and half-amused at all the different over-the-counter brands. We went with the strongest one, then drove to his house. Once we read the instructions, we realized we needed to put our clothes in a bag and change. He lent me a pair of Nike shorts and a Pythons shirt, which I shamelessly intend to keep. Hopefully, he hasn't seen me sniffing it.

We cleared the island countertop and studiously reread the directions and got to work. I applied his lice medicine, and he applied mine. Now, we're in his office, waiting for our forty-five minutes to be up. We've played darts and pool; then he gave me a tour of his memorabilia. He tells me he has more in boxes in a special storage unit that he hasn't unpacked yet. My guess is they're still packed because he doesn't plan to stay.

The timer on his phone goes off, and he eases Dog out of the way and stands. "My master bathroom has two sinks. We can rinse at the same time. That good?"

I nod and follow him into his bedroom upstairs. It's painted a deep gray, the duvet a soft white. I browse past pictures of him and stop.

He comes back to find me. "Those are my sisters and mom."

It's an old picture, and he's maybe sixteen, still in that awkward stage of teetering between an adolescent and an adult. He's handsome, his hair to his shoulders, a smirk on his face. His sisters are younger, and he's got his hand clasped on either one. His mom is behind him, smiling, her arms spread wide around them as they huddle together. My throat prickles.

"You're thinking about your mom?" he asks softly and puts his hands on my shoulders from behind.

I lean back against him, and my shower cap rests on his chest, but he doesn't seem to care. The moment is spontaneous and uncomplicated—two people who fit together effortlessly. I sigh. Why does it feel as if we've known each other forever?

"A little. Mostly, I was just thinking about how happy you look." I pause. "I want that one day. A family, kids . . ."

"You will—I mean, when you meet the right person."

"What do you want?" I ask. "You know, besides football."

"More football. Friends. And like you said, to live a meaningful life, and for me, I guess that means helping others. That's what the bookstore is. I don't technically own it or manage it. I donated it to the town after I bought it and requested they hire young people to run it. It's good for the community and the kids. Someday I'd like to open a free camp for kids to come and learn football from pro players. It's just an idea, I guess."

I recall that literacy billboard he had in New York, his perfect face, that wide smile that said *I own the world.* Was he as kind then as he is now? I think so. Only now, he's a man who keeps people at a distance to preserve his heart. The only exceptions seem to be Toby and the team. I've watched him on the field, the light in his eyes when he coaches. Will he miss that when he leaves? Will he miss me?

"Do you want a family someday?" I ask.

He tenses, and I turn around as his blue eyes darken, vulnerability in their depths. "I always wanted them, you know, before, but now . . . I can't see it." He looks away from me and shrugs, chewing on his bottom lip.

He and Whitney had plans for kids, and I wait for jealousy to hit me, but it doesn't. Tenderness rises inside of me, for his pain. For his loss.

I've lost my parents but never a soul mate.

I smile. "We'd better get this off of us before it burns our heads."

Chapter 16

Ronan

My body is hyperaware of Nova as she stands between my legs blow-drying my hair. She hums under her breath as her fingers massage my scalp. We've spent two hours rinsing out the medication, then combing nits out of each other's hair. Since hers is long, it took a while. I enjoyed it, showing her the comb, then watching her gross out. We laughed until tears ran down our faces. Lois brought over tea tree oil shampoo, and we each shampooed our hair three times. She also gave us tea tree, mango, and rosemary oils for future use as repellents. Those little fuckers better be dead.

"I could have dried it myself," I say when she clicks off the dryer. Hers is already dry, lying smooth and straight down her shoulders. I reach up and rub the glossy strands between my fingers. I love her hair.

"It gave me another chance to make sure your scalp was good," she murmurs.

I look up at her from the vanity seat. My hands land on her hips, my thumbs caressing her skin through the shorts. I can't stop myself. I'm in Nova overload, drunk on her proximity.

"Was that the only reason?" *Did you want to be as close to me as I want to be to you?*

She bites her lip. "Let's get your place cleaned up."

I stand and stretch. I'm wearing loose joggers and a black tank top. I picked it out of the bureau on purpose, knowing it shows off my jacked forearms. I've caught her gaze lingering there several times since we started this "fake" relationship.

Right now, her gaze lands on the tent in my crotch, and I laugh sheepishly. I really don't care if she sees I'm turned on—which is the exact opposite of how I should act. Apparently, the primitive side of me has taken over my brain.

My arms fall to my sides. Must do better.

"Thank you for helping me out." It's one of the things I like about her personality—her willingness to help others.

"It's called *teamwork*, darling," she says sweetly. "And you're going to help me after we're done here."

"Deal."

She's a bundle of energy as we sweep through the house, tossing linens and my duvet in the washer. She's wiping down my bedroom while I vacuum, humming "Jolene" under my breath. I finish and flip it off. When I turn, she is behind me and pulls her phone out and takes a pic. "'Coach Cleans after Lice Scare at Blue Belle.' This will go viral on social. Gives you a real homespun appeal."

"You better not." I walk over to her and reach for her phone, but she tucks it behind her back and twirls away from me, laughing.

"You didn't know it, but I snuck some pics of you with the plastic cap on your head."

I hated that cap! "You didn't!"

"I did, and I'm going to tag the Huddersfield coach. He'll love it," she calls as she runs out of the room.

I chase her down the stairs as she hits the bottom, turns the corner, and disappears.

"I'm going to find you," I sing out. "And when I do . . ."

I check the extra bedroom downstairs, looking under the bed and in the closet. I move to the bathroom and rip back the shower curtain.

I stalk to the den and circle the perimeter. Dog barks from the sofa, then jumps down and trots to my office door. I pet him. "You've got some use after all."

I ease the door open and step inside. The place is spotless from when we both cleaned earlier.

I check under my desk, then the shadowy corners behind the recliners. I half expect her to jump scare me.

There's a crash from the kitchen, and I run out, bumping into Dog. I glare at him. "You're helping her? That's it. We're over, Dog." I slide past him and run my gaze over the kitchen. Nothing looks out of place, so what fell? I do a systematic patrol, then check the cabinets under the sink, then laugh under my breath. Where is she?

Dog trots to the pantry door and sits. I narrow my eyes at him. "This better not be another one of your lies."

He sneezes, throwing slobber everywhere.

I move him out of the way, then fling the door open. It's a big pantry, lined with shelves on either side. Lois organized it—canned goods in order on the left, dry goods on the right.

Nova reclines on the back wall, not a flicker of surprise on her face as she munches on a vanilla wafer.

"Found you," I growl.

She pops another one in her mouth and chews. "Took you long enough, jock. These are so good. My mama used to use them to make the best banana pudding. I think I want to try her recipe."

I plop down next to her, and she hands me the box.

"How many can you get in your mouth at once?" she asks. "I did three. Nearly choked. That's when the can of peas fell. I guess you heard it?"

I pop an eyebrow. "Yep. Let's see. I bet I can get five. You on?"

"Stakes?"

"A boon."

Her full lips curl up. "You're on. You have to eat them all at once." She hands over a water bottle. "You'll need this, which I stole from your amazing pantry. You could throw a small party in here."

"I'd call my pantry . . . *lavish*."

She snorts.

"Let's do this." I take her water and twist off the top.

She hands me five, and I open my mouth and cram three in, then four, then five. My cheeks puff out, and she giggles as I tilt my head and chew and chew and chew.

"I'm here if you need the Heimlich," she says.

I swallow and guzzle the water. I stick my tongue out, and she claps.

"I'm a badass," I say.

Her eyes roll. "God, you're so easy. I knew you'd get five. Don't be so arrogant."

"So you just wanted to see me make a fool of myself?"

"I should have asked you to put a bra on first."

"When is everyone going to forget that?"

"Never ever, ever, ever."

I toss an arm around her shoulders, and she leans against me. A feeling of contentment rises as the moments tick past. "I'm ready for my boon."

"What is it?" She gazes up at me.

"You never told me your secret the night of the dart game."

Her chin gets a defiant tilt, one I've come to recognize. "That was an emergency—my foot hurt, and then I saved your ass from the sheriff—so that boon is null and void. You can't repeat it."

"Look at you. Getting all territorial over one little secret. You must have hundreds. I don't see what the big deal is . . ." I grin.

"Technically, I told you about accidentally stealing Ryan Reynolds's toilet thingy. No one knows that."

"Accidentally, right."

She rolls her eyes.

"You didn't even tell your old roommate?"

"No." She winces. "What if it's worth money, like it's fourteen-karat gold? What if it was a family heirloom? What if—"

"Damn, you're cute. I should call him up and tell him."

"You know him?"

"Hmm. I know lots of famous people. He follows me on Insta."

"Pompous ass."

I smile. "Have you ever wondered why we keep meeting in closets?"

"Technically, this is a lavish pantry."

"Feels the same. Just me and you, and the whole world is out there. Like we're alone," I murmur and trace my fingers over her shoulders.

"Technically, we are."

"Smart-ass."

She smiles. "Thanks."

"Tell me another secret. I insist."

Her fingers trail down my forearm to my hand, light teasing touches over my fingers but not quite taking my hands. Tingles ripple over me.

"Okay, here's one: I'm kind of disappointed in you," she murmurs.

"Why?"

Her fingers dance back up my chest, then toy with the neck of my tank top. "You asked for a boon, and all you want is a silly secret."

"I want to know you."

"Hmm, but knowing me is a dangerous thing, isn't it?"

I pause, seeing that serious glint in her eyes. "Yes." I stare at her lips. "What should I ask for, then?"

She moves her body and settles herself gently in my lap.

I groan, long and guttural.

With her hands on my shoulders, she swivels her luscious ass over the bulge in my joggers. "If I were you, I would have asked for a kiss . . . or something else . . ."

My breath hisses out. "Jesus . . ."

She puts her fingers on my lips, her voice husky. "Think hard, Ronan. What does the man in you want?"

I arch my cock up to grind against her center, the heat of her making me dizzy. "I want to fuck you."

A shaky breath comes from her lips. "How do we begin? Tell me."

My lids lower as I wrap my arms around her waist, my hands tracing under her shirt to tease the skin around her ribs. *Fuck.* So soft. "Take your top off."

Her blue eyes dilate as she pulls the Pythons shirt up from the hem and over her head. Her hair cascades around her slim shoulders. She's wearing a black lace bra, the tops of her breasts creamy as her chest heaves.

"Goddamn, you're sexy," I groan.

"What else?"

"The bra. Remove it."

She reaches behind her, unsnaps the clasp, and then eases it off, tossing it over her shoulder. "Sorry, but you can't wear this one."

I growl, and she tosses her head back and laughs, joy radiating from her.

My heart stutters in my chest. She's magnificent. Proud and uninhibited.

I drape my eyes over her tits, the red nipples that stand erect, as if aching for me to touch them. I don't. Not yet. This is her game, and I'm playing it.

"Take your shorts off. And the underwear," I demand.

She stands up and toys with the waistband of the shorts, a smile curling her lips. "You sure? Once these come off—"

"Take the motherfucking clothes off."

She eases them down to her ankles. With deft fingers, she separates her thong from the shorts and twirls it around. "Off."

My hand pushes down on my dick at the sight of her. The lights are bright and show every perfect curve of her body, the line of her throat, the fullness of her curves, the flat stomach, the arch of her hips, the pussy between her legs.

"What now?" she asks, watching me with heavy eyes.

"Spread your legs, and stand over me. Put your hands on the wall behind me."

She steps over, with her feet on either side of my legs. Her palms slap the wall. I shove my joggers and underwear down to my knees, and she gasps, her lashes fluttering.

"Keep those pretty eyes on me as I finger fuck you," I say, arching my neck up to stare at her, my tone guttural. I pump my cock as my other hand brushes over her pussy. She swivels her hips as I tease over her outer folds, then delve into her center, my fingers coming out drenched. I stick them in my mouth and lick them slowly. "Better than vanilla wafers, babe."

In this position, I can see everything—her swollen clit, her wet entrance, which is grasping for more of me. I touch her with both hands, spreading her gently, then stroke inside to her dampness with one finger, then two. I spin her clit with my thumb, my gaze searching her face. I want her to come hard. I want to watch her fall apart.

Goose bumps rise on her legs as she rides my hand. Her pants and moans fill up the room as I pump in and out of her, looking for that sensitive knot on her upper walls. Finding it, I stroke the area softly, satisfaction rippling over me when she clenches around my fingers, spasming.

"You're the most beautiful woman in the world," I purr as I adjust her position, my hand on her ass as I tug her down. Scooting down, I lie on the floor, and she follows, placing her knees on either side of my head.

I trace little designs up and down the silky skin of her legs as I give her a cocky grin. Fuck, I love this position.

A nervous chuckle comes from her. "My vagina is, like, right in your face."

"It's an exquisite pussy," I murmur. "Want to ride my face, Princess?"

She starts to laugh, but at the first touch of my mouth, she shudders, a sharp cry of need erupting from her.

I eat her greedily, with relish, like a man starved. My tongue flicks at her clit slow at first, rubbing over the stiff top and the sides, learning her body, then faster as my teeth bite gently. My fingers piston in her entrance, rubbing her G-spot. My other hand palms her ass, guiding her into a back-and-forth rhythm. Breathing heavily, she glides against my mouth as I groan, the reverberation of the sound making her shiver.

"You like that?" My lips trace over her pink skin.

"Yes," she gasps.

Fingering her, I flick at her nub, my chest humming a low, long growl. "Fall apart for me."

Stiffening, she grabs my hair and yells my name as she comes. Time stretches as she rides the wave, her channel sucking at my fingers as I skim over her.

Fuck, I like how she orgasms. Wild and needy.

We're breathing heavily as she moves away and leans against the wall. "That was incredible," she whispers. "I'm still vibrating."

"Come here," I say.

Sitting up, I put my back against the wall. She climbs in my lap, facing me, and I put my hand on her nape.

"Kiss me."

She grabs my face and takes my lips hungrily, urgently, her teeth nipping at my bottom lip. She slips her hands around my neck, and we turn ravenous as I make a meal of her mouth, twisting and fluttering with her tongue, tasting her teeth, the sides of her mouth, the roof. I want to inhale her until we're one. I trace the outline of her lips, then bite her top lip and suck it into my mouth. We're dirty and rough, licking and biting at each other. I drag my mouth to her jawline, to her throat, an invader, hungry to own every part of her. I roam to her ear. "Fuck me."

She leans back, her hands on the floor for balance as she rubs her wetness on me, tracing over my cock. Small motions, soft, then faster. She's completely exposed to me, mouth parted, desire on her face. My hand goes between us and thrums her clit. I feel a bead of come oozing from me, and I dig my fingers into her legs and lift her and mount her on my crown. Holding her tight, I push in, then out, barely inside her.

"More," she begs and sinks farther down.

A blaze of fire washes over me, and my heart pounds so hard I'm sure she can hear it as I slide all the way home and grind against her. Our fit is exquisite as I stay where I am, relishing the tightness.

"I want you desperately," I whisper in her ear.

When I move, it's with no holds barred. My mouth meshes with hers as my hands clasp her lower back, and we fuck. I thrust inside her, deep and hard, the pleasure vibrating over every inch of my skin. Our breaths are loud, gasping, as I pump in and out. She tightens her muscles around me, and I groan.

"Do that again."

She rotates her hips and tightens her pussy as I tilt her face up and kiss her. Again and again.

This is what I've wanted. That primal part of me that recognizes its prey. Her.

"I want to fuck you every which way I can," I growl.

She kisses down my neck, then bites me. "How?"

"Against the wall. I'll stand."

I slip out of her, my dick swollen and red, aching. We stand up, and I pick her up as her legs lock around my hips. I flip her around to the wall, then push inside her. She groans as I delve deep in her channel, angling my hips to rub against her upper wall. A bead of sweat drips down her face, and my tongue takes it. My head lowers to her neck as I breathe in her scent. Shivers dance down my spine as she tugs my hair, pulling my lips back to hers.

She slips a hand between us, her fingers moving.

"You're mine," she breathes into my mouth as she orgasms, and the fact that *she* says such a possessive thing is so hot it sends me over the cliff. My cock expands inside her, then jerks, my body shuddering as I wring it out, diving into her depths, not wanting it to be over. Juices drip down our legs as electric pulses skate over me. My arms quake, and I ease her to the floor and lie down with her over my chest. My heart pounds erratically as I try to slow my breathing.

We don't speak for several minutes, our bodies tangled together.

She props her head up and gives me a wry look, one that makes me smile.

"What?" I ask.

"I'm sticky, and this floor has got to be killing your back."

"I'm fine." I ease up and reach over, grab some unopened paper towels, and tear off a few. I slide down to her waist and clean her gently, then toss them in the trash by the door.

The floor is uncomfortable, yet we lie side by side and look at each other. She has a glow on her face, a satisfied look in her eyes, one that I put there, but something else takes front and center. I want to enjoy this moment, but . . .

"I didn't wear a condom," I say, grimacing.

She chews on her lip. "I know. I'm, um, on the pill . . ."

I exhale. "I haven't had sex without a condom in years."

"Oh. Okay, so you're good?"

"If you mean if I've had an STD test, I have. Have you?" I ask.

"After Zane, yes."

My mood darkens. I hate that bastard, and it has shit to do with football.

And why is that? the logical side of my brain asks.

A slow panic builds in my chest like a heavy boulder, growing bigger and bigger. Sure, part of it is about the lack of a condom, but the other side . . .

My head races with thoughts as I lay out the facts: I'm insanely jealous of Andrew, of any man who's had her attention, and I look forward to our games in the teacher lounge. Hell, I rush from class to get there first just so I can watch her walk in. Honest? If it took lice to have her in my house, dancing and singing, then I'd do it all over again. It's not even about the sex, which is intoxicating; it's the emotional, needy side of me that's humming for *more*.

As that kernel of truth hits me, the air in the room thins as my anxiety turns to full-blown fear.

My hands tremble, and I tuck them behind my head, hoping she doesn't notice. Reaching for control, I suck in deep breaths, wrestling with my head as I battle an undeniable tug toward her combined with this awful, sinking dread . . .

I mean, let's be honest. I'm no good for Nova. I'm no good for anyone.

Point blank: I'm not what a girl like her deserves.

I can't be relied on. I can't protect people. I'm leaving!

She's trying to start a new life, and here I am, screwing it up. I'm going to hurt her. I am!

I swallow and find my voice. It sounds normal. Thank God. "I shouldn't have done that. I mean, the pill isn't one hundred percent effective . . ."

Our gazes cling, and she's quiet, scanning my face. Okay, maybe my voice shook a little.

I drop my eyes. She's an intuitive person. *She knows.*

"You should have said something before," she says in a tight voice.

"There wasn't time, and I wasn't thinking clearly."

"Really." Her eyes narrow.

I scrub my face. "Will you let me know when you start your period?"

She eases up. "Huh. I see. Okay, well, it's due soon. I'll be sure to keep you updated on my menstrual flow."

I try to take her hand, but she evades me. "Hey," I say. "Don't be upset."

"Don't tell me how to feel."

I sigh. "I'm not prepared to be a father, Nova. I don't want a surprise baby or entanglements—"

"I told you I'm on the pill, so chill. You won't have any *entanglements* from me." She stands and jerks up her thong and shorts, sliding them on. Then her bra and shirt.

"Nova—" I sit up.

She holds her hand up. "No. We finish some spectacular sex, and you immediately . . . ugh. You really suck at pillow talk."

"It's a valid topic. We shouldn't have—"

"Regrets already, Ronan. How predictable." Her lips twist.

I groan. "I said I was sorry for New York, Nova. It's bothered me for years, wondering who you were and if I hurt you. I know I did, and I hate it, okay, hate it. I'm not that kind of guy. I was with *you* that night. Totally. What we did, it was all *us*. Did I regret it? Initially, yes. It came at a weird time, and I felt guilty, but in the end—"

"Stop talking." She tosses my shirt at me, and I catch it before it hits my face.

I pull it on, then put my hands on my hips. "Okay. You talk."

Her jaw clenches. "I don't like that you're pulling away mentally five minutes after we've had sex. We both know exactly what this was. A get-it-out-of-the-way fuck. Hey, there's one to add to my list. No need to repeat it, especially since you *regret* it."

Shit. "I never said I regretted this."

"You didn't have to!" She heads to the door, her eyes shiny.

There's a burning sensation in my chest. "Nova . . . wait . . ." I open my mouth to try and explain my anxiety, but nothing comes out.

She pauses and looks over her shoulder at me, her hair messy and tangled, her lips bruised. "You want to know my real secret, Ronan?"

My heart stutters at the emotion in her eyes. "Yes."

She breaks my gaze, her eyes darting around the pantry as if looking for answers. She comes back to me, a resigned expression on her face. Her hands clench. "My secret is . . . that night at the Mercer Hotel . . . by the time we got to your room . . . I was already half in love with you. The way you danced with me, the way you kissed me in the elevator—boy, that was the clincher . . . and now you're here in my hometown, and we're spending time together."

Then she whips out the pantry door, and I lean back against the wall, winded by her words.

Half in love with me . . .

You fucking know what it means, Ronan. Feelings.

Adrenaline spikes as my heart races, nearly exploding. Fear rushes, that sensation of things moving too quickly for me to process. Somehow, I follow her out of the pantry, and she's at my front door.

I watch her, hating myself. My head flashes with images of what could be with her, and part of me yearns for that, wants to run to her, but my limbs won't move, frozen in the foyer. I feel dizzy, my head spinning.

Stop her, stop her.

If I do, I'll slip toward something dangerous, toward an ocean I can't swim in. I've drowned before. I loved and lost. I ruined it. And that pain is excruciating.

She clicks the door shut.

My eyes close. My heart truly is made of stone . . .

Chapter 17

Ronan

Saturday rolls around with another win in the books for us last night. Only a few games left until the end of the season.

I step out of my Suburban and scan the parking lot the Tylers have set up across the street from their mansion in an open field.

I find Nova's Caddy. She's a few rows over, leaning against the car. Tucking my hands in my gray slacks, I walk toward her, unease in my gut. It's been a cold week with us, even in the staff lounge.

My eyes take in her clingy black dress, above-the-knee length with a mandarin-style collar. Yellow roses splash over the fabric, snug against her curves. My groin tightens.

"You should have let me pick you up," I say when I reach her, smoothing down my jacket. I sent her a text this morning, but she replied she wanted to drive.

She smiles tightly with red lips.

"I like your hair," I say, reaching for normal. It does look pretty, swirled up in a complicated twist that frames her face.

"Thanks. Sabine did it." She straightens up from the car. "As long as we walk in together, then that's all we need. I'm ready for a drink."

I exhale. "Nova . . . about the other day. I never want to hurt you—"

She stops me with a narrowed look. "We had sex. It's done."

Tension fills up the warm night as we stare at each other.

I don't want it to be done . . .

Someone in the parking lot calls my name, breaking our connection.

"Fine," I say, then crook her arm in mine as we walk toward the French-country-style mansion across the street. She stares straight ahead, a pinched look on her face.

"At least try to enjoy it," I mutter.

"I will, darling," she says, her accent thick.

Some of the players see us and jog to us, ending any other conversation. They're dressed in khakis and button-downs, and I give them a nod of approval. We do fist bumps all around. Toby gives me a hug, and I squeeze his arm and tell him he looks great in his slacks and shirt.

Melinda and her dad are in the foyer when we enter. Melinda rushes to us, gives me a blinding smile, and then puts her hand on my other arm. "Ronan! I've been waiting for you. You remember my dad, of course."

Before he can step forward, Nova leans in. "I'm going to get us drinks."

My hand clings to hers longer than it should. I'm not ready to let her go, and I have a feeling she isn't coming back . . . "Sure," I finally say, my gaze searching her face.

Melinda eases her arm through mine as her dad shakes my hand. They lead me through the spacious house and to the grounds outside with acres of rolling hills in the distance. A huge white tent is set up with a DJ in the back. White-covered tables, champagne fountains, an elaborate buffet, and caterers dot the area. We end up at a table with other men who played football back in the day with Mr. Tyler. I get introduced around and say the usual things: *Glad you came. Thank you for the support. Yes, the team looks incredible this season.*

A few minutes later, I head to the podium and give a welcome speech to the guests. My eyes search for Nova and find her in the back with Sonia and Andrew and a few other faculty members. I pause mid-speech, my gaze locking with hers.

I was already half in love with you . . .

What a crazy thing to say. Incredible, seemingly impossible, yet—

She sends me a fake adoring smile, then tips her glass of champagne up at me. I clear my throat, find my place, and finish. The partiers erupt in applause. Then Lois joins me and presents a slideshow of the games this season.

After the speeches are over, someone grabs me a water and a plate of food as I survey the crowd. The DJ plays a fast song, and I see several of my players dancing, along with Sonia and Nova.

Lois appears next to me wearing a floor-length maroon dress and her Stetson. "Nova's having fun."

"I see that," I grunt.

She munches on a quiche. "You two look good together. You think it might be serious?"

I give her a pointed look. "Stay out of my love life."

"You're the one who asked for her to be your PA. I wasn't going to meddle any longer after the party, but you insisted we give it to her." She takes a drink of her champagne.

"She doesn't know I got her the job." My head tumbles with thorny thoughts, deciphering the reasons why I wanted her. She needed a job, and she loved football. Plus, I owed her something after that night in New York. The analytical side of me thought it would be a great idea after that kiss in the bookstore to ask her to fake date me. I even covered it with HR beforehand, although if the answer had been no, I still would have given the nod for her to have the job.

Skeeter slides in next to me, watching the crowd on the dance floor. He nudges me with his elbow. "I don't see Sonia's date."

I shake my head at him. "Skeeter, she broke up with that accountant months ago."

He starts. "She did?"

"She mentioned it at lunch when it happened. You might have been on your phone."

"I never liked him. He didn't like football. I tried to talk to him at the last party, but it was like talking to a calculator."

"Ask her to dance."

"Why does she talk British? Is that weird?"

I chuckle. "She's quirky. Embrace it."

He squints, lasering in on Sonia. "I'm just a country boy. I like fried chicken and mashed potatoes on Sunday, shooting guns, and fishing. She likes science and *lice*." He tosses back his glass, draining it. "I need to be drunk to dance."

I grab another stem of champagne from a tray passing by. "Have another, then."

He takes it, his forehead furrowed as he munches on a shrimp. "I'm a jock, and she's smart. I live with my mama. My last girlfriend broke up with me and got married a month later. I didn't even know she'd been seeing that cowboy and me!"

"Stop talking yourself out of it. Win the heart, win everything," I tell him.

Midbite of his next shrimp, he shoots me a surprised look. "That's only for football, Coach."

"Is it?"

Before he can reply, Melinda's father juts in, nodding at me and Melinda. "You two are young and spry. Get out there and dance."

"Yes," Melinda coos and leans in, her perfume heavy and thick.

"Go on; enjoy the party," her dad insists as he slaps me on the back. "Does that leg injury keep you from dancing?"

"No."

His buddies smile at me, nodding.

I exhale noisily. To refuse now would be rude to the Texans. And Nova's avoiding me, so . . .

"All right." I set down my plate, then lead her out to the floor, a few feet away from Nova and Sonia.

Nova looks at me, then does a spin in her dress, the fabric billowing around her long tanned legs. She grabs Sonia's hand, and they move to the other side of the floor.

My gut churns as my eyes follow her. Oh, she sat next to me in the lounge this week, pretending, but there was a difference. My chest panged for her unreserved smiles, the way she'd brushed her lips over my scars.

"Electric Boogie," by Marcia Griffiths, blares from the speakers, and several people rush out to do the Electric Slide. My jaw clenches when I see Andrew joining Nova for the line dance.

I tear my gaze off her. Once I leave Blue Belle, I want to do it with a clear heart, and that means no serious relationships.

Another girl joins us on the floor, sliding in next to Melinda, then another, then another, until I'm encircled by young women. Another song comes on. I should leave and go back to the table, but I also want to see what Nova is doing. In other words, I'm losing my mind.

The guitar-focused song "Say You Won't Let Go" hits the speakers, and I jerk to a stop, remembering the Pythons party.

"Dance with me," Melinda says, her hands sliding up my jacket.

"Melinda, catch a clue. I danced to be polite. You and I are never going to happen. It's Nova, and this song belongs to her."

She gapes at me as I turn around, maneuvering through the crowd.

Andrew's hand rests on Nova's shoulder as he grabs her another glass of champagne off a tray. He leans down to whisper something in her ear. With their backs to me, I acknowledge the crazy mix of emotions boiling in my chest—part possessiveness, the other side something

I can't put my finger on. Maybe rage. She spent years with him. She fucking loved him. Maybe she still does.

"Excuse me; it's our song, babe," I say gruffly, then turn her around.

She smiles up at me, her eyes unusually bright. "Darling! Andrew was just telling me about his vacation home at the beach in Galveston. He wants to know if we'd like to visit—"

"I prefer the Pacific Ocean. Bye, Andrew." Using my shoulders, I push him away with a slight bump, then lead her out to the dance floor.

She exhales. "Rude."

"Don't care." My hands encircle her waist. "You seem to be having a good time."

She twines her arms around my neck as her throat bobs. She looks away. "Right back at you."

"You left *me*, Princess," I grind out.

She shrugs, then leans her head on my chest. A long exhale comes from me as our bodies connect, some of that earlier tension ebbing away.

"I thought our song was 'Jolene,'" she murmurs. "Of course it's a song about a woman begging another woman to leave her man alone."

"I like this one."

She sighs, her fingers playing with my hair. "Have you ever listened to this one the whole way through?"

"Yes."

She looks up at me. "Oh?"

"It's about a man who falls for a girl the night they meet. He wants to spend his life with her."

"Then it doesn't fit us at all," she says. "Does it?"

Her face tilts up as her gaze searches mine, and something about the shadows in her eyes . . . I inhale a sharp breath as clarity dawns. I see her face that night in New York, clear as day, the impish smile when we met, the way her eyes burned for me. Subconsciously, that morning after I awoke, my brain erased her face. Sure, I had a rationale for it, that

I was drunk, but the truth is . . . I felt a visceral connection to Nova, my loss clinging to her joy—and my head couldn't handle the guilt that it was so close to Whitney's anniversary.

She drops her gaze and swallows thickly. "Ronan . . ."

"Yeah?"

She presses her face into my chest. "I don't feel so good . . ."

I stop our dancing and tilt her face up. "What's wrong?"

Her lashes flutter as sweat beads her face. She licks her lips. "It's so hot in here. Please—"

My chest seizes as the blood leaves her face. "Nova?" My voice carries across the crowd, and I feel eyes darting to us.

"Air." She tries to get out of my arms, then stumbles, and I reach for her, straightening her before she falls. I sweep her up and shove us through the dancers, bumping them out of the way. As soon as we clear the floor, she pulls away from me and runs through the yard into a garden with statues and manicured landscaping.

"Nova!" I catch up with her as she stands behind a cypress tree, gulping in air. Even for late October, it's hot and sticky. She holds her stomach, then bends over and throws up.

I rub her back. "Let's get you out of here."

"I just ruined an azalea," she breathes out, wiping her mouth with her hands. Her body weaves.

"Fuck the plants." I take her up into my arms again and stride through the lawn, bypassing the tent and walking around the house. My eyes dart from her tense face to the dark path. Her hair has fallen and lies over my arm as I dart across the street, holding her close to my chest so I don't jostle her.

"I can drive," she gasps out when we reach my car. "You're supposed to stay at the party. Take me to my—" She stiffens, her eyes widening, and I ease her down. Her hand hangs on to me as she vomits again, her shoulders heaving.

When she stands, I open my passenger door, pick her up, and strap her in. Grabbing napkins from the side pocket, I wipe her face gently, then clean her dress. "What's wrong? Was it the champagne or—"

"If you're thinking I'm pregnant, I'm not." She sucks in a breath. "Turn on the air, please."

I get in and crank the car, blasting the air conditioner, pointing the vents in her direction. "Do we need to go to a hospital?"

She leans back on the headrest, shaking her head. "No. Roll my window down. In case."

"Tell me when to pull over, okay? Just don't take off your seat belt."

She winces. "Vomit is on your jacket. I'm sorry."

"Shh, it's fine. Hang on." Whipping out of the parking lot, I drive past the big houses, pointing the car toward her place. My heart pounds. It's just vomit, so why am I so worried? It's not the pregnant thing; I believe her when she says she isn't, but . . .

I ease my hand over, find hers, and hold it tight.

Chapter 18

Nova

Ronan's drawn face bends toward me as he carries me into the house. "How are you feeling?"

"Like I want to hurl," I say, willing the boiling lava in my stomach to settle.

He pushes through the door and rushes into the den.

Sabine stands up from the couch. "What's wrong?"

My stomach rumbles again, and I wrestle out of Ronan's grip. He doesn't want to let me go but finally does. I cling to the staircase, my head spinning. "I don't know; I never do this . . ." I stop, frowning. Unless . . .

Sabine reads my mind. "Did you eat shellfish?"

"You have a shellfish allergy?" Ronan bellows. "Why didn't you tell me? Where's the goddamn EpiPen!"

Sabine cocks her head at him. "Remain calm. She doesn't need an EpiPen. It's not that serious. Shellfish allergies can occur at any time, mostly when you're an adult. It started when she was twenty-five and had lobster while we were on vacation in Maine. After that, Mama declared Maine was the worst place in the United States. Her reactions have happened two times since then, all by accident. Once she had clam in soup; the other was sushi. Mama said she never should have gone to that sushi place."

"I ordered the veggie rolls," I say weakly.

She ignores me. "Regardless, something went wrong. Nova doesn't eat most seafood or chicken. I'm not sure why she hates chicken, but she does. When she eats shellfish, she feels faint, vomits, gets a rash on her stomach, and sometimes has diarrhea—"

"Okay, that's enough," I say, my shoulders slumping as I trudge up the stairs. "There might have been crab or lobster in the quiche. I didn't ask, and I should have. I only had a few. Bring the Benadryl, Sabine."

After clicking down the air on the thermostat, I make it to the bathroom next to my bedroom and throw up again. Leaning over the sink, I wash my face and pat it dry. The door opens, and Ronan walks in with the medicine.

Wearing a frown, he sits on the edge of my tub and pulls out his phone, scrolling.

I take the Benadryl, then grimace at my white face in the mirror.

His voice is abrupt. "Are you having difficulty breathing, swelling of your throat, or a rapid pulse?"

I chug the Sprite he brought. "Don't look it up on your phone. It will only scare you. I'll be fine in a few hours. You should go back to the party. For real. This is just a mild reaction."

He stands, a scowl on his forehead. "If you think I'm leaving you, you're crazy."

I exhale. "Fine. Help me out of this dress." I put my hands on the sink, clinging to the edge.

He unzips the back, easing it off my shoulders. His fingers trace a line down my back. "I've never seen you sick."

"It happens."

"You're always so peppy and . . ." He takes a step away from me, picking up my dress and laying it over the hamper.

"This will pass," I assure him. "And I'll go back to being pissed at you."

Wearing my thong and lace bra, I take small steps and hang on to the wall as I edge past him and turn on the shower. I glance at him over my shoulder. "Privacy?"

"Nova . . . there's something I want to say. I fucked up the pantry moment for us." He tugs at his hair, his face grimacing. "There's a wall of fear inside me. I froze up and didn't know how to handle us." He lowers his head, then looks at me. "I hate us being at odds."

Part of me relishes this open side of Ronan, but the other part, self-preservation, doesn't want to be hurt. I push up a smile. "Okay, I'm glad you said that. May I shower now?"

He bites his lower lip as his eyes skate over my face. "What if your throat starts swelling? We need to make sure your reactions don't worsen with each exposure. I want to hang around in the bathroom."

"Ronan . . ." My words stall.

"I just want to make sure . . ." He scrubs his face. "Whitney died on my watch, Nova."

"That wasn't your fault. It was a storm. And I'm not even close to being that sick. I've been worse off with the flu."

I notice the tremble in his hands. "Inside, I know that—I do—but . . . I feel like I'm at a crossroads, you know, a big one, and I'm going to screw it up because I can't be relied on. I can't. I worked all my life to be the best; I came from nothing, and I attained what some people never do. The Heisman. An incredible career. A team who admired me. A girl I loved. It's like my world was so perfect for those years that I never imagined anything bad would happen, and I let down my guard! I failed!" He heaves out a breath. "This week has been shit, and tonight, seeing you sick just brings back those feelings of inadequacy. Even with this town, I worry about disappointing them, about leaving my players. They think I'm this great coach and person, but what if I let them down too? They can't imagine it, but what if I *can't* get them that trophy? They want it so much, and they've put all this responsibility on me, and sometimes it feels tougher than playing for the Pythons. At least then, I depended on other people in the game, and I have other coaches, but it's me, all me. These people love me; they've put me on a pedestal, and that terrifies me. Their expectations, the belief that I'm going to save them. I talk big and bolster them up—hell, I'm great at getting people to believe in themselves, but I don't believe in *myself*! I'm not brave anymore! I lost it somewhere along the way, and I don't know how to get it back. How fucked is that?" He jerks to a stop. "Jesus, you're sick, and here I am, bugging you . . ."

My heart softens at his admission. "Ronan, no, let it out. It's good for you. Speaking your truth puts it in the universe so you can conquer it later."

He turns and looks at me. His eyes shut. "The things you say . . . I've missed you—"

I sigh, interrupting him. "Ronan, I'm here for you as a friend, but . . ."

"Let me finish." He inhales a deep breath, then swallows. "Nova, that night in New York, when we met, I think I f—" He stops abruptly, his hands clenched as he stares at the floor.

I manage a smile, unsure of what he's trying to say, as my stomach churns with more nausea. "It was a tumultuous experience for both of us. Can we put a pin in this?"

"Are you okay?" He rushes over to me.

"The quiche isn't going to keep me down."

He searches my face, then nods. "Okay. I'm sure you're right." He drops the lid on the toilet. "Get in and shower, Princess. I'll sit here in case you need me."

Fifteen minutes later, I'm out. He stood outside the door while I dried off, then grabbed me an old NYU sleep shirt. My wet hair hangs around my face in a tangled mess as I walk to my vanity. I sit, and he brushes out my hair, then holds my arm as we walk to the bed. He whips back the covers on the left, and I slide inside. He tucks them around me.

He holds up the *Art of War* on my nightstand. "Are you reading it?"

"Don't be weird about it."

He gives me a half smile. "What's your favorite part?"

"The part about musical notes and colors and tastes. How there's only a handful of each, yet they each produce millions of sounds, hues, and flavors."

"I know the one."

"Of course you do. Your brain . . ." I mimic something exploding.

He smiles, then fiddles with a picture of me and Mama and Sabine on my nightstand. "You deserve all the wonderful things in the world, Nova. I'm not it."

Our eyes cling. His words were soft, and I heard the ring of truth in them—that he believes. I don't allow the sadness and disappointment I feel to surface. I push them down because I do deserve something awesome. And someday I'll have it.

I pull my hand out of the covers and take his. "Hey. Here's another quote I like, just for you. There's a thousand battles and a thousand victories, and through it all, you must believe in yourself . . . and stuff like that. It's not exact, but then you already know I'm not great at memorizing quotes."

He squeezes my hand. "Funny."

Sabine walks in the door. "Are you okay?" There's an edge to her voice. "Mama went to bed and never woke up."

Ah . . . I imagine after the flurry downstairs she's had time to worry. I spread my arms wide. "Right as rain. You can sleep with me if you want." She did for the first two weeks I was here.

She rubs her ring, her eyes darting to Ronan, who's plopped down in a puffy chaise chair next to my side of the bed. Sparky walks on the back of the chair, then jumps down from Ronan's shoulder and curls in his lap. Ronan gives him a dark look but doesn't move him. "Weird-ass cat."

"Is Coach going to stay?" Sabine asks.

I look at him.

He pets Sparky. "I'll leave if it bothers you, Sabine."

"It doesn't," she says. "I like you all right. Just don't snore, 'kay?"

A smile flits over his face as he leans his head back on the cushion. "Got it."

My limbs grow heavy as I relax into the cool cotton sheets. "Crawl in behind me," I tell my sister.

"Can we sing?" she asks.

"Absolutely."

"Dolly?"

"Who else?" I reply.

"'Islands in the Stream' or 'Here You Come Again'?"

"You decide," I say.

Wearing her shorts and a baggy shirt, she crawls in behind me, wrapping her arms around my middle. I clutch her hand, threading our fingers together as her voice croons "Here You Come Again." I sing the chorus with her.

"I'm never leaving you," I tell her, my voice groggy. She snuggles closer.

My eyes meet Ronan's across the shadowy room. He hasn't taken them off me.

Go home, I mouth.

He shakes his head. *No.*

I sigh, and before I can think of what else to say, exhaustion and sleep tug me under.

Later, I don't know when, I feel hands on my head, the brush of his lips against my forehead, and then I'm back in dreamland, in a place where Ronan isn't afraid to love . . .

Chapter 19

Nova

"I don't see why we can't strut out to 'We Are the Champions,' rip some practice jerseys off, do a roar, punch our chests, then do a body roll," Bruno says. He demonstrates by rolling his torso, then running his hand down his chest to his groin. "Am I right? The crowd will go nuts!"

Several football players nod and elbow each other, laughing.

"And I'll be fired. You will not touch your privates, Bruno. Am I clear?" I rub my forehead. We're in my room, the desks pushed to the side as we work on the pep rally for the Huddersfield game next week. No one can agree on a song or what to do.

He grins. "It might start a riot anyway."

"Technically, you aren't champions yet," Sabine says from the floor, where she and Toby sit working on a poster that says **Free Lambert!**

Toby looks up. "True that. We don't want to jinx ourselves."

"If you're stuck on Queen, a better song would be 'We Will Rock You.' The beat is bloody great," Sonia says as she eats her salad next to me.

"We did 'We Will Rock You' last year," Milo says. "Might be bad luck."

The players nod. Superstition and bad luck are a real thing in football. Since we lost to them last year, we must do everything different this time.

"What about 'Eye of the Tiger'?" another player says as he chows down on a sandwich.

"We aren't tigers. We're Bobcats," Bruno mutters. "There is a difference."

Leaning against a desk, I run a hand through my hair, twisting it up with a rubber band into a messy bun. It's important they make decisions themselves. They weren't given much leeway before with Melinda, and I want them to feel as if they're creating something that's all theirs.

"We need a routine, y'all! Something lit!" Bruno says to them as he faces his team and lifts his hands up. "Hit me with the ideas!"

"A line dance?" Milo offers. "I can boot scoot and boogie. Granny taught me."

"I'm not wearing cowboy boots," Bruno says. "Texas isn't a stereotype."

"It's early November. Maybe dress up like turkeys? Flap some wings, then do the chicken dance," a player says.

Bruno heaves out an exhale. "Whoever said that . . . what the fu—heck no!"

"The Macarena?" another player says. "It's fun."

"No," Bruno says and crosses his arms. "I'm in charge of this, and it has to be right!"

"It's important to listen to everyone's ideas," I remind him.

"I like the Carlton or the 'Y.M.C.A.' Old school," Sonia offers.

"Eh, I don't know," Bruno says, scrubbing his face. "We want them foaming at the mouth for us. Toby, you're our captain. Thoughts?"

Toby is currently laughing at something Sabine is saying. After I supercleaned the house from the Great Lice Debacle, they had their first date. We had pasta and watched *Clueless*. He's been over to do homework a few times. I met his mom when the four of us got together at the bookstore and had dinner.

She's not allowed to be alone with him. I've told her she must wait until she's sixteen. My own love life is the pits, but when it comes to Sabine, I'm doing what Mama would want. Protect her. Guide her.

Feeling all eyes on him, Toby glances up. "Oh. Um, I'm not really a dancer, but maybe a country song? We could walk around and pump our fists. Maybe lip-synch?"

Bruno winces. "We don't want some sad 'Let me go drive my truck and drink a beer' song."

Toby's lips quirk. "Ms. Morgan, what do you think?"

I tap my chin. "'Boom Boom Pow' by the Black Eyed Peas is upbeat."

Bruno nods. "It's not terrible, but . . . I don't know . . ."

"Bullocks. You're hard to please," Sonia tells him.

Bruno runs his eyes over the team that came to the meeting. "I have high expectations. We're gonna beat those bast—I mean Rams, and I want to jump-start it good." He heaves out a sigh. "We need the perfect song."

"'Gangnam Style,'" says a voice from the door. Caleb. There's a burrito in his hands as he leans against the doorjamb. "It gets people on their feet."

"Hey!" I say with a smile.

Caleb gives me a jerky nod. "Hey. I—I was just coming by to chat and overheard you guys."

He's been by twice since he came back to school, *Just to say hi,* he says, but I think he needs people. Grief can isolate a person. "Come in and help us," I say.

Bruno waves him in. "Yo! I like it, dude. It's got smooth moves." He proceeds to shake his butt and wave his arms like he's riding a horse. "It's fresh, a little country with the horse move, and the rest is sexy—which will drive the girls crazy. I love it! Yeah, yeah!" He turns to the players and pumps his fist. "Can we do this, guys?!"

They mumble among themselves while I bring up the song on my phone and play it.

A few heads start nodding at the electric beat. Bruno does the horse-riding move, then a lasso one as a few of the guys get up and attempt to dance. Sonia tosses her salad in the trash and gets out there with them.

Caleb sets his burrito down and stands in front of them and does all the moves, adding some popping, spins, and robot moves.

I shake my hips and twirl my finger in the air. "Go, Caleb!"

He smirks, then finishes the song by dropping to the floor and break-dancing as the guys cheer him on.

"You're really good. You think you can help us get that together?" Toby asks Caleb after they've finished.

Caleb shrugs.

"We're meeting in here for lunch this week to figure it out." I pause, recalling seeing his school record with the counselor. "Didn't you do drama last year?"

Caleb nods. "Yeah."

"Great!" I exclaim. "Then maybe you can help us with wardrobe as well?" I give him a "Please help us" look.

Bruno juts in. "We need pull-apart jerseys."

I pat Bruno on the arm. "We all know you have muscles under your shirt."

"Your hot cheerleader girlfriend knows too," Sonia calls, and a few of the guys laugh.

I give Bruno a pointed look. "Give it up."

He lets out an aggrieved exhale. "Okay, so what should we wear?"

"Boots and jeans," Milo calls.

"A furry Bobcat outfit," another player calls.

Bruno rolls his eyes. "We can't dance in a hot-as-heck fur outfit. What do you think, bro?" He looks at Caleb.

Several moments pass as Caleb squints and paces around the room, studying the players, his forehead furrowed, an animated quality about him I haven't seen before. "Suit jackets and dress pants from the Goodwill or something sharp in your closet you don't mind ruining. Fedoras if we can find them. Sunglasses for sure. We loosen the seams on the clothes; then halfway through the song, you jerk them off. Maybe twirl them around"—he smirks—"kinda like a striptease. Your jersey and football pants are underneath."

"Yeah, yeah, I like it. Can you come tomorrow?" Bruno asks him.

Caleb looks at me. I give him a pleading look and hold my hands up in a prayer.

He laughs. "Okay."

"Good." Toby slaps Caleb on the back. "Be prepared. Half of us can't dance, me included."

"This is true," Sabine says as she comes over. "I tried to teach him a TikTok dance, and he tripped over the coffee table."

"All right," Toby says to Caleb. "The game is next week. Does that timeline work?"

Caleb nods. "Who's going to loosen the seams?"

Sabine raises her hand. "I can help."

"Me too," I add.

"My granny will," Milo adds.

"I'm in," Sonia offers.

We decide to ask a few others to help with the wardrobe. Sabine makes a list of names and offers to make the calls.

The bell rings.

I clap my hands. "Okay, guys, same time tomorrow. Pick up your lunches, and toss them in the trash, please."

Toby gets mine, Sabine's, and his, then throws them away as they walk out the door together.

Bruno ambles over to me. "Thanks for, you know, taking this on."

"Aw, you're welcome, Bruno," I say. "Don't forget to answer your poetry questions."

He rolls his eyes and walks out the door.

"Ms. Morgan?" says a deep voice.

I glance up as Andrew files in, maneuvering between the students as they leave.

"Hey," I say to him.

"That wanker wants to shag you," Sonia says under her breath as she grabs her bag, then leans in. "I have a class, but I can wait a few if you want?"

"No, I've got this," I murmur. "Go on."

She sashays past him, nodding a hello.

"I've been missing you for lunch," he says as he comes closer. He rakes a hand through his blond hair, his dimples popping as he smiles at me.

"Yeah, we've been busy." I catch my reflection in the glass. No lipstick, my hair is a tornado, my royal-blue dress has a mustard stain on it from my sandwich, and I'm shoeless. I pad over to behind my desk and slip my heels on. I quickly brush some gloss over my lips. I turn back.

"Is everything okay?" I ask with a benign smile as I grab my satchel. We keep things light and easy. We talk about school and sports. I've clocked the smoldering looks he sends me, the way his hands linger . . . I've ignored it.

He gives a pointed look to a few of the kids who dawdle, looking over the posters we've made.

"Can we talk in private?" he asks. "This is my planning period, so . . ."

I frown. "I'm supposed to be at the field house."

"Just a few moments. Please."

I debate. There's nothing pressing in Ronan's office except answering his phones . . .

Andrew and I are always surrounded by other people, even at the fundraiser, and maybe I've been wondering what we'd say if we *were* alone . . . "Sure."

We walk out together, and he leads me to the same closet Sonia and I use. He opens the door and clicks on the light while I reach up to the top shelf and grab one of the e-cigarettes. I offer him one, and he says no while I suck on one, willing myself not to choke. My goal is to appear to be a nonchalant badass.

Vapor billows in the small space. "What's up?" I ask.

He leans against the door, a pensive look on his face.

I hold his gaze until he blinks and glances away from me.

"Andrew? We're here to talk."

"I've missed you."

Just three words . . .

Several tense moments pass, then . . .

My carefully constructed walls crumble. Anger flares in my chest. Maybe it's because I've been around him for several weeks, unsaid words brimming in my head. "You have no right to say that."

A slow blush rises on his face. "I know, Nova. I—I'm sorry I hurt you. Paisley and I . . . if it's any comfort . . . we weren't happy. We tried, we really did, but once she realized I wasn't . . ." He sucks in a breath. "We stayed in the same house for years, getting along, living our own lives, but now that Brandy is older, we both realized—"

"I don't want to hear about you and Paisley. I don't care," I say sharply, banked emotion rising higher. "You came to *me*. You flew to New York to beg me back; you got on your knees and looked in my eyes. You promised it would work. And when I woke up the next morning, you were gone—like a coward."

His face falls. "I know . . . you said we could try again, but you *saw* me and Paisley. I knew you'd never forget it."

"You wanted your daddy's money," I mutter.

"And I've been unhappy ever since!" he shouts, then sobers, breathing rapidly. "God. I'm sorry. I just . . . I don't regret the time I've had with Brandy—I love my little girl—but if I could have had you both, I would have, Nova. I loved you."

I look away from him.

I'm glad he left. Marrying him would have been a horrible mistake.

"Seeing you here at school that first day . . . it was like the sunshine came back. Nova, I *still* love you. I never stopped." He moves to take my hands, and I'm so shocked by his words that I let him.

I frown as I take him in—the earnest face, the burning intensity in his topaz eyes. I recall that first day *I* walked in the school, how devastated I was to see him . . . I've wondered over the past weeks if maybe *I* still carry a torch for him in my heart . . .

"I don't feel that way about you, Andrew. That part of my life is over."

"You cared about me once. Just . . . forgive me. If you could let it all go, then maybe, I don't know, there might be a chance . . ." He searches for words. "I know it's crazy, but . . . you came back home. That means something. What if it was always meant to be us?"

A wave of feelings hits me as he twines our hands together.

His double betrayal has eaten at me for years, tiptoeing down the hallways of my head, digging its claws into me. I've used his sins as a shield of protection, painting men with the same brush. I wasted so much time thinking about him when I could have had real relationships.

Forgive him?

When he changed *who* I was inside?

I swallow thickly.

But . . .

Forgiving is for you, Mama used to say.

I glance away from him, my head tumbling.

It's been years . . .

What happened, happened. We can't change it.

In the end, he did me a favor.

And the idea that he and I were meant to be? Unbidden, a smile slips over my face. Fate didn't bring me to Blue Belle for Andrew . . . it was Ronan. I believe that, as sure as Mama's roses are yellow, as sure as I love Sabine. The odds of us meeting again were too tiny, too impossible. What we do with those chances, well, that's up for debate—

"Nova?" He's moved closer to me, cutting off my train of thought.

I glance at him and blink, refocusing.

He squeezes my hand, and clarity arrives like a rush. Letting go of the hurt doesn't mean I have to forget, but it does mean when I see him in the hall, I can smile and mean it.

"I forgive you."

"And us? Why not try?" His eyes shine down at me.

"I'm with Ronan, and I care about him." Truth.

I recall the feeling when we met, as if we'd already had a hundred conversations before, as if our souls saw a commonality. I love his scars, his geekiness, his stark vulnerability . . .

Being with him, even though he's still finding out who he is and what he needs, is like peeking into possibilities. He said I deserve better, and I get where he's coming from—a place of incredible loss, and climbing that mountain isn't easy—but I'm not one to give up easily.

Mama raised me to believe there's a tiny light inside everyone, a wonderful place of possibilities for your life. It's up to you to find your "glow" and turn those possibilities into certainties.

Make the impossible real. Reach for the stars, even if they burn, Nova.

I blink. Wow. I haven't thought about her "glow" idea for a long time. Why now?

Because . . . I love Ronan. Deeply. It may have started in New York, but now that I've seen who he really is—a flawed man who cares and loves intensely . . .

"Nova?"

He's been saying something, and I've missed it. "Go on," I say, my tone distracted.

"Ronan isn't staying here."

My stomach drops. "I know."

"And he calls you *babe*. You hate that word."

I frown. Where is he going with this?

"And when you call him *darling*, your accent kicks in." He touches my cheek. "There's something fishy. You're barely in town, and then suddenly you're dating the one guy who hasn't shown interest in anyone? And the way you act in the teachers' lounge is strange, almost as if you wanted to rub it in my face."

"I did." A small smile curls my lips, and he huffs out a laugh.

"So you do feel something for me, then?"

Regret. The energy I wasted. The insecurities I allowed.

He bends his head, and before I can move, he presses his lips to mine—

The door swings open, and he's pulled roughly away.

I gasp, stepping back.

With a flushed face, Ronan grinds his jaw as his hands clench, then open.

"I should fuck you up right here," he hisses as he shoves Andrew in the chest. "But this is school property, and I don't want to be arrested for putting you in the hospital. Keep your hands off Nova."

Andrew stumbles, then comes right back at Ronan. He gets in his face and points his finger at him. "This is between me and Nova—"

"Stop this!" I say as I step between them. "This isn't the place. And there's no point!"

Andrew backs up and straightens his shirt while Ronan takes several deep breaths, then turns his eyes to me, ice blue and cold. "You're late for work." Then he flips around and stalks out.

I turn to Andrew, my voice low. "Don't do that again. You and I will never be together."

He exhales and shakes his head. "Nova—"

Cutting him off, I shut the door and quick step to catch Ronan. He's been gone for three days to a coaches' conference in Austin, and my gaze eats him up. On Sunday after the fundraiser, I woke up around six, and he was still asleep in the chair. He woke up disheveled, his tie loosened, his face dark with a shadow. He inquired if I was okay, then said he had to go. There's been an anxiousness inside me ever since.

He was here this morning—I saw his car—but I came in a tad late and skipped the staff lounge and went straight to my classroom.

He's wearing his teaching clothes, a pair of gray slacks and a long-sleeved tailored blue shirt with the cuffs rolled up. His back is tense, his strides long.

"Ronan, wait," I call, but he keeps going.

I'm out of breath by the time we step outside to the sidewalk that leads to the field house.

I glance at his hard, chiseled jawline. "I started my period."

His nose flares.

"You told me to tell you," I remind him lightly.

"Good," he bites out.

"What you saw, it wasn't what you think. He asked to speak to me in private. It was good—"

He jerks to a stop, putting his hands on his hips, his face flat. But those eyes. Boy. They are blazing. "Was it? I guess so. He had his hands all over you. And his mouth!"

"He kissed me," I say calmly. "I didn't want him to."

"I didn't see you pushing him off!"

"You didn't give me time. You came looking for me?" I give him my sweet smile.

"I've been gone. I wondered where my goddamn PA was," he says, then starts walking again.

I glare at his back, then take off after him.

He swings open the door to his office and marches in. I follow and slam the door, then jerk the blinds shut on the windows. If he wants a showdown, we'll have one.

He's already stomped to his closet when I turn. A sharp inhale comes from me when I take in what's on his desk: a dozen or so yellow rosebuds with bright-green magnolia leaves tucked around them in the vase. A Dairy Queen Blizzard with M&M'S, my favorite, sits next to them.

My breath hitches. I carefully pluck one of the buds from the vase and twirl it between my fingers. The creamy petals haven't unfurled yet, and I rub it against my cheek.

I open the closet door. His back is to me as he whips off his shirt and tosses it on the floor with force. He stops and scrubs his face. "Leave me alone, Nova. You don't want to be around me right now."

I clear my throat as I enter. "He and I . . . we never had closure, and he wanted forgiveness." I stare down at the rose. "That story I told you in the bookstore? I never finished it. Andrew came—"

"Don't say his name," he growls.

I huff. "Fine. *He* came to New York before his wedding, and we made plans. I was going to leave NYU and come back to UT. Then he changed his mind and left."

He turns around, legs planted wide, arms crossed. "You still have feelings for that asshole."

"No. I mean, it *was* a shock to see him after so long that first day. Regardless . . . I want to forgive him. It gives me peace." I take a step toward him. "He made the wrong choices, but it worked out for me."

He captures my gaze, holding it captive. "Really."

"Mm-hmm." I ease closer, wary, as if I'm approaching a tiger, taking in his sculpted chest, the six-pack on his abdomen, the way his slacks hang on his lean hips.

His lashes flutter. "Jesus. You were all I could think about in Austin."

"Me puking or the awesome sex in your pantry?"

"Mostly the sex."

"Honest. I like it." I twirl the rose across his chest, grazing his collarbone, over to his shoulder. "You bought me flowers."

"I missed you," he growls. "I got them myself. No one did it for me."

"Wow, you're a big boy." Smiling, I come closer and lean my head on his chest as I wrap my arms around his waist. "And the Blizzard?"

"Is melted." His fingers land on my hips as his chin rests on the top of my head.

"It's my favorite," I whisper. "I'm glad to see you. We didn't get to talk before you left."

He sighs. "I recall saying a lot in your bathroom. About a crossroads . . ." He exhales. "I—I need to tell you something."

I start at the uncertainty in his voice. "Okay."

"One minute, I was sitting in a restaurant in Austin with five other coaches discussing the new regulations for next year, and this girl walks in and . . ." His words trail off.

"Was she pretty?"

"No, it wasn't that. She rushes up to this guy at the bar, and he picks her up and swings her around, then kisses her. Like, really lays one on her. People around them hooted and clapped. They sat down and ordered drinks but barely drank them. They just kept smiling, leaning in, and touching each other's faces. You know what I saw when I looked at them?"

"What?"

"Joy. Pure rapture. It's as if no one else was in that room but them, you know? Not the customers. Not the bartender or servers. Then before I knew it, fifteen minutes have passed, and the coaches are waiting for me to answer a question I never heard . . ."

"What were you thinking about?"

His arms tighten around me. "You and me. Imagining us as that couple. It wasn't hard."

"Oh . . ." My heart leaps with hope. The man wants me. He cares. And he got me this job. (Yes, Lois told me this week.)

He traces a hand down my spine, his fingers circling the small of my back. "I needed the break from Blue Belle so I could think. Seeing you sick, on one hand, reminded me of how scary it is to have someone, but later . . . I thought about how fleeting life is and . . ." He pauses, his chest rising. "And maybe, I don't know, that I needed to reassess everything I've been telling myself for the past few years."

We stand there silently as I soak in his words. I hear the fear, but I also hear courage. Irrepressible happiness washes over me, emotion clogging my throat. I press closer to him, digging in, and he sighs, running his hands through my hair.

"I'm really scared, Nova," he whispers.

"Life will always be scary. It's better when you do it with someone."

His hands tilt my face up, and his thumbs graze my lips. I lean into the touch, and he presses his forehead to mine. "I don't want to hurt you, but when I see you"—he brushes his lips over mine—"you break down all my walls."

"My adorable beast, we'll take it one day at a time." I will crush those walls.

His throat bobs. "You'll take a chance on me?"

Yes, yes, a million times. I nod.

He gives me a wide smile, then brushes his nose with mine. "Hey, it's good to see you."

"You too," I murmur.

He winces. "Guess I blew up back there, huh?"

"It was spectacular. Let's do that every week."

He grunts. "I can't stand him near you, Nova. If he touches you one more time, I'm going to beat his ass."

I shiver. "I like you all growly, but I made myself clear."

"No more closets for you and Andrew. I fucking mean it."

That glow inside me flares bright.

Yes, being with Ronan comes with risks. He's afraid to accept love, to reach out and grasp it . . .

And he's leaving.

But . . .

I want to touch the stars, even if I get burned.

"Do you believe in possibilities?" I ask.

He studies my face for several moments. "Yes."

"That's all I needed to know." I graze the rose over his crotch.

He grins. "You really do dig yellow roses."

"And the man who gave them to me."

"This 'thing' between us is crazy," he says, a bit of wonder in his voice.

"I happen to embrace crazy," I murmur.

"Come here." He pulls us over and leans against the table in the closet, positioning me between his legs. We hold each other.

"Where's the team?" I ask.

"Skeeter took them out so I could find you."

"And you marched in like a caveman."

"I marched in like Han Solo."

"God. You need to get over *Star Wars*. There are other movies."

"Come over to the dark side, Princess." He slants his mouth over mine. "Did you lock the door out there?" he breathes in between kisses.

"No clue."

"I don't care," he says as he unbuttons the top of my dress, revealing my blue lace bra. He bends down and sucks my nipple through the fabric as my hands curl around his head, clutching him.

"I'm not having period sex with you," I say as he tugs the material down. His fingers strum one nipple, tugging it, as he flicks his tongue over the other. My head spins at the desire that rushes over me.

"Whatever you say," he mumbles as he uses his mouth, plucking, dragging his teeth over me.

"I mean it," I say, a lack of conviction in my voice.

His laughter rumbles against my skin as he pushes my dress down to my waist. "I'll clean us up afterwards, babe."

"That's just gross."

Heat jolts through me as he cups both of my breasts in his hands and pushes them together, his tongue tracing their outlines, skimming his mouth from one to the other. Soft, then hard.

"We really need to talk about this *babe* thing, darling," I push out through heavy breaths. "You're saying it to annoy me—"

"You stop *adorable*, and I'll stop *babe*." He laughs against my skin, and I laugh with him, leaning back to give him more room.

"Coach?" comes from somewhere in the hall.

I squeak and press myself against Ronan. He straightens, holding me, and calls out, "Lois? Give me a minute. I'm—"

She appears at the closet door and tips up her Stetson. "Oh. Well. Good, good, I see. Sex play."

I glare at her.

She lets out a wistful sigh. "I remember those days of not being able to keep my hands off Bill. Anyway . . . I just came to talk about the game plan for next week—"

"Lois, shut that damn door so I can finish putting on my practice clothes," Ronan says.

"Yeah, put your 'practice clothes on.' Got it." She shuts it slowly, eyes dancing.

Chapter 20

Ronan

"Sonia, um, I brought two meat loaf sandwiches. My mom made them. I thought . . . do you want one?" Skeeter says as we gather around the table in the lounge.

Sonia looks up from the other side of the table, her eyes big. "I—I'm a vegetarian."

He makes a disgusted sound. "What? Why? This is cow country!"

Nova shifts in her chair next to me, leaning in to watch her best friend and Skeeter. My hand curls between her legs under the table, drawing little patterns on her knee.

Sonia sets down her hunk of broccoli. "I eat clean to prevent heart disease and live longer. Plus, I love animals."

He takes a bite out of his sandwich and chews, then wipes his mouth. "I like dogs, but we're talking about chickens and cows and pigs here. There's a difference. We're at the top of the food chain for a reason. It's just instinct to eat 'em."

Her shoulders stiffen. "You've seen me have lunch in here for years. Haven't you noticed I don't eat meat?"

He pauses. "Yeah?"

"No, you didn't!" she says. "And . . . I refuse to debate my choices with you. I do it because I like it, so leave it alone."

He drops his sandwich and blinks. "Wait . . . are you mad at me? I brought you food!"

"You brought me meat!" she counters.

"That's what a man does! Jesus ate fish! Lions eat animals! It's the circle of life! And, and . . . cows might take over the world if we didn't eat them! I don't know if that's true, but there's a website about it . . ."

My lips twitch, and Nova squeezes my leg to stop her laughter.

"There's no point in arguing with you," Sonia says as she gathers up her lunch, her face red as she looks at me and Nova. "Excuse me, guys. I need to go."

"Where are you going?" Skeeter asks, rising up.

"My special place," she mutters, then flounces out the door.

Skeeter shakes his head and lifts his hands in exasperation. "What did I do? I thought she'd like a sandwich!"

Nova sighs. "It's what you didn't do. You didn't notice her eating habits. You didn't ask her to dance at the fundraiser—"

His eyes widen. "Did she want me to?"

Nova nods slowly. "Yes."

"I assumed she ate real food at home or maybe she was dieting. I didn't know! And I can't dance. Even with champagne." He blows out a breath. "Where is her special place?"

Nova smiles. "The closet by the bathrooms. Oh, and she might be vaping."

"I thought she wanted to live longer!" he bellows. "Someone needs to make her stop."

Nova shrugs. "Or you could just meet in the middle and agree to disagree . . ."

"Dammit, women are peculiar." He gathers his stuff in his box, handling the meat loaf with care. He paces around the lounge for a few moments, then huffs. "I'll go find her."

"Take your time if you need to," I tell him.

He squints at me. "What do you mean? We've got practice."

Nova lets out a groan. "Skeeter! Catch a clue!"

"What?" he yelps.

"Do you *like* Sonia?" she asks.

He shifts from one foot to the other. He stares at the floor. "She's pretty. She's not dating that calculator guy anymore. I was wondering if she wanted to maybe go to the Roadhouse. They have all-you-can-eat wings tonight. I usually wolf down about thirty when I go, but now . . ." He puts his hands on his hips. "I might gross her out."

Nova smiles. "They have vegetarian options. Go and tell her you're sorry, and invite her out."

He exhales, then glances toward the door, a look of determination on his face. "I might be late, Coach."

We watch him go, then laugh, our heads bending together.

Nova rubs her hands together. "I'd love to be a fly on the wall of that closet. Obviously, the lice incident wasn't enough to get them together. Maybe this will."

I gaze down at her upturned face and smile. These past few days with her have been exhilarating. You know those people who shine so bright you gravitate to them, wanting to bask in their warmth? She's that. A little star.

"Melinda and Andrew didn't come to lunch today," she murmurs.

"I know. Good for us." I kiss her, my hand curling around her nape.

She pulls away slowly. "I need to go check on Caleb and the guys. I left them in my room."

"I'll see you at the field house. Dinner at my place? You and Sabine?"

She stands, her hand running over my shoulders. "Sounds good."

"I can grill. What should I make?"

She pauses, a light growing in her eyes. "Chicken. I want chicken."

I laugh as she sashays out the door.

◆ ◆ ◆

After lunch, I'm walking out to the field house when my phone rings.

"Yo, Reggie, how's it going?" I ask my agent.

"Hey! How are you doing?"

"Great, great. About to head to practice."

"Sounds good. Hite called me this morning. It's not official, but Dunbar is going to resign. The drug addiction is all over the media, and they can't keep a lid on it. There'll be a press conference in a few days. Hite's itching to nail you down for the short list."

"Reggie—"

"Stanford is at the top right now. You could be part of that team and work your way up. Hite will retire in a few years."

I reach the field and step out on the grass, frowning as I wait for the wave of calm that usually comes on the field, but it doesn't. Instead, anxiousness tugs at me.

"Ronan? He'll want to meet with you."

My hand taps my leg in frustration. "Look, I'm about to play the biggest game of the year next week. I can't fly to California and interview for a job I don't really want."

"Uh-huh. They've had a great season, and they'll get a bowl game. You could be there for it."

"Reggie . . ."

"Look, I hear the reservation in your voice," he says. "I get it. I do. You've been there for almost two seasons, and you want to finish, but life happens, and shit changes. You can pay out your contract with Blue Belle and go to California."

Toby sends me a wave as he runs into the field house.

"Ronan?"

"What?" I mutter.

"There's no harm in getting on the list. You can always say no, right?"

There's truth in that.

"Okay, fine, add me to the list, but keep it private. I need to go, Reggie."

"Wait! Ah, well, there's something else I heard through the grapevine that's simmering. I don't have all the deets, but—"

"What? Where?" My gut clenches, and I can't decide if it's hope or fear of an opportunity I can't say no to.

"I'll get back to you with facts once I get more info."

"Can you give me a hint?"

"Ah . . . well, it's close to home."

"Chicago?"

"No. Look, I've said too much already. I don't want to get your hopes up. I'll call you soon."

He clicks off, leaving me annoyed. I stalk out to the center of the field and stare at the Bobcat.

Moving up to the next level is what I want

But . . .

My chest tightens, and I stop and bend over to catch my breath.

It's going to rip me apart to leave this team—and Nova.

Chapter 21

Ronan

A woodpecker bangs on a nearby tree as I gaze down at Nova. The weather is warm, and she's wearing cutoff shorts and an old BBHS shirt. Her hair is everywhere as we lie in a hammock next to the pool.

We won our game last night on the road in Brighton, about two hours from Blue Belle. She and Sabine stayed home, and when I pulled up around one in the morning, I unlocked her door and headed upstairs to her room. I crawled in, tucked her in my arms, and slept the best I have in a while. We got up for Sabine and then made pancakes with Dolly playing. It's a Morgan Girl family tradition.

She stirs and opens her eyes, a slow smile curling her lips as she stretches. "Hello, handsome. I didn't mean to fall asleep."

"I don't mind."

She's here. *With* me.

"Where's Sabine and Toby?" she asks.

"Lois's house. Milo is there, and they're playing video games. I hope that's okay?"

She bites her lip. "Does this mean we're alone?"

"They've been gone for maybe an hour, so . . ."

She grabs her phone and fires off a text. "I'm telling Lois to keep them there for a while. Maybe order them a pizza. It's close to dinnertime, and Sabine loves Domino's gluten-free . . ."

I grin. "What will we do without them here?"

"Fun and games . . . give me a head start, 'kay? About twenty seconds," she says as she stirs around in my arms to get out of the hammock.

"What do you mean?"

She stands. "We're going to play a game. Keep up, Fancy Pants." She darts around the pool toward the house. Dog raises his head from the lounge chair he's asleep in, then snuffles out a disgusted sound and lies back down.

I heave myself out. "Don't you think we're too old for hide-and-seek?"

"We're never too old for games!" she calls out from the french doors. "I won't be hard to find! FYI, I'm off my period!" The door slams behind her, and I count to twenty, then take off after her

I go to the pantry first, then circle back to the kitchen, then head for my office. I swing the door open, and she's leaning against the pool table, a stick in hand. She's already racked the balls.

"See. Told ya it would be easy."

I drape my eyes over her body. "Are we going to play pool?"

"Hmm, I'm not very good."

"I don't believe you," I murmur, walking closer to her, grazing my hand down her arm. "You go first."

"Done!" She turns, lines up her cue, and shoots, sinking two solids.

"Damn," I breathe. "You're good."

"Take off your shirt, Coach."

"Oh, it's that kind of game, huh?" I pull at the neck of my Pythons shirt and toss it to the ground. Her eyes track over my chest, lingering on the V of my hips.

"Nice tent in your pants," she murmurs, then scratches on the next turn and pouts.

I grab my cue and line up and sink two stripes.

She cocks her hips. "Well . . . what do you want?"

"Your shorts. They have to go," I purr.

She unsnaps them and eases them down, revealing a black lace thong. Her legs go for miles, and my tongue darts out to lick my bottom lip, my teeth digging in. "Nice."

I scratch on the next turn, and she lines up to shoot, bending over the pool table, her ass on display. My hand twitches to touch her. As if she knows, she throws a look at me over her shoulder. "No touching the goods," she says. "That's for later."

My cock thickens.

Like she's done it a million times, she adjusts the cue and sinks a solid, then turns to me. "Secret time. Tell me one."

My lids lower. "I'd rather take my pants off and get this party started."

"Secret. Now."

I shift my feet, my gaze going to the closet door where Leia is. "I didn't like the Leia because her hair wasn't blonde."

Her mouth parts. "You wanted a me-Leia?"

"Hmm." I didn't understand my dissatisfaction with the wax figure when she arrived, but . . . she wasn't Nova, and I wanted something closer to the beauty I'd met.

She smiles. "Ah, that might be the sweetest thing you've ever said . . ."

I roll my eyes. "Just go again. I'm ready for my turn to happen."

She misses, then gives me room to make a shot, grazing her hand over my crotch as she slides past.

I groan, adjusting my breathing from her touch, then lean over the table and sink a stripe. I tap my chin, eyeing her. It's so clear what I want. Her naked. Completely. "The shirt. Off."

She pulls at the hem slowly, her hips swaying back and forth as she tugs it over her hair and tosses it over her head. My chest rises at the sight of her in her black bra and panties. Our eyes lock. "You like?"

"Mm-hmm." I turn and attempt another shot, and miraculously it goes in.

"Bra. Lose it," I demand.

She unsnaps the front, dangles it on her fingers, and then throws it at me. "Get ready to wear it."

I laugh, turning away from her luscious tits, and sink another stripe. "Yes!" I call out and pump my fist.

She curses.

My gaze takes in her erect red nipples. "You cold, babe?" She glares at me as I lean against the table. "What next . . . hmm . . ."

She puts her hands on her hips. "Just say it."

"Underwear. Off."

"You're still dressed!"

"Those are the rules, babe." I cock an eyebrow.

She grabs her phone and turns on music, "I Knew I Loved You," by Savage Garden.

"Is that your stripping song?" I ask. "Or are you stalling?"

She flips me off, then sways her hips to the song, humming along as she tucks her thumbs in the sides of her panties and teases them up and down. The lace dances down her hips, past her thighs, to her knees, and then to her ankles. She picks them up and tosses them to me. "Your turn to go again. Or are you stalling?"

My mouth drying, I eat her up with my eyes. My knees feel weak, and with a groan, I turn and make my next shot. My hands are unsteady, but I manage to sink the ball.

I turn around and face her, trying not to gloat.

"Well?" she asks in a low, sultry voice. "What's it gonna be, darling?"

"Get on the table. Spread your legs."

Her breath hitches. "You dirty, dirty man. You still have the eight ball."

"Fuck the eight ball. I want you. Now."

She walks toward me, and I meet her halfway. I pull her face to me and kiss her. It's a stormy kiss, explosive, throbbing with need as our tongues fight for dominance.

"I love kissing you. Each time is different," I murmur as our breaths mingle. "Now get your sweet ass on the edge of the table so I can eat your pussy."

"You're so poetic," she says as I sweep her up in my arms and set her down on the table, shoving the rest of the balls out of the way so she can lie back.

I trace my hand down her throat, letting it rest at the bottom. It's a possessive "You're mine" hold.

Her fingertips graze my arm. "If you're into choking, I need to know."

"And if I am?"

"Then I only ask that you let me do you first."

I chuckle as I lean in and take her lips gently, skimming over that lush bottom one, stretching it with my teeth. "I'd never hurt you, but someday . . . maybe . . ."

"Possibilities are endless," she murmurs. "Now make a meal of me." Propping her feet up, she leans back on the green table.

I inhale at the image she presents. So willing. So hot.

I swat her ass, and she glares at me.

"Just checking," I chuckle and lean over and kiss her softly, then trail down her throat, sucking on the skin.

"Ronan . . ." She curls her hands in my hair.

I skim over her succulent nipples with teasing touches, plucking, tweaking. She arches, and my tongue dips down to the valley between her breasts and traces down to her waist. I kiss her hip bones, playing over her belly button. My thumb grazes over her nub as my tongue tastes her. With my other hand, I shove my shorts and underwear down and grasp my cock. Little spasms flutter from her folds as I feast on her skin. Her clit swells as I suck it into my mouth and flick over it, lingering, exploring her secret places. She calls my name, her body quaking and shuddering as she rubs against my face. Her back arches up, and she pulls my hair and comes with a shout, her body quivering.

I stop pumping my length and prowl on top of her. She opens her arms and scoots up to let me get on the table. Fire blazes under my skin as I get on my knees and pick up her hips, her legs falling over my forearms. Her ass rests against my upper thighs. My chest heaves as I slide inside her slickness and groan, need rising higher as her tits bounce with my entry. I swivel my hips to get deeper, yelling out as I hit home.

Her eyes glaze, her pupils blown. Sweat drips down my face, my gaze trained on her, memorizing her features, the way her hair splays out behind her. I play with her nipples, skimming my tongue over the tips, then sucking them into my mouth.

Her hips rise to meet me as I work her, my shoulder muscles flexing as I slide out and thrust back with a need that curls down my spine. She tightens her legs around my hips and gazes up at me, our eyes locked

We're in a bubble, the only two people in the world, and all that matters is this second, this feeling. The air crackles as something powerful and beautiful passes between us. A gift. A rare moment. The world tilts as my throat prickles with need for her. My mouth parts to gasp.

"Nova . . ."

She tugs my face to hers, and I let down her legs to lie on top of her, easing between them.

I slow us down, dragging out the thrusts, my face in her neck. We turn languid and unhurried, stretching out the moments I'm inside her. She feels like silk, tight and hot. I rise as I slide out, my crown rubbing over her clit before I thrust back inside.

"Nova . . ." I can't find the right words for what's happening between us.

"I'm here. I feel it too," she breathes out.

With tender lips, I kiss her throat, her ear, her collarbone, her breasts. I want to consume her, have my smell on her skin.

Her hands clutch my ass, her nails digging into the skin, and I'm gone, euphoria ripping through my skin, my bones, every molecule inside me. I roar at the sensation, the ultimate pleasure, my body riding the wave. She tips over with me, our hands clinging to each other.

With her caged below me, I give her another kiss. "You're beautiful. That was beautiful," I tell her as we turn on our sides and face each other, our legs and feet tangling together. I push the hair out of her face, and the moments tick by as we stare at each other.

She smiles. "You're gonna have a damp spot on your pool table. Can you recover it?"

I laugh. "This can be our sex table. I'll put it in my bedroom." My eyes eat her up—the flushed cheekbones, the dainty nose.

"I want to show you *Star Wars*," I murmur. "Just you and me. I want to sit next to you and watch your face when you realize how awesome it is."

Her hands toy with the ends of my hair. "You're going to torture me with a galactic saga?"

"Come on; you know you're dying to see it." I rest my chin on her head.

She lifts her face. "Do you still have some vanilla wafers?"

I nod. "You can have the whole box, but I wanted to cook us dinner. I have steaks in the fridge. I picked them up today. On my own."

"Such a big boy. Do you have potatoes and garlic bread?"

"And salad stuff." I pause, holding her hands in mine. "Will you stay the night?"

"Sabine—"

"Lois has already said she'd stay over with her."

She squints at me. "Did you have this all planned?"

"Hmm. I want you alone for one night."

She lets out a gusty exhale. "This movie better be good."

I smile broadly and kiss the tip of her nose. "You're going to love it."

She swats my ass. "Cook me dinner."

Chapter 22

Nova

We're in Ronan's bed. I'm propped up on the bed with pillows behind me. My fingers play with his hair as his head rests on a pillow on my legs. He strokes my legs, drawing little circles on my inner thigh. The movie reaches the end, and the credits begin to roll.

He turns his head and looks up at me. "Well?"

I smile.

"You hated it?" he says.

I open my mouth, then shut it.

"Tell me!"

I grimace. "The acting is bad, especially from Luke; the lines are cheesy; and the Stormtroopers . . . how on earth do they see out of those costumes? And they can't kill anything with their weapons. Somehow, the main characters all manage to avoid getting blasted—well, except for poor Obi-Wan. Supposedly it's set in a galaxy far, far away, but everyone speaks English?"

"Yes," he growls.

"Hey, boo-boo, I loved it."

He sits up, the sheets sliding against his bare chest. "Liar."

I laugh as he pulls me down on the bed and cages me in underneath him.

"How will I punish you?"

"No. I promise. I do! Han Solo is awesome. He kills a lot of people. Chewie is my man. And R2-D2 is my favorite. I love him! May the Force be with you!"

"I don't believe you." He tickles me, his fingers dancing around my ribs. I squirm around him, giggling, trying to get to the edge of the bed. He drags me back. "You're not escaping me."

I gasp. "I swear!"

He leans over and kisses me slowly. "I'll forgive you. I'll let it go. I can live with you not loving it. On one condition."

"What?"

"That you never change. That you'll always be happy . . ." He stops, his eyes dark with emotion.

I blink. "Okay."

He rolls over to his nightstand and opens a drawer, then comes back and places a small box in my hands. His words, when they come, are hesitant. "I got you something in Austin on my last day. I hope you like it. As soon as I saw it, I knew it had to be yours."

I sit up, smiling at the silver wrapping paper. "And it's not even my birthday."

I tear at the paper, tossing it on the floor, then settle the black velvet box in my lap and open the lid. My chest hitches at the gold necklace inside. I lift it up, and there's a star dangling from the chain, outlined in gems. It's simple yet elegant, the type of classic jewelry I'd pick out for myself. "Are those real diamonds?"

"Would I give you fake ones?"

"I mean, I'd love it either way. It's beautiful . . ."

"Here, let me." He takes the necklace, and I lift my hair so he can slide it around my neck and connect the clasp. He picks up the star and settles it on my chest. His fingers stroke the star, making my skin hum.

"Because you're a burst of light," he says softly. "Because you believe in people. Because I can't look up at the night sky without thinking about you. You're a star."

My heart swells with emotion, at the tenderness in his gaze. "Ronan . . . I'm in love with you. I love you."

The room feels hot, and my thoughts scatter as he inhales a sharp breath.

I see hesitation in his eyes. Loneliness. *Fear.*

I see a man standing alone on a precipice, needing to take that one step . . .

My lips quirk ruefully as I hold his gaze. For the first time since Andrew, I'm all in with a man, my cards on the table. "Too soon?"

He flounders for words, his eyes searching my face. "Nova . . . I'm on the short list for Stanford. It's not what I want, but I'm looking into it to make sure. I'm being up front and honest. I don't know the future." He licks his lips. "Be patient with me. I don't want to . . . screw us up. Remember possibilities? That's what's happening here, okay? Life is happening, and I don't know how it will all shake out, but you . . . you make sense."

I nod jerkily as he pulls me to him, his fingers stroking my back. I wanted him to tell me he loves me too, but . . .

I'm going to be brave and go with us as we are and savor each moment we share. If it flays me alive and cuts me open in the end, then fine, I took a chance, and in the end that's all a person can do to find happiness.

He kisses the top of my head. "How about a game?"

"Rules?"

"This time you tell me what to do," he says.

"Okay. Put my thong on, Fancy Pants." I lean over and grab it from the floor and dangle it in front of him.

"Hell to the no."

"Cheater. My rules . . ."

He narrows his eyes at me, and I try to keep a straight face but end up laughing, pushing the earlier emotional moment aside. "I'm sorry, but your face . . ." I stop as he tosses me back on the bed and tickles me. I flail around underneath him as he captures my wrists and pins them above my head. His lower body rests on top of mine as we breathe heavily. My head arches up, and I take his mouth in a demanding kiss, and he groans, our lips meshing over and over.

"Jesus . . . you're . . ." He stops and puts his face in my neck, taking deep breaths.

"What?" I ask.

"Everything a man could ever want. I need you right now. I need to be inside you."

I press into his hips, and he moans, rotating against me. His length is hard and thick on my leg, his mushroom-shaped crown wet. "Take me like this," I demand. "And look me in the eyes and tell me you need me."

"I do, Princess," he murmurs as he sinks into me slowly, his gaze locked with mine. "I need you, I need you . . ."

Chapter 23

Nova

"How was your date with Skeeter?" I pass Sonia an e-cig, and she takes a long toke, vapor billowing in the closet.

She grimaces. "So it was going well. We came in separate cars, you know, just in case things went south. We sat down and ordered. He was eating his chicken wings, and I was munching on my salad. I was nervous. Quiet. I needed to pee but didn't want to get up. The restaurant was packed. And he just keeps talking and talking, probably because I'm not. Then I gulp water and get choked. It went down the wrong pipe, and the coughs just kept coming and coming.

"My face turned red. My hands flailed. My glass spilled, and my salad tumbled to the floor. Lettuce and carrots and cheese on my pants. People stared. I mean, it got quiet as a church in the Roadhouse. I grabbed my throat; then Skeeter jumped out of his seat. I'm sputtering, and my stomach is jumping from all the coughing, and I think I just might hurl—or pee—then he tries to do the Heimlich on me, and I'm gasping, trying to tell him that it's not food lodged in my throat, just fucking water! Finally, I get free and dart for the restroom, where I pee forever and get my breath back. I stayed in there for twenty minutes, hoping he'd just leave without me, but oh no, he comes looking for me, like, knocks on the door and then comes in, and there I am, crying on the toilet! And that's how it bloody went!"

I burst out laughing.

"I know." She shakes her head. "I can joke now, but it was the worst first date ever. I'm sure it's our last. He hasn't texted, and I refuse to reach out. That man will have to come to me."

The door flies open, revealing a tall, handsome, auburn-haired carnivore.

"You're vaping?!" Skeeter calls out. "I told you how terrible that is for you!"

"Shut the door!" Sonia says. "I lost my lungs at the Roadhouse anyway!"

He clicks it closed, then snatches the e-cig out of her hands, holding it over her head. "These things will kill you!"

She shoots to her feet, a flush rising on her cheeks. "Meat will kill you, you big wanker!"

Skeeter glares at her, throws the e-cigarette to the ground, and then takes her in his arms and lays one on her. She hesitates, her arms bouncing; then she moans as her hands curl up around his neck—

And that's my cue.

I slip out of the closet and shut the door.

"Hello, darling," I say as I enter the staff lounge and sit down next to Ronan. The *darling* has stuck, and truthfully, I dig it. I brush my lips over his cheek.

He gives me a smile. "How was class?"

"Good." I unwrap my sandwich. "We're doing art or music for the poetry unit. I'm doing it along with them."

"Which one?" He puts his hand on my knee under the table, drawing circles there.

"'The Road Not Taken' by Robert Frost. I'm painting a forest with a forked road. I really love it."

"Ah, a poem about the choices we make," he says, a hesitant look on his face. "Good one."

"Hmm, yes." In class I'd realized the poem was a metaphor for us. A decision from him is coming, either to stay or to go.

My fingers toy with the star around my neck. There's no point in worrying about something that hasn't happened yet. Just like I told him, we're taking it one day at a time.

So why do I feel as if something awful is coming?

Chapter 24

Nova

Excitement fills the gym a few days later. The cheerleaders finish their dance routine to "Another One Bites the Dust," maroon-and-gold plaid skirts swishing as they run off the court. The crowd claps, standing on their feet and whooping. Several students hold up signs. **Go, Fight, Win, Bobcats!** Then **Free Lambert!**

Sabine sits on one of the bottom rows among students, her eyes trained on the entrance of the concession area, where I'm with the players and coaches.

Bruno adjusts his brown fedora. "Do I look lit, Ms. Morgan?"

"Of course. You all do!" I put my eyes on each of the players. There's about twenty of them dressed in suits, the seams loosened by Sabine and me and Sonia. Not everyone wanted to do the dance. Those players are waiting on the other side of the gym in their uniforms. They'll run out in the middle of the song and pump the crowd up.

"One minute till we go!" Caleb shouts as he stands next to the sound system.

Toby, Milo, and Bruno line up at the entrance.

I glance over, and Ronan is on his cell, his face animated as he talks to someone.

"Wait a second," I tell Caleb and turn to go to Ronan.

"He doesn't care about us," Melinda says as she slides in next to me. "He's itching to leave, and you know it. He's going to go somewhere better, and then you won't have your *darling* anymore."

You can't argue with a scorned woman or whatever she thinks she is, but I know how to handle her. Be direct. No mercy . . . "Fuck off, Melinda."

"So rude," she snips behind my back as I hurry off.

"Sounds good! I can't wait to see you." Ronan clicks off his cell and turns. "They ready?"

I study his face, wondering who he was talking to. I nod. "Yep."

I wave at Caleb to start the music.

We watch from the sideline under the basketball goal as the players swagger out on the court. They get into a line formation, then dance, shaking their butts and doing the lasso. In unison, they fall to the floor and do push-ups as the crowd cheers. They hop up, popping and doing the robot. Hats and sunglasses fly off and scatter on the floor. The end of the song approaches, and the suits burst open. Jackets and pants fly off and are swung around their heads, then tossed to the ground. The people in the stands jump to their feet as the guys dance the last part in their uniforms, then move to the stands, slapping hands.

"Bloody hell, they make a grown woman wanna be in high school again," Sonia says. "Oh, wait, we are!" She laughs and gives me a hug. "You did great, Nova."

"I didn't do much."

"Ah, but you're the one with the patience. Those guys adore you."

Warmth fills me.

A few feet away, Ronan and Principal Lancaster are in a deep discussion, their backs to us. They stride out farther in the concession area and look outside through the glass doors. My heart drops when I see several TV vans and reporters climbing up the steps to the gym, cameras aimed our direction.

I frown. I had them scheduled for five o'clock—and they were supposed to show up at the field house.

The players wrap up with the students and jog into the concession area, high-fiving and patting each other as they laugh.

Toby sees me and rushes over. "Where's Coach? The crowd is chanting his name . . ." He stops when he sees the people outside. "What the heck? I thought they were coming later."

I shake my head. "I don't know."

"Something must have happened," Toby says as Bruno and Milo join us.

I leave them to head to Ronan. He's frowning as he looks at his phone. "Why are they here?" I ask.

Principal Lancaster grimaces. "Apparently someone tipped them off that Coach might be leaving."

My forehead furrows. "How did they know we'd be in the gym?"

Principal Lancaster exhales. "We announced the pep rally online, so . . ." He lifts his shoulders and looks at Ronan. "Look. They're on school grounds uninvited. I can call the police or go out there myself and tell them to leave. It's up to you, Coach."

His lips tighten. "It doesn't matter. It got out. They're here, and I'll have to deal with it sooner or later. Reporters don't just disappear."

"What can I do?" I ask.

"Nothing. It's already been blasted online." He shows me an article, but I don't have time to read it before Toby is next to me.

"Coach? What do they want?"

Ronan flinches, then opens his mouth to reply, but nothing comes out. Unease is written all over his face. With a grimace, he strides away from us to the glass doors and steps outside.

Foreboding crawls over me as I follow him.

He can't face this alone.

Chapter 25

Ronan

A November breeze blows my hair, and I settle my Bobcats cap down on my head. Swallowing down unease, I approach the edge of the concrete ledge that leads down to the steps of the gym. I sweep my gaze over the myriad of reporters gathered at the bottom. At least five cameras are pointed at me, one of them ESPN.

The plan, months ago, had been to do an interview with local stations before we played Huddersfield, letting the guys get some camera time, maybe catch a few college scouts' eyes. But this isn't about my players; this is about me.

They rush forward, a local guy managing to push out ESPN. He shoves a microphone in my face, a gleam in his eyes. "Michael Collins here from WBBJ in Austin."

I nod at him, my face flat. "Hmm."

"Ronan, we received a tip you're on the short list for Stanford. Can you confirm if this is true?"

My jaw grinds as all eyes focus in on me. I hear shuffling sounds and throw a glance behind me as Nova and several players spill outside and gather around me. My shoulders tense as I adjust my stance. Whatever I say, it's going to be wrong. It's going to ripple through my team, eroding their trust, messing with their heads, which need to be straight for the game.

Michael steps closer. "Coach Dunbar, the quarterback coach from Stanford, has resigned, and Coach Hite confirmed you were on the short list. Is it true?"

"Yes," I mutter. So it was Hite who spilled . . . not a good way to start. Unless he wanted to force me to decide. Dick move.

A sharp inhale comes from a person next to me. Toby.

The reporter edges closer. "Are you aware that when the news was announced by Hite, the student body started a petition this morning to get you to the top of the list? So far, they have five thousand signatures."

I shake my head. "While I appreciate the support, I'm focusing on my team here."

Another reporter edges forward, a woman. "How will this affect the Bobcats? You have games coming up. Will you be here for those?"

"I plan on it. Next question," I snap.

"How will this affect your team's morale for tonight's game?" She's looking at Toby.

"My team is ready," I say on a growl. "And you aren't talking to my players. Not later either."

She eases back as the guy from ESPN finally nudges forward. There's a gloating expression on his face that gives me pause. His camera girl follows him as he points a mic in my face. "Hey, Ronan." He gives me a thin-lipped smile.

I narrow my eyes. "Keith. You're a long way from New York."

"We follow the news, and you are news. Good to see you back in the spotlight. How do you like living in small-town Texas?"

"I love it. The people, the players, the school. Next?"

He chuckles. "You're abrupt. Nothing new there."

I exhale. "Do you have a question, Keith?"

"Yeah." He leans in and looks at the camera. "Hello, from Keith Bridges. We're here in Blue Belle, Texas, a hot spot for talented high school football. Ronan Smith, former quarterback for the Pythons, is here with us. He's been coaching here for two seasons. Last year he took them to state, and this year they're hopefully going to finish the season undefeated. Isn't that right, Ronan?"

I nod.

Keith smiles at the camera. "Earlier today, Stanford announced him as being a contender as their quarterback coach, and this station also got another tip . . ."

I inhale, my eyes widening.

He looks at me. "Is it true you're slated as the next quarterback coach for the New York Pythons? I bet those Stanford people are going to be devastated"—he glances at the people around me—"as well as Blue Belle."

Breath whooshes out of me. How the fuck? My old coach called me this morning; then Tuck called before the pep rally.

My hands clench as I force a smile. "You're on private property without an invitation. Disperse, or the police will be alerted. Thank you."

"Ronan, just answer the question!" he calls, but I ignore him.

My players have walked off ahead of me, their shoulders stiff.

Skeeter eases in, his hands in his pockets. "That was a surprise." He watches the reporters pack up their gear. "Is it true?"

"It's true New York called me, yes."

"Ah, I see." He looks away from me, his jaw tense. "We've got practice. I'm gonna head out to the field house and get 'em started if you need a minute to figure out what you're gonna say."

"Skeeter, look, I'm sorry. I just found out about the New York offer. Stanford isn't going to happen. I just—"

But he's already striding away. My jaw flexes. Now I can add him to the list of people I've hurt.

I look at Nova.

She's wearing her cream leather skirt with a navy blouse, a Bobcats button pinned to it. Her hair is up in a high ponytail, accentuating her face, which is currently blank.

She picks up the necklace I gave her and runs it through her fingers. Her words are soft. "You said you'd be honest with me."

"It happened this morning. Reggie and Coach Hardy called me. Then Tuck. I didn't think anyone else knew, but . . ."

"We had lunch together."

I sigh. "Nova—"

She grimaces. "New York is the perfect place for you. It's your home."

It *was* my home. It's where my team is. Friends. Memories.

After I don't reply, she lets out a little sigh. "I bet your phones are ringing off the hook. What do you want me to say?"

"Tell them nothing."

"Got it. Just like you told me. See you in the office."

Then she's gone, headed back inside the gym.

I want to chase after her, but my ghosts from the past, the ones that still have their claws in me, hold me back.

Later, it's game time in the locker room, and I haven't had a chance to talk to my team. By the time I came to practice after the reporters showed up, the guys were already running plays on the field, and I needed time to think, so I left it alone, but now, there's no avoiding it.

Dread hits me as I take in their downcast faces.

Then Toby walks in.

"You're twenty minutes late," I say as he plops his duffel down on the bench. "The rest of the team is dressed out and ready to play."

He tugs out his clothes, then puts his back to me as he puts on his pads.

"Toby?"

The other players dart their gazes from me to him.

"You're the captain, Toby. Answer me."

He turns and lifts hard eyes up to me. "I'm still captain. Are you still our coach?"

Bruno grumbles under his breath, "Yeah, that's what I'm sayin'," then dips his head.

I rock on my heels, searching for the right words. I don't know if I have them.

Toby jostles around for his helmet and face mask, then shrugs. "My mom didn't feel well. I stayed with her as long as I could. Sorry."

Worry inches over me. "Do I need to send someone to check on her?"

"No."

"Are you sure? I can send one of the assistants or Lois—"

"No!" he calls, then takes a deep breath, his chest rising. "She's fine. It's the usual. It's nothing."

Once he's outfitted and sitting with the other players, I clear my throat and stand in the center of the room. My hands tap my leg. "All right. I know you have questions about what happened today after the pep rally."

Bruno sits with his legs spread, his eyes not meeting mine. Milo slumps over, cupping his face. Toby stands, his jaw tight. Skeeter glares down at his clipboard. Lois wipes at her face with a tissue.

A long exhale comes from me at their silence. "As you know . . . from earlier . . . I'm on the short list for Stanford, but that isn't going to happen, and I'm being considered for the Pythons. That's no reflection on you. We've come far together and—"

"Are you going to leave?" comes from Bruno.

I take off my hat and rake a hand through my hair. "It's a possibility."

"You've had two offers!" Toby snaps out.

"Right now, *you* are my team, and I'm standing right here." I sweep my gaze over them. "You're the heart of this town, not me. We've won every single game in the toughest district in Texas. Together. This team is going to state, and there's going to be a gold trophy in that case." I point to the shelves behind me, already lined with previous championships.

They look at me with lackluster eyes.

I pinch my nose, anxiousness rising as everything from earlier crashes into me. The shock and hurt I saw on my team's faces. How Nova walked away, her shoulders bent.

"It sucks, okay; it sucks! I can't give you an answer!" I declare as I put my hands on my hips. "That bullshit today wasn't meant to happen. You think I'm disloyal. You think I'm deserting you—go ahead; be angry!" I slam my fist into the palm of my other hand. "But remember the tape we've watched, the strategies we've worked on since summer camp. Think about each other. How close you've become. How the players on this team are family. We adjust. We pivot. We are Bobcats!"

A few heads lift and nod, murmuring under their breaths, "Yeah, yeah," but several don't. Bruno still looks sullen, and Toby won't look at me, his eyes fixed somewhere above my head.

Skeeter pumps his fist in the air. "All right, Bobcats! Who's with me? Huh? Huh? Win the heart, win everything!"

Their reply is half-hearted, and it cuts into my heart.

I heave out a breath and follow them out the door.

By the end of the third quarter, the score is twenty-eight to seventeen, and we're losing. I pace the sideline and run a hand through my hair, my cap gone since I tossed it on the ground earlier. My offense jogs off the field, shoulders slumped. On our last play, Toby threw an interception, his second, letting the Rams score again.

He jogs over to Skeeter—not me—and I walk over to him.

"Look at me, Toby."

He whips off his helmet and chews on his bottom lip so hard it looks painful.

"It's my fault," he grumbles as he rubs his face and stares at the ground. "They're beating me on the routes . . ."

"They've been studying. They know your habits. Listen to me."

It takes him a moment, but he finally looks at me.

"Okay, look, you're angry with me, yes?"

He nods tightly.

I sigh. "The best quarterbacks learn to have amnesia. Pretend today never happened, okay? For the team's sake."

"Not sure I can. I don't want you to leave."

I hear the pain in his young voice, and my hand goes to his shoulder, like it has a hundred times. "That's not the way I would have told you. You're important to me, you hear?"

He starts the lip chewing again.

"You are. I see myself in you, Toby. You have a big future ahead of you, and tonight is just the beginning."

He shrugs and looks away from me.

"Think about the day you saw those stuffed animals on our field. Remember your anger? Take that, and form it into determination. Huddersfield thinks they got one over on us. But we're stronger, smarter, meaner. I already know you're the most talented high school quarterback in Texas. Prove it to *them*."

He nods, his gaze narrowing on the other team across the field. *That's it. Focus.*

I pull the rest of the team in. "All right, we may be down, but we're not out. Defense, tighten up your lines. Their center took a hit earlier. Press him. He's not on his best game. Offense . . . we're gonna focus on the running game and some screens. Bruno, be ready for the ball. After that, downfield will open up. Everybody good?"

They nod.

"I need more enthusiasm, boys!" I lean into their huddle. "Whatever you think, whatever opinions you might have about me, leave it on the sidelines. Think back . . . those players snuck into our school and trashed our field. They made a mockery of our mascot. Don't you think it's payback time?"

"Yeah!" they call.

I clap. "Make it happen!"

They huddle, their arms around each other, chanting.

I glance up to the stands, my gaze searching for Nova, not seeing her. With a long exhale, I turn back to the field.

With thirty seconds left in the game, we're down by four points.

Our offense is on the Rams' fifty-yard line, and it's third down and ten. Toby catches the snap and drops back, looking for his receiver. Milo is covered; then Bruno misses a block. Toby scrambles, fake pumps the ball, and then tucks it under his arm and darts. I run down the field with him, waving my hands. Behind us, the crowd screams. He dodges a tackler, spins, and then hits the end zone. I bend over and clutch my stomach, then rear back up and pump my fists.

Bruno picks Toby up and twirls him around in the end zone. Milo and the rest of the offense join them. They do the lasso from the pep rally, and I wave them in before they get called for celebrating.

Our kicking team runs out and kicks the extra point, and we lead thirty-one to twenty-eight.

I gather the defense around me. "There's fifteen seconds left, and all they need is a field goal to tie. We can't let them score. Anything can happen. They can throw a Hail Mary, a hook and lateral, or just run for it." I pull out the note the Huddersfield guys left on our field and wave it around. "I've been carrying this around, waiting for the right time to show it. It says they're going to tear us apart piece by piece! It says we're losers! Are we going to let that happen?!"

They pass it around, faces darkening. "No!"

I slap their helmets. "Go kick their asses."

Their offense snaps the ball, and the quarterback throws a pass—which is intercepted by one of our linemen, a burly fellow who can't run but tackles like a pro. I bellow out a "Heck yeah!" as he blunders and stumbles through their offense, hops over a player, uses an arm to hold one back, and then slowly runs to the end zone. It's a dream come true.

Our sideline goes nuts, players and coaches jumping and screaming, faces red and sweaty as they cheer. After the field goal, the score flips to thirty-eight to twenty-eight.

The buzzer goes off, and fans, parents, and cheerleaders swarm the field. Milo picks up the Gatorade and dumps it over Skeeter. I laugh, standing back and taking it in. Sabine jumps into Toby's arms and kisses him. Sonia dashes on the field and runs straight to Skeeter, hugging him, then drying him off with one of the team towels.

My eyes search the field, loneliness creeping in when I don't see her.

"Great game, Coach," the opposing coach says and shakes my hand.

I nod and say the same. People run past me, shouts going up: "Go Bobcats!" and "All the way to state!" I keep my head down, victory and a sense of loss mixing inside of me.

A booming voice pulls my gaze up.

"Look at you. Big shot. Beat the fuck out of that team. My best goddamn friend in the whole world! He's a badass! That's what I'm talking about!" Tuck throws his arm around me and gives me a bear hug, then slaps me on the shoulder. "Texas football is legit. Fans are rabid! Some old lady mowed me down to get on the field! That game was"—he kisses his fingers—"chef's kiss, bro. Fucking fantastic!"

I grin. "It's good to see you!"

He preens and flips his hair. "I know."

"How was the flight?"

"Got here just before the game started. For real, Ronan, your players are a force." He smirks. "'Course, it helps that you're the best coach ever."

I smile broadly. "Come on. I want you to meet them. Don't be surprised if they ask for an autograph."

"This old injured dog?"

I chuckle.

He tosses an arm around me like he used to on the field. "Me and you, man. We're a team. Yo, I hope Dog remembers me. He tried to get in bed with me last time. I kinda want a pet, was thinking about something small, like a Chinese crested, sweet and cute, but if it pees my place up, I don't know—maybe I need a pet and a dog walker . . ." He continues to talk, and my eyes wander to the stands. Still no Nova.

Chapter 26

Nova

I stare at myself in the mirror. My lipstick is cherry red, but my eyes have shadows under them, and my face is pale. As I apply blush, I picture a BBHS without Ronan, and my hands set down the makeup and cling to the edge of the sink.

He's going to choose, and I already know which one makes the most sense—

My throat prickles with emotion I've been holding at bay for hours since the reporters showed up.

Gathering my things, I tug my Bobcats shirt down over my skinny jeans and walk out of the stadium restrooms. Sabine and I watched the game from the top row of the stadium in the shadows of one of the overhangs.

My heels click on the tile as I enter the field house. With most of the players dressed and gone, it feels strange and quiet after such a huge win. Most of the team has headed to Randy's Roadhouse for the party. Normally, I'd be gone, too, but I left my work satchel in Ronan's office and need to grab it. I waited until I thought he'd be gone.

I frown when I see that his door is partly open. I hear voices.

"Back to the Pythons. Coach Dixon seemed all right, but I guess he's worsened. He's a fine man, and I know you admire him. It sucks that he has cancer, but it's your chance . . ." The voice sounds familiar—I think it's Tuck. I saw him on the field talking to Ronan.

I can't hear Ronan's reply but catch bits and pieces of Tuck's words.

"The whole team is chanting your name. It will be great to have you back, man. You can stay with me or find your own place, whatever." Tuck pauses. "I imagine it's gonna be hard. Those kids . . . you took them far. What about Nova? You said it was getting real with . . ."

My heart thuds painfully as I inch closer to the door.

"Leaving with no entanglements. That was the plan," Ronan says with a ring of finality.

"You've got two victories, bro. Your win tonight and your win tomorrow in New York . . ." Tuck chuckles.

I need you . . .

I don't know the future . . .

Both of those are his truths.

I close my eyes, my chest rising. He never made a commitment. I was the one who put my heart on a platter. I knew him leaving was a possibility—I did, but I jumped off the cliff straight into the volcano.

I lean against the wall, gathering myself.

Sabine and Toby appear at the end of the hall, and I straighten up and hurry toward them. They dashed off earlier to grab a few posters to keep.

"Your face is wet," Sabine says. "Were you crying?"

I wipe at my face. I hadn't realized.

Toby frowns. "You okay, Ms. Morgan?"

"Right as rain," I reply to his earnest gaze.

"But were you crying?" Sabine insists.

"Just a little, but it's fine now. The game really got to me. You played amazing, Toby. I took tons of video for Bonnie. Let's go see her and show it to her," I say, anxious to get away from Ronan. My satchel can wait until Monday.

We grab take-out food, then head to Toby's house. We devour our food in the kitchen, then head to the den for Bonnie to watch Toby's big plays. I chat with her while Toby and Sabine sit side by side on the floor, her head on his shoulder, his hand playing with her hair. He leans down and kisses her cheek, then murmurs he loves her, and she says the same, then snuggles into his chest.

Later, we pull up at the house, and Darth Vader is still in my window. I wince, pulling my gaze off him. Sabine heads to her room, and I sit on the couch, with something on TV that I'm not watching. My head feels blank. A little numb. My phone is next to me. It's been blowing up with texts from Ronan since this afternoon. I never went to his office after the press conference. I stayed in my and Sonia's closet, my head churning with thoughts. He sent more texts before the game. I can't bring myself to reply.

Around eleven, I put Sparky's leash on him and head outside. We turn right, away from Ronan's house, and head to the front of the neighborhood. He prisses along but pauses to look at me a few times.

"I'm fine," I tell him.

He seems to narrow his gaze.

I blow out a breath. "I swear!"

He turns back, sees a small frog, pounces, and then eats it delicately.

Crickets resonate, still hanging on to the last bit of warm air in Texas. Next week is Thanksgiving, and I center my thoughts on which of Mama's dishes I'll make.

We walk past Caleb's house, make the turn at the stone entrance, and then start back. I'm almost to my house when I see a tall, broad form ahead of me, leaning against an oak tree in my yard.

My stomach pitches, my steps slowing.

I can't avoid him. Words need to be said.

I walk over to him, stopping a few feet away. Sparky rubs in between his legs, and I pull him back, then undo his leash and tell him to go to the porch. He licks his paw, gives me a sniff, and then prances up the steps and goes inside the cat door I put in.

Twisting the leash between my fingers, I take in Ronan. He's changed into Nike shorts, an old shirt, and sneakers. There's no hat, and his hair waves around in the light wind. His arms hang down his sides, an uncertain expression on his face.

"Hey," he says, his eyes searching mine. "Sabine said you went for a walk."

"Yes."

He straightens up off the tree and walks to me. "I wanted to tell you about the new offer, but school wasn't the right place—you were focused on the pep rally; then the reporters showed up . . ."

I nod. "I get it."

"The Stanford thing . . . I called Hite and took myself off their list. It never felt right."

"But New York does?"

His hand brushes at my hair, his fingers rubbing the strands between his fingers. "Their quarterback coach, Dixon, has terminal cancer. They kept how serious his diagnosis was under wraps. When I found out he was sick a while back, I assumed it was temporary, because that's what they told everyone. I didn't dream they'd come to me. I don't have any experience on that level and . . ." He drops his hand and rubs the back of his neck. "You probably don't want to hear all this."

"They'll need you right away." I know how football works. I also realize that on the NFL level, he'll have to devote his life to it, especially since he doesn't have experience. He won't have time for a relationship with a girl in Texas.

"I'm flying out tomorrow to meet them. Nova . . ." His fingers skim down my arm. "This isn't easy for me—"

"You wanted no entanglements. That was the plan, right?"

He tenses. "That was the plan, yes, but that's not what happened."

"You told me exactly how this would end. With you leaving."

He takes me in his arms, his movements slow, his eyes soft under the glow of the streetlights. "You have every right to be angry."

The smell of him lulls me, and I press my face into his chest, my hands clenching his shirt. "Yes," I say shakily. "I promised myself I wouldn't be, that I knew this was coming eventually, but I just thought . . ." That a job he wanted wouldn't come for a while? That he'd fall just as madly in love with me as I am with him?

My arms go around his waist, and we lean against each other.

I close my eyes and think about the good things, how he left me a rose on my first day at school, how he took care of me when I was sick. He's a wonderful, kind man, and I'm losing him.

I place my cheek against his chest, and he rests his chin on my head. "I never planned on you. I never imagined this could be . . ." He stops, his voice unsteady.

"What?"

His hands tighten around me. "I'm terrified of so many things. Leaving you. Not leaving you. I've dragged you into this relationship, and I'm hurting you—the last thing I want to do."

I nod.

"Nova, look at me."

I lift my face to his, and our eyes cling.

"You said you were half in love with me that night in New York—but I was half in love with you too. The fierce way you wore that outfit, how you didn't care what anyone else thought, the way we clung to each other . . . I was drunk—I was, okay, I know—but you had so much joy. Maybe, I don't know, you gave me back some of mine or at least some hope that I could get my life back. In an indirect way, you're the reason I ended up in Blue Belle. How's that for fate?" Not waiting for a reply, he presses his forehead to mine. "I swore I wouldn't ask, that I wouldn't put you in this kind of situation, but would you consider coming with me? You and Sabine."

My eyes fill with water. I've thought about this since the moment I found out. If he'd ask me—and what I'd say. "This is her home. I followed Andrew to UT. I almost followed him again the second time. Following a man? It's not who I am anymore. I never planned on ending up here, but . . ." I pull away and clasp his hands, threading our fingers together. My eyes linger over Mama's rosebushes, Lois's apple trees, the home where I grew up. I think about Sabine, about singing songs with her in our kitchen, about Caleb and Toby and Bruno and Milo. I think about Sonia and Skeeter and Lois. They've become my family. The longer I stay, the deeper those threads will grow, bloom, and then flourish.

Mama gave me roots and wings to believe I could be anything, live anywhere, but Blue Belle is where my heart resides. With Sabine next to me. Her roots are here, and I want to give her those same wings. To watch her fly.

I found my glow. It's Ronan. But it's also home.

He closes his eyes. "Nova. I lov—"

I put my finger to his lips. "I don't think I can take those words. Just kiss me, and say what you came to do."

"Nova—" His face falls. "I—I can't say goodbye."

My throat thickens, and I squeeze his hands. "Listen. Find your glow. Discover all the possibilities. Reach for the stars. No one deserves this more. You're a hell of a coach. You care about those kids and what happens to them. You have integrity. Loyalty. Perseverance. There was a reason you got the Heisman. You are the best quarterback I've ever seen. And this? This is your second chance to be close to what you had. I want the world for you. I want everything for you, Ronan: goodness and love and success and all the football achievements and accolades . . ." My voice breaks, and I tug it back. "You deserve your dream job. You do. Take it. Grab it and be happy."

"God. Nova . . ." He closes his eyes. "Please. You're killing me."

I get on tiptoe and press my mouth to his. He parts his lips and clutches me tight, his arms picking me up. I hang on to his shirt, and the kiss hardens, desperation mingling as we yearn for more.

I pull away, gasping for air.

His chest heaves, his gaze bright with unshed emotion. "Nova . . ."

"Go get 'em, darling." I push out a watery smile, tug myself out of his arms, and then go inside the house.

Chapter 27

Ronan

I step off the helicopter, and a chauffeur ushers me and Tuck to a waiting black SUV. The driver asks if everything is to my satisfaction, and I tell him yes before we pull out of the heliport in lower Manhattan and head toward the offices of the owner of the Pythons, Damon Armitage II.

The morning started with Damon's personal jet picking us up at a private airstrip in Austin. We landed at JFK Airport, then hopped in the helicopter. All of this was intended to impress me. I smooth down my blue slacks and white dress shirt. My hands tug at my silver tie.

"You look a little pale," Tuck says as he settles into the SUV. He picks up one of the bottled waters and hands it to me. "It was a bumpy ride."

I set it down and scrub my face. "I didn't sleep last night."

"Adrenaline from the game. I get it." His hazel eyes study me.

"Yeah, right." I lean back on the seat.

I couldn't sleep because of her.

Her words. That goodbye kiss.

I stare out the window at the financial district. People walk up and down New York, coming and going, heads down as they move from one place to another. The bustle, tall buildings, and honking horns are an adjustment. I've visited Tuck several times in the off months, but this time, the city feels busier, more intense. I think about my hammock in Blue Belle.

We're ushered out of the SUV and greeted by Damon's personal assistant. I leave Tuck and get on the elevator with the PA and head to his office.

He's not there when I arrive, so I pace around the room, my heart thudding, a feeling of surrealness inching in. For two seasons, my life revolved around kids in Texas, trying to help them be champions. I came up with our motto, *Win the heart, win everything,* and those words sit like a lump of cement in my gut.

What's Toby doing right now? Is he working a shift at the bookstore? Is he worrying about his mom? Dammit, I should have checked on her last night . . .

Bruno . . . he'll be planning a date with his hot cheerleader girlfriend.

Milo . . . he'll be at Lois's playing video games.

Skeeter? He'll step up as head coach and take the Bobcats to state.

Maybe Andrew will apply and get the job next year.

And Nova . . .

My heart splinters. I shut my eyes and force myself to push the images of her away.

Blowing out a breath, I make my way to the trophy case on the right side of the room.

"If all this works out, I'll need another case," says a raspy voice behind me.

I turn to find Damon Armitage II, the owner; Coach Bruce Hardy, the head coach of the Pythons; and my agent, Reggie.

Leaning on a gold-tipped cane with a snake on it, Damon walks behind his desk, then sits. Wearing a black tailored suit, complete with an ascot and a boutonniere, he's in his seventies, rich as fuck, and known as an eccentric firebrand. "I'm glad you were able to fly in, Ronan. We could have chatted over the phone, but then I wanted you in the room." He waves his arms around at his spacious office. "Nothing beats seeing a man face to face and getting the measure of him."

"True," I say.

"We all met in the elevator," Reggie says with a nod. "Good to see you, Ronan!" Around forty, he's dressed in a slick suit, his dark hair clipped around the ears.

"Same," I say, and the four of us shake hands.

Coach Hardy grins at me. A tall man in his late fifties, he sat by my bed in the hospital for three days after the wreck. He flew my mom from Chicago to New York on the team jet the night it happened. When I woke up the first time in my room, the two of them were there, waiting.

We make small talk, catching up, then chat about his new quarterback, Lucas Pine, a fresh kid from Iowa. He's having trouble with the transition from college to professional, missing snaps and play calls.

"How's Coach Dixon doing?" I ask a few minutes later. "Tuck said he was flying to Houston for treatment."

Coach Hardy sticks his hands in his khakis. "You probably passed him somewhere over Indiana. We're going to miss him on the field. A hell of a man and coach."

Reggie takes a seat. "It's a tragedy." He looks at me. "But it gives Ronan a chance to step in. I was thinking we'd start with what Dixon was making—"

"Hold on," I say sharply as I slide into a leather chair. "I appreciate the urgency, but there hasn't been an offer made or one accepted. This was just a discussion."

Reggie starts, glaring at me.

Damon frowns, straightening his ascot. "Don't be coy, Ronan. The salary will be there. We know you, your talent, your work ethic. We've seen what you did with that team in Texas. You're our pick, hell, before

Stanford snatches you up!" He slaps the desk and lets out a wheezy laugh.

I lean back and smile, pretending to be calm when I'm anything but. My stomach just won't settle. "I called Hite and turned him down."

Reggie nods, and the other two smile, clearly happy.

I clear my throat and steeple my hands. "The thing is I've made commitments, Damon. The high school playoffs start December first. Will this wait until afterwards?"

He picks up the pipe on his desk and lights it. "No. Sorry. We want to announce Dixon's leaving the team, as well as his replacement, on Monday. Our staff's covering the game Sunday, but we've lost two already, ones we should have won."

"I'm aware," I say. "I see the mistakes, the bad calls."

He stares at me with beady eyes. "Why don't you and Coach Hardy catch up, go meet the staff, maybe some players, then take a walk in that stadium." He puffs on his pipe. "You've got memories there. Hell, I get a hard-on every time I sit in the owner's box. Not bad for an old man, eh?" He slaps his desk and lets out another laugh, then sobers, considering me, raking over my face and posture. "All right, all right . . . I hear you; I do. You've spent some time in Texas and need some time to mull this over."

"Yes."

He nods decisively. "I'll be in touch with Reggie about the money by the end of the day; then I'll need your answer by tomorrow. All right, boys, I have a phone call with a senator. So . . ." He waves his hands for us to leave.

Reggie, Coach Hardy, and I walk out to the foyer. Coach heads to the restroom, and Reggie pulls me to the side, a furrow between his brows.

"Your part is to win the interview," he says. "You're acting like you're having second thoughts."

"That was barely an interview. He wanted my ass in New York so I'd feel nostalgic."

He shakes his head. "Why are you hesitating? This job is a no-brainer. It cuts years off your plan to be in the league."

True. Scoring an NFL position wasn't something I expected so soon. I love my old team. I love the staff I used to work with. This *is* my dream job.

I stare out the window. So why does it feel wrong?

◆ ◆ ◆

Later that day, it's dark when the cab drops me off in front of Tuck's building. They wanted to put me up at a hotel, but I chose to stay with him. Earlier, he left us at Damon's office and went to his physical therapy appointment.

Wearing joggers and an old shirt, he's waiting for me in the den, Chinese takeout already ordered, a drink poured in a glass. He hands it to me.

We walk in the kitchen, where he grabs a cheese-and-fruit plate out of the fridge and sets it on the island like it's the Hope Diamond. He gives me a smile, batting his lashes. "How was your day, dear?"

"You'd make a great wife, Tuck, but I prefer blondes."

He flips me off while sticking a cube of cheddar between his lips. He chews and swallows it down. "So? Give me the deets."

I nod and sit on a stool. "It was good. Met the new guys. They seem great. Jasper has a great arm. I like his enthusiasm. I caught up with some people on staff and a few players. The stadium, ah, it was fucking great to walk inside. I closed my eyes and pictured a hundred thousand fans on their feet for us . . ."

"Like coming home?"

I pause, glancing around at his modern apartment, the one I shared with him for years. The gray leather couches. The expensive, fancy Swedish swivel chairs he insisted we had to buy. The mirror coffee table that broke once when one of his girlfriends danced on top of it. (He ordered another one.) The bright yellow painted on one wall, black on the other. My eyes end on the floor-to-ceiling windows.

The curtains are spread, and the view of Manhattan twinkles like stars in the distance.

Stars.

Nova.

I take a steadying breath, feeling the loss of her like an uppercut to the face. It's Saturday, and we could be hanging out, playing pool or darts, watching a movie, watching football . . . I never showed her my comic book collection. My lips twitch. She'd fall over laughing. Then there's the Matchbox cars and video arcade machines. I wonder if she likes *Ms. Pac-Man*—

"Ronan?"

I look up. "Yeah, man, it felt like home. It was awesome."

"Hmm, I see." There's a question in his tone, but the doorbell rings, and he leaves to grab our food.

Later, after we've eaten, I clean up the mess while he tells me about his ankle, his therapist, the new neighbor who plays music too loud, his new yoga class . . .

He lets out a breath. "All right, then. I've told you everything. Whew. What should we do tonight? There's a new club I want to hit—"

"You can't dance on that ankle." I toss a dish towel over the faucet to dry.

"No, but I can talk to pretty girls."

Several moments tick by as we lean in over the island.

"Well? Hot chicks or stay at home?"

"Let's take a ride somewhere," I say, easing up.

He nods, not asking me where. He already knows.

He grabs keys from a drawer and dangles them. "Ferrari or Maserati?"

I roll my eyes. "You got a new sports car?"

"Meh. Got rid of the Escalade."

A few minutes later, we back out of his garage in his silver Ferrari. He lets the car idle at the exit. "Connecticut, I presume?"

"Yeah."

He pulls out on the road and points the car away from the city.

I gaze out the window at the passing buildings. I roll my neck. This entire day I've been unsettled, a pricking sensation eating at my insides. It's fear, that I'm fucking something up, but I don't know how to stop it.

"You're quiet. Whatcha thinking?" Tuck asks a few minutes later, glancing over at me.

I smirk ruefully. "That you're my best goddamn friend in the whole world. I might not be where I am today if it wasn't for you. You got me dry. You sent me Leia. Like a boss. You bought an outfit and found the perfect girl. Fuck. I love you, man."

I hear him sniff. "Asshole. Why are you making me cry like a girl?"

I huff out a laugh. "You're almost a girl anyway."

It's close to ten by the time we pull into the landscaped and well-lit memorial garden. Tuck drives through the park, around the curves and hairpin turns. We stop at the bottom of a hill, park, and get out. He leans against the car and crosses his legs. "Take your time, bro."

I nod and walk to Whitney's grave. It's set next to her grandparents', a gray stone carved into a heart that ends in a flat stone on the bottom. Her parents picked it out, and I feel like she would have loved it. I sit down next to it and stare at her name, the date she was born. It's been over two years since I visited. In the beginning, it was a lot, sometimes with Tuck, sometimes without. It usually involved a bottle of whiskey.

The last time I came was the day after the Mercer Hotel.

I settle my hands on the stone. Is it possible to have two (or more) loves in a lifetime? Does fate select your possibilities, and if the stars are aligned, you meet them? Is it possible to love them differently?

Whitney was the first girl I let into my heart. Our love bloomed into a gentle thing, sweet and uncomplicated. I planned a happy life with her. Then watched her die.

Nova. Jesus. I'm in deep with her. I love who she is. How strong. How sure she is of her feelings for me. How she treats others. How she's devoted to Sabine. How she puts up with Lois. How her accent thickens when she's pissed. Her hair. Her smile. Her damn cat. Her spunk. Her old cowboy boots. Her words about living a meaningful life, and fuck me, I miss her.

I glance up at the night sky, stars gleaming. I swallow thickly. Whitney's up there in heaven, scowling and huffy. I bet she has her little round glasses on, the ones I said made her look like a professor. She's pointing her finger at me, telling me I'm a fool, that I need to let go and live my life.

I exhale. My gut knows that to feel alive, to taste what life has to offer, I must conquer my fear of losing people and letting them down. I need to loosen the guilt that burdens me. Fear and guilt have built a fortress in my heart, the stones laid with anguish and pain. It's whispered to me that it's safer to just skim through life, lurking in the dark, never living in the light.

But . . .

Now I have another chance, and I'm too scared to reach out and grasp it.

Nova called Andrew a coward.

I bend my head, unable to look at the stars.

I'm. The. Fucking. Coward.

Chapter 28

Nova

On Monday morning, I park the Caddy in the school parking lot. Sabine and I head up the sidewalk and step inside. It feels like any other day. Teachers arriving. Kids milling around the hall, leaning against lockers, and chatting. Spirits seem high, despite the absence of Ronan.

I wonder where he is, if he woke up with the same sense of loss I did. I touch my hair as I catch my reflection in one of the lockers. It's clean, but I let it dry on its own last night. Untamed, it hangs around my face in chunks. Sure, I brushed it, but it's unruly. I prefer to wear it straight with a flat iron. Maybe I should put it up in a messy bun—

"Nova?"

I stop, blinking. "Yeah?"

Sabine cocks her head. "I've been talking to you about New Zealand. You're just staring off into space."

I ease out of the way of a passing student. "I do that sometimes."

"You did it all day yesterday."

I wince. "Sorry. I love New Zealand. Isn't that the place with the caves lit by worms?"

"Correct. Waitomo Caves. That glowworm species is only in New Zealand. People take boat rides to see them."

"I hear the beaches are amazing too. We could check out the caves, then scuba dive?"

"We'd need classes for scuba." She points at my black silk blouse. "You didn't button it right."

I look down at the pearl buttons. Dammit. I skipped one. I quickly fix it, brush down my slightly wrinkled red skirt, and then smile at her. "How do I look?"

"Sad. Messy. Kind of out of it."

I make a fist and pump it. "Just the look I was going for."

"Funny. I'm going to find Toby." She pauses. "If you need me, you know where my classes are. Pull me out, and we can talk or go home. We can hang out, and I'll sing 'Little Sparrow' for you."

My heart swells. "Go find him. I'm great. Or I will be. It just takes a minute to recalibrate."

She nods, and I head to the lounge. I don't see anyone I want to talk to, so I grab my coffee and leave.

"Morning, Ms. Morgan," comes from a few students who've come early, and I wave as I walk to my desk. I get ready, pulling my canvas off the wall and propping it on an easel so the kids can see it. It's a blurred landscape painted in shades of gray, brown, and green. In the center is a lone unisex figure, standing at the fork of two narrow roads. A forest of sparse pine trees lines the paths. I wince. It's kind of dark for me.

"I like it," Caleb says. "It makes you think."

"Thanks! What did you pick for the assignment?"

"I compared Emily Dickinson's 'Because I could not stop for Death' to Green Day's 'Wake Me Up When September Ends.' It's a lot of death and stuff, but . . ." He waves a typed paper at me. "I liked it. Pretty cool. You're not a terrible teacher at all." He blushes. "Um, I don't think that came out right."

"It's fine," I say with a smile, then pause. "Hey, I was wondering if you and your grandmother wanted to come over for Thanksgiving.

Toby and his mom are coming, and we'd love to have you guys too." It goes unsaid that I know how hard this first holiday will be for him.

"Ah, yeah, I'll check with her." He turns to leave but turns back. "Um, thanks, you know, for everything . . ." He trails off, and I think I know what he means. Just for showing up at his house. Everyone needs to know that someone cares.

"Just no Dairy Queen, right?" I give him a thumbs-up.

"Yeah." He laughs as he takes his seat.

By the time my classes are over and lunch rolls around, I'm less fuzzy but tired from pretending. I said the right things in class. I took up homework and gave assignments.

I'm on autopilot. Maybe the kids know. I noticed the questioning, almost careful looks they sent me.

I try to shake it off as I walk to the vaping closet, but Sonia and Skeeter stand in the back, fingers laced together as they kiss.

I exit quickly, then pass the lounge, my silver stilettos clicking.

I do not want to see Melinda's "I told you so" face.

Remembering that my satchel is in the field house, I focus on getting there. That's it. It will be nice and quiet, and I can gather myself before Skeeter and the players show up.

With hands that slightly shake, I put the key in the lock and open his door. The phone is eerily silent. I glance around for my satchel but don't see it. Frowning, I ease into the closet.

Once there, oh fuck, I'm lost.

The entire space smells like him.

I touch his dress shirts, sliding my fingers over the fabric, then move to the practice polos. I go back through them, picking my favorites, taking shirts off the hangers, and then tossing them on the floor. I find the maroon shirt he wore Friday night on the table. I rub it through my hands as I picture him running down the sideline, yelling for his team.

He is magnificent. A king.

A beast.

A sexy, beautiful lover.

Generous. Funny. Crazy smart.

I want him to be happy. I do, I do, but . . .

My chest hurts, and I wonder if it's possible for a heart to break for real. A pained sound comes from my throat, and I plop down to the floor among his shirts. I lie back on top of them, arms spread, my vision blurring with wetness.

The fog in my head, the exhaustion. Depression. That's what this is. It's okay. Totally fine. I'll get over it. Right?

I pick up his pale-blue dress shirt, the one that matches his eyes, and push my face into it, inhaling a deep breath. God. I've lost it. This level of hurt can't be normal—

The office door creaks open, and I jerk up to sitting, swiping my face as I wonder who's here.

"Nova?"

My breath hitches. "Ronan?"

"Are you in the closet?"

I stumble up, wobbling on my heels. "Don't come in here!"

He opens the door and blinks at me as I cling to the table. God, he looks amazing—okay, maybe a little tired and haggard. There're shadows under his eyes, and his hair is everywhere, messy pretty, accentuating his sharp jawline.

"What are you doing here?" My eyes eat him up, from the deep-blue shirt to his snug gray slacks.

I glance down. My blouse became untucked on the floor, my skirt is askew, and my hair spills out of my rubber band.

He steps inside. "Are you rolling around in my clothes?"

"No. Yes. For a second. Low blood sugar probably."

His lips twitch.

"Don't you say a word! I was just . . ." I sigh. "Sniffing shirts and plotting which ones to steal."

"I'd like to see you wearing them."

My hands clench. "You haven't called or texted or—"

He comes forward and sweeps me up into his arms, bridal-style.

I squeal. "What are you doing?"

His eyes capture mine. "I missed you."

My lips tremble. "I didn't miss you."

"Liar. I've been looking for you. The lounge, the closets, your room . . ."

"I wanted to be alone."

"With my shirts?"

I exhale, trying to ignore him, but it's hard with the adoring looks he's giving me.

Without letting me down, he strides out of the closet, somehow manages to lock the office door, and then sits down on a small couch.

I wiggle and rearrange myself, straddling him near his knees, not caring that my skirt is up to my hips.

He lets out a long exhale. "We need to talk. First, I turned down the job."

My mouth parts, and I slap him on the arm. "What? Why? That was what you wanted!"

A wry expression crosses his face. "A person can want something at one point in their life, then want something entirely different later, especially after they've realized what's important."

My heart flies, hope fluttering inside me that he's not leaving, but . . . "Use real words."

He chuckles as his fingers graze over my cheek and down to my throat. His hand rests at the base of my neck. "Where's my necklace?"

I sniff. "I forgot it this morning."

"I'm gone for two and a half days, and you're already moving on? I can't ever leave you alone again." His hand goes around my nape, and he pulls me to him and kisses me hard. I gasp and cling to his shoulders, devouring his taste, the feel of his lips. He's an invader, delving deep, his fingers digging into my scalp. We end with smaller, gentler kisses, soft brushes over and over . . .

Our breaths mingle when we part.

He holds my face and peers deep into my eyes. "I. Love. You. With everything inside me. I love your . . ." His voice thickens. "Wow. I had this whole speech planned out, but it's up in smoke."

"Do continue."

He brushes his fingers over my swollen lips. "Princess, when I love someone, it's with my soul. It's full commitment. It's a relationship that will grow, evolve, and change to fit us. I won't ever stop trying to be the best man I can be. I won't give up on us, through thick and thin."

"Is that why you said no to the job?"

"It affected it, yes. As soon as I left Texas, something wasn't right. I wanted you. I missed Lois and Skeeter. I wanted my team. I wanted to be celebrating with them at Randy's Roadhouse. Do I want to coach in the NFL someday? Maybe. Would I like it to be the Pythons? Sure. They're a great franchise, and New York was my home—in a different life. The truth is I'm not ready."

I trace his scar. "You can do anything you want. I believe in you."

He smiles. "I need more experience; that's for sure. I don't know everything I need to know right now about coaching. I need more trophies and time with the Bobcats. More talks with you. If I took that job, it would take over my life. Life is too damn short to be lonely, Nova. It's too short to give up on having something real with the one person I love."

I sigh. "Oh."

"My gut knew New York wasn't the right choice." He pauses and cups my face. "I knew exactly which road to take, and it was back to you, but I had to get past my fear of losing you, of letting you down . . ."

"Did you?"

He hugs me close to his chest, his hand running down my hair. "Honestly, I may never stop being overly cautious or a nervous Nellie about some things, but we can deal with it as it comes. I want love. It's a gift. My heart is yours. You took a sledgehammer and beat the shit out of it."

I pump my fist. "Score."

He bites his bottom lip, a strange expression on his face.

"What?" I ask.

"So . . . I was on the plane, thinking about how to tell you all this, and I had this idea of getting on the intercom, maybe playing my guitar and singing 'Jolene'; then I realized there's a lunch lady named Jolene and I can't sing. Plus, it felt cheesy—"

"Totally. Dorkish. Downright stupidly romantic—"

"Do you want me to get on the intercom and tell the whole school how I'm going to be your man until the end of time?"

I swipe away a tear. "No. We'd be *those* ridiculous people I roll my eyes at."

He laughs softly. "Ah, then how about I sing 'Say You Won't Let Go' now? I've been working on it. There's no guitar, but . . ."

My heart soars as he sings the words softly, a song about a guy who meets a girl at a party—yes, there's alcohol involved. The years pass, and he's waiting for her to see him as he dreams of them growing old together.

He finishes the song. "I'm sorry I was a selfish dick from the moment we met."

"I'm sorry I sneered at your necklace this morning, then rolled around in your shirts, then slapped your arm."

He chuckles, then sobers, his eyes glinting with emotion. "My glow is not in New York, Nova. It's right here with you. The team is extra. I've never loved someone like this."

The enormity of his words settles over me, and I kiss him tenderly, then graze my lips over his scarred cheek to whisper in his ear. "Same, darling."

We get sidetracked, our hands tracing each other, seeking solace from the days we spent wondering what the future held.

I lean back. "Have you told the players?"

"Principal Lancaster herded me in the office when I walked in. He announced it on the intercom: 'Coach Smith turned down the Pythons to stay at Blue Belle.' I could hear the cheers from the office. I guess you didn't hear it because you were in the closet."

"I was depressed."

"Poor girl . . ." He brushes his fingers over my breasts, caressing my nipples through my blouse.

I ease out of his lap.

He grunts. "What are you doing?"

I unbutton my shirt and toss it off, exposing my black velvet bra. I unzip my skirt and kick it off. My shoes fell off earlier when he picked me up.

His chest rises as he watches me. "Is this a sex game? We only have about fifteen minutes before everyone gets here . . ."

"This won't take long." I sashay back, sit on top of him, and swivel my hips. "Would you like a lap dance, sir?"

"How much?"

He catches on quick.

"Twenty for the dance, fifty for a blowie, a hundred if you want to fuck, sir."

"I have two hundred bucks in my wallet. Also, can you always call me *sir*?" He runs his nose up my neck, breathing deep.

My hips rub slow circles against the bulge in his slacks. "Sir, two hundred gets you dinner later. Definitely a walk with my cat," I say as he unsnaps my bra, then throws it over his head.

A minute later, his pants are off and he's thrusting inside me.

My hands tangle in his hair as emotion ripples over me. "I love you," I gasp out.

He presses his forehead against mine. "My beauty. We're gonna have the world."

Chapter 29

Ronan

"You need more butter, Tuck. Southern women use a lot of butter, dear. It's why those city girls are so skinny. They don't get enough fat in their diet," Lois explains as he stirs potatoes in a big bowl. He's wearing one of Nova's aprons, just like I am. His has pumpkins on it; mine has squirrels eating acorns.

Lois then goes into a spiel about how he needs to work on his running game.

It's Thanksgiving at Nova's. I've already called my mom and sisters and checked in with them. Hopefully, I'll see them after we've finished the playoff games for state.

Nova stops chopping celery to peer inside Tuck's bowl. She sticks her finger inside, then puts it in her mouth. She holds back a gag. "Did you put milk in it? No wonder it's hard to stir!"

Tuck flashes a grin, then jogs to the fridge and grabs the milk. "Oops. Guess I should read this recipe better."

Nova puts her hands on her hips. "Don't be a slacker, Tuck."

"Where's that jelly recipe?" Lois asks as she flips the pages of the sacred cookbook.

Nova scoffs and curls her lips. "I took it out and locked it up, Lois. I'll be making Mama's jelly this year for the fair."

Lois hisses. "You wouldn't."

Nova grins. "I might."

Sabine comes in from the den, a serious expression on her face as she contemplates Tuck's form in the art of mashing potatoes. She walks around him carefully. "I thought NFL players were strong. The potatoes are chunky. I like my potatoes smooth." She looks at Nova. "What's wrong with him? Why isn't he using the mixer?"

"There's a mixer?" Tuck stops and exclaims, panting slightly. He wipes his face, and a piece of potato plops on the floor. "Don't tell me I've done all this for nothing!"

Lois elbows him. "The mixer is broken."

Nova stifles a laugh. "Right."

Bonnie giggles as she makes a chocolate pie.

Tuck cocks a hip. "Oh, I get it—be mean to the new guy. Y'all are pulling one over on me, and here I was thinking Texas women were sweet. Didn't I help Ronan deep-fry the turkey? Didn't I stay up all night worried about what you guys would think of me? Okay, that really didn't happen, but for real . . . where's this mixer at?"

"I think they just wanted to see how you moved, Tuck." Toby chuckles from the table, where he's been put in charge of making squash casserole. He's taking it seriously, carefully slicing the squash, kind of like me as I break apart corn bread in a pan for the dressing.

Nova wraps a boa around Tuck's neck, as an apology, maybe, then hands him a mixer she grabbed from the pantry. "Have you ever handled one of these?"

"Never," he says seriously. "But I love toys. How fast does it go, and can I have fun with it?"

She gives him her teacher look. "Start on low, and work your way up to blend. And don't get potatoes on my walls."

"Yes, ma'am," he says as he fluffs his boa. "Tuck's famous mashed potatoes coming up!"

I laugh under my breath. Two peas in a pod, they are, and they haven't shut up since he showed up last night at my house. First, he wanted a minute-by-minute recounting of the night she'd burst into my birthday party; then she wanted a detailed list of every model I'd ever dated. I'm pretty sure she took notes.

I smile at no one, realizing suddenly that my best friend and Nova are going to be tight, and it's the best feeling in the world.

"Are they always like this?" Tuck rolls his eyes at me, indicating Nova and Lois as they swing their hips to a pop song while Sabine sings the lyrics.

I nod. "Pretty much."

Sparky darts in and runs in and out of Tuck's legs, meowing, then laps at the piece of potato on the floor. Tuck glances down at him and, under his breath, says to me, "That cat is freaking messed up, man. How can you walk it? It's ridiculous looking."

I walked Sparky *and* Dog at the same time this morning when we arrived at Nova's. She was busy prepping and needed the help, and a gut instinct just told me to try and see what happened if I got them together. Sparky and Dog took one look at each other, shrugged, and trotted down the sidewalk, ready for their business.

"Sparky's a Donskoy of Russian heritage. They're quite expressive without hair," I say as corn bread gets under my fingernails. "I owe Nova a new cat, actually. I'm thinking Christmas."

Nova overhears, gives me a look, and then throws back her head and laughs.

Sonia and Skeeter arrive with a broccoli dish, making us hoot at Skeeter, who doesn't think it's funny; then Caleb and his grandmother bring a pecan pie.

Two hours later, a pan of yeast rolls is burned—my fault—but no one cares. Everything else is beautiful. Nova and I put the leaf in her dining room table and set it with her mom's rose-patterned dishes. She sits at the head, with me next to her and Sabine on the other side.

I look at them both, feeling that familiar happy sensation that's been going on since I drove back into Blue Belle.

Nova is mine, and the relief is so acute that my throat clogs. If I had chosen the Pythons, I would have regretted it for the rest of my life. I lost my heart in New York, but I found it in Texas.

Visiting Whitney's grave was a cleansing for me, a rebirth into possibilities. Life is too short to hold back, to not let love in, to not make real commitments, and sometimes you must trust that everything is going to be okay. My spark is back, my hope, and my joy. All it takes is a little faith, something I lost along the way.

This town, the people, my team—I want to give them my heart. Like Nova, I want to plant roots, grow them deep, and see what happens.

"I'm thankful that Coach stayed. He's the best coach and man I know. I'm glad my mom is with me today," Toby says quietly as we take turns going around the table talking about things we're grateful for.

"For hot girls who adore me," Tuck declares, then sobers. "Seriously, though . . ." He shoots me a look, then grins. "I'm just glad that I can say I fixed these two lovebirds up. Who's the man? I am."

Sabine blinks. "You are amazingly conceited."

He tips his glass. "Thank you, my dear, and my mashed potatoes *are* smooth, so . . ." He lifts his brows.

She smirks. "Thanks?"

"That's it. Just go with it." He clinks their glasses together.

"I am," Sabine says dryly.

I huff out a laugh because she sounded *exactly* like Nova.

Lois blinks away the tears in her eyes. She's eating with us, then heading to her daughter's house for their meal this evening. "For me, I'm just happy to have friends who love football as much as I do."

Skeeter clears his throat and stands. He glances at me, then Sonia. A long sigh comes from him. "Well, it's a toss-up between having Ronan back as coach and hooking up with Sonia—"

She straightens in her seat, her face flushing. "We haven't 'hooked up'!"

He rolls his eyes. "Right, right, I know—we're dating; I just meant we reconnected after knowing-each-other-in-high-school kind of thing . . ."

Caleb says he's grateful for his grandmother, and she says the same about him. Bonnie murmurs that she's thankful for her son, and Sonia says she's grateful for new beginnings—and we all know what she means.

Sabine clears her throat. "When my mama died, it was the worst day of my life, and the only person who could make that better is sitting next to me. My sister. She is the best person I know. That's all." She stares down at her plate, and I see Nova taking her hand and squeezing it under the table.

I stand. "I've told my team if you win the heart, you win everything, but I'm not sure I truly understood it until now." My gaze lands on Nova. "I do now, and I'm ready for the rest."

Lois sighs, dabbing at her eyes.

"And we're going to win state!" I declare, and the group whoops in agreement.

Nova raises her tea glass in a toast, a mist in her eyes as she sweeps them over the table. "If you'd asked me a year ago whether I'd be living in Blue Belle and loving every minute, I would have laughed, but it's my anchor, as you all are. Thank you for coming to my home and being part of my family." Her sapphire eyes drape over me, lingering, a softness there. "I hope we spend many, many holidays together. And win state! Go Bobcats!"

Cheers go around the table.

I lean into her, brushing my lips over her cheek.

Turns out her words are prophetic.

For we do spend many holidays together. And we do win state, many, many times as we spend the rest of our lives together.

Epilogue

Ronan

Several years later

Cleo, my oldest at five, gets a defiant tilt to her chin as she cocks her hip. One hand flips her long blonde hair. "My rosebush is best."

"Yours was first, yes, so it's bigger, but all the bushes are awesome," I reply diplomatically.

"I guess. Mine was first, so I win."

"If you say so."

"I do."

I bite back a grin as we head to the truck, where I pull out the new bush we bought in Austin at the same store where Nova's mom got hers.

A few minutes later, two-year-old Lia wobbles down the steps of the house, then teeters, making me inhale a sharp breath. Standing in the flower bed, I let the shovel fall and dash up to grab her, setting her on my hip. I push the riot of curly dark hair out of her face. "Who let you out, sweet pea?"

She takes her thumb out of her mouth. "Me!" Then she glares down at her sister, a look of triumph on her face. "Mine!"

I huff out a laugh. I don't know if she means I'm hers or her rosebush is the best. Maybe both. Born close to my birthday, she's the most like me so far. Competitive—and a *Star Wars* fan. Granted I've shown her only the first one, but she's the one who watched with wide eyes while Cleo said it was boring, then flounced off to play outside.

Their two yellow rosebushes are planted side by side in our landscaping, just like Nova's and Sabine's next door. My gaze goes to Nova's house. We have some amazing memories there: that first Christmas, a big championship celebration after we won state, birthdays, and then our outdoor wedding in the side yard that connects the house with mine. It was a small affair with family and close friends under a white tent in the spring. She carried flowers from her mom's garden and wore a stunning white V-neck wedding dress. Nova would never sell that house, and we've spent time on it during the off season, painting the outside and modernizing the kitchen. In fact, I think Lia was conceived the day we worked on the kitchen. One minute I'm putting up a backsplash, and the next, Nova is eyeing my muscles, then stripping out of her frayed shorts and Bobcats shirt.

"I be good," Lia says, then squirms out of my arms and joins her sister. She peers down at the hole I dug, then looks up at me with bright-blue eyes. "What goes there?"

Cleo pokes her sister's arm. "Don't you remember? They put in a note. Let's ask Daddy; he knows everything. Right, Daddy?"

The trust in her eyes, combined with *Daddy*, makes my heart swell.

I ruffle her hair. "That's right. Mommy and I write a special note for you, about all the good things we want for you. Then we set the plant in and let the roots grow around it."

"It's for our glow," Cleo tells her younger sister in a sage voice. "We all have it because we're special."

"Glow!" Lia announces and looks around the dirt. "Where is it?"

Cleo palm slaps her own face. "Gah, she's stupid!"

"Not!" Lia says.

I bend down to Lia and tap her chest. "Your glow is right there in the center of your heart."

"Special!" she says, then pouts. "No Oliver. I'm best!"

Cleo rolls her eyes. "He gets one too, silly. It's his first birthday." She frowns. "I wish we got presents for his birthday, but Mama said no."

"Presents!" Lia calls out.

"Your present is you get to help set the bush in," I say, and they squint at me with identical disdain.

I hear the front door open, and Nova steps out.

Wearing a red sundress with her hair framing her face, she gives me a rueful smile as she takes in my dirt-stained shirt and shorts.

I lift my hands. "I make a mess of this every time. I wasn't made to work in gardens."

She laughs. "You'll need to change before we take pictures. Lois will be here in fifteen; then we're heading to the Roadhouse to meet Skeeter and Sonia and who knows who all Lois invited to his birthday party."

"Most of the town, I bet." We're doing a special thing tomorrow just for us since it's Saturday and Sabine will be here.

My gaze goes to the birthday boy in her arms. With a crown of dark hair and dark-blue eyes, he takes my breath. Two girls and a son. I want more if Nova agrees, but so far she says three is the magic number.

He sees me and jumps for me as Nova sets him down. I meet him before he reaches the steps. Solid and big for his age (like me), he crawled at six months and walked at nine.

"You'll get him dirty," Nova chides as she joins us.

I grimace as I look down at him. "He isn't wearing this, is he?" I already know the answer, but I love to rile her up.

"Yes," Nova replies. "See the detail on the smocking on the collar? It's got little balloons, and the blue color of the romper matches his eyes perfectly. I know it's girlie, but smocked outfits are a southern thing."

I don't care what he wears, whether it's girlie looking or not. He can play with Barbies or whatever he wants. I kiss his cheek, then hand him back to Nova.

She brushes at the dirt on his outfit/dress while I dart inside to change.

A few minutes later, we're lined up around Oliver's new rosebush. My hand is intertwined with Nova's. She's my love, my everything. She brought the sun—and stars—right to my soul. She brought me a family—not just our kids but the people in Blue Belle. We've collected four state championships since I've been here, and I've no plans to leave. Maybe someday, when our kids are bigger and the time is right. My football career here gives me joy, and when you have joy, why would you go and look for anything else?

Oliver stands between his sisters as they clasp his hands, rather tightly to keep him still. Sparky sits next to Dog while the cat I got Nova, Dimitri (because he's Russian, and I got to name him), is on the end next to Cleo. He's been her cat since day one and is never far from her.

"All right," Lois says as she picks up the camera. "Let's get this picture for the album!"

Before she can click, a white Honda pulls into the driveway, and Sabine jumps out of the car. She rushes up to us, straightening her red sundress to match Nova's. "Wait for me, y'all."

"You told me you couldn't make it until tomorrow!" Nova says.

Nova asked Sabine if she wanted us to wait for the weekend so she could be in the photo, but she'd said no, that the picture must be taken on the actual birthday. Nova told her we'd do another one tomorrow, and we'd put them side by side.

Sabine smiles. "I tried to call you, but you never answered."

"I have three kids. My phone's probably still charging—on silent," Nova admits.

Sabine shrugs. "I skipped my classes today. I emailed my professors and said it was my nephew's birthday and I had to take one picture. I'm sure they'll understand."

I laugh. Right.

"Sabby!" Lia calls, and it's chaos after that as she runs across the yard. Cleo chases her, determined to get to her aunt first. Oliver plops down in the dirt, then sticks a rose in his mouth.

Nova groans and pulls leaves and petals out of his mouth as Dog chases Dimitri—he does not like that cat and never will. Sparky raises an eyebrow at the show, then pounces on a lizard.

Nova picks up Oliver, gives him a kiss, and then motions to Sabine and the girls. "Get in here with us."

We line up again, smiles on our faces. Lois clicks the photo, several of them, and years later when I look at them, at all of them, from Nova's to Sabine's to our children's to Sabine's children's, I thank the stars for my glow.

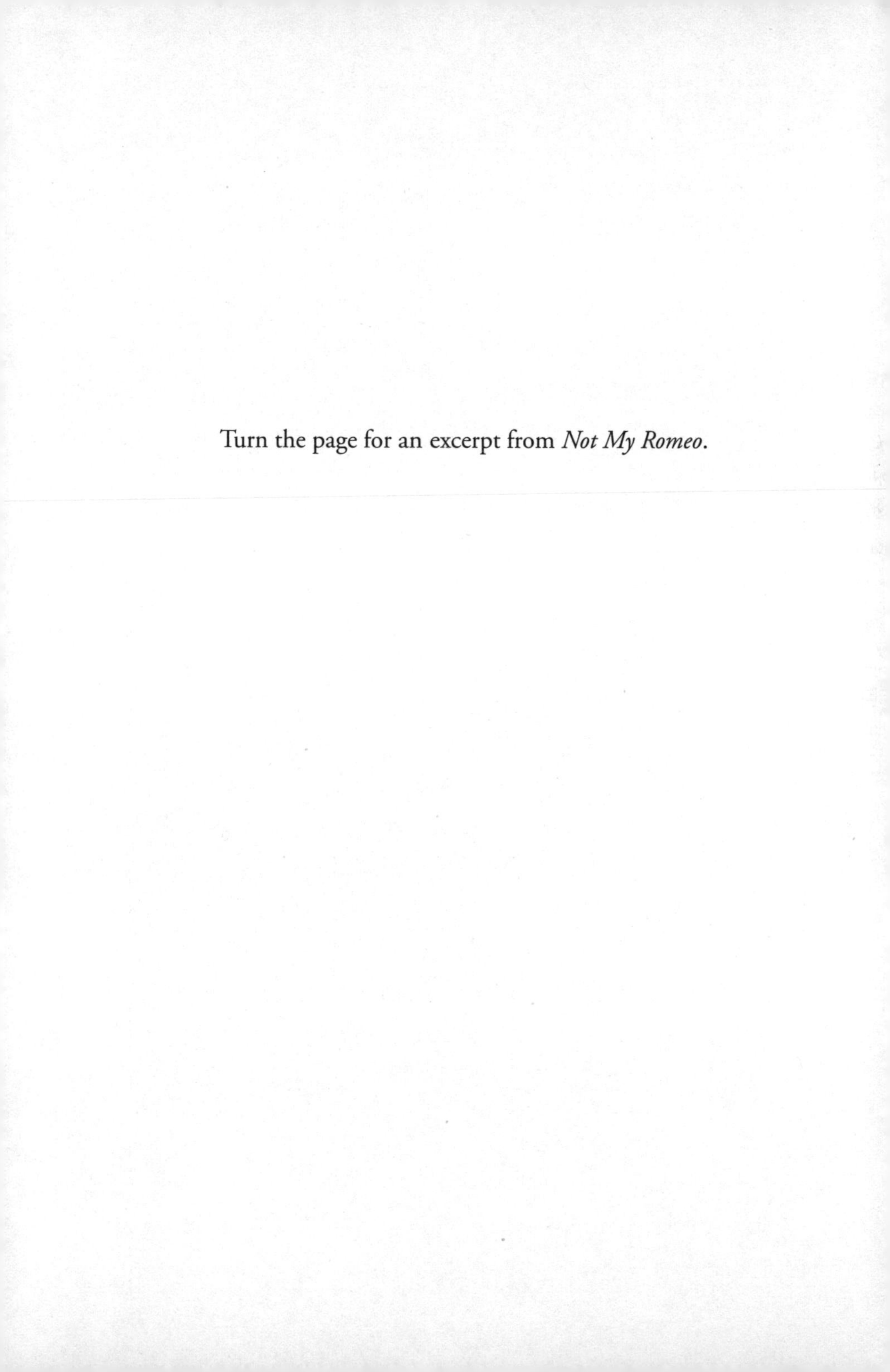

Turn the page for an excerpt from *Not My Romeo*.

Chapter 1

ELENA

If I smoked, I'd have one in my mouth right now. Maybe two.

But I don't, so I settle for chewing on my thumbnail as I whip my little Ford Escape into Milano's jam-packed parking lot. Glancing around, I take in the stone-and-cedar exterior, the flickering gaslights by the door. It's a five-star restaurant, one of the best in Nashville, with a monthlong reservation wait, yet my date managed to get us one on short notice. Points for that.

A long sigh leaves my chest.

Who, *tell me who*, agrees to a blind date on Valentine's Day?

Me, apparently.

"I'm breaking the seal!" I announce to no one.

That's right. Tonight, I'm meeting Greg Zimmerman, the local weatherman for the NBC affiliate here in the Music City. Supposedly he's tall, dark, handsome, a little nerdy, and fresh from a breakup. Perfect for me. Right?

So why am I so anxious?

For a brief moment I contemplate a pretend headache. Dang it. I can't do that. For one, I promised my roommate, Topher, I'd follow through; two, I have nothing better to do; and three, I'm starving.

And this is *just* a quick dinner, no matter what Topher says. I recall him in the library today. He'd been wearing his Grateful Dead T-shirt and skinny jeans, bouncing up and down in the romance section as he mimicked riding a horse. *Straddle him like a thoroughbred, Elena. Take those reins, dig your spurs in, and ride him until you can't walk the next day. Pound him so hard he can't even say "Cloudy with a chance of snow" the next day.*

I blow at a piece of hair that's fallen out of my chignon, then tuck it neatly behind my ear. No horsing around tonight. I'm here for a nice meal. Italian *is* my favorite, and I'm already picturing a nice bowl of pasta and garlic bread.

Just say hi, be nice, eat, and then get out.

Besides. What can go wrong from meeting someone new?

I pull down the rearview mirror and check my appearance. Pale as paper. After scrambling around my bag, I pull out my cherry red and roll it over my full lips, then blot them with a tissue. I sigh, studying my features as I adjust my pearl necklace and matching earrings. The truth is there's nothing spectacular about me. My nose is a hair too sharp, and I'm annoyingly short: five feet, three inches and a quarter in bare feet. That quarter is very important. Floating somewhere in between a true petite and the "standard" size, I'm stuck with clothes either too long or too short. If I want something that fits well, I make it myself.

Another glance in the mirror. Another sigh.

I hope Greg isn't disappointed.

I get out of the car and approach the beautifully stained oaken double door, where a doorman dressed in a black suit gives me a smile and opens the door. "Welcome to Milano's," he murmurs, and I swallow down my qualms as I step into the foyer and squint around the dark interior.

Dang.

Dread inches up my spine.

Why did I insist on not seeing a photo of Greg before the date?

Mostly I just wanted to be . . . surprised. When your existence is as boring and mundane as mine, it's the little things that spice it up. Instead of my normal coffee, let's try the peppermint latte. *Mind blowing.* Instead of wearing my hair in a bun, let's make it a messy topknot. *Amazing.* Instead of seeing a picture of your blind date, go anyway, and look for the guy wearing a blue shirt. Sounded exciting at the time, but I'm cursing myself as I check out the interior. There's no one waiting for me in the foyer. I did text him to let him know I was caught in traffic, yet I got no response back. Perhaps he's already seated and waiting for me.

The hostess whisks a lovey-dovey couple to their seats in the back of the restaurant, leaving me alone and fidgety. I brush down my black pencil skirt. Maybe I should have changed into something flirtier? I do have a closetful of slinky dresses Nana left me—

Nope.

This is the real me, and if he doesn't like what he sees, then, well, he can suck it.

I am who I am.

After five more minutes have passed and the hostess still hasn't come back, my nerves have ramped up, and I've broken out in a small sweat, the nape of my neck damp. Where did she go? Is she on a break?

I take a seat on a long bench, whip out my phone, and send him another text.

I'm here in the foyer, I send.

No reply comes back.

Annoyed and running on hunger fumes, I decide I can find him myself. Feigning confidence I don't have, I waltz out of the foyer and make a quick perimeter of the restaurant. A few minutes later I feel like a stalker as I peer at the patrons, so I move to stand in the shadowy alcove next to the restrooms, scanning for men alone on Valentine's Day.

Topher should have chosen a different night for us to meet, considering I have a horrible history with Valentine's Day. At my high school Sweetheart Dance, my date, Bobby Carter, drank so much spiked punch that he barfed all over my white dress. My college boyfriend's idea of a romantic night was ordering in sushi—his favorite—then playing video games with his friends online. I can't recall one decent Valentine's Day in all my twenty-six years.

Bam. My eyes land on a tall dark-haired man wearing a blue button-down, the sleeves rolled up to his forearms. He's in the far corner, sitting apart, almost tucked away. His table has several empty ones around it, and I find it curious that he's managed to get privacy on such a busy night. A waiter sets down his food, and my lips tighten.

He's eating without me?

I spy his phone next to him on the table. The nerve! Why hasn't he responded to me?

He's taller than I expected, judging just from how he sits in his plush leather armchair—

Wait a minute. He *does* look vaguely familiar, like a face you've caught briefly but can't put a name to. Mama and Aunt Clara always have the TV on at the beauty shop, so it's possible I have actually seen him on the news.

I pull my white cat-eye glasses out of my purse and slide them on for a better look. My heart flip-flops as butterflies take flight in my stomach. Oh heck no. That can't be him. He's . . . he's . . . freaking gorgeous, and I don't mean regular handsome but like a movie star: dark hair swept off his face, the strands wavy and unruly with copper highlights, soft and silky brushing against his cheeks, and too long for a newscaster, in my opinion—but what do I know? I don't own a television.

He lifts his arm to shove his hair back, and my eyes pop at the tightly roped muscles of his forearm and biceps straining through the fabric, the impossibly broad shoulders that taper to a chest.

Well, would you look at that.

And this has to be him, right?

I'm in the right restaurant. He's alone. He's wearing a blue shirt. He has dark hair. Odds point to yes. Usually the most simple explanation is exactly what it appears. Therefore, he must be my date.

The man in question turns to look out the window, tapping his fingers on the table impatiently, and I take in his profile. Long straight nose, full dark arching eyebrows, and a sharp, bladed jawline. Sensuous lips, the lower one decadently full. Almost wicked. He's the kind of hot that draws your eyes over and over just to make sure it's not a mirage. I knew guys like him at NYU—sexy, athletic gym types who played a sport. And those types never gave me a second look. I'd watch them work out while I fumbled my way around one of those god-awful butterfly machines, while beautiful, tall, svelte girls who weren't sweating fawned over them, bringing them towels, water bottles, and sexy promises.

He isn't beefy, though, like those brawny guys with thick necks and flushed faces. His muscles are taut and powerful, nothing too overstated, yet tight and no doubt firm—

Elena. Enough with the body. It's to your taste. Move on.

He takes a sip of an amber liquid, his long, tanned fingers grasping the fragile container as his eyes rove across the room. They prowl around the restaurant, as if he's assessing every person in sight, and I feel the sizzle of him even from twenty feet away. Prickles of awareness skate down my spine. Greg has massive raw animal magnetism coming from him in waves. *I'm the alpha,* his body language yells. *Come and challenge me.* I watch as a few ladies eye him—even some of the guys are turned and checking him out. Some are whispering. Interesting. I guess he has quite the following on the news.

His gaze drifts right over me without stopping.

Not surprised.

I duck back into the shadows.

Dang it. My hands clench. I wanted nice and nerdy, not this . . . sexy beast!

And judging by the scowl on his face, he's grumpy. *Life's too short to be dour, Mister.* And what is he annoyed about? I am here!

And he did see a picture of me. Topher said so.

Yeah, maybe he doesn't really want to meet you.

Maybe he's hoping you won't show up.

I tap my foot. I should leave. Really.

I have a ton of things to do at home. Some sewing, snuggling up with Romeo—

The smells of Milano's waft around me, spicy and tantalizing, and my stomach lets out an angry howl. I move from one foot to the next. Every place to eat between here and Daisy is going to be packed. I could always hit a drive-through on the way back home—but how pathetic is a Big Mac and fries on Valentine's Day? Plus, I'll have my entire nosy family to answer to tomorrow. They've built up this blind date so much: *Oooooh, Elena has a date with a weatherman. Ask him if that's a barometer in his pocket or if he's just glad to see you.* That nugget came from Aunt Clara. If I chicken out now, there'll be hell to pay, because no matter the brave face I put on, everyone knows I haven't been myself in months.

I give myself a mental pep talk.

Grow some balls, Elena.

You can't keep living life on the sidelines.

Sometimes you have to go out and take what you want.

So what if he's hot enough to suck the dew off a rose.

So what if he's got a dangerous look on his face.

You are hungry. Do it for the pasta.

He is your date. Go get 'em, girl.

I gather my resolve, point my little black pumps in his direction, and start marching.

ABOUT THE AUTHOR

Wall Street Journal, New York Times, and USA Today bestselling author Ilsa Madden-Mills pens angsty new adult and contemporary romances. A former high school English teacher and librarian, she adores all things *Pride and Prejudice*, and of course, Mr. Darcy is her ultimate hero. She's addicted to frothy coffee beverages, cheesy magnets, and any book featuring unicorns and sword-wielding females. Feel free to stalk her online.

Sign up for her newsletter and receive insider info about new releases and exclusive giveaways: www.ilsamaddenmills.com

Facebook: @authorilsamaddenmills

Join her private reader group on Facebook: www.facebook.com/groups/ilsasunicorngirls/

Instagram: @Ilsamaddenmills